AF535081

MULE

sands press
Brockville, Ontario

MULE

Peter Parkin & Alison Darby

sands press

sands press

A Division of 10361976 Canada Inc.
300 Central Avenue West
Brockville, Ontario
K6V 5V2

Toll Free 1-800-563-0911 or 613-345-2687
http://www.sandspress.com

ISBN 978-1-988281-65-0

http://www.peterparkin.com

Cover Design by Jason Russell
Edited by Sparks Literary
Formatting by Renee Hare
Publisher Sands Press
Author Agent Sparks Literary Consultants

Publisher's Note

For information on bulk purchases of this book or any book published by Sands Press, please call 1-800-563-0911.

1st Printing March 2019

In honor of the victims and survivors of the seemingly endless progression of unthinkable man-enabled calamities.

This book is dedicated to the memory of dear friend, Lynne Galster (nee Hyde), who broke our hearts by leaving us far too soon.

Plots, true or false, are necessary things,

To raise up commonwealths and ruin kings.

(John Dryden, Absalom and Achitophel)

Prologue
February 13, 2003 - 9:00 a.m.

Mitch Joplin looked in the mirror as he went about his morning routine. Not bad looking after all these years, he thought. Tall, well-built, still lots of hair. And his most striking feature of all—his eyes—still penetrated, right back at him from the mirror. Those eyes had seen a lot over his sixty-five fast years, and unlike most people his age he wished he could forget more than he could remember. But that was not to be, and he was haunted by the trauma those memories produced in his dreams, every single night. It wasn't much better when he was awake either, Mitch realized, as he popped his morning Prozac.

He shaved as usual, being careful not to chop off the mole on the left side of his cleft chin. Every time he made that boo-boo, it would bleed for hours... and he didn't have hours to spare today. He ran his fingers through his hair, and pulled on his favorite "activity" shirt—one in a family of shirts he wore only when he had something eventful to accomplish. Mitch's entire adult life had been one event after another. On this day there would be another mission, but one that was his alone for a change.

He ambled out to the kitchen of his spartan apartment and began the preparations to scramble some of his patented eggs. He knew it would be a long and agonizing day, and he needed the energy to get through it. As he pulled the spatula from the drawer he soberly reflected that he might not even see the end of this day.

He had been trained to always believe that the day, or mission, would end in victory. That discipline of mind had probably helped to make every one of them a success. That also depended of course on how you defined "success." Up until now he had defined it as simply getting out alive. His superiors had a different definition entirely, and his survival wasn't part of it. Mitch had always accepted that as an inescapable fact with his particular line of work. His chosen occupation was behind him now and had been for over a year. What he had done was not behind him; it was always staring him right in the face. Most of his actions he could neatly categorize under "love of country." But there was one act—his last before he had retired—that was tearing him apart.

Today was the day he had chosen to get closure, and for the first time in his life he felt butterflies in his stomach. He had never experienced closure before. He completed his deeds like a robot, detached from reality. He was talented at what he did, and those talents had been well rewarded. He had put faith in his masters and did what he was told. Most of what he had done took place in faraway lands, which gave an almost fairy-tale quality to his memories. Hard to feel guilt. But once or twice upon a time he had done things closer to home.

He looked around the ugly apartment. This was the last time he would see it. Rented under a phony name, paid in advance for eighteen months to avoid credit checks on a name that didn't exist, the lease was now almost up. But that was okay…he had somewhere else to go. His dog was waiting for him there right now as a matter of fact. After this long day, Mitch would return to that apartment and leave this one behind. It had been rented under his real name, a nice change. He visited there yesterday and left enough food and water for his pet for at least three days. He liked this new apartment, located on the ground floor with a fenced backyard. A trap door allowed his dog to let himself in and out. Perfect for Mitch and his little buddy. He had also recently sent a note in the mail to his daughter, letting her know of the apartment address, and asking her to take care of his dog if anything happened to him.

Kerrie, what a treasure. And what a waste of his life that he had missed so much over the years. He intended to make up for lost time if he survived the day…and if she let him after learning what he had done.

He finished his eggs, gulped down his coffee, and turned on the television. A CNN headline of yet another terrorist warning, this time in the Los Angeles area. Mitch shook his head—what this world had become in the last couple of years. He thanked God that Kerrie had never had children, even though he would have been thrilled to be a grandfather. What a world for kids to grow up in. And what on earth would society look like in twenty years? He wasn't sure he wanted to be around to see it.

Time to get on with things. He rose from the couch and strode in his trademark swagger to the bedroom. He pulled out his belt holster and glock, snapping them into place. Then he carefully removed a heavy, multi-pocketed vest from a separate closet, expertly donning it over his activity shirt. A black trench coat and gloves completed the look.

He took one final glance in the mirror, and was a bit startled at how menacing he looked. He wondered why he had never really noticed that before.

Well, today that menace would come to an end. In more ways than one, he thought, and for more people than just himself. Today was probably the first unselfish day of Mitch Joplin's life.

February 13, 2003 - 10:00 a.m.

Connie Reynolds rushed for the shower, beating her younger brother by a hair.

"Ladies first," she said apologetically, opening the door.

Her brother glared back at her. "If you were a true lady, I wouldn't mind so much!"

She grabbed a towel and playfully flicked it at him. He jerked out of the way before it caught him in the crotch. "I'm going to be late for work John, so I promise I'll be quick, okay?"

She closed the bathroom door while hearing John mutter, "Every morning, the same thing, and I always lose."

Connie jumped into the shower and turned on the soothing hot water. She knew she didn't have the time to luxuriate under the pulsing settings, but she picked her favorite one anyway and let it roll over her body. Just a few minutes. John could wait; he was already pissed at her anyway. She didn't want to be late for work. Her job at the bank was fun, and even though she was just a teller she felt important. Dealing with customers all day was right up her alley; she loved people and hers was the perfect job for that. She had a knack for calming people down when they were upset, and she knew when to call upon someone more senior if the problem was beyond her authority.

Connie was twenty-three now, and had had to grow up well before her time. Both of her parents were killed in the World Trade Center on 9/11. They had been visiting their investment advisor in the South Tower that morning. Hoping for early retirement, they were planning to be a little more aggressive in their investments, drop out of the rat race in five years, and still have enough to help out their two kids as well. They were wonderful people, and she and John missed them terribly. John was sixteen and becoming a man very quickly. Connie had assumed the position of legal guardian of her brother, and the two of them were left equal interests in their parents' estate, including this little house on Long Island. They were well taken care of thanks to their parents' foresight; except for the emotional part. They also received a considerable sum of money from the "Victims of 9/11 Fund," which Connie had carefully put aside in safe investments for herself and John. It was amazing how much she had had to learn over the last eighteen months, and it was even more amazing to know that she could actually learn these things that used to be so foreign to her. It showed her what a person was capable of when there was no other choice, and when there was no one to lean on anymore.

It had been a tough eighteen months, but her memories were finally becoming more pleasant. Before, they had been tainted with bitterness and anger. Connie and John had spent many an evening looking over photo albums of family vacations and get-togethers. She remembered how they both had made fun of their mother for insisting on whipping out the camera at every moment and snapping away. They always had to stop what they were doing and pose. Mom believed in being prepared, to not catch people at their worst. She felt that everyone had the right to look his best in something as important as a photo. Connie regretted now that she had made fun of her mom at these photo-ops, and when she thought of those moments she always felt a tear in her eye. She wished there were more photos.

Now she was a substitute parent, and raising her brother to manhood was not easy. Particularly since boys didn't wear their emotions on their sleeves the way girls did. She really had to step up to the plate in those first few months after 9/11, to help her brother deal with his grief. He had become angry and withdrawn, which affected his schoolwork, as well as relationships with teachers and other students. John was the only one in his class who had lost parents in the disaster, and he was having a tough time coming to grips with why—why him. Connie lost count of how many visits she had made to the school for parent/teacher conferences. However, what seemed to make a difference and help turn John around, was just Connie's persistence in talking to him, caring about him—whether he liked it or not. She guessed that he just needed to know that someone still cared. And Connie sure cared about her little John. He had absolutely refused to attend grief counseling, so Connie knew his only hope was her own determination. It paid off.

After dealing with John's grief, Connie began to make time for her own. She missed the comfort and security her parents had given her—the affection, the advice, always being there; hell, just shoulders to cry on.

It was sad, she thought, how much she and John had taken their parents for granted when they were still alive. They were supposed to have been a part of their lives forever—invincible—and then to lose them in such a horrifying, shocking and public manner, cut her to her core. She so longed for the midnight chats with her mother over tea, the boisterous games with her father at the lake, and Sunday dinners with all four of them together. Those times could not be repeated—and new experiences would never be. Her father would not walk her down the aisle, her mother would not help her pick out a wedding dress, and her children would not be visiting grandma and grandpa on weekends. Her children would never know their wonderful grandparents.

They held a burial for their parents, carefully chosen clothes and personal effects the only items inside otherwise empty coffins. No remains were ever found, which was sadly the case for hundreds of victims. It was tough to get closure without the remains, but Connie found some peace by visiting Ground Zero. That was her parents' real grave. What a tangled mess of destruction, and it hurt her to know that those tons of material had come down on her beloved mom and dad. It was astonishing to read the reports of victims' passports and credit cards being found in the rubble, but very few tangible remains. How was it possible that all evidence of human life could be extinguished so easily, but temporary creations of paper and plastic could hang around virtually intact? They also apparently found passports for a couple of the terrorists who had hijacked the planes, and she wondered how that was possible with impact explosions of the magnitude that she had seen on T.V. And those terrorists' passports, in her mind, had no business being in the same rubble that contained her mom and dad.

For a long while after the attacks, she couldn't help but hate the face of every Arab she saw on the streets of New York. The barrage of media coverage of these terrorists, their roots overseas and the apparent hatred that their world had for her world, was more than the normal brain could process. Connie's feelings were normal, she guessed, but they weren't nice to carry around, day in and day out. So she had attended anger management counseling to help her deal with these unfamiliar and poisonous feelings. Thankfully, she was now able to isolate the perpetrators of the attack without broad-brushing an entire race or religion. However, most New Yorkers hadn't bothered with counseling and the feelings of most people were still centered in hate and fear, albeit more subdued now than in 2001. A period of relative calm had now settled in around the city, since nothing else had terrorized them in the same way since.

Connie teasingly tapped her brother on the back of the head and ordered him to get his books and head off to school. "Okay, okay, who made you the boss?" John cried out, then caught himself. " Just kidding, Sis." He went over and gave his big sister a rare hug, and she hugged him back. Both of them knew it was just the two of them now, and they had to hold onto each other to survive.

They headed out the door together, and Connie offered to drive John to school, only a few blocks away. He agreed. Connie knew that he would. All modesty aside, she knew that she would be considered by most teenage boys as a "hottie." Being seen dropped off by his "hottie" big sister could only be a good thing for John. A guy needed every advantage he could get at sixteen. In fact, she remembered that with teenage girls it was similar—being judged by association was a reality in high school.

Of course, John never admitted to her that he thought she was hot. Connie just knew it, and knew that he was proud to be seen with her. And why shouldn't he be? She had long auburn hair—the same color as John's—which contrasted with her milky white skin making her look younger than her age. And she had been told by former boyfriends and even a scout from a modeling agency, that she had the face of an angel. Of course now that she was older and less naïve, she knew that they all probably had ulterior motives when they told her that. But, being as objective as she could possibly be, she tended to agree with their assessment.

Connie knew that status for teenage boys was terribly important, and being accepted within a peer group was almost a daily obsession for them. John had admitted these things to her during the time she was helping him with his grief. He was only fourteen when their parents had died and just barely cracking into the "cool" crowd. Then, all of a sudden everyone was tiptoeing around him, afraid to say anything. He had tearfully confessed to Connie that he felt like he was now on the outside looking in. He grieved for his parents, but also in typical teenage fashion felt that it was unfair that they had died and put him in the position he was now in.

Connie counseled him to simply grab the bull by the horns and control the situation—not wait to be talked to or included, but instead initiate things himself. To be outgoing and cheerful, even though he might still be crying inside. Teenagers didn't like to be around kids who were "downers," and would tend to avoid those kids at all cost. John should save his misery to share with her, or to keep for his private moments. Connie wasn't even sure at the time that she was giving him the right advice—she had just been following her instincts when she talked with him. But gradually over a period of months, everything began to click for John. His confidence and sense of belonging returned. Connie loved seeing him smile again, and vowed that she would always give him every possible advantage in life that she could—even the simple things like being the "hottie" who dropped him off at school.

They said their goodbyes at the school, and Connie headed off on her commute to Manhattan. She worked at the NY State Security Bank right downtown, not far from Ground Zero. It was one of the smaller banks, but she liked that. Smaller banks tended to be friendlier. A person wasn't just a number or an anonymous face in the crowd.

Many of her fellow workers, some quite good friends, had left to work in the suburbs after 9/11. Not Connie. It was weird, but she felt as if she'd be abandoning her parents if she gave in to the fear and left the area where they had perished. Her counseling sessions had helped her deal with both the fear and anger together. She had learned that they were very similar emotions, and had almost identical physiological effects on the body. She came to believe that this entire tragic process had made her stronger, and she was glad that she hadn't run away. That would have been very easy to do, and indeed many did.

She made it downtown in record time, left her car in the parkade where she held a monthly pass, and walked the five blocks to her building. Monthly parking was expensive in Manhattan, but she preferred the privacy and relative safety of her own car. It was one little luxury that she allowed herself.

She checked in with her boss and waved hi to her fellow workers. Today was going to be a good day. It was Thursday, and Thursday had always been her favorite day of the week—it meant that the most relaxed day at work was the very next day, with the weekend just around the corner. Most people liked Fridays best, but she preferred Thursdays because of the anticipation of Friday. Weird. Also, this was the thirteenth of the month which meant that it should be a lucky day, unlike Friday the thirteenth. She had to admit she was a bit superstitious, and had a tendency to search for the good in almost everything.

She went to her usual teller station and began preparing for her day of greeting customers. She had some favorites who always waited in line until her station was free. That was nice for her to see; it made Connie feel appreciated, needed. This branch wasn't as busy as one might expect for a downtown bank location. With so much on-line banking being done nowadays, and instant tellers, the traffic to human tellers was diminishing. She worried a bit about this. One day her job would be gone. That's why she had put her name forward to be enrolled in management training at her bank. She hadn't been accepted yet, but she was keeping her fingers crossed.

Connie smiled at her first customer of the day. This was indeed going to be a good day. She could feel it.

*****

Mitch moved slowly, but purposefully, through the streets of Manhattan. It was a beautiful day for a walk, but he couldn't enjoy it. He was preoccupied with how the day would unfold. He never usually worried when he was on a mission, but then again, he had never planned missions or taken responsibility for their outcomes. He merely executed them. This time was different.

As well, he had been expertly trained—or more appropriately, brainwashed—to be detached from his actions. There had never been any passion, only cold efficiency. But time and retirement had eroded his protective shell. This time there was real passion fused with absolute frustration. More than that though, he felt wasted, deceived, and guilty. Thank God for Prozac, or who knows what kind of shape he'd be in.

In his line of work, the substantial money helped keep things covert most of the time. Money always kept a lot of people quiet. But there were also the threats that came with the assignments. Betrayal of classified material, no matter how moral the motivation, would most certainly lead to a conviction of treason. This was made clear in no uncertain terms. The greater good of the country superseded everything else, and most of the robots bought into this. That patriotic pledge crap succeeded in keeping most things secret, along with, of course, the promise of money. If those tactics didn't work, there was always what was referred to as "leverage"; a cruel kind of blackmail that the government used to remind the robots who was really in charge of their lives. Mitch still remembered his "leverage" as clear as if it were yesterday, although it was actually a long time ago…

Even though all of the methods the government employed seemed to keep things in order and the electronic age made secret information less accessible, Mitch was amazed at how much of a paper trail still existed for actions that were carried out by operatives. It was a good thing he had already taken full advantage of that Achilles heel. After today it all would have been buried so deep…

He saw his target building up ahead: NY State Security Bank, right downtown in the heart of it all. He banked there under his real name. The place was public and he felt no fear there. Also, he had no reason to believe he was under surveillance. However, where he had been living was a different story entirely. He wanted to sleep at night. Having the tenement apartment under a false name felt better to him. His life would change dramatically today, or end. He knew that, but he had to turn this page to regain his soul.

As he walked along, he stole a glance at his reflection in a store window. An old man looked back, which of course he was. In his own mirror at home, he never thought he looked that way. Foolish vanity. He walked through the front doors of the bank and glanced at his watch: 12:00 noon. She should be here, at her usual spot. There she was, looking pretty as usual. She reminded him so much of his daughter at that age, not in looks but in personality. Thankfully, Kerrie had never had to endure the kind of living hell that Connie had. She was a sweet girl and vulnerable, but also strong; he knew that from their many conversations. He regretted that after today she would hate him.

*****

Connie was getting through her customers fairly quickly today. Few wanted to chat for long, which was unfortunate. That was the part she enjoyed the most in her job.

Then she saw him, her favorite customer. He was next in line, and he always waited just for her. Mitch was one of those special "it" people, with a magnetism and intelligence that shone right through those incredible eyes. His charm and words of advice always brightened her day. She had confided in him many months ago about what she had endured with the horror of her parents' deaths. He was the one who had encouraged her to seek counseling, and the power of his words made her feel that she had to do it to survive. He made that clear in very few words. Mitch didn't need a lot of words—his eyes said it all. She knew he was retired but had no idea what he had done for a living. She had asked once but he didn't answer, so she never asked again. She knew that whatever it was, it was important, because he seemed so self-assured. Mitch had seen a lot of life, she was sure of that. He was worldly and confident, with a "Don't fuck with me" look about him. Connie found that strangely intriguing.

For an older man she thought him attractive as well, but never told him so. She didn't think he would take well to hearing such a compliment, and was afraid that he might also take it the wrong way. Connie didn't want anything to hurt her friendship with Mitch. He was more important to her than she would ever have the courage to tell him.

He made his way to her counter. "Hi, Connie."

Connie smiled warmly. "It's so good to see you, Mitch. Are you here to clean us out today?"

He stood there, not joking in his usual way, and looked distracted. She could tell he was thinking of something other than how much money he was going to withdraw. "Mitch, are you all right?" Silence. Something was wrong. This was not the way their encounters usually went.

"Connie…there's something…" She saw a tear in his eye, something she never expected to see from such a cool, tough guy. And he had never stammered or seemed at a loss for words before.

"Mitch, can I get you a glass of water?"

Mitch shook his head and then, almost instantly, the sadness and discomfort left his eyes, replaced by an intensity that caused her heart to skip.

He leaned in towards her over the counter, and said, "Connie, you're going to be frightened today. I have something very serious to do here. I don't want you to be afraid, but I know you will be anyway. I can't help that. I demand your cooperation with whatever I ask you to do. But I want you to trust that nothing is ever quite what it seems."

Connie stared at him, dumbfounded. Then she started to laugh. "Good one! You're testing me, aren't you, Mitch? You want to see if my counseling sessions have worked?"

Suddenly she saw a sharpness and focus in his eyes that she had never seen before. It scared her. For the first time she felt fear as she looked into Mitch's eyes, which she had never in her wildest dreams expected to experience with him.

"I promise that you will not be harmed, but right now I want you to press the hold-up panic button under your counter," Mitch said under his steely glare.

"Is this a hold-up, Mitch? Are you holding me up?" Connie said with a quiver in her voice. She could feel her knees go weak, and her mouth go as dry as sandpaper.

"Push the button, Connie," Mitch demanded in a voice that couldn't possibly have been his. Connie couldn't help herself—she screamed and buckled to the floor as her knees finally gave out. Mitch leaped over the counter as if he were bouncing off a trampoline. He wrapped one strong arm underneath her and gently helped her up—as he did, she could see him reach under the counter and press the button himself. He seemed to know the exact spot—no fumbling around. He slid his arm up around her neck. Connie was vaguely aware of his free hand sliding into the side pocket of her suit jacket. She could hear the faint crackling of paper as he slid his hand back out again. Had he put something in her pocket?

That same free hand was now holding a long pistol, a type that Connie had never seen before, even on cop shows. Mitch was holding it high in the air with the barrel pointed to the ceiling—he clearly wanted everyone in the bank to see it. Connie couldn't take her eyes off it, nor could she catch her breath. It was coming in labored gasps. Mitch seemed to notice, and released the pressure slightly from around her neck.

Mere seconds had gone by since Connie had screamed, but it seemed to her to be much longer. Terrified faces stared at her and Mitch. Everyone had heard the scream and had watched as the imposing black-coated man leaped over the counter. Now all six feet, four inches of him was holding a petite helpless teller around the neck, brandishing a gun. They were all stunned into absolute stillness, afraid to move.

One of the vault managers, Tim Moffat, said in a very calm voice, " Sir, can you tell us what you want please? No one needs to get hurt here."

Mitch ignored him and announced in an authoritative voice, loud enough for all to hear: "Remain in your spots! Do not move! If you follow my instructions, no one will be hurt. The alarm has been pressed, and the police will be here shortly."

Moffat persisted, again calmly. "Sir, the bank cameras are running. You can't escape with any money. You'll be caught."

Mitch addressed him directly this time. " I don't want money, and the cameras are just fine with me. There will be more cameras shortly."

He then summoned the closest other teller, a cute Hispanic girl with eyes as big as saucers. Connie knew her only by her first name—Conchita. They had enjoyed coffee together a couple of times. She tentatively walked toward them and exchanged a questioning glance with Connie.

Mitch pulled out a piece of paper from his pocket, handed it to her, and said, "When the police arrive, I want you to walk out of the building with your hands in the air. After they grab you, which they will, give them this sheet of paper." Conchita nodded nervously and walked through the secure gate to the public side of the counter, waiting for the sirens.

Mitch followed with Connie in front, one arm still around her neck, and the gun in his other hand at the ready. No one approached him, no one moved.

Once he was in the outer area, he released his arm from Connie's neck and ordered her to stand still. Connie froze in position, and could feel that all eyes were on her at that moment. She was more frightened than she had ever been in her life, and could not believe that this man whom she was so fond of could be this same monster standing behind her now.

A million questions were going through her head, not the least of which was why on earth he had pushed the silent alarm button. Surely he knew he would get caught. What did he want? What was in that note he had passed to Conchita? Would he hurt her?

She could feel him moving behind her now, removing his trench coat and dropping it to the floor. Then she heard gasps from the customers. Connie turned her head and saw that Mitch was wearing a vest, with what looked like tubes or bars poking out of thin pockets across the front. He was now undoing the vest carefully, slowly. She guessed what this vest was, and it chilled her to the bone.

He was now speaking to her, softly. "Put this vest on, Connie, and be very careful." She did as she was told, and started crying as she did. She couldn't help herself. All she could think of was what her little John would do without her.

Mitch was still holding the gun, and with the other hand he pulled a contraption out of his pocket. Long wires with a connector at one end and a mechanism with one red button at the other. He plugged the connector into the side of the vest which Connie had now done up around her chest. He then stood several feet back from her and pushed the red button on the contraption in his hand.

"This is a bomb, as you've probably all guessed," he announced to the crowd. "I'm holding down the detonator button, and if I let go, this bomb will go off. Please continue to stay where you are."

Connie was sobbing uncontrollably now as she stood all alone in the middle of the concourse. Everybody was staring at her and she could see the pity in their eyes, but also the fear. There was probably no doubt in anyone's mind that if that vest exploded, it would not just be Connie who would go with it.

They all waited for what seemed like an eternity.

The sirens could be heard now, and several police cars screeched to a stop across the street from the bank. No one was walking by the building, so the area must have already been cordoned off. Mitch nodded to Conchita, and repeated his instructions to her. She did as she was told, and Connie watched through the window as the teller was pounced on the second she stepped outside. She could then see her being hauled away to a police car. All Connie could think was, "She's the lucky one."

*****

Outside, the young officer in charge read the note:

I have a bomb. I also have something to say. Once I've said it, I will surrender and no one will be hurt. I am a retired government officer, formerly of the CIA and Special Forces.

I am an explosives expert, so please take my words seriously. My thumb is on a detonator and a teller is wearing a bomb vest. If I am harmed and my thumb is accidentally released, the bomb will explode. It is powerful enough to kill more people than just this teller.

I want a television crew brought into the bank to record, live, what I have to say. I will want to see the broadcast as it unfolds, transmitted through the closed circuit T.V. system in this bank.

Mitch Joplin

This note was too much for the young officer. He'd handled bank robberies before, but this was way more than he was trained to do. He immediately dialed his superior and read him the note. Within minutes, a host of unmarked vehicles arrived on the scene, and a rather officious-looking man in street clothes took over, along with his own personal entourage. A bomb disposal unit arrived, and it became a hive of activity.

Several city blocks had been cordoned off around the bank site, and buildings were evacuated quickly. This process was surprisingly well organized and people obeyed without question. The 9/11 disaster was still fresh in people's minds, and no one seemed to want to linger too long.

*****

Connie was still standing. An hour had passed since the second shock of her life began to unfold. She looked around and saw that most people were now sitting on the floor, and many were holding their heads in their hands. She had to go to the bathroom in a bad way. Her bladder was ready to burst, but she didn't dare ask Mitch if she could. He was still standing behind her with the gun in one hand, and the detonator in the other. He was pressing the red button so tightly that the blood had drained from his thumb. She turned her head and looked into his eyes. He winked at her and nodded his head as if to assure her that this would all pass soon. For some strange reason, she suddenly felt better. She thought this was odd considering what was strapped to her chest. But it was those eyes of his. They could convey messages without speaking, and they were saying to her, "Don't worry."

Suddenly the closed circuit televisions hanging in the interior of the concourse crackled with static, and changed their images. Connie now saw a television reporter at the mike, and it looked like he was on the street one block down from the bank entrance. The headline "Breaking News" was scrolling across the screen, and the monitors came to life with sound. Connie realized this was the first time she had ever heard sound coming from these monitors.

The young reporter seemed out of breath as he spoke, and she could tell he was barely able to contain his excitement.

But his words came:

"...has a bomb strapped to the chest of a bank employee. We don't know her name at the moment, but we'll get that to you as soon as we know. We do know that another bank employee was allowed to leave the building, and we have chatted with her already, although she refused to give her name or appear on camera.

"This is what we do know from her, however. She was given a note that she passed along to an officer when she came out of the building. She read the note while still inside the bank, and it apparently says that the robber wants a television crew brought inside for a live announcement.

"We are told that his name is Mitch Joplin, a retired government agent and military explosives expert. This Joplin is holding a detonator, and if interfered with and his finger slips off the button, the bomb will explode.

"This is all we know at the moment. An obviously tense situation here in New York City, a city whose citizens know all too well the fear that can take hold and rip their hearts out at a moment's notice. We will bring live updates as more information becomes available."

Connie stared at the monitor, her heart pumping in her throat. Mitch had watched the broadcast also, but he seemed detached...almost bored. Most of the other hostages in the bank were crying and trembling after hearing the reporter. Connie had never felt so alone in her life. She had felt scared and vulnerable when she learned of her parents' deaths, but at least then she and John could hold and hug each other for support. This time she was completely on her own.

*****

The officious-looking man in the command vehicle outside the bank dialed a number on his satellite phone. Hundreds of miles away, a man answered.

"Yes, I just saw the broadcast. Has anything else happened since you read me the note?" The man in the vehicle replied, "No, all stable at the moment."

"We never predicted this one, did we?" said the man from Virginia. "Why didn't we see this coming? We set them loose, and just trust."

"Well, we have to deal with it now," answered the man in New York. "He wants a television crew. Do we bite?"

"Yes, we bite. We'll be using the Ark Team for this one. I've already ordered them in and they should be on the scene shortly. The police know that they're out of it now. I've already talked to the chief. Make sure our team is protected, but as always, they know the risks."

*****

Time was passing very slowly in the bank. The pain in Connie's groin was becoming unbearable, and she had no choice but to finally just let it go. It was a rush of relief, as the warm urine gushed down her legs and pooled on the floor at her feet. She felt no embarrassment, just relief. She glanced at Mitch. He stared back at her with what looked like pity in his eyes. Suddenly the doors to the bank opened and a man dressed in what must have been a bomb-proof suit entered. He stopped just inside and addressed Mitch in a muffled voice.

"We have the television crew you asked for. If we can proceed now, you can say your peace and we'll hold you to your word that we can end this peacefully. Your call."

Mitch simply nodded, and the bomb guy motioned for the two additional men behind him to enter. They came in slowly, both dressed in the same cumbersome outfits and carrying large metal shields. One held a large camera, and the other carried a microphone attached to a pack on his hip. They positioned themselves in front of Connie. Mitch stayed at his place behind her and to the left. He wasn't hiding behind her; he didn't seem to be concerned about that at all. Also, at well over six feet tall, there were few people he could hide behind.

The lead man said, "Okay Mr. Joplin, we can proceed."

Connie glanced back at Mitch, and could see him stare with unblinking eyes at the lead man. Then he turned his eyes toward the other two. Suddenly she saw a new expression on his face—a frown and an open mouth, as if he was going to address one of them. Connie turned her head to see which one he was looking at. It was the cameraman, and all she could make out were eyes that were much older than the other two men, gazing intently through the mask at Mitch.

All of a sudden the man's camera flashed, momentarily blinding Connie. Blinking her eyes, she whirled around, aware now of an unexpected sense of motion behind her. In shock she watched Mitch lurching downward.

The next second or two moved in slow motion. Connie saw Mitch collapse to the floor with a perfect hole now between his eyes, fist unfolding, thumb coming off the wicked red button. She dove to grab the detonator, but knew it was too late. The button popped up with a resounding "click" that she decided, in that one horrifying moment, was the loudest noise she had ever heard in her life.

Chapter 1
January 2009

Winter had hit Calgary with a vengeance: howling winds, sheets of snow mixed with hail, cars sliding into every inanimate object imaginable, plus a few animated ones. The sidewalks were mostly empty of human activity, staying indoors being the smart choice today. Jack Howser was the lone figure on Poplar Street, aggressively shoveling snow, and losing the battle. A beautiful Border collie, adorned with striking black and white patterns, romped along beside him, enthusiastic in the effort to try to herd the snow. Every fling of the shovel saw the dog hunch and lunge at the pile. He was enjoying himself, but his partner clearly wasn't. With each lunge the dog pushed the snow back onto the driveway again.

Jack leaned on his shovel and surveyed his progress. Not much to look at, but he knew that if he didn't get the snow out of the way as it fell, the pile would be too high to shovel later. At fifty-five it might be too much for him. He silently chastised himself for not springing for that snow blower in the fall while they were still in stock.

His dog suddenly leapt at Jack's waist, his snout grunting noisily into his pocket in search of a treat. Jack laughed and gave the dog an affectionate rub on the head. Mule is as smart as they come, he thought, almost human. He dropped down into the snow and wrestled with the strong and agile animal. Wrestling matches that always ended with Mule on top. No exception this time either, as Mule gently held his master's arm in his mouth, as if daring him to say "uncle." Jack rolled over, picked up all forty pounds of dog, and threw him into a snow bank. Mule looked like he had a grin on his face, and clearly seemed to enjoy every second of this roughhousing. This was the life—a partner who fed him, walked him, and wrestled with him. A dog's world couldn't get much better.

Jack let out a whistle and led the way back into the house. Time for lunch. He'd had enough of this snow-shoveling shit for now. His house was a small bungalow, wartime built, but handsome in its curb appeal. Located in a nice older area of the city, the trees were huge, and in the summertime draped themselves lazily over the street, nearly touching each other. Jack was always amazed at the canopy of shade the trees provided. From the back of the house his lawn sloped, punctuated by several arbors and a romantic gazebo, right down to the shore of the Elbow River. A scenic and peaceful spot to relax when the weather was nice, which unfortunately wasn't very often in Calgary. The river was also great entertainment for a dog that loved to dive in for a swim whenever the moment grabbed him. He was one hell of a swimmer, and the current in the river was never a problem for Mule. Once in a while, Jack would paddle out in a rubber raft with his athletic pet swimming along close by. The dog seemed to know that his claws might tear the raft, because he had never even attempted to climb aboard.

Jack walked over to his gas fireplace and hit the switch. He actually preferred the authentic wood-burning ones, with the crackling sound and the hypnotic flames. But there was no choice anymore within the city of Calgary, for environmental reasons. Clean-burning gas fireplaces were all that were allowed now, although those lucky enough to have already had a wood one were grandfathered.

He moved into the kitchen and made himself a sandwich, cutting off a piece to share with Mule. While this was an old house, Jack had completely renovated it, retaining as much of the original charm as he could. The kitchen had new nickel-plated appliances custom-made in retro style, which blended in nicely with the immaculate original pine floors. All the old woodwork around the doors and windows was refinished now, leaving the house with a cozy warm feeling. There were two bedrooms down the hall, and Jack used one as his office. There was a basement too, but really nothing more than a crawl space that he used for storage. The house was small but it suited him fine, and there was only him and Mule so how much space did he really need? He loved the neighborhood more than anything, and it was exclusive enough to keep out the riff-raff. A small house like Jack's would fetch close to a million now, just for the location alone. In fact Jack felt that whoever bought it from him one day would buy it for the lot on the river, tear his little house down, and build a monster. Calgary's old neighborhoods had a habit of allowing that to happen. In a decade's time, Jack knew that a lot of the old-town charm would be gone forever as new replaced old, and trees were removed to make way for triple-car garages.

Calgary is a rich city, located in the second-most western province in Canada, bordering the majestic Rocky Mountains. The mountains were only about an hour's drive from the city limits, but Alberta's splendid visibility made them seem within walking distance when viewed from western-facing backyards. The city's fame and fortune came from oil and gas, with the head offices of virtually all of the energy companies located in Calgary, having moved out of the eastern city of Toronto over the past decade or so. While Toronto had always been the financial capital of Canada, it seemed foolhardy for the oil companies to continue to have their head offices thousands of miles away from where the action was—and the action was in Alberta. Within the oil sands of northern Alberta lay the second largest oil deposits in the world, next to Saudi Arabia. But since the Saudis are so secretive about how much they really have, Alberta may actually have the mother lode.

Jack himself was a product of the shift of head offices from Toronto to Calgary. He had been CEO of the Canadian operation of an American oil and gas firm, and moved his company to Calgary back in 2003. Most of his 1,000 employees made the move as well, giving up the warm swimming lakes in Ontario for the mountains of Alberta—and most never regretted it. Calgary was a smart city from a development standpoint. It wanted to attract easterners and knew that they would miss their beloved lakes. So developers were encouraged to build new communities around beautiful man-made lakes. The more elite homes backing right onto the lakes had their own docks and were basically designed to imitate cottage life. But Calgary cottage life meant no long-weekend commutes and the lake was available 365 days a year. The summers were perfect for swimming and fishing, and the winters for skating and pick-up hockey games. The easterners loved this lake-living concept, so when they moved to Calgary, they stayed. It certainly wasn't even close to the romantic notion of having a cottage on a rustic lake in Ontario, but it was a decent compromise if a person had to make one.

Jack had retired from his job last year, and so far had not regretted leaving that stressful life behind. However he did find the change to be a shock, from going 150 miles per hour, down now to a virtual snail's pace. Boredom came to be his new enemy; a problem he'd never had to worry about before. His executive life had been stressful, but certainly never boring. Retirement was a serious adjustment for an overactive mind. Jack also didn't have a lot of friends, certainly none that he would consider close. He had not spent time cultivating friendships during his career years. He had had a lot of business friendships, but they came to an end when he retired. Nothing in common anymore. And the people in his company all directly or indirectly worked for him, so in that position he really couldn't make friends. Although his relationships with his staff and management team had always been cordial, he had to maintain his distance for objective and authoritative purposes. That distance created a barrier that needed to exist for proper chain of command and efficient business management. Jack accepted those realities back then. He was a bit lonely now, and rationalized that that was the price to pay for the many years of high income. It was indeed true that "it was lonely at the top", and even lonelier when you left the top.

Jack dated occasionally, but his heart wasn't really in it. There were a few nice ladies out there that he had gotten to know, and he had even slept with some of them. But that had been more for physical need than any particular fondness. They were willing, and he was still able. End of story.

The thing is, none of them had yet been able to hold a candle to Susan.

*****

He lost her back in 2001, on that fateful day of Sept.11. Susan had been a prominent insurance broker with a global brokerage firm. She was based in the Toronto office, and had to visit New York on a regular basis. On that day, she was attending a breakfast meeting at Windows on the World. That famous restaurant spanned both top floors 106 and 107 of the World Trade Center north tower.

Jack remembered that day painfully well. He guessed that everyone remembered where they were when the planes hit, but particularly those who lost loved ones. That day would be seared into their memories and their nightmares forever. He had been off to a late start that morning, enjoying his coffee at their downtown Toronto condominium. He'd just talked to Susan at 7:00 a.m. that morning. She mentioned the breakfast meeting she had to attend, and was looking forward to her noon flight out of JFK back home to Toronto. She said she hadn't slept well and could hardly wait to get home to her own bed. He had blown her a kiss over the phone and told her he loved her, and missed her. She suggested they go out to dinner when she got back. Jack thought that was a splendid idea.

He turned on CNN for the news at 9:00 a.m., and within minutes saw his life turn on a dime. He thought he was watching the filming of a movie as Flight #175 slammed into the south tower of the World Trade Center. And in the second it took him to process that shock, he noticed smoke already billowing out of the north tower. He knew that the north tower was where the restaurant was and the smoke seemed to be coming out of a gaping hole several floors down from where the restaurant would be. He quickly learned from the live newscast that Flight #11 had hit the north tower seventeen minutes earlier than the flight that hit the south tower. He panicked, phoned his wife's cell. No connection. He browsed the internet for the Windows on the World phone number and dialed it. Nothing but silence, not even a ring. He browsed for the WTC Administration offices and dialed that number. Busy signal. He phoned Susan's office and talked to her secretary. She and everyone else in her office were watching the same newscast and were in the dark as to how Susan or any of their other colleagues had fared. She promised to let him know as soon as she heard anything at all.

Jack sat transfixed in front of the television, knees shaking, tears streaming down his cheeks, praying for the first time in his life. There was nothing he could do except wait and force himself to watch and listen. He convinced himself that there would be a rescue. After all, the plane hadn't hit her floor directly. He was thinking maybe they could get up on the roof if a helicopter could land there. He was hoping she had headed upward instead of down.

Then the horror got worse. At about 10:00 a.m. he watched as the south tower heaved and crumbled to the ground, neatly, and in a matter of seconds. It hadn't leaned or toppled sideways. It just kind of shuddered and fell in its own footprint. Jack's hands started to shake. He tried to console himself by thinking that the south tower must have been more severely damaged: it was the second tower to get hit, but the first to collapse. Susan would be okay. They were probably rescuing her right now. The north tower must be in far better shape. It wouldn't fall down; it couldn't.

Then about thirty minutes later, Jack's world collapsed along with the north tower. He couldn't believe the nightmare unfolding in front of his eyes. And the building fell in exactly the same way as the south tower—straight down, in seconds, in its own footprint. He prayed that Susan had gotten out in time. But she hadn't.

In the days following the disaster, it became clear that his lovely wife had not been rescued, had not been wandering in a daze throughout the avenues of New York like so many others had.

Instead, her body, smashed almost beyond recognition, had been found under the rubble, on the concrete promenade in front of where the north tower had once stood. She had been one of the 200 or so who had jumped.

Almost eight years had passed since that horrible day, but it seemed like yesterday to Jack. While the agony and despair had long since passed, the emptiness and sense of loss remained. He had loved Susan very much. She had been beautiful, compassionate, intelligent and absolutely full of life. She loved adventure, going on trips to faraway places. She had enriched his life with her enthusiasm for life. Susan had never been negative about anything; she always took the optimistic view, and since Jack wasn't always like that, he found her good example motivating. They had been married for twenty-five years, which seemed to Jack as his entire life. Life began for him with Susan. So, getting back out there hadn't been easy for him. He always found himself comparing lady friends to Susan, which wasn't fair to them. He knew they could tell too. He certainly had no problems attracting women, being blessed with movie star good looks. Some women even compared him to Paul Newman with his dirty blonde hair and captivating blue eyes. He was of moderate height, standing close to six feet tall, and did not have an inch of fat on his body. However, he knew that while his dates were attracted to him, they were also annoyed whenever he talked about his wife—which was often. He knew he had to snap out of this eventually; in fact he made a pact with himself to do it soon. Susan wouldn't want him living like this—regretful, lonely, regressive.

Jack was in good shape because he worked at it. Years ago he had obtained his black belt in karate. He never really looked at karate as a tool of defense; more as an aggressive means of staying in shape and achieving something difficult. He was achievement-driven and curious to a fault. If there was a mystery in life or in business, he had always wanted to solve it. He loved history and the unsolved mysteries that existed in the past. He wanted nothing more than to solve one of those old mysteries himself. This curiosity and drive is what helped make Jack a rising star in business, and successful at whatever he tried to take on. However, that same drive brought him to virtual burnout on the job—the main reason why he knew he had to finally leave his career behind, or die in it.

His daily routine included his karate kata—a sequence of movements simulating attack or defense positions. This was good exercise for him, and good practice at agility and coordination. But more importantly, it kept his skills sharp and his memory of the movements current. He also found it to have a calming effect, probably the same way yoga did for its practitioners.

Mule was a product of his loneliness. Jack was so desperate for another living creature in the house that he adopted Mule back in 2005. He had never owned a dog before, and had never really had a desire to, but Jack became a quick convert when he saw him at the animal shelter. There was no known history for Mule. He had been found wandering Calgary's streets, hungry and skinny. But he had clearly been trained by a master. Not only was he a classic Border collie in his stealth and agility, he actually seemed to be a good guard dog as well, which Jack found surprising for a Border collie. Mule seemed to take to Jack quickly as well, even behind the bars of the shelter. They made a connection and Jack couldn't leave without buying him. He had nursed him back to health, and since then the two of them had been inseparable. Mule was friendly and fun, but also very protective of Jack and the house. He wasn't averse to growling at strangers until he saw that Jack approved of them. Then they were best friends. He always watched Jack's reaction to people and then he reacted accordingly. Jack found this loyalty and trust heartwarming. They clearly had a bond.

The shelter had no idea what his real name was so Jack called him Ranger, a name that the dog took quite a while to warm up to, then seemed to reluctantly accept. The shelter also advised Jack that his new buddy had a microchip implanted beneath the surface of his skin, around the neck/shoulder area. This chip would likely contain an identification number that could be tracked through the chip manufacturer's registry, who could provide him with a name and address. However, the scanners that the shelter used could not read the chip. The attendant surmised that either the chip was faulty or another type of scanner would be needed to read it; a fairly common problem apparently. Jack took Ranger to a local veterinarian for a check-up and to see if he had a scanner that would be worth a try. No luck. The vet suggested that it was possible that Ranger might be an American dog and a vet or shelter in the states could possibly retrieve the information off the chip. The scanners used in Canada were quite different from the ones in the states.

Jack made a mental note to do that some day, but without any real urgency. Ranger belonged to him now and he didn't know if he really wanted to track down the old owner. But eventually his natural curiosity got the better of him, as he knew it would.

The summer of 2008 resurrected Jack's urge to investigate Ranger's background. They had been together almost three years at that point, and had become so close that Jack felt almost like he was betraying Ranger by not finding out his history. Either that or he was bored out of his mind in retirement and needed some kind of distraction from the routine.

Working on the hunch that the dog was from the states, he decided he would drive down to the closest state to Alberta, beautiful Montana, and see if he could find a vet who had the right scanner. So he bundled Ranger into his Audi A6, with the twin turbo engine that Jack just loved to hear whine, and headed off down Hwy #2 south to the border. Border crossings were more delayed now since 9/11, but Jack thought that to be a good thing. It had been far too easy before, and God only knew how many crazies had freely crossed between the two countries before the World Trade Center disaster. Border guards were finally armed too, which Jack thought was kind of a no-brainer.

There was the usual lineup of cars when he arrived at the border. As he patiently inched his way along, he counted three cars in the line up ahead that got pulled over into the compound. By the time he arrived at the gate, they had been cleared by a separate crew of guards, and were on their way. He showed his passport to the officer in the booth and displayed Ranger's vaccination certificate. He asked Jack to pop the trunk, and he also took a peek under the hood. Then he announced that Jack was good to go. This whole process had taken about an hour since he had pulled up at the back of the line. Not too bad compared to some other trips he had made down this way.

He headed directly to Whitefish, an area he had vacationed at quite a bit over the last few years. The lakes in Montana reminded him of Ontario lakes in appearance, although they were a bit on the cold side. Whitefish Lake was a gem, and he had rented cottages there many times. It was a busy lake, but well worth the stay. He headed down the main drag and stopped at the first veterinary clinic he saw. He hitched up Ranger and headed in the front door. It wasn't too busy. There was an old lady filling out some papers in the waiting area, a cat with a bandaged paw laying on the floor beside her. Jack kept his distance. He had an allergy to cats that wasn't pleasant. The old lady handed the girl at the counter her papers, picked up the cat and headed for the door, giving Jack a friendly smile as she passed.

"Can I help you, sir?" The girl at the counter was wearing hospital garb, and she looked to be in her early twenties. Cute too—short, brown hair, and eyes that sparkled as she smiled. Jack thought she looked outdoorsy. A tanned face, and sinewy wrists that had probably had to restrain more than their share of large dogs.

"Hopefully you can." Jack summoned his most charming smile. "My name's Jack Howser. I live up in Calgary and I adopted Ranger here about three years ago. I understand from my vet that there's a microchip under his skin. Unfortunately, up in Canada, we don't seem to have the same scanners as you folks, and I'd like to check my dog's background."

"Are you concerned about anything in particular?"

"No, not at all. Ranger is healthy and friendly. I'm just curious. Would the doctor be free to do a scan for me?"

She smiled patiently at Jack. "I am the doctor, sir, and I'd be pleased to help you."

Jack gulped and turned different shades of red. "Um, um, I'm sorry, I just assumed…"

She laughed. "Call me Meagan. Please, don't be embarrassed. I do look a little young for my age."

Jack sighed. Off the hook. Thankfully she assumed it was an age thing rather than a sexist thing. Meagan escorted him and Ranger back to a rear examining room, and Jack lifted his dog up on the table. She brought out a wand and flipped a switch. It had a long handle with a grip and it widened near the end in almost a triangle shape. Set in the triangle was a screen. It looked similar to the one his vet in Calgary had used, but Jack kept his fingers crossed hoping that the technology was different. She waved the triangle end over Ranger's neck and shoulders. The wand beeped and the screen came to life.

"We're in business," Meagan said. "We have the data." She looked down at the screen, and hesitated for a second. "That's strange," she muttered. She shook her head slowly, and then made a few notations on a piece of paper.

"What's strange?" Jack asked.

"See for yourself." Meagan handed him the sheet of paper. While Jack read over what she wrote, Meagan sat down at her computer and tapped away at the keyboard. She wrote out some more information and handed it to Jack. "Call this number here. This is the manufacturer for the type of chip that Ranger has. Ask for the registry, then recite the code number from the chip on that other note I gave you—R207—and they should be able to give you the critical information from Ranger's file."

Jack looked at the piece of paper, and frowned. "What's this other stuff here?"

"I haven't the slightest idea. I just copied everything down for you. I've never seen additional information like that on a chip before. Usually they just have the code number and the manufacturer's identification."

Jack looked at it again, puzzled. This was very strange. A curious phrase and numbers, with no apparent meaning: *"Tell her she has the key to her Soul within her reach. 15/15/14."*

"Are you sure there's nothing else?"

"That's all there is—but I think that's enough, don't you?" She chuckled.

"Yes, this will keep me busy for a while just pondering what it means! I'm actually amazed that all of that information can be crammed onto a chip. How big are they?"

"Only a bit bigger than a grain of rice. And they can actually hold a lot more than what we found on yours."

"Wow, simply amazing technology, eh? You've been wonderful, Meagan. I don't know how I can thank you—other than paying the bill of course!"

"Don't worry about it, no trouble at all. Charging you isn't worth the paperwork. Consider it a favor from a Yank to a Canuck."

"Well, that's mighty neighborly of you, Meagan. Much appreciated."

"Just remember me the next time you're passing through, Jack. Maybe you could buy me dinner?"

Jack felt a tinge of excitement and considered staying an extra day, but quickly came to his senses. "I might just do that."

He made a quick exit before things got too complicated. Jack was only interested right now in finding out about Ranger's past.

On the drive back to Calgary, Jack thought about the pretty young vet, and wondered why he couldn't get his priorities straight. He had chosen to investigate a microchip instead of enjoying a nice dinner with a young lady who was clearly flirting with him. He wondered if maybe age was starting to catch up to him. Once home, he hustled Ranger into the house, and went down the hall to his office.

The next part was easy. He dialed the number to the chip manufacturer, gave out the code #R207, and had what he was looking for. Lo and behold, Ranger's name was actually "Mule" and he had been implanted with the chip back in 2002. Jack thought Mule was a strange name for a dog. He liked Ranger a hell of lot better, but figured that maybe out of courtesy he should ask the dog and see what he thought. He called out to the living room where Ranger was lounging, and said, "Mule, come here, boy!" The dog was there in seconds flat, looking strangely revitalized. "Mule, sit." The dog obeyed and raised his right paw. He had never done that before. Jack accepted the outstretched paw, and then his little buddy started licking his hand. Ranger had never been a licker either. Jack took this as a sign that the dog was happy to be called by his real name for a change. He must have awakened some memories in the poor little fellow.

From that day forward, Ranger became Mule, and both man and dog were happy as clams.

The code number from the chip also gave Jack a dog license number for the bureau in New York City. Jack wondered how it was possible that Mule could have landed in a shelter in Calgary. He called the licensing bureau in New York and gave them the tag number. Jack learned that Mule had been born in 2001 but became orphaned in 2003 when the owner, a Mitch Joplin, had died. There had been a transfer of ownership to the late owner's daughter, a Kerrie Joplin, but the license had not been renewed due to an apparent move by the daughter from New York to Kalispell, Montana.

Interesting, Jack thought. He had been very close to Kalispell earlier this very day. He could have looked her up had he known.

Oh well, never too late. He checked with directory assistance for Kalispell, but there was no record of a Kerrie Joplin. Her number was probably unlisted. Jack was disappointed, but for now he turned his attention to the mysterious phrase and numbers extracted from the chip. Did they have meaning? Or were they just gibberish? Was he looking for a mystery? He fretted over this for a few hours, until finally telling himself that he was probably demented and needed to get a life—badly.

*****

Now on this wintry day in 2009, Jack found his mind wandering. Bored, and in need of something different, he went into his office and turned on the television. There was a retrospective show about the Kennedy assassination. Jack knew more about that event than any documentary could teach him, so he surfed the channels. He stopped at another documentary about pet safety, and saw that they were in the middle of discussing the trend toward micro-chipping pets. An interesting segment.

It reminded him of the strange data from Mule's chip. It had been a few months since he had tried to track down the late owner's daughter. He rummaged around in his desk and found his notes. "Aha!" he exclaimed out loud. "Maybe worth another try?" As Jack pondered this, he said partly to himself and partly to Mule, "What the hell. What better things do we have to do today, eh boy?"

Chapter 2

The quiet stillness of the lake was shattered by the roar of a lone snowmobile, a silver streak snaking its way along the shoreline. When it reached its apparent destination near the snow banks of the bay it made one last burst of speed leaping and twisting in the air as it hit the drifts. The silver demon came to rest beside a stately old home that had seen better days.

A slim figure in a stylish red suit jumped off the machine and strolled up to the front porch. Removing her helmet, she shook her head as her long blonde hair flowed out over her shoulders. She plopped herself down on an old Muskoka chair and sighed contentedly. How lucky she was to live in such a setting. There really was no nicer view than Flathead Lake, even in the winter.

It was a cold January day in Bigfork, Montana, and Kerrie Joplin was enjoying every second of it. She had moved to Montana in 2003, and lived the first couple of years in Kalispell while she worked on designing the specifications for renovating this old house by the lake. It was more than a house though; it was a bed and breakfast, or at least it would be a bed and breakfast once the finishing touches were done. Bigfork was a beautiful little town, very "artsy", located on the northeast shores of the biggest lake in the western United States. The shoreline circumference was 160 miles and the lake covered 200 square miles. It was a deep lake too at 300 ft., making the fishing challenging but also spectacular for those who had patience. Monster Mackinaw trout up to 50 lbs. prowled the lake, and more than one fisherman had fallen into the water trying to hook one.

The lake was pristine—a boating and swimming paradise—and snowmobiling in the winter was fabulous, as was the ice fishing, as long as you stayed close to the shore in one of the bays. Flathead Lake seldom froze over completely. And for skiers, two major areas, Whitefish Mountain and Blacktail, were within easy driving distance of Bigfork, as was the larger center of Kalispell. It only had 20,000 people but at least the shopping was more varied than what Kerrie could obtain in Bigfork.

But Bigfork was cute. Not only did it have the recreational amenities that a bed and breakfast needed, but it was a quaint town that offered gourmet restaurants and an incredible array of arts and crafts shops, galleries, and uppity gift stores. Tourists loved it—it seemed to be right out of a Norman Rockwell painting. Kerrie had just taken down all of her Christmas lights and decorations—always a sad tradition. The old house had looked incredibly warm and inviting, she thought. Since her home would be open for business in just a few days, she knew that next Christmas would be very special, with guests staying for the holidays. She had taken the opportunity this year to get some good photos for her website, showing off the Christmas splendor. Even though the house still looked tired on the outside, good color photos with the Christmas lights and decorations fooled the average eye.

However, it wasn't just her home that took the holiday season seriously. The entire town and surrounding area had the nickname "Christmas Town" in some media circles. The most incredible array of lights and decorations in the entire country could be found in Bigfork. Everyone took great care to maintain the tradition, and the town began to look like Christmas almost right after Halloween. Kerrie figured every town should have an image, and what better image than to be known as "Christmas Town."

She hoped to be able to attract some winter guests in a few days' time, and then truckloads of people through the summer. She had a fleet of seven snowmobiles that guests could use (after signing a waiver, of course) and three water-ski boats for summer fun. Her dock was on shore right now due to the winter ice, but it was one of those that slid easily into the water in the spring with the help of a few strong guys. It anchored itself quite handily to pilings sunk deep into the lake bed, and its length was able to accommodate boats and sunbathers alike.

She was proud of her old house and of the wonderland she lived in. What a change from her former life in New York.

Kerrie had moved here in 2003 after the violent death of her father in an apparent bank robbery. But instead of a bank robbery, it was actually some kind of media stunt that her father had attempted to orchestrate before he was shot and killed. He had been holding a bank full of customers and employees hostage, along with a teller wearing a bomb vest. He was still hanging on to the detonator when he was felled by a single bullet to the head. When Mitch was shot, the bomb didn't detonate. Turned out it was a dud, and the gun he had been brandishing wasn't loaded. She knew her father was an expert in explosives, so he would never have created a dud by accident. And since the gun was empty, it was apparent to Kerrie that Mitch never intended to hurt anyone. What was also apparent was that he had something important to say and he wanted the world to hear it through the media. Somehow he felt he had to force the media to put this message on the air, and he needed something spectacular to do that.

Either that, or her father had completely lost his mind, a possibility that she had considered seriously over the last few years. During the couple of years leading up to his death, her dad had become strange, despondent, paranoid at times, and had fallen into depression. He went on medication for the depression, but on some days even that didn't seem to help. Mitch became over-protective of Kerrie, and even paid for firearms training for her as a Christmas present one year. Kerrie rejected the present, but Mitch was so insistent and persuasive that she relented and gave in. She adamantly refused to buy a gun though. She drew the line there. But her dad was relieved she at least had learned how to use one, and that she had actually developed into a pretty good shot. He even took her out into empty fields to practice what she had learned. He was determined that she would be well equipped to defend herself. Against who or what, Kerrie had no idea.

For most of her dad's life, his career had been secretive. Kerrie and her mom knew some of it, but not all. There was military work, extensive explosives training, and secret trips away in the middle of the night without even a goodbye. By the time her mother had died of cancer in the mid-eighties, her father's career was so busy Kerrie wondered if he had even noticed she was gone. And his career was troubling him more and more all the time. He became distant, though never abusive. After 9/11 he seemed to go over the edge. The whole world had been horrified by that event, but Mitch seemed to take it personally. He was never the same again. He seemed angrier, more distant than ever before, and acted almost desperate at times.

He had retired a couple of months after 9/11, from whatever it was he did, and Kerrie was glad about that. Then in 2003, after his death, she found out through the media that her dad had been CIA. While that came as a bit of a shock, she wasn't really all that surprised. She knew he had some kind of career that wasn't easily talked about, and she didn't even know if her mother knew what he really did. All they both knew was that he worked for the U.S. government—in what capacity they had no idea. She guessed that he was probably forbidden to talk about it to anyone. Sad that he had no shoulders to cry on; carrying around the dangers, fears, and burdens with no one to confide in or confess to. No wonder he seemed wound up so tight.

The publicity from that bank incident was beyond spectacular. National media picked up the story and ran with their speculations for weeks. Kerrie was relentlessly pursued 24/7 by the paparazzi in their attempts to pin her down on personal views about what her father had done. Grim photos hit the front pages—her father lying in a pool of blood with a hole in his forehead. The media could be so insensitive and sensational, it defied understanding. Anytime there was blood, it was the lead story ad nauseum. She loved her father despite his secrecy and brooding. He always made time for her when he was around, and was so protective, all the more so in the last two years of his life. He was a gentle giant; confident, handsome, piercing eyes, threatening swagger, but affectionate and probing. He always wanted to know how people felt, always showed an interest in people that belied his menacing size. She knew her father was caring, but she was sad that he seemed so troubled.

Well, maybe he had finally found his own way of destroying his demons, with that end-of-life media stunt. Or, as she'd almost convinced herself, maybe he had just lost his mind. She couldn't understand how that special team of government killers could just gun down her father while he held his finger on a detonator. Those goons were apparently fully protected in bomb-proof suits, but the staff and customers in the bank sure weren't. The message to the media afterwards was that they had been able to easily identify that the bomb was fake, but wouldn't give specifics as to how they knew. And if they knew that it was a fake, then why did they have to kill him?

They obviously figured upon entering the bank that the bomb might be real, otherwise they wouldn't have been dressed the way they were. And if they discovered the truth only once they got close to Mitch, why did they come in with a fake video camera—a gun disguised as a camera? That meant in her mind that they intended to shoot him from the beginning whether or not the bomb was a phony. Kerrie figured they just got lucky. They intended to shoot him and take the chance that everyone else except them might be killed. Collateral damage. That thought always gave Kerrie the shivers. And the media lapped up the government's statements as usual—no questions asked, no logic challenged. No one wanted to be locked out of the next big political story or scandal so best to just show the blood on the front page, paint her father as a loose cannon and move on. Don't piss off the big boys. Whatever speculations certain braver media outlets dared to voice died off without follow-up.

Well, that was almost six years ago now and Kerrie had moved on with the mystery unsolved. She had resigned herself to the fact that that was the way it would remain. She had a life to live and her father, no matter how troubled, would have wanted her to move on.

In his own way, he had helped her do just that. In his will he had left Kerrie almost $400,000 in cash—and the biggest surprise of all—this old house in Montana. Another brick in the mysterious life of Mitch Joplin. In fact, a lot of bricks; most of them had needed repairing over the last few years. This house was a mess when Kerrie first showed up to look it over. The inside needed gutting, the outside needed virtually everything, and the shoreline was decrepit. She figured that was why Mitch had left her so much cash, knowing she would have no choice but to fix it up. It sure was big though—a huge living and dining area, large country kitchen, eight bedrooms, ten bathrooms, and a beautiful sunroom. As soon as she saw it, she thought "bed and breakfast," and then immediately threw her heart and soul into restoring it.

However, the place had been a target of vandals and the homeless; the evidence was everywhere. She was so afraid that the place would deteriorate further while she lived in Kalispell designing the renovations, that she hired a security firm to camp out there 24/7. It was expensive, but she felt she had no choice but to protect her dad's investment. Then, once the work started, she rented a trailer and had it set up next to her house so she could keep an extra set of eyes on the place herself. She was relieved now to be no longer living in that stupid trailer.

The house still looked tired on the outside. Wood treatments around the windows, porch, and gables needed paint. Patios and stone walkways were badly cracked and had to be replaced. The windows themselves were still the originals, and probably wouldn't survive another winter. But the inside was now gorgeous and almost ready for patrons.

In the reading of the will, there was a surprising guest who had been invited. The poor little teller that Mitch had held hostage. Kerrie couldn't remember her name now, but Mitch had left her $200,000. Kerrie wondered if they had been having an affair, but after chatting with the girl it became apparent they were just acquaintances. The girl had been as shocked as Kerrie that she had been included in the will. She seemed appreciative but Kerrie could tell that the poor girl was still shaken to her core. She trembled throughout the will reading, with her bloodshot eyes constantly looking down at the floor. At the time the will was read it had already been a month after the incident, but the shock that the girl had experienced that day was still with her. Kerrie had advised her to seek counseling, which she promised to do.

Then after that she never saw her again. She hoped she was doing well. But the whole thing about that teller added another element of mystery. The will had been re-written about a month before Mitch's death, and the teller had been singled out in the bank incident as the hostage of choice. So it seemed Mitch knew who he was going to use, knew she'd survive, and wanted to leave her something as a token of thanks or consolation. Kerrie had wracked her brain over this part of the mystery for months. None of it made sense.

Kerrie left the front porch and went into her grand foyer. She lit the fireplace that already had some nice dry birch piled up in it. It was a wonderful fireplace, functioning as a two-way between the living room and the hallway. The roaring fire would welcome guests as they entered the house, and then greet them again as they sat down in the living room.

She wiggled out of her snowsuit, marveling at the good shape she was still in, despite the unhealthy eating she tended to do sometimes. She knew she was a stunner—a beautiful body that every man watched as she walked by, long blonde hair, and an almost perfect face accented by the most alluring green eyes. She was thirty-five now—not vain by any means—but proud that she had some natural gifts. She knew she had gotten most of them from her father, including a slight cleft chin that added some extra character to her persona. She could do without the freckles on her nose, but makeup usually took care of that nicely. When she was a little girl, her mother had always told Kerrie that she took after her father. Kerrie usually protested saying that she wanted to be more like her mother. As she grew up she couldn't ignore the physical similarities any longer. Her mother had been right. She always wished, mainly for mom's sake, that she had a sister or brother who looked like the other side of the family. However, her mom's long fight with cancer prevented her from having any more children. Kerrie was an only child and the apple in her father's eye.

She possessed her dad's brains as well, but regretted that she had had to give up her career in New York after Mitch's death. She had been a corporate lawyer with a prominent law firm. Still only an associate but on the list to be partner within only a few months. Her dad's stunt had changed all that. The senior partner had called her in to his office a few weeks after the heavy media blitz had ended, and asked her to resign. He said the publicity of her father's death and the mysteries surrounding it were far more than the firm's reputation could handle. He wasn't kind about it either. He was actually quite angry, as if he blamed Kerrie for what had happened. Kerrie had protested, even threatened legal action, but she figured there was no point in pursuing anything public. She doubted there would be any court sympathy with the shame that her father had brought onto her.

She settled for a large severance package and went on her way, with no thanks of any sort from the firm for her years of loyal service and no goodbye party from her colleagues. She had been shunned. She tried to land a job with other law firms but never got past the first interviews. The legal community in New York was a surprisingly tight one—everybody knew everything and everybody. Kerrie was pretty sure she had been blackballed.

She decided that it must be fate—it was in the stars that she would run a bed and breakfast and her father had helped create that fate for her. So off she moved, lock, stock, and barrel, to "Big Sky Country."

Kerrie had also inherited Mitch's prized Border collie, Mule. Kerrie and Mule had always gotten along great. She could tell that the dog missed his master, but he took to Kerrie as a reasonably acceptable surrogate. Unfortunately, the partnership hadn't lasted very long. In the summer of 2005, on a trip through the Rocky Mountains of Alberta, Mule had been lured away from a picnic area by a small animal. His instinct took over and off he went. Kerrie took chase but couldn't catch up. She looked for Mule for a couple of days until she finally gave up. She prayed that someone had found him and was giving him a good home. Guilt ate her up inside. Her dad had entrusted Mule with her and it was the last living link to her dad that still existed. He had loved that dog and she dearly hoped that if he was looking down from heaven, or up from that other place, he would forgive her.

It was getting late in the afternoon now, and the western sun was streaming through the front windows. Kerrie went about her daily routine of closing all the sunshades. Even with the sun low on the horizon at this time of the year it could become blinding in the house. Before Kerrie installed the shades she actually had to wear her sunglasses in the house at this time of day. She moved robotically through each western-facing room, pulling down the custom shades. She had made a good choice with these: most of the harmful rays were blocked and her guests could sit comfortably in the late afternoons after a day of activity, yet some light was still allowed through in a lazy diffused glow.

She entered one of the upstairs bedrooms and suddenly caught movement out of the corner of her eye. She stared out the window for a moment or two to see if it was only her imagination. There it was, a figure moving along the side of her house closest to the lake.

She ran downstairs to the kitchen and pulled a large carving knife out of the block. Kerrie wasn't one to hide under the bed. At times like this though, she wished she still had Mule by her side. The Border collie had actually been a darn good watchdog, and very protective of her. She cautiously walked to the front door, knife in hand, and peeked out the window to make sure that whoever it was out there was not on her front porch. Coast clear, she slipped on her boots, opened the door and tentatively stepped outside.

There he was, with an armful of her firewood, making his way down to the frozen shoreline. Kerrie shouted. "Hey! What are you doing there?" The man turned and started back towards her. He was dressed in a black snowsuit, expensive looking, and a black toque. His face was familiar.

"Hi there. I didn't know if anyone was home or not. I knocked but there was no answer." He spoke in a deep baritone voice, and had a friendly manner about him—not just in how he spoke, but the way he walked.

But Kerrie was still on her guard. "Don't give me that bullshit, I've been home the whole time. I would have heard the knock."

He looked at her, seemingly hurt by her outburst. "I'm sorry. That's one big house; you could have easily missed my knock."

Kerrie conceded he was probably right. "What are you doing walking away with my firewood?"

"I'm sorry, Kerrie. I ran out of wood back at my place, and thought you wouldn't mind if I borrowed some. I'll bring you back some wonderful pine as replacement, once I get a new supply."

Kerrie furrowed her brow. "Do I know you, sir?"

"I helped with your dock in the fall, me and that skinny friend of mine."

Now it hit her. Of course. Last summer had been the first time she had launched her new dock, with some workers from town helping out. Come fall though, she was in a pickle trying to figure out how to deal with it for the winter. Two men had been walking up the beach and saw her contemplating her dilemma. They both pitched in and helped her pull it out. This guy did look a lot different in a toque though; it didn't do his good looks justice at all. Kerrie remembered thinking at the time that he might be a neighbor worth getting to know.

"I'm so sorry. I feel so foolish for not recognizing you. Of course you can have the wood. It's the least I can do to repay you for the heavy lifting."

"Well, you did give us some beer, so I considered that payment enough at the time. I promise you, I will replace this wood." Kerrie relaxed and felt silly standing there with a mega-knife in her hand.

"I'll introduce myself again—name's Bob Trundle. I live four houses down the lake. I would have stolen wood from my other neighbors, but you're the only one who seemed to have an adequate supply." He laughed.

"Hello again, Bob." She waved the knife at him. "It's not very neighborly of me to be brandishing this knife at you. Sorry about that."

"Hey, no problem. I'll come armed to the teeth the next time I steal your wood!"

Kerrie laughed, and thought that he seemed like a very charming man. She felt sheepish. "Would you like some coffee? You can drop your wood there and pick it up on your way out."

Bob dropped it without any further convincing. "That would be wonderful. Nice way to take the chill off."

Kerrie led the way through the front door, and Bob just stood there in shock.

"Wow, this is absolutely gorgeous! You wouldn't know from the outside how incredible it is in here!"

Kerrie was beaming. "Thanks. It's been a long haul, but I think I'm almost there." They took their boots off in the hall, and Kerrie put the knife back in the block on the kitchen counter.

"So tell me, Kerrie, what do you need a big house like this for? You're single, right?"

Kerrie felt some unease. "How do you know I'm single?"

"I just assumed. You didn't have a husband helping you with that dock."

Kerrie breathed a little easier. She didn't like people knowing her personal business, at least not virtual strangers. "This is going to be a bed and breakfast. I've already arranged the permits, and I should be open in a matter of days now."

"That's exciting. I'll have to pass the word to some of my friends who travel up this way from time to time. It will save me having to cater to them!"

Kerrie laughed, knowing full well that men didn't go to too much trouble for guests anyway, at least not to the extent women did.

Bob took off his snowsuit and hung it up on a hook in the foyer. He wandered through the living room. Kerrie could see him running his fingers along the windowsills, admiring the wood trim and its smooth finish. "You didn't do this work yourself, did you?"

"Why? A woman can't handle this manly stuff?"

"Well, no…I…"

"I'm just jerking your chain," Kerrie chuckled. "I hired out most of the work, but I did all the design and specs myself. I wanted it to be exactly as I envisioned it to be. It's taken me about four years work plus two years planning to get it just right. All that's really left now is the outside work."

Kerrie went into the kitchen and turned on her coffee maker. Strong coffee was the order of the day, and she didn't really care whether Bob liked it that way or not. He continued to wander around, looking at the dining area, sunroom, and parlor. "This house has so much character. People are going to love staying here. Do you mind if I wander upstairs?"

Kerrie thought that was rather ballsy. She didn't like the idea of him going up there alone.

"While the coffee's brewing, I'll go with you," she said. "There are four bedrooms down here, and another four upstairs. They've all been re-done in kind of a Victorian look."

They both walked up the staircase, Kerrie leading the way. She felt a little odd bringing a stranger to the upstairs bedroom area but Bob didn't really alarm her too much except that he seemed a bit pushy. She kept her wits about her just in case. They wandered down the upstairs hall, peaking into each bedroom. Bob was impressed with the attention to detail. Then he stopped in the middle of the hall and looked up at the ceiling. "It looks like you have an attic up there. Have you re-done that as well?"

Kerrie looked up at the trap door with the old-fashioned handle. "My contractor asked me if I wanted to do that, and I passed. The house is big enough as it is. I sure don't need any more room."

"Have you gone up there?" Bob asked.

"No, the contractor showed me how the trap door brings down a staircase, but I haven't bothered to go up there yet."

"Should we go up and have a boo? There might be some ghostly things that could prove interesting. This house must be at least a hundred years old. You might find some surprising treasures waiting for you up there."

Kerrie shook her head. "No, I'll do it in my own good time. That's all I need right now—to find more junk in this house that I have to dispose of. I'd rather not know." Bob seemed disappointed. Kerrie thought that he was probably a nosy sort in addition to being pushy.

They went back downstairs and sat at the kitchen table. Kerrie poured two steaming mugs of her strong coffee, and offered Bob some doughnuts. She pointed out that they were a day old, but he didn't seem to mind. They continued to chat about the weather, the beauty of the scenery, and the neat little town of Bigfork. Kerrie found out that Bob had lived here for four years and she thought it strange that she'd only seen him twice in that time. She told him that she had started renovation work on her home about the same time as he moved into his, and that she had spent her first two years in Kalispell working on designs and materials. Bob didn't share her enthusiasm for renovation work.

He told her he traveled a lot, and when he was home he liked to keep to himself. Kerrie didn't believe that last part for a second. Although it did indeed look like he traveled—unusual for this time of the year for someone to have such a deep tan as Bob's. And she could tell he was muscular in an athletic kind of way, so the outdoors was probably something he enjoyed. He was certainly an attractive man. She guessed he was over six feet tall, and with his dark hair and complexion he looked almost Hispanic.

"So what do you do for a living, Bob?"

"I'm semi-retired. Made some money in the stock market as a trader and dropped out early." He looked quite young to be semi-retired. Only about forty-five, Kerrie guessed.

"Must be nice," she said. "For the part of you who is not retired, how do you keep busy?"

"I'm a writer," he replied. "Freelance stuff. I tend to do a lot of travel writing for magazines—been doing that for years. And I'm in the middle of writing a novel. So between those two things, I keep as busy as I want to be. And I'm single so being away from home a lot isn't really a problem. So, Kerry, aside from being a nouveau hotelier, what do you do?"

"That's all I will be doing, and I'm looking forward to it. Should be a nice lifestyle for me."

"No other ambitions? You seem like a bright lady."

Kerrie blushed at the compliment. "Well, I am a lawyer and I practiced in New York City until six years ago when I moved out to Montana."

"Why did you leave all that behind? Not that this isn't nice, but it's a far cry from the excitement of New York City."

"A long story. My father died and left me a sizeable inheritance, including this old ramshackle house. I decided to make a life change."

"Sorry to hear about your father. How did he die?"

Kerrie didn't like this line of questioning at all. "He just died."

"Okay, sorry to pry. It's none of my business. My parents died a few years ago in a car accident, so I guess I'm sensitive to what other people go through having gone through it myself."

Kerrie felt a bit ashamed of herself after hearing this. However, the way her father died was a lot different than a car accident and she still didn't want to talk about it.

"It was nice that he left you enough to be able to change your life," Bob commented. "Not many people get a second chance, so you're pretty lucky.

Did he just buy this house sight-unseen, or did he have a chance to visit it? It's a long way from New York to Montana."

"I don't know whether he visited this place or not. It was a surprise to me that he owned it. He never told me about it."

"Your dad must have been a secretive guy. Wonderful for him to leave this surprise for you though. Maybe he just liked surprises?"

Kerrie started to squirm. "Well, Bob, I have to get on with some more chores if I intend to open this place for business in a few days. I'll have to kick you out unless you want to start paying me my daily lodging rate."

Bob laughed. "I can take a hint. I'll just grab my firewood, your firewood I mean, and be on my way."

Kerrie laughed as well. She thought this guy was pretty charming, despite being a bit on the nosy side. Must be just a guy thing. They had to know everything so they felt in control.

Kerrie watched Bob walk down the shoreline with her wood, and thought that she would probably bump into him again now that they knew each other a bit better. And she had the feeling that he would be more likely to engineer it than her. Either way, she sort of looked forward to it. She hadn't dated in quite some time and this guy did seem interesting; as a bonus he was easy on the eyes.

She went back inside and sat down in front of the fire. Kerrie really didn't have any urgent chores today. She had cut the conversation short because she wanted to avoid any bad memories and just get on with her new simple life.

But then her phone rang.

Chapter 3

Newly energized once again towards investigating Mule's history, Jack's first call was back to the microchip manufacturer to see if they could share any insights about the strange notations. No luck. Their answer was basically that anyone could put anything they wanted on a chip. The only information the manufacturer kept on file was related to the basic identification of the dog to allow the animal to be returned to its owner.

Jack looked at his pet and gave him an affectionate rub on the head. "What information are you carrying, boy? Lottery secrets? Poker tips? Or maybe just words of wisdom from a fortune cookie? You could be more valuable than I gave you credit for!" He laughed to himself and Mule seemed to laugh along with him. The dog scampered over to the front door and pulled his leash down from the coat rack.

"Okay, okay, I get the message, fella."

Jack put on his coat and they went outside. He looked at the shoveling mess that still awaited him, and decided it could wait another day after all. The snow had stopped so it wasn't going to get any deeper.

They walked down the street and took a public pathway down to the river. It was completely frozen over now with several skating rinks cleared off for the kids to use. There were a few playing hockey on one particularly smooth sheet of ice, so he and Mule ventured on down to have a look. Jack let him off his leash, and the dog was off like a shot down to the hockey rink, sliding on his rump as he hit the smooth ice. The kids were laughing as Mule tried to regain his footing, while at the same time leaning his body in the direction of the puck. Mule somehow managed to grab the puck in his mouth as he slid by it and then got some serious traction. He dodged and deked his way around the boys, sliding in circles as they chased him. One of the goalies started banging his stick on the ice to get Mule's attention. It worked. Mule did a one-eighty, and started barreling straight toward the goalie, but lost his footing when he tried to turn away and slid head-on into the net taking the goalie down in the process. One of the kids from the other team yelled, "He barks, he scores!" What a heartwarming sight this was—Mule playing his own version of hockey, and the kids rolling around on the ice with laughter.

Goalie and Border collie were struggling to get themselves out of the mesh. Mule's front paws were caught up in the back part of the net, so Jack slid his way over to get him untangled. The goalie looked up at him with a big grin on his face and said, "Next time, can he be on my team?"

Jack hooked Mule up to his leash and they headed on their way, the kids yelling enthusiastic goodbyes. They had clearly enjoyed this little intermission to their game, and so had Mule. He loved kids and they seemed to act as a magnet that he could never resist. Jack thought it was sad that he and Susan hadn't had children. Dogs and kids belonged together. But then again, so did dogs and lonely adults.

They headed back to the house. It was late afternoon and already starting to get a bit dark. This time of the year in Calgary, the days were short, too short. Jack could hardly wait until the summer when the sun stayed out until around 10:00 p.m. for a few weeks. When he was still working he had been able to put in a full day at the office, eat dinner, and still get in eighteen holes of golf before dark. He always thought that was so wonderfully weird, but that was the way Calgary was. Weird weather at times, but also some surprising benefits to being this far north.

Once back inside the warmth of the house, Jack parked himself at his desk and pondered once again the strange phrase and numbers on the chip. It was time, he thought, to be a little more persistent in tracking down the former owner's daughter. What was her name again? He pulled out his notes... Kerrie Joplin. The last time he had tried was this past summer, but he hadn't tried too hard. Now in the dead of winter, he found himself more bored and more curious. So he tried directory assistance for Kalispell again ... nothing.

She could have moved to another town close by, or really any town in Montana. Or she could have left Montana completely. He figured he would concentrate first on the area surrounding Kalispell and see what turned up. He got out his map and started with the town of Lakeside. No luck. Then the town of Polson. No luck. Then Somers. Struck out again. Finally directory assistance gave him some good news. A woman by that name lived in the town of Bigfork, right on the shores of Flathead Lake and only about thirty minutes from Kalispell. He figured this must be the same girl. There couldn't be too many people, especially in sparsely populated Montana, with the unusual name of Kerrie Joplin.

He poured a scotch and decided to phone her. He needed some liquid courage to take his snooping to the next level, so he took a large swig and picked up the phone.

"Hello?" came a soft voice at the other end.

"Hi, is this Kerrie Joplin?"

"Yes, who is this please?"

"Hi Kerrie. My name is Jack Howser from Calgary, Canada, and I've been trying to track you down for some time now. Are you the same Kerrie Joplin from New York whose father was Mitch Joplin?" Silence at the other end. Jack waited and held his breath. "Kerrie, are you still there?"

Suddenly the phone connection was gone. Jack looked at the phone, puzzled, wondering if he had hit the wrong button by mistake. He dialed again. After five rings, she picked up. "Who are you and what do you want!" she demanded.

"I'm sorry, Kerrie, I didn't mean to upset you. Did I say the wrong thing?"

"You phone me up out of the blue and start asking personal questions? Of course you said the wrong thing!"

Jack took another swig of the whiskey. "I only phoned to track down the owner of a dog that I adopted here in Canada. A Mitch Joplin came up in the records as the prior owner before a Kerrie Joplin adopted him. I was hoping you were that same person." Jack could hear her sigh at the other end, clearly one of relief.

"Mule? You have Mule?"

"Yes, I do. So you're obviously the person I'm looking for then. Do you feel better about me now?"

"I guess I do. I'm so sorry for my outburst. I've been trying to put my father's death and history behind me, and it shocked me to hear a stranger phone and ask about him. Tell me about Mule! How is he, and where did he turn up? It's been over three years since I lost him." Jack could finally hear some excitement in her voice.

He filled Kerrie in on Mule's health, how he tracked down the dog's real name and original home from the microchip, and how he had been trying to find her just out of curiosity. She told him about the inheritance of the house, her short-term move to Kalispell, and subsequent move to Bigfork to open a bed and breakfast, and finally her trip to Alberta in 2005 when Mule took off on her.

Jack enquired about her dad's death, but she clammed up. He decided to change the subject to the one he was most curious about. "Kerrie, did you know your dad had that microchip implanted in Mule?"

"I had no idea," she replied. "I guess that's becoming more and more common these days."

"It seems to be," Jack said, "but what doesn't seem to be common is having unrelated information transferred onto these chips. For some reason, your dad had some weird additional notations put on the chip that don't seem to have anything to do with the dog."

Kerrie was silent.

"Kerrie?"

"I don't want to comment on that. My dad did a lot of things that were secret, and I don't want to go into them."

"Okay, fair enough. Maybe we can talk about them some other time then, when you're feeling better?"

"I'm feeling fine, and my feelings are none of your business. I don't even know you."

Jack could sense that he had lit another fire. "I'm sorry once again, Kerrie. You're right, it is none of my business."

A moment's pause, then, "I'd like my dog back, please."

Jack hadn't seen this coming. "That's not going to happen. It's not your dog anymore. I've legally adopted Mule."

"He is my dog, and if you were a decent person you would give him back to me."

"You couldn't have looked very hard for him, Kerrie, and you didn't even leave your name and number with the local SPCA in the event they found him. When I discovered him in the pound he was a frail version of what he is now. It's a good thing I wanted him, otherwise they probably would have euthanized him."

"He's still my dog, and he has tremendous sentimental value for me because of my father."

"I thought you didn't want to talk about your father. You very clearly said you wanted to leave his history behind you. Isn't this dog part of that history?"

All Jack heard next was, "Go fuck yourself!" Then the line went dead.

*****

Two men were talking on a secure phone line, thousands of miles apart. The man in Virginia said to the man in Montana, "We heard something that may be of concern. It has to be checked out."

The man in Montana expended a weary sigh and said, "Why do you people in Langley seem to think those of us in the field have nothing better to do than go on your wild goose chases? We have active assignments to take care of that require more of our attention than these ghosts from the past."

The Virginian was getting testy. "Listen to me! The new administration cannot have these loose ends turning into catastrophic tight ends. Our job is to keep them under wraps, while at the same time giving the politicians plausible deniability. And your job is to do what I say your job is. So whether you like it or not, loose ends are part of what we do, and have to do for survival."

The other man chuckled. "Why don't you just kill all the loose ends? Then we wouldn't have to do all this stupid listening and surveillance on top of the other more important things that require our expertise. Sometimes I think we've become very expensive babysitters."

The Virginian was yelling now. "I don't care for your sarcasm, and you know full well that we can't just kill everyone who knows anything or is in possession of something. Not only does it draw a lot of unwanted attention, but a lot of people like you and I would be dead as well. Who would ever agree to carry out company assignments if they knew they would likely end up on a slab afterwards? We have always used, and will continue to use, other methods to ensure secrecy, except in drastic cases like Mitch Joplin. He gave us no choice. But for most of the others—and there are many—we will listen and watch, probably for the rest of their lives. Some we may have to kill but that would be a last resort."

"Okay, okay, quit the lecture. What do you want me to do?"

The Virginian's voice was calmer now. "We listened in on a phone call that a Canadian man made to Ms. Joplin. That dog that her father owned has turned up in Canada. And it seems there's a microchip, containing something other than just the dog's identification. This Canadian, a Jack Howser in Calgary, did not mention what it was but it sounds like the kind of thing Mitch would have done. He was brilliant and as sly as a fox. It might be nothing, but we have to find out. We need that dog."

*****

It had been a couple of days since Jack's uncomfortable phone conversation with Kerrie Joplin. He wished he had never contacted her at all. The nerve of that girl thinking he would just give Mule back to her. How could she think that after more than three years she'd be entitled to have her dog back, just like nothing had ever happened. He knew that both he and

Mule would be brokenhearted. They were really used to each other now and had formed a strong bond. He couldn't imagine life without his dog.

And wow, did she ever have issues with her father. What was that all about? Whatever it was, she was having a tough time putting it behind her. She sure had a nice voice though, until she swore at him. But even then he found it rather captivating, albeit rude as hell. He liked a woman with spunk. He figured this lady could hold her own with anyone.

And now she was opening up a bed and breakfast. Jack had a flicker of a thought that maybe he should go down there and be one of her first customers. He'd like to put a face to that voice and spunk. No, what was he thinking? She'd probably slam the door in his face. He kept thinking about two of the words she used to describe her father: "history" and "secret". Two words that a curious guy like Jack took to like a duck to water. Words like that were a narcotic to Jack. He decided that he should try a search over the internet for 'Mitch Joplin', and see what popped up. Probably nothing, he thought, but worth a try.

He wasn't prepared for what he read in not just one, but several articles dating back to 2003. Jack sat at his computer in shock, and was suddenly sympathetic with Kerrie's reaction to his questions about her father. He remembered reading about that horrible bank incident in the Canadian papers. It had received a lot of press for a couple of days afterward, as any bomb-related event throughout the world did in the wake of 9/11. It all came back to him. He remembered being intrigued by the story back then. It was one hell of an unusual story, for sure. And the CIA connection. This explained Kerrie's reference to her dad's secrecy.

Jack poured himself a scotch, and could feel the adrenaline pumping in his veins. He wanted to know more, wanted to get inside the head of Kerrie Joplin and perhaps through her, into the head of Mitch Joplin. He began to make some notes.

A couple of hours later Jack took a needed break and threw a couple of rib-eye steaks on the barbecue. Then he added some asparagus and a baked potato as side dishes. He dropped some pieces of steak on the floor for Mule, who gobbled them up instantly. Jack needed a breather from all of this Joplin stuff. He could feel that he was starting to get obsessive about the microchip now that he knew who Mitch Joplin was. The mysterious words and numbers were starting to develop some serious relevance in his mind, and he couldn't shake the feeling that there was something to all of this.

Fresh air. That's what he needed. Jack and Mule headed out the front door together and down the street. As usual, in this cold weather, the street was empty. They headed along their usual route, rounding the corner up the street toward the park. This is the path they took every day, with the occasional detour down to the river.

Once they reached the park, Jack let Mule off the leash and they both walked along the edge of the park next to the street. He was vaguely aware of a slow-moving van coasting along beside him. He looked over at it just as it spun its tires. It skidded to a stop about twenty yards ahead, right beside Mule.

What happened next seemed to be in slow motion. The side van door slid open and a man jumped out and pounced on Mule, cruelly yanking him into the air by his collar. He could see Mule kicking as the man swung the dog toward the open van door. He missed, slamming him up against the side of the van instead and then Mule fell alongside the curb, squealing in pain. Jack was already in full stride, closing the distance fast to the van. He yelled at the man, who ignored him and tried to lift Mule up from under his belly. Jack was on him before he could get any heft, grabbing the man by the neck and twisting him backwards. The fist came hard and fast to Jack's face as the man whirled around. Jack went down and the man turned his attention back to Mule.

The van's engine was still running and another man was peering out the passenger window. Jack got to his feet and spun, landing a wicked kick to the assailant's head before he could get Mule into the van. He grunted and went down. Jack leaped on top of him and rammed a flat hand to his nose, hearing the awful crunch of splintering bones. Blood was now spurting out of the man's nose like a fountain.

The passenger door opened, and the other guy jumped out, holding a knife. Before Jack had a chance to react Mule leaped in the air to the man's chest level and chomped on his neck. A howl of pain broke the still evening as he went down, with Mule still holding on. The thug shoved the dog off and struggled to his feet, blood streaming from his throat. His knife out of sight, he went down into a fighting stance facing Jack, and advanced. Jack matched him, and threw a punch to his head, faked another punch, and then brought his foot up into the thug's groin with incredible force. The guy grabbed at his crotch in pain just as Jack was driving his other foot up at his unprotected face. Crunch. Another broken nose. The driver of the van started leaning on the horn, and both men reacted by struggling up to crouch level and hurling themselves through the van's open side door. It spun its wheels before speeding off down the street.

Jack strained to see if he could catch the plate number, but it was obscured by slush and mud. He then walked over to Mule, who was standing gainfully off to the side watching the van disappear from view. He bent down and examined his pet, applying some pressure to his side and legs. All seemed fine. No telltale whimpering or flinching. The only sign of the battle was the blood from the man's neck wound staining the white of Mule's chin.

Jack would have him checked over by the vet anyway just to be sure. He could feel a pretty good bruise starting to come up on his own left cheek where the would-be dognapper had nailed him. Tears welled up in his eyes as he petted his dog, realizing how bravely Mule had come to his defense. He marveled at the instinct of this animal to leap for the man's neck, and it warmed his heart to know that his buddy had been by his side in this ridiculous battle. What the hell had this been all about? Sure, Mule was a beautiful animal, but this attempted dognapping seemed like overkill.

Jack stood there on the street, trying to make sense out of the surreal event. He played it over and over again in his mind, looking over the scene on the road, seeing the blood-stained snow, realizing it hadn't been a dream. He also realized that this was the first time in his life that he had ever had to use his karate to defend himself or a loved one. An ominous milestone, he thought.

Chapter 4

"We've recovered the knife, Mr. Howser, so we'll run it for prints. We also noticed the large amount of blood at the scene; so it looks like your dog did quite a job on that guy," said the young officer sitting in Jack's kitchen.

"Well, he most likely saved my life," Jack replied. "When that guy jumped out of the truck brandishing a knife, I thought I was a goner. But remember, some of that blood came from two broken noses too, not just the throat injury Mule inflicted."

"Has your dog had training as a guard? The way he reacted seems to have been a taught reflex, similar to our dogs on the force."

"He might have. I bought him from the pound over three years ago, so I don't know what kind of training he's had. Unusual though for a Border collie to have had that kind of training. I suspect he just acted on instinct to protect me."

The officer frowned as if to say 'get real, buddy,' "Has your dog ever drawn blood before?"

"No, this is the first act of physical aggression I've seen, although he will growl at strangers. He growled at you when you came in."

"I'd keep an eye on that dog of yours, if I were you," the officer said. He turned a page in his notepad and wrote something down.

Jack felt frustration starting to build. "I'm a little confused here," Jack said. "Who's the victim? I called you because some thugs tried to take my dog and physically assaulted both of us. We defended ourselves. Why do I get the feeling that Mule and I are considered the bad guys?"

"I'm sorry, sir, didn't mean to make you feel that way. Just exploring all avenues. I'm curious as to whether or not you and your dog had made some enemies. Do you know of anyone who may wish to harm or steal your dog?"

Jack caught himself before he answered. He didn't want to talk about the strange microchip. He didn't know if it had any meaning or not. No sense opening up a can of worms and involving more people than necessary. Also, the cop's question made him immediately think of Kerrie Joplin. Could she have arranged this? Did she have the means to orchestrate this attempted dognapping? He knew she wanted her dog back, but would she go to this extreme? He decided not to mention her either at this point.

"No, no one at all. We get along well with our neighbors and pretty much keep to ourselves. Everyone seems to love Mule."

"Excuse me for asking, but why in hell would you call a beautiful dog like that 'Mule'?"

"It just came to me one day, and it seemed right," Jack lied.

The officer slowly shook his head, probably thinking Jack was some kind of flake. "So, can you give me a description of the two guys? I think you said there was a driver, too, whom you couldn't see?"

"I can't tell you anything about the driver, but the other two guys were both about six feet tall, athletic builds, one blondish and the other with dark brown hair. Both of them seemed to know martial arts, although thankfully not as well as me. What also stood out to me was that they didn't fit the stereotype I have of thugs. They were clean-shaven, and wore expensive winter jackets, as well as arctic-style boots that would be found in the higher-end shops. These guys did not seem to be street types at all."

"Hmm …how about a license plate number?"

"I couldn't see it. It almost looked as if it had been smeared over deliberately. It was perfectly covered so you couldn't see even one letter or number. I thought that was odd. Even their exit was prepared. The driver seemed to know when enough was enough and it was time to scoot. He honked the horn with two short bursts and these guys reacted quickly to get themselves back into the van, as if that was a pre-arranged signal."

The officer nodded in agreement. "Okay, Mr. Howser, I think I have enough for now. We've alerted the local hospitals to let us know if anyone comes in with smashed noses and throat wounds. We've also taken blood samples from the snow, and we'll do a DNA enquiry into the data bank. Of course, we'll see if we can get some prints off the knife. We normally wouldn't go to too much trouble for mere dognappings, but this one does seem more brazen and violent, so it's worth checking into. We'll let you know if there's any progress, or if we have more questions for you."

Jack thanked the officer and showed him out, then promptly sat down on the floor with his dog. He felt so lucky to be able to do this. If he had been a second or two later in reacting, he would be sitting here by himself right now. Mule reached up and licked Jack's face. Normally Jack didn't like this, but he sure as hell appreciated it right now as one of life's little pleasures.

He felt a little guilty for not being totally honest with the cop about the chip, and about Kerrie's expressed wish to have her dog back. The more he thought about Kerrie, the angrier he became. Could she have actually done this? He didn't know the girl so he couldn't form a judgment, but at least over the phone she didn't seem to be the type.

That dognapping would have been quite the thing to organize in just two days' time from all the way down in Montana. Her father, having been former CIA, would probably have been able to pull off something like that pretty easily, but it was hard to believe that an average citizen could. Did Kerrie inherit some of Mitch's contacts? But then, why would someone go to that much trouble and that much risk for a dog?

The CIA. All he knew was what he had learned from movies. His impression was that these spooks moved in secret circles, and could seemingly do things above the law, with resources that would astonish the average Joe. Jack decided to search the internet for more information.

He discovered that there were mounds of data on the CIA. It was an organization based in Langley, Virginia, just a few miles from Washington D.C. Its primary official role was the collection and analysis of information about foreign countries, corporations and individuals, and then subsequent advice to the U.S. government on its findings. It sounded like the CIA had been a lone cowboy prior to The Intelligence Reform and Terrorism Prevention Act of 2004, which brought it under the Director of National Intelligence. In addition to overseeing the CIA, this Director had to oversee all sixteen different intelligence agencies. Jack found it ridiculous to think that the U.S. needed so many intelligence collectors. With that many running around doing their thing, it was hard to believe any of them could be really and truly controlled.

He saw reference to a secretive outfit in the CIA known as the Special Activities Division (SAD), and there was no specific information at all as to what this group did, only generalities. There seemed to have been some conflict over the last few years as to how the CIA was to relate to the FBI and Homeland Security—some "lines in the sand" as to who would handle domestic security intelligence. However, it seemed to be acknowledged that the CIA would indeed get involved when collection of information from outside the U.S. might impact domestic matters. And of course the CIA was supposed to be in constant contact with the Department of Defense, which one would expect.

Jack found himself starting to develop a headache when he read about the various divisions of the CIA: Foreign Broadcast Information Service; Directorate of Science and Technology; National Open Source Enterprise; The National Clandestine Service; The Office of Near Eastern and South Asian Analysis; The Office of Russian and European Analysis; The Office of East Asian, Latin American, and African Analysis; The Office of Terrorism Analysis; The Office of Transnational Issues; The CIA Crime and Narcotics Center; The Weapons, Intelligence Nonproliferation, and Arms Control Center; The Defense Threat Reduction Agency; The Counterintelligence Center Analysis Group; The Information Operations Center Analysis Group; The Office of Collection Strategies and Analysis; The Office of Policy Support...and so on; probably much more than he could ever research, or even be allowed to research. Jack couldn't help but laugh a bit. Trust government to make everything so convoluted, bureaucratic, and confusing. No wonder taxpayer deficits would go on and on forever; at least in the U.S.

His internet search hinted that there were also purported CIA front corporations, airline services and the like, that the normal person would never know about.

Jack was particularly interested in that secretive CIA arm—Special Activities Division (SAD). He figured that title pretty much covered everything that either fit or didn't fit into all of these other divisions. Apparently this Special Activities Division reported in to another CIA division known as The National Clandestine Service. This service was responsible for collection of foreign intelligence—which seemed to be what all the other divisions were for as well—and covert paramilitary operations. They seemed to work in high threat or hostile areas, and did their work in situations where the U.S. government needed the deed done without the government being associated with it. The officers of this SAD group could not wear any clothing or carry any objects that would identify them with the United States, and it was well accepted that if they were caught or compromised in any way, the government would legally deny their status and any knowledge whatsoever as to the nature of their mission. They were truly 'lone wolves.' And prior to the Act being passed in 2004 in response to the 9/11 intelligence failures, these people must have had even more freedom than they did today. Scary.

Jack figured the guys and girls in this SAD division were the real spooks. While they did not have the protection of the government and they well accepted that risk, at the same time since they weren't protected it would seem that they could freely operate outside the law with no rules. It was rumored that these agents were also extremely well paid for the risks they took. They seemed to be the elite, and very highly trained.

Jack thought of Kerrie's father, and wondered what it must have been like for her growing up under such a cloak of secrecy. Jack also wondered which division of the CIA Mitch had worked under. Could it have been SAD? Interesting acronym, he thought; probably aptly described how these agents felt about their lives. Or perhaps they just loved the rush and excitement so much, the acronym more appropriately described how the people in their lives felt.

Jack printed off what he needed and turned in for the night. Maybe tomorrow he would phone Kerrie and pose the dognapping question to her.

*****

Kerrie stood back in the snow on the shoreline and surveyed her house. In need of a paint job, but the new signs sure looked good. She'd had them installed on the entrance from the road, as well as above the porch that looked over the lake. They gave her house a real professional look; in fact, it looked like it had always been a bed and breakfast. She had asked that the signs be antiqued for an older authentic look. They were large and carved in the shape of lighthouses.

Kerrie had decided to call her place Lighthouse Inn, as she always thought that it slightly resembled a lighthouse. It was situated on the point of a beautiful bay, and the house had a very unique feature—the southwest corner that looked out on the lake had a three storey cylindrical structure that you could enter from inside the house. It was like a little tower and had its own spiral staircase up to the third floor 'widow watch.' Kerrie thought this feature gave the house real character, and offered a wonderful view of the lake. It was like a separate little wing of the house, and really served no purpose at all except to give the house a different dimension. It needed some fixing up still, so Kerrie didn't intend any guests to go up to that third floor lookout room just yet. She was afraid that the floor wasn't quite secure, but at least that little section of the house helped give the bed and breakfast its name.

She went back into the house and started preparing dinner. Spaghetti tonight, she thought. She found it hard to believe she would be opening up her little inn to guests in just a few more days. Her website was launched now, along with all the wonderful Christmas photos. Her on-line application and credit card processes had been tested and they worked. All that was left were a few finishing touches on the inside.

As she was making her pasta, she thought back to that phone call a few days ago from that Canadian—what was his name?—Jack. She was glad to know her dog was alive, and in hindsight thought that she had been kind of nasty to that poor man on the phone. She didn't like the questions about her father, but how was that guy supposed to know her history? She had treated him unfairly and she knew that. She was relieved that Mule had a home and was safe. She had been a brat to suggest that Jack give the dog back to her. That was how she had felt at that moment. She was calmer now, and thought that maybe she should call Jack and apologize. She looked for the number near the phone…she had copied it down from the call display. Kerrie had just picked up the phone when the doorbell rang. She peeked out and saw a man in a suit standing on her porch. He was carrying a clipboard and looked pretty serious. Kerrie opened up the door, and he boldly stepped into the foyer.

"Are you Kerrie Joplin?" he asked, squinting at his clipboard.

"Yes, I am. What can I do for you?"

"Hi Kerrie, I'm Jim Nesmith with the Flathead County district, the building inspector. I understand you're pretty much finished your renovations and I need to check things over to make sure you're okay for occupancy. I understand you'll be operating a bed and breakfast here?"

Kerrie couldn't hide the puzzled look on her face. "I'm a bit confused. I've arranged all of the permits and have already received the occupancy certificate. Another gentleman was here a month ago and gave me the green light."

Jim handed her his card. "No need to be alarmed, Kerrie. We won't cause you any unnecessary grief. This is just a routine final check."

"Well, okay. I've cooperated in every way possible so far, so I'm not going to change my attitude now. Please feel free to wander around."

"Thanks, Kerrie. It's nice to get cooperation. You wouldn't believe how many people give us a hard time, when we're only here to help."

Jim began his tour, starting with the kitchen and moving throughout the rest of the main floor—opening cupboard doors, checking the plumbing where it was accessible, and testing out the electrical system. He then went upstairs. Kerrie followed him for this part of the tour. He went through the bedrooms and tested all of the bathrooms, then stopped in the hallway. "Ah, I see you have an attic. Any rooms finished up there?"

"No, I haven't even been up there yet. It has a staircase that folds down, but I don't intend to use it. I don't even know if it's safe to walk around up there. I'm afraid that someone might fall through the ceiling." She laughed.

Jim ignored her, jumped up, and grabbed onto the handle of the trap door. The staircase folded smoothly down to the floor. "Well, that works pretty good," he said.

"Hey, what are you doing?" Kerrie exclaimed. "I told you it might not be safe! I don't want to take the chance that my ceilings will fall in!"

"For safety reasons I have to check it out," Jim said. "This is part of the overall inspection."

"That doesn't make any sense at all. I told you that the attic won't be used, so why does it have to be inspected? Go inspect the basement—you haven't even asked about that yet. That's where all the heating and plumbing originates. I would think you'd be more interested in that."

"Lady, I'll look at everything in the order I want to look at it," he snapped.

Kerrie noticed a definite change in Jim's tone, and she felt an alarm bell ringing in her head. Jim started up the staircase.

"I'll ask you one more time. Get down from those steps now, or I'll phone the police. You do not have my permission to go up there."

Suddenly Kerrie flew back against the wall and collapsed to the floor. She raised her hand to her face in disbelief, feeling incredible pain in the side of her jaw. She was afraid that it might be broken. The stranger on the staircase above her, whom she now realized with trepidation was not a building inspector, had savagely kicked her. Kerrie started to struggle to her feet, but her knees gave out on her and she fell back down again. Too shocked to say anything, her brain was having a difficult time processing what had just happened. The man rapidly descended the stairs and looked down at her with a twisted smile. He had an ugly hawkish nose and a pock-marked face; Kerrie was surprised she hadn't noticed this before now.

"You want to play rough with me, lady? You don't tell me what to do, bitch!" He reached into his pocket, pulled out a roll of duct tape and ripped her silk scarf off her neck. Kerrie screamed as loud as she could. He smacked her hard across the face, causing a fresh jolt of pain through her jaw-line. He stuffed the scarf into her mouth as far down as he could. Kerrie gagged, and kicked out hard with her feet. He hit her again, in the stomach this time, roughly taped up her hands and feet, and shoved her up against the hallway wall. He then pulled out a cell phone, punched in a number and said just one word: "Presto."

"Now, you be a good little girl while I finish my snooping. If you're lucky, I'll leave you in that spot when I go, without hurting you any more. If you misbehave, you and I may have to get more intimate."

Kerrie trembled, knowing full well what he meant. She couldn't believe this was happening to her. It was like a bad dream. This creep was some kind of thief looking for treasures—seeing nothing of interest in the house, he must think she has the good stuff hidden up in the attic.

She was angry that she had been duped so easily. She should have called the County offices to check on this guy before she let him in. She was usually more careful than this.

The imposter was halfway up the staircase when Kerrie decided to try to shuffle herself slowly down the hallway, to see if she could reach a phone in the next bedroom. If she could knock it off its cradle, she might be able to dial 911. She didn't think this guy would just leave her alone when he finished searching the attic. She was certain that he would do what he just threatened to do.

Kerrie heard a sigh from the top of the staircase as she began to move. The man climbed back down again wearing an impatient look on his face as if he was being inconvenienced. He came straight towards her, raised his foot back and hefted it into her side. Kerrie screamed through her scarf—a muffled scream that had the effect the man apparently wanted to hear.

Kerrie was seeing stars now—the pain was severe. She rolled herself into a ball and held her breath. Her attacker smiled as he watched, then turned and started back up the stairs again.

Suddenly Kerrie heard the doorbell. The phony inspector heard it too, and jumped off the stairs, flattening himself against the wall inside the doorway of one of the bedrooms. She could just barely see him from her angle as he stood frozen. The bell rang again. Kerrie could feel her heart beat faster and faster with each second that passed. She had never been so scared in her life.

The front foyer door opened, and a voice called out, "Kerrie, are you here?" She recognized the voice right away; her neighbor from down the beach, Bob Trundle. She summoned all of her strength to arch her back and lift herself off the floor and back down with a thud. The intruder peeked his head out the bedroom door and glared at her. He showed her a knife and held a finger in front of his mouth. Kerrie ignored him and did it again.

"Kerrie, are you all right? Talk to me!" Bob yelled out.

She could hear the sound of his feet on the stairs as he made his way up to the second floor. At that moment Kerrie felt a pang of guilt, knowing she was bringing this nice unsuspecting man into a trap, thinking he could save her. What chance did he have against this man who would ambush him from behind with a knife?

Bob reached the top and peered around the corner into the hallway.

Kerrie could see the look of utter shock on his face when he saw her lying there. She aimed her terrified eyes at the doorway that the man was hiding behind, hoping Bob would look in that direction. But he didn't. Instead, he ran to her side in a panic and pulled the scarf out of her mouth. Kerrie didn't have the chance to warn him. The man lunged from the doorway and plunged the knife into Bob's shoulder. Kerrie screamed, wild-eyed and frantic. Bob yelled out in pain as he grabbed his shoulder and saw the blood on his hands. He whirled around to face his attacker. He rose from the ground and his feet went to work, leaping in the air and moving in bicycle fashion as he struck two lightning hits to the man's head. The guy went flying back against the wall. Blood was pouring out of Bob's shoulder but he didn't seem to notice. He rammed his finger tips into the attacker's throat, and the man started making choking sounds. Bob then grabbed him by the ass and hurled him down the stairs.

He then turned to Kerrie again, and pulling a jackknife out of his pocket began cutting away the tape from her hands and feet. Kerrie could tell by the stare he gave her that he was noticing the rising bruise on her cheek and jaw area. She winced in pain as he helped her to her feet. Her side felt like it was on fire.

"Stay here, I'm going to check on our friend," Bob said, out of breath.

He disappeared down the stairs, while at the same time Kerrie heard the sound of a car engine starting up and the spin of tires in the snow as a car pulled away.

She heard Bob curse. "Damn bastard! I should have killed him!"

He came back up the stairs again and told her that the man had escaped. At that point she didn't care. She was just glad to be alive, and so relieved to have a neighbor like Bob. Together they hobbled down the stairs and into the kitchen. Kerrie grabbed a dish towel off the stove, gently pulled off Bob's jacket and wrapped his shoulder, tying a knot at the end.

"Tell me what happened," Bob said in a soft tone, as he turned on the tap and poured her a glass of water.

Kerrie took a deep breath and related the whole incident to him, sheepishly admitting that she had been careless and naïve. "I was so anxious not to have any roadblocks for the opening of the B&B, that I let my guard down."

"Don't be so hard on yourself," Bob said. "It's only natural you would be anxious and hurried. When we get like that, we overlook things that we normally would be more careful about. You had no reason to doubt him. He did have identification."

"We'd better call the police." Kerrie said, almost as an afterthought.

Bob picked up the phone. "I'll dial it for you Kerrie. Are you up to talking to them right now?"

"Let's just get it over with while it's all fresh in my mind."

Bob pressed '9', then stopped and looked over at Kerrie. "You know of course that this will get some publicity once we report it."

Kerrie frowned. "You mean the press?"

"Yes, local press jump all over stories like this, particularly one that has some interesting elements to it—a new resident, a little inn just about to open, a mysterious attic, a phony building inspector. They'll probably be foaming at the mouth to write this story. Not much happens in these small towns."

Kerrie looked at him thoughtfully. "I wasn't even thinking about that, Bob. The publicity is a scary thought, but I can't just let him get away with this."

"He's probably long gone by now, and I doubt if he'll be back again. Anyway, it's up to you, Kerrie. Right now, let's just make sure you're okay. At the very least we should get you in to see a doctor, and you can think about the police matter while we drive in to town. We can do both at the same time if you decide to report it."

Kerrie started to tremble, and Bob wrapped his blood-stained jacket around her shoulders.

"You're going to be shaken over this for awhile. We need to get you to see a doctor right now, okay? You may even need something for the stress. You can't just brush these things off."

"Okay, let's go." Her voice quivered. "But you need to have that shoulder looked at too."

"It's just a flesh wound. I'm not too worried about it. I've had far worse. By the way, I'm going to stay here with you tonight and I don't want to hear any puritanical arguments against it. I'll stay as long as you need me to, but I can't let you be here alone right now."

Kerrie wasn't in the mood to argue about anything at all.

Chapter 5

The sun streamed through the window of Kerrie's main floor bedroom. She squinted her eyes and groaned. The clock showed 9:00. She had slept in. She struggled to the side of her bed and felt a jolt of pain up her side. So, it hadn't been a bad dream after all. What happened yesterday really did happen. She limped to the bathroom and gasped as she looked in the mirror. The entire right side of her face was swollen a hideous red/purple color. "Even makeup won't hide this," she rasped.

Sounds from the kitchen gave her a start, until she realized she had agreed that Bob could stay overnight in one of the other seven bedrooms. She told him he could have his pick. She put on her housecoat and moved slowly down the hallway to the kitchen.

"Good morning, sleeping beauty," Bob said cheerfully.

Kerrie frowned at him. "You're seriously in need of glasses, buddy. Look at my face."

"It's not that bad. It looks awful because it's just one side of your face. If we could get the left side to match, you'd look balanced."

"Very funny. How did you sleep last night, and where?"

"I slept great in that charming east-facing bedroom upstairs. Nice to get the morning sun."

"Tell me about it. My room down here faces east too. I usually enjoy the sun waking me up, but not this morning," Kerrie said.

"How are you feeling?"

"Just more stiff than anything else. The face looks bad, but it doesn't hurt unless I touch it. It's more the side that hurts, where that bastard kicked me. How about your shoulder?"

Bob moved his arm up and rotated his shoulder. "It's okay. Like I said, just a flesh wound. Those things heal pretty fast; it's the muscle tears that take time."

Kerrie poured herself a cup of coffee. "Bob, thanks again for driving us to emergency last night. Thank God my jaw wasn't broken and there were no internal injuries."

"You're a very lucky lady. Bruises take time but they clear up. Just a bad reminder in the meantime."

Kerrie took a long sip from her cup and savored the strong caffeine rush. "I've never been so scared in my life, and I consider myself a pretty tough cookie. I don't think I'll ever forget that guy's face—evil personified!"

Bob picked the intruder's business card up off the kitchen table. "Yeah, he was pretty ugly, wasn't he? I phoned the County office this morning and asked if they have anyone working there by the name of Jim Nesmith. They've never heard of him. By the way, I found his knife in the upper hall this morning—must have flown from his hand when I kicked him. Do you want to keep it to give to the police?"

Kerrie quickly shook her head. "No, just get rid of the damn thing. I don't even want to see it. And I've decided to leave the police out of it. The publicity of a home invasion and assault, and the fact that he's still at large, could kill my little business here before it even starts. I can't take that chance."

"But if you don't report it, that guarantees he'll always be at large." Bob said with concern in his voice.

"I know. That's a chance I'll just have to take. What you said last night is probably correct anyway—I don't think he'll come back here."

"I just want you to consider everything carefully. I do believe the publicity would be bad, but I'm also concerned that you won't feel safe. Maybe you should consider an alarm system?"

Kerrie pushed her chair back, grating against the hardwood floor. "That wouldn't be practical for an inn that has guests coming and going at all hours. I don't want to restrict my guests to curfews, and I sure wouldn't want to have to give the alarm code out to each guest, and then have to change it after each guest leaves. That would be ridiculous."

"Then maybe a good watchdog?"

Kerrie allowed a wry smile from her swollen face. "Funny you should say that."

"What do you mean?"

"Nothing. Private joke." She got up to refill her coffee.

"Okay, so how do you like your eggs? I make a mean fried egg."

"I prefer scrambled. Kind of a habit my dad got me into. He was good in the kitchen, particularly his breakfasts."

Bob got up and walked over to the fridge. "Okay, scrambled it is, and I found some overdue bacon in your fridge too. It might still be safe to eat, especially if I burn it!"

Bob scrambled up the eggs, fried the bacon as crisp as he could get it, and they both sat down and enjoyed it. The coffee was strong and the toast was perfect. Kerrie thought she could get real used to a man cooking for her.

"Bob, I still can't believe my luck that you showed up when you did yesterday. Thank you so much for risking yourself like that."

"At the time I didn't know I was risking myself. I'm probably a coward at heart, so I don't know what I would have done if I had known a maniac was upstairs and you were taped up like that."

Kerrie gave him a disbelieving look. "Somehow I doubt that. You're just being modest. It sure looked like you knew how to handle yourself. How did you learn those fancy kicks, and that thrust to his throat? I've never seen anything like it before except in a Bruce Lee movie!"

Bob smiled. "Old military training—the first Gulf War. Some things you never forget."

"Good for me that you didn't. I was sure that I was finished last night. I can't believe I was so careless to let a nut case like that dupe me. I want you to know I'm usually much more careful."

"Kerrie, we all have careless moments that we wish we had back again."

"It was strange. After he tied me up, he took the time to make a call on his cell. All he said was "Presto" then hung up. Now isn't that a weird thing for a burglar, or rapist, or whatever he really was, to do? What do you make of that?"

Bob grimaced. "That is strange. Maybe he had an accomplice with a truck or something. They intended to clean out your attic of whatever was in there. Perhaps that was the signal for him to drive up to the house?"

"But when you saw him driving away you didn't see a truck too, did you?"

Bob shook his head. "No, I didn't, and it was too dark by that time to get a license plate number on the guy's car."

Kerrie sat at the table re-living last night, knowing she shouldn't do that but she felt she had to. So much was going through her head, now that she could think more clearly.

"Bob, I forgot to ask you in all the chaos. Why did you come to the door last night?"

"I was checking on you to see if you needed any last minute help on your house." Bob hesitated and began to blush. "And I wanted to ask you out to dinner. There, cat's out of the bag," he said sheepishly.

"Boy, did you ever get a surprise. Not exactly the kind of date you imagined, eh?"

"No, but definitely one I'll always remember you for. Not everyone can boast of a first date as memorable as that!"

Kerrie laughed, then went silent again as she thought some more. "How did you get in the front door? I always keep it locked."

"I was surprised myself. When there was no answer to the two doorbell rings, I tried the handle and it was open. I hope you don't mind my letting myself in."

"Normally I would, but under the circumstances, I'll overlook it! I am really surprised that the door was open though. After I let that creep in, I remember turning the lock—which is almost second-breath for me."

"Well, you must have just thought you did. Sometimes things are so automatic, it's hard to remember whether or not we do them, kind of like thinking you left the stove on when you're already a half hour's drive away."

"True," Kerrie said. "That must have been what happened. All I can say is thank God I was careless about that last night, or I may not be sitting here with you right now!"

Bob cleared away the plates, and Kerrie started stacking them in the dishwasher. Her opening was in a couple of days and she thought perhaps she should delay it a week or so, until her jaw and side felt better. Picking up after guests might be too much for her. Also, she really didn't want to be greeting guests with one side of her face looking like a watermelon. At least she hadn't received any bookings yet, as it was the slow season. She could probably delay it without any real impact.

"So, your dad was a good cook, eh?" Bob broke her thoughts.

"Yes, he was. When I was lucky enough to see him."

"Too bad that the line of work he was in took him away from you a lot. How did you handle that as a kid growing up?"

"I just got used to it, I guess." Suddenly Kerrie felt her stomach in her throat. How did he know what her father had done for a living?

"Bob, what do you know about my father? I don't recall discussing him with you."

Bob paused for a moment, just enough to make Kerrie uneasy.

"Last night, after I brought you back from the hospital, you mentioned a few things about your father. You probably don't remember too much because of all the codeine they gave you."

Kerrie started easing up. Yes, of course, she had forgotten about the painkillers. They always affected her in a dizzy way. She knew she had to stop being so paranoid on the subject of her father.

"You're right, Bob. Sorry about that. It's not that I don't remember *too much* though; I don't remember *anything* about that discussion!"

"That's good, Kerrie." Bob now had a sly smile on his face. "That must mean you don't remember anything else we did last night either."

Kerrie flicked the dish towel at him. "I would have remembered something like that, don't you worry!"

They both laughed. Kerrie thought it was good to laugh after a trauma like last night, even with her jaw hurting.

She felt comfortable with Bob. He seemed like such a nice man, and she felt very indebted to him now after how he had saved her life. She felt safe around him, and she had to admit to herself it was nice having a man around the house, at least for the moment. She did like her privacy, and wasn't ready for anything permanent with anyone, but right now it just felt good. Probably just a post-traumatic reaction, she thought.

"Do you want me to stick around for another day or two, or at least come here at night since I've already messed up the sheets upstairs?"

"I think I'm okay. Knowing you're just down the beach is a comfort to me. Just write down your phone number before you go, and that will be perfect."

"Okay. So how about dinner some night when you're feeling better, or at least less self-conscious about your jaw. That is, after all, why I really came here last night."

"You know, I would really love that. Why don't you just leave that thought with me and I'll call you? There are some things I need to do around here for a couple of days. I think I'll delay my opening for a few weeks. That will give me time to get everything just perfect. I think I was pushing it anyway trying to open so soon."

"No problem. Maybe I'll wander down from time to time just to check on you." He paused for a second, then in a more serious tone said, "You should consider checking out that attic. What if there is something of value up there that perhaps some scumbags out there know about? You don't know anything about this house during the time your dad owned it, or how many people may have been in here as guests of his. The fact that that guy wanted so desperately to get up there should cause you some concern, or at the very least, curiosity."

Kerrie sighed. "You're probably right. I should check it out."

"Why don't you think about it, and when you're ready I can go up there with you. It will be less dangerous for you in case you fall through the ceiling or something. Then I can rescue you again."

Kerrie laughed. "I will indeed wait until you go up with me. I wouldn't dare go up there alone."

Bob came up to her and gave her a hug and a big kiss on the cheek, her good cheek.

"Don't worry about anything, Kerrie. You're okay now and everything will be just fine. As I said, these burglars don't usually make repeat appearances, especially when they've been beaten up so badly. But don't forget to lock your doors, and don't let anyone in if you don't know them. Okay?"

"Okay, Bob, I promise." She kissed his cheek too. "Thanks again for your chivalry. I'm so grateful to have you as a neighbor."

"It's an honor, m'lady." Kerrie watched him as he walked back down the beach toward his house. He was a good looking man, no doubt. And charming.

And boy, his timing was incredibly good.

*****

It had been several days since that attempted dognapping incident, and Jack still hadn't gotten around to phoning Kerrie. He had pretty much decided in his mind that she couldn't possibly have arranged it. However, the coincidence weighed on his mind, so he still wanted to talk to her.

He had been busy the last few days with a boy that he occasionally spent some time with. Jack was a Big Buddy to a ten year old who had lost his father to a car accident a couple of years ago. The mother was a wonderful lady who was really struggling as a single mom. While Jack usually had a set day every month that he spent with the boy, sometimes Heather called him to spend some extra time when she felt he needed it. And this week he needed it. He had been getting into trouble at school and crying in his room quite a lot. Jack picked him up from the basement apartment that his mother rented, and took him to a Calgary Flames hockey game. Josh loved hockey and was always so excited when he saw Jack. While Jack had never been a father, he found that he related well with kids. He particularly enjoyed the satisfaction of cheering up this sad little soul and giving him advice when he felt that he was receptive to it.

Then on the second day with Josh, they took Mule out for a run in Fish Creek Park—a huge urban wilderness, the largest of its kind in North America. They saw some deer, a moose, and several coyotes. Mule kept the coyotes at bay with his energetic herding style. It was always funny to watch these wild animals head for the hills whenever Mule went to work. It was easier for them to just run than stick around and try to figure out what made a Border collie tick.

After the two days spent with Josh, Heather called Jack to thank him. The boy was so much more relaxed and settled, and she knew Jack's efforts had paid off. She was so grateful, which made Jack a little uncomfortable because he felt that he hadn't really done that much. It just goes to show, he thought, how the little things can mean such a lot in a young person's life. Josh was missing his dad in a serious way, and Jack, while being a poor substitute, was at least filling some kind of void for the boy. Jack felt good about that.

He was just making lunch when there was a knock at the door. Mule barked, went running into the front hall and put his front paws up against the door. Jack looked out the window and saw a white SUV parked in front, with the words "Calgary Animal Control" painted on the side. Shit, he thought, what now!

He opened the front door and was greeted by a nice-looking woman in a uniform and cap, standing on his front porch. She smiled at him. "Mr. Howser?"

"Yes, I'm Jack Howser, how can I help you?"

"Sorry to disturb you, sir, but we received a report from the police about the incident with your dog last week. I'm here to meet your dog and ask a few questions. Just routine, I assure you, but we have to investigate every reported dog attack."

"I thought we had put this matter to rest. We were attacked, and we simply defended ourselves. The police should be out there trying to catch these thugs, rather than reporting to you about my dog."

"Can I come in for a few minutes, sir? I assure you it's just routine, but we have a job to do totally separate from the police investigation."

Jack capitulated. "Okay, I do hope this won't take too long."

They went into the living room, and sat down. She gave him her card: Ashley Wright, Animal Control Officer.

"So, Ashley, how do you want to do this?"

She reached into her bag and pulled out a muzzle with a leash attached to the neck portion. "I need to put this on your dog while I examine him."

"Hold on. Mule's not going to like that."

"It's a requirement, Mr. Howser. Your dog has already attacked one person. I can't take any chances."

"He attacked in self defense...okay, go ahead. Let's just get this over with."

She summoned Mule, and he came over to her willingly. He had accepted her as soon as Jack had allowed her to sit in the living room. She deftly slipped the muzzle quickly over his jaws and snapped it in place around his neck. She was too fast for Mule to react, but he started shaking his head from side to side once it was in place, trying desperately to dislodge it. Ashley petted him and talked to him in a soothing voice. Jack liked the sound of her sexy voice, and it occurred to him that if she insisted on putting a muzzle on him too, he would probably agree to it.

She felt around his jaw area and flashed a penlight into Mule's eyes. Then she looked in his ears and examined his genital area.

"Mr. Howser, Mule looks okay at first glance. As you can appreciate, one of the things we worry about when there is an attack is rabies. He doesn't appear to show any signs whatsoever; however, I would like to see his vaccination records if you can get them for me. Otherwise, I'll have to take him in for quarantine and testing."

"There's no need for that. I always keep Mule's vaccinations up to date. If you can wait here for a few minutes, I'll go get them for you. Would you like a bottled water in the meantime?"

"Sure, that would be very nice, thank you."

Jack went to get the water, anxious to have this over with. He could be more pleasant with her now, knowing that he had the records she needed to see. And she did seem like a fair and reasonable lady, as well as being quite attractive. This indeed made it easier to be nice.

Jack handed her the bottled water with a glass, and then headed down to the basement where he kept his file cabinets. He had to duck his head going down, as his basement was basically a crawl space, with a height of only five feet.

He pulled out Mule's file and started heading back up the stairs. Just then he heard the front door slam shut. What the fuck? He took the steps two at a time, forgot about the ceiling height, and hit his head on the rafter. Down he went, head throbbing.

He shook it off and got to his feet. He ran through the hall. Sure enough, lady and dog were gone. Jack sped to the front door and yanked it open just in time to see the SUV pull out from the curb and head down the street. What the hell was going on with this dog!

Jack grabbed his keys and didn't stop to put on a jacket or take off his slippers. He leaped off the porch stairs and jumped into his car. God, it was cold. He spied his leather driving gloves and slipped them on as he haphazardly backed out of the driveway.

He could see the SUV turning the corner at the end of the block and he headed after it, his heart pumping fast. Jack could feel his breathing become more difficult as the stress and excitement caught up to him. He was puzzled, frightened, and angry all at the same time. And he was terrified that he might never see Mule again. What did they want with his dog? He knew this must be related to the incident last week, and was reasonably sure now that this pretty lady was no animal control officer.

He screeched around the corner and could see the SUV about a quarter mile away. He hit the accelerator and allowed the twin turbos of his Audi to kick in. He knew the SUV was no match for his vehicle, and within a minute he was right on her bumper.

She turned at the next corner and Jack followed suit. Seeing the street empty of traffic, he floored the Audi around the SUV, spun the wheel, and slammed on the brakes. He was about twenty feet ahead of her, positioned so that his vehicle blocked her way. Ashley skidded to a stop within inches of Jack's car.

He jumped out and ran to Ashley's door. As he got close he could see that she was stunned, with blood dripping from her forehead. He figured she probably hadn't taken the time to put on her seatbelt and had hit the steering wheel when she came to a sudden stop.

Once Jack reached the window, he tried the door. It was locked. He could see Ashley shaking her head to clear the cobwebs, then she turned and looked straight at him through the window. In an instant her hand shot over to the glove compartment and pulled out a gun. Jack reacted fast and on pure instinct. He reared back his right arm and slammed his fist forward, into and right through the side window. In the same fluid motion, while his hand went effortlessly through the thick glass, it continued on to the back of Ashley's head and rammed it forward into the steering wheel again. This time she appeared to be more seriously dazed and her fist opened dropping the gun to the floor-mat.

He reached down and hit the unlock button on the armrest. Jack then moved to the rear of the SUV and opened the tailgate. Mule, still muzzled and leashed, came leaping into his arms as if he had been waiting. He carried the dog back to his car, afraid to put him down, and eased him into the back seat. Jack removed the muzzle and turned back to face the SUV. As he did, its wheels spun and it went into reverse at full throttle. Ashley manipulated the car into a 180 degree turn like the expert that she probably was, and sped off in the opposite direction.

He gazed after the fleeing white vehicle and thought of giving chase, then just as quickly changed his mind. He decided that there had to be a bigger picture involved here than Ashley or the other three dognapping thugs. This was all just too weird.

Chapter 6

When Jack arrived back home, he was relieved to be able to just sit in his living room and enjoy the sanctuary of it. What another crazy day. He was certain it was no coincidence that two attempts had been made to steal his dog in less than two weeks.

These had to be coordinated attacks—and for a very important reason for those kinds of chances to be taken. And they were both broad daylight attempts. He wondered when the night attack would come. He also wondered when his luck would run out. The only thing different today from almost six months ago, was that Jack now had knowledge of the strange message on a microchip implanted in Mule. And the only thing different today from three weeks ago, was that he had actually talked about this chip and its message over the phone—to Kerrie. While he had not given any details about the message, he did mention it.

There were two possibilities: Kerrie herself had arranged both of these attempts to get her dog back, or his phone call to Kerrie had been listened to by a third party who wanted the information off the chip.

Using his business logic, he didn't see any other possibilities. He could have accepted the first attempt as a simple dognapping. But after the second attempt, he discarded that idea. Too much of a coincidence. They were both brazen attacks. And the first dognappers didn't dress like one would expect scum to dress, they knew martial arts, and one of them had a knife.

And Ashley, or whatever her real name was, was slick and professional. She had official-looking identification, drove an official vehicle, drove it like someone who was well-trained at fast maneuvers. Last but not least, she had a gun. A plan like hers required some major planning and organization.

In Jack's mystery-obsessed mind, he had come to the conclusion that this was all about the microchip. Jack couldn't resist. He had to pursue this, even though he was starting to fear that owning Mule could actually cost him his life. It was getting that crazy. However, he was being driven by his curious mind, and it had to be satisfied.

Who were these people? Terrorists? Had Mitch uncovered something in his work that he had tried to expose when he was alive, but as a back-up plan wanted to expose it from the grave? Were they a criminal cell that had far-reaching abilities? This was Canada, and Mitch had been an American—these people seemed to be able to reach across borders with impunity. How had they listened in on his conversation with Kerrie so easily? How else could they know about the microchip unless they had listened? Was his phone bugged, or was it Kerrie's? He needed to talk to her, warn her, perhaps get down to Montana to see her. So far he had put off calling her back in light of how badly he had upset her the first time, but he knew he would have to stop procrastinating and at least try to get her to listen.

It dawned on him that there was one other way some bad elements could have found out about the microchip message—the cute veterinarian in Whitefish: Meagan. Yes, that was possible. It may not have been a phone bug after all. That vet had written down the message for him off the scanner. Perhaps she had memorized it, or the scanner had a recall feature that she accessed. However, the more he thought about it, the less likely that it was Meagan. His contact with her had been last summer, and these attacks started almost right after his phone conversation with Kerrie. Meagan was probably a long shot for that reason.

Now, how on earth was he going to handle this latest attack? He struggled with the idea of reporting it to the police. They didn't seem too impressed with him after the first attack. Now what would they think? Would reporting this one open the can of worms even further? If he didn't report it and someone on the street or in one of the houses or businesses had witnessed his altercation with the Animal Control vehicle, and got his license plate number, how would it look for him if they reported it and he didn't? Indeed it would look like he was trying to hide something, which of course he was.

Jack mulled these things over while he enjoyed a scotch neat, and finally decided that he had no choice. He had to report it.

Reluctantly, he picked up the phone.

*****

Jack poured the two officers coffee as they sat around his kitchen table. One of the officers was the same young cop who had visited him after the first incident. He introduced Jack to the other guy, a drug enforcement detective named Al. Jack had a sick feeling as to which way this was headed once he knew what this detective did. He now wished he hadn't reported it.

The uniformed cop deferred to the detective as the questions started flying.

"Mr. Howser, do you realize how unusual this is to have two attempts to steal your dog in such a short time?" the detective asked.

"Yes, sir, I sure do."

"Why do you think somebody wants your dog so badly?"

"I have absolutely no idea. We live a quiet life, and I'm a retired widower. My dog is my only company."

"Do you earn any money on the side, Mr. Howser?"

"How do you mean?" Jack asked.

"Anything at all you want to tell us about, that might reflect on why your dog is so popular?" Jack detected sarcasm in his voice.

"I live off my pension and my savings. I have no other sources of income."

"You must be pretty well off then. You're not too old, you live in a very expensive neighborhood, and you don't work. Must be nice."

"Yes, it is." Jack was having trouble holding his temper. This guy was starting to piss him off with his 'working class hero' shit.

"We checked with Animal Control, Mr. Howser. No surprise that no one by the name of Ashley Wright works there, or has ever worked there. Also no one even close to the description you gave works there. In addition, a vehicle containing some uniforms was stolen off their lot last night. They only discovered and reported the theft this morning, before your incident occurred. The vehicle has now been found abandoned a few miles from here, along with the discarded uniform. We'll check for prints, and also run the blood found on the steering wheel into the DNA data bank."

"Good, some progress then."

"Not really. We found no prints on the knife from your first attack, and the DNA did not show up in the data bank. We expect if this woman is part of the same crew, we'll find nothing for her either. We usually find something from scenes unless they wear gloves. According to you they didn't wear any, so your culprits were arrogant enough, or confident enough, not to bother."

"Yes, they didn't fit the stereotype, that's for sure. But tell me, how could there be no prints on that knife from the first attack?"

"Smarter people than me might be able to answer that, Mr. Howser. In any event, I'm asking the questions here, not you. Have you traveled to any foreign countries within the last year?"

"No. Oh, yes, I'm sorry. I drove to Montana with Mule for the day last summer."

"Oh, really. And what was the purpose of that trip?"

"Just a day trip. Some shopping and sightseeing."

"You don't look like the shopping type, Mr. Howser. What did you buy?"

"Nothing. I just browsed through some of the shops in Whitefish, cruised around Whitefish Lake and looked at some of the cottages for sale, stuff like that. Then I drove back."

"Do you always take your dog with you when you go on day trips to the U.S.?"

"Yes, I do. Do you own a dog, detective?"

"No."

"Well, then I guess you're not familiar with their need to go to the bathroom several times a day, are you?"

"No need for attitude Mr. Howser. We're just trying to figure all of this out."

"Perhaps then we could spend more time talking about the bad guys, rather than focusing on my personal habits." Jack was finding it harder and harder to hide his resentment.

The detective ignored this remark.

"We've checked up on you, Mr. Howser. You've never even had a speeding ticket. But I'm curious. Have you ever done drugs, or dealt in drugs?"

"No."

"When you were in Montana, did you come in contact with any nefarious types, buy drugs of any kind?"

"I just told you that I've never done or dealt in drugs."

"Yes, indeed you did. Sorry, Mr. Howser. Moving on then, in both of these attacks, you seem to have been able to take rather heroic measures to save your dog. Is it worth risking your life for a dog?"

"I just reacted, not much time to think. I guess if I had had the chance to sit back and analyze the safest options, perhaps I wouldn't have done what I did. However, I do love my dog and I am indignant about anyone violating my life, and he's a big part of my life."

"With the damage you inflicted in both attacks, it's apparent that you have had professional defensive training. Tell me about that."

"Years ago I obtained a black belt in karate, merely for exercise and the challenge. I never expected to have to use it. Now I've used it twice."

"Where did you obtain your black belt?"

"In Toronto."

Detective Al put his cup down with a decisive clunk, signaling to Jack that he was finished with him. "Mr. Howser, thanks for your cooperation. I must inform you that I don't entirely believe everything you've told me. These attacks are just too much of a puzzle for me not to think there is something going on with this dog. We need to take your dog down to the station and conduct an examination."

Jack squirmed in his seat. "Is that really necessary? Can't you examine him here?"

"No, sir, we have to take him."

Jack started wondering if this week could possibly get any worse. Now he was worried. He consoled himself for the moment by telling himself that if they found the chip he would just deny that he knew about it. But then, how would he have known to change the dog's name from Ranger to Mule? The records would show that he did that shortly after his trip to Montana last year. He could feel the sweat start to drip down his arm.

"Okay, you can examine him. But I'm not letting him out of my sight. I'll follow you down to the station in my car and Mule will ride with me."

"No problem, Mr. Howser. By the way, why did you name that dog Mule?"

The young officer in uniform smirked at this remark by his colleague, and said, "Al, I asked him the same thing when I was here a few days ago. He said it just came to him."

They both laughed mockingly, and the detective said, "Good thing the dog doesn't know how funny that name sounds, eh?"

Jack said without smiling. " I like the name."

"Well sir, let's hope that name isn't indicative of the dog's occupation, for your sake."

*****

When they arrived at the main precinct for the Calgary Police Service, the officers directed Jack to a back entrance. They went through double doors into a rather noisy compound. This was obviously where they housed the police dogs, as the barking was overpowering. It reminded Jack of the pound where he had bought Mule. They went down a long hallway away from the noise, and he and Mule were ushered into a large examining room, which also looked like it functioned as a laboratory.

Detective Al went off to summon the vet, while he and Mule sat down in the reception area. Jack was finding this experience rather intimidating. He hated lying and he was always fearful that when one lie led to another lie, eventually it all would come crashing down. However, he just wasn't prepared to give up what he knew. He was stubborn that way, sometimes to a fault. He guessed that somewhere in his formative years he came to truly believe that 'knowledge is power.'

The vet came in and introduced himself, a Dr. Wilson, the chief vet for the police service. Jack was instructed to lift Mule up on the examining table. Good old Detective Al continued to lurk around. Jack really didn't like that guy.

The vet then explained to Jack about what they were examining Mule for. "Mr. Howser, I'm sure you've heard of people being used to transport drugs around the world, sometimes in their luggage but more often of late, inside their bodies. They're referred to as Drug Carriers, or more commonly, Drug Mules. In the last few years we've seen animals being used in a similar fashion. Drugs can be swallowed in protective packages, to be expelled by the animals at a later date. We find that this usually causes constipation, which the drug dealers like because it gives them sometimes a few extra days before they have to worry about recovery of the package from the animal's feces. Not good for the animal, but good for the dealer. This is, however, a difficult and undependable method of transporting drugs. Sometimes the dogs do not just gulp the package down—they chew it and overdose."

Jack said, " I can assure you that Mule has not been constipated."

"Yes, sir—well, we'll find that out for ourselves." Jack wondered what he meant by that.

Dr. Wilson continued his explanation. "We've also found that animals have been used to transport drugs that have been inserted under the skin, usually by a slight incision and sewn up by sutures. These are hidden nicely under the hair, so long-haired dogs tend to be used for this method. Your dog is long-haired."

"Yes, he is, but again I assure you that there is nothing to find."

"We'll find that out for ourselves also, Mr. Howser."

Al piped in. "Maybe now you understand why I made that crack about your dog's name?"

Jack turned his head slowly toward the detective. "I knew why you made the crack, detective. And do you really think I would be so stupid as to name my dog Mule if I intended to use him as a drug mule? Get real." God this guy was a piss-off. Jack felt like smashing his nose in.

Dr. Wilson then explained to Jack that he was going to do an enema on the dog. Jack protested but to no avail. He asked Jack to hold Mule steady while he inserted a large syringe up his rear. "This won't be pleasant," he said.

The substance had an almost instant effect. The vet had to practically jump back to avoid getting splashed. Mule wasn't all too impressed either.

The vet said that there was no sign of constipation, and that the quantity that came out was a normal daily amount. However, what faintly resembled a mouse carcass was part of the contents. Detective Al came to the table with his gloves on and held the deformed, and substantially chewed body up by the tail. The vet then examined the body to make sure it was not a fake mouse. He then put it down on the table and slit open its belly. No drugs. No surprise.

Dr. Wilson then explained to Jack that the next thing they needed to do was shave about half the length of Mule's hair off from all over his body, so that he could examine more easily for any sutures. Jack sighed. There was nothing he could say or do to prevent this. He just wished it were a warmer time of the year. Mule would feel the cold more now with half his coat gone.

The vet brought out his shears and went to work. Jack had to admit, the man was being very careful to do the job evenly and not disfigure Mule in any way. Mule would still look like a Border collie, just not as full. Jack was glad the vet was doing this job rather than his new friend Al.

Once the hair was shortened enough, the vet went to work with a careful examination all over Mule's body. Jack admired the dog's patience. He was behaving very nicely, probably because Jack was standing beside him. Dr. Wilson brought out a large magnifying glass and slowly moved it over Mule, his eye right up to the lens. He was looking for any stitching, and he was being very thorough. He then stopped at Mule's shoulder area, and parted the hair carefully.

Jack's heart skipped a beat. He waited for the inevitable.

"Mr. Howser, it looks like there's some old scar tissue between Mule's shoulder blades, up close to the neck area. Can you tell me what that's from?"

Jack was careful not to let his voice crack. "An identification chip was implanted years ago in case Mule got lost."

The vet nodded as if he already knew what it was, and was just testing Jack. "Yes, those things are wonderful innovations. Every dog should have one."

Jack slowly exhaled and allowed himself a glance at Al. He was standing there looking bored, and didn't seem to react at all to the scar tissue comment.

Dr. Wilson stood upright, and announced, "This dog's clean, Al. No evidence of any drug transportation activity either in the stool, or under the skin. I think we can let Mr. Howser take his dog home now."

Al looked disappointed. "No other tests can be done?"

"No, Al, we're done here. Mr. Howser has been inconvenienced enough already."

"Okay then. Mr. Howser, you're free to go. We'll let you know if we get any results on the prints or blood DNA."

Jack nodded and picked Mule up off the table. He shook hands with Dr. Wilson and thanked him for his courtesy. He ignored Al and started walking down the hallway. Al followed close behind.

"Watch yourself, Mr. Howser. I have the feeling that you're into something way over your head."

Jack had to admit that the prick was probably right, but he wasn't in the mood to hear it from him. He turned on his heel and said, "Go catch the real bad guys, detective."

"Sometimes bad guys don't look like bad guys, Mr. Howser. Sometimes we're staring right at them and we don't know it," Al said with a smirk.

Jack put his face close to Al's, studied him for a second, and said, "You know, I think you may be right."

Chapter 7

The next few days Jack spent researching home alarm systems. There were so many available, and so many different price ranges, it was hard to decide. He finally reasoned that to hell with price, he would go with the best.

He arranged to have all the windows and doors protected with contacts. He preferred not to go with motion detectors due to the prevalence of false alarms with those types of systems. He did however have the system connected to a central monitoring station that gave him the added security and peace of mind. The alarm company installed a sign on his front window also, alerting any intruders to the existence of an alarm.

Once they were finished with the installation, Jack set his pass code and breathed a sigh of relief. Before the installers left, he asked if they could check for listening devices in his home. The guy in charge looked at him kind of quizzically, but went out to his truck and came back with a detection instrument. After covering the entire house he assured Jack that there were no devices on his phones or anywhere else in the house. Jack breathed another sigh of relief.

Mule's hair was already starting to grow back in. It didn't take long for these collies. Jack could tell the dog noticed the difference. He didn't stay out in the back yard too long when he had to do his business, and he would frantically rub himself along the carpet. The shorter hair must have felt strange for him, or itchy, and Mule seemed to think that rubbing would make it grow back in faster. These kinds of dogs were meant to shed, not be clipped.

Jack pulled out his papers on the microchip phrase and started fiddling with the words. He had taken another run at this last night, and nothing seemed to make sense to him. He stared at the words and the numbers, hoping that something would jump out at him: *"Tell her she has the key to her Soul within her reach. 15/15/14."*

Strange, he thought, really strange. He figured that it might be a message to Kerrie—some inspirational words Mitch had wanted to share with her? But what did the numbers mean? Was the operative word in the phrase "key"? Did

Kerrie have a key and she perhaps wasn't aware of what it was for? Why did the word "Soul" begin with an upper case letter? His concentration was jolted by the phone ringing.

"Hi Jack, it's Heather."

"Hey, Heather, nice to hear from you. How are you and Josh doing?"

"Wonderful, Jack, just wonderful. Josh has been on top of the world since the last time he saw you. Things have been going so much better for him."

"I'm glad to hear that. He's such a great little guy, and I really enjoy my time with him too."

"It's so nice for me to hear that. I always worry that we're imposing on you."

"Nonsense. Spending time with Josh is good for me too—and remember, I volunteered to be a Big Buddy, so it's something I wanted to do. Sometimes I wonder who's helping who more."

"That's so nice of you to say, makes me feel less guilty. The reason I'm calling is to see if you can spare some time today. Josh is so excited. He has a surprise he wants to show you, and he can't wait another day."

"Well, now you've piqued my interest. Of course I have time. I'll always have time for Josh."

"Wonderful, can you come over this afternoon?"

"No problem. How's 3:00?"

"That would be great. And, Jack, could I ask that you leave Mule at home this one time?"

"Oh, okay, Heather, if that's what you'd prefer."

"Don't take offense. We love Mule, but I think you'll understand when you get here."

"Okay, now I'm really intrigued. See you this afternoon."

Jack hung up the phone and walked over to Mule. "Sorry, boy, have to leave you at home. You're not wanted today." At least he now had an alarm system, so he felt safe leaving Mule alone.

He sat down and looked at his papers again. Shit, he thought, this was driving him crazy. He needed to get in touch with Kerrie again very shortly. She had every right to know what was on the chip, and perhaps together they could figure it out.

Assuming of course, she wouldn't hang up on him again.

*****

Jack arrived at Heather's basement apartment at 3:00 on the nose. He parked his car on the street and walked up to the separate entrance at the side of the house. As soon as he knocked on the door, he knew what the surprise was. He heard the barking of a dog from inside.

Josh opened the door with a big smile on his face, and Jack was almost bowled over by a big rush of fur. He couldn't believe his eyes. He was staring at a carbon copy of Mule. The dog had his front paws on Jack's chest and was licking his chin furiously. "Do you like him, Jack?" Josh asked.

"I love him, but of course you knew I would."

"I wanted to get a Border collie just like Mule, and Mom finally agreed!"

"That's wonderful, Josh. He's a fine looking dog."

Heather walked over and took Jack's coat. "Come on in, Jack. Now you can understand why I didn't want you to bring Mule today. This dog is just getting used to us, and we don't know how he'll be around other dogs."

"This is amazing," Jack said. "He looks just like Mule, at least before Mule got shaved."

"Why did he get shaved?" Heather asked, as she hung Jack's coat in the hall closet.

"Oh, just this little procedure that Mule had to have at the vets, nothing serious." Heather accepted his explanation. She knelt down on the floor with Josh, and they both started teasing the dog with a ball.

"How old is he?" asked Jack.

"Supposed to be about five years old." Heather's reply was muffled as the dog crawled over her head. "We got him from the shelter. He seems to be nicely house-trained, and very friendly with Josh. So he must have been raised with kids."

"So Josh, what's his name?"

"I decided to call him Buster. He looks like a Buster, doesn't he?

"You know, that's exactly what I would have called him. I knew it as soon as I saw him."

"You did not! You're pulling my leg."

"No, honestly. You couldn't have picked a better name."

"Can you stay for dinner?" Heather asked eagerly. "You can educate us on how to take care of a dog like this."

"That sounds great. I'd love to."

While Heather made dinner, Jack and Josh took Buster out for a walk and a run in a nearby park. Jack noted that this dog was pure Border collie—the same athletic nature as Mule's, and the same curious approach to groups of people or groups of birds or squirrels. He would go into the classic Border collie hunch, and approach with stealth and caution. The dog clearly was having fun practicing instincts he truly didn't understand.

Josh was in his element. This was his dog, and he was so proud. Jack was thrilled that Josh had been influenced enough by his time with Mule that he convinced his mother that no other dog but a Border collie would do. This really made Jack feel good. He now realized that he had had more of an impact on the boy than he had given himself credit for. He knew that Buster would be good for Josh, give him a purpose and teach him a sense of responsibility at his young age that he perhaps hadn't felt since his father's death.

They put Buster back on his leash and headed to the apartment. Josh was walking along with Buster, trying desperately to control him, but Jack could tell that Buster was not used to walking on a leash. He might have even lived on a farm. This would take some practice or obedience training. He showed Josh a few tricks in trying to get the dog to heel. He stressed that Josh needed to practice these things every day in order for Buster to get the message. Border collies were one of the most intelligent breeds, so with persistence he would learn eventually.

Jack also recommended the treats in the pocket trick. Josh listened intently, obviously determined to learn all that he could to care for his new friend. Jack suspected that this was probably how it felt to be a father—seeing that admiring look in the boy's eyes as each word of advice sunk in.

"Your mom probably has dinner ready, so we should get back. Perhaps we can both hang on to the leash and Buster can just pull us!"

Josh laughed. "I'm sure he's strong enough! I think Buster is the strongest dog in the whole wide world, next to Mule of course!"

As they walked along, neither of them noticed the dark van that was slowly following a block behind them.

*****

Dinner was great, and Jack really enjoyed spending time with this wonderful little family, now made a little bit larger by Buster. He also took more notice of Heather this time than he had in the past. She was a very attractive lady, about thirty-eight he guessed. She had the cutest dimples that made their appearance every time she smiled. And she smiled a lot. Her hair was jet black, and cut short in a way that curled around her chin and framed her face. Her skin looked incredibly smooth. Jack had to work hard resisting the urge to run his hands over her shoulders.

He knew that Heather would attract a lot of attention everywhere she went. She projected a classy image. Her eyes, though, held sadness. They betrayed her overall image. There was the slightest hint of dark circles that she had probably tried to hide with makeup. There was redness around the edges of the eyeballs, and there were small crinkle lines under her eyebrows. Heather bore the stresses of a single mom who had lost the love of her life. The eyes told the story for her.

Jack felt sorry for her, losing her husband at such a young age, and raising a young boy all by herself. He knew that she was a legal secretary, and while she made good money, it wasn't much in terms of getting ahead. Her husband had left them with only a small amount of life insurance, and while they had owned a house together it had been heavily mortgaged. When money got tight this past year, Heather had been forced to sell the home with very little profit. The recession had eaten into any real equity they had gained over the years, so renting this basement apartment was all she could afford for now.

But she remained cheerful despite her circumstances, and Jack could easily tell that she was totally committed to her son. Josh was her life, and Jack wasn't surprised she agreed to buy him a dog. She knew it would make him happy, and that was all that was important to her. There was genuine love between mother and child, and Jack was envious of that kind of connection.

"Okay, Josh, time for bed. You have no school tomorrow and it's my day off, so we're going to do some things together. We'll make it a big day."

"Aw, can't I stay up a little bit longer? We have a special guest tonight!" Josh looked over at Jack, probably hoping for some reinforcement.

"No, young man. Off to bed."

"Can Buster sleep with me tonight?"

"Well, okay, we'll try it for tonight and see if he's okay in the room with you. But if he keeps you awake, you have to promise me you'll chase him out."

"I will, Mom. I promise." Josh ran over and gave his mother a big hug and kiss. Then he held out his hand to Jack like a little man, and Jack shook it. "I love you, Mom, and I love you too, Jack."

Jack could feel his eyes tearing up. Josh had never said this to him before and it felt nice to hear it. He ran off to bed with Buster following eagerly. Heather opened another bottle of wine and brought it over to the couch where Jack was sitting.

"Oh, I don't know if I can handle any more, Heather."

"Sure you can. This is a special occasion."

Jack quickly relented. "Okay, you've made your case." He held out his glass and Heather poured. She turned on the stereo and found some soft relaxing music, making the wine taste even better.

They spent the next two hours talking about their lives, loves, and careers. He had never told Heather before how he had lost his wife, and he could see some tears rolling down her cheeks as he told the story. It touched her, probably because of the violent way she had also lost her husband. She could relate to the sudden shock that Jack had felt.

They had, at the very least, this in common.

Jack began to realize how easy Heather was to talk to, and what a special person she seemed to be. Most of his time had been spent with just Josh, and the occasional casual conversation with Heather. This was the first time he and Heather had really shared with each other. He also figured the wine was helping both of them relax.

They were sitting there quietly enjoying the music and the wine, when Heather slowly leaned over and gently kissed his lips. "You're a very handsome man, Jack Howser."

Jack kissed her back in the same gentle way, and said, "You're not so bad yourself, Heather McIntosh."

They began necking like teenagers, and eventually Jack could feel Heather's fingers sliding down to his crotch. He responded by sliding his hand up her blouse, rubbing her breasts. She moaned appreciatively and deftly snapped open his jeans. In an instant her head disappeared and he could feel her tongue on his penis. It was his turn to moan.

Neither of them gave a second thought to the fact that they were in the living room and Josh could come wandering out at any moment. Reckless for sure, but this impulsive moment was one that was not going to be denied.

Jack's head was spinning. Part of his brain said this was wrong, that it was a conflict with his Big Buddy duties, and the other part said, "Fuck it, this is nice." He gave in to the latter. Jack gently shifted her prone to the couch, pushed up her skirt, and pulled down her panties. He entered her in one smooth motion. Her passion was frantic and Jack responded with his own. They were in sync and both were enjoying the closeness. Jack marveled at how passionate she was and how good she felt. Her skin was so soft, the softest he'd ever touched, and he felt an emotional intimacy with Heather that he hadn't felt with the other women he had dated. When he reached orgasm at virtually the same time Heather did, it was an ecstasy he hadn't felt since Susan.

He looked down at her and smiled. She smiled back in a lazy, relaxed sort of way, and stroked his face with her fingers. "That was nice," she said in a soft voice. "You should know that I haven't been with a man since Steven died. I must think you're pretty special."

"You're pretty special too, Heather." Jack meant it.

But in the back of Jack's mind, something was bothering him. He couldn't put his finger on it—a feeling of inevitability, or conflict—he wasn't quite sure.

But he was sure about one thing. He would see her this way again.

*****

There was a three-way call taking place between a man in Virginia, a man in Montana, and a woman in Calgary.

"He's got the dog staying with a mother and son that he seems to know. He must be getting nervous," the woman said.

"Pick up that damn dog and get this over with," snapped the Virginian. "We've wasted enough time on this already."

"Consider it done," the woman replied forcefully.

"And where are we on that Joplin lady?" the Virginian asked.

The man in Montana paused for a moment to collect his thoughts. "We have a slight problem."

"What now?" the Virginian sighed with mounting anger.

"Our man's cell phone is missing. We think it fell out when he tumbled down the stairs at her house."

"All the field phones are disposable, they can't be traced."

"You're forgetting one thing," the Montanan said. "These phones have a call history."

"They're supposed to be erased every day."

"Well, he doesn't recall when he last erased it. And of course if he had known he was going to lose it falling down the stairs, he would have pushed delete on the way down."

"Spare me your typical sarcasm. Maybe you need to question your judgment as to the quality of operatives you hire for these spot jobs."

"He's a good man. He's done a lot of great work on special projects for us. This is not his fault."

The Virginian thought for a moment and then said calmly, "Try to get the phone back without drawing attention, and in the meantime as a precaution, instruct all field operatives who he could have phoned to erase their histories and throw their phones away. They should buy new ones, and then you can set up a new directory of numbers."

"That should deal with the problem. Then there's really no need to get the phone back—the history of numbers on it will be useless," replied the Montanan.

"Sure, but can we take that chance? What if this idiot phoned a land line?"

"I doubt it. Our instructions were always very clear, but I see your point. We'll get it back."

"And what are our new plans for getting access to Joplin's attic?" the Virginian asked.

"We're working on it. Trust me, we'll have a look at it in due course. We can't have any more violent encounters at that house. We were lucky the first time that nothing more developed from it, but we may not be that lucky the second time."

"No, we don't want attention. But we may have to eventually throw caution to the wind to get some answers." The Virginian's tone had become harsh again.

"I agree. Leave it with me." The Montanan grimaced as he hung up the phone. He thought that these relatively simple domestic tasks, where "being careful" was the most important thing, were a hell of a lot more difficult than dangerous overseas assignments where the rule of thumb was "no rules."

Chapter 8

Jack woke up the next morning with a headache and mixed feelings. He knew the pounding head was from the excessive amount of wine that he had consumed with Heather, but the mixed feelings were not as easily explained.

He had enjoyed himself with Heather, and found her extremely attractive. His relationship with her son made the affection even more intense, because he knew her as a caring mother, not just a caring lover. But he couldn't shake the feeling of betrayal—to his Big Buddy role, and the vulnerability of a mother who was going through a tough time. However, he knew he hadn't taken advantage of her—she had made the first move, after all. But he felt in his heart that he should have resisted. She shouldn't be just another roll in the hay. Heather was a classy lady who was warm-hearted and dedicated to her son. This was not his usual date.

He also couldn't deny his attraction to her. She was gorgeous, funny, and a pleasure to be with. They had experienced similar tragedies. And he couldn't stop thinking about her. He made up his mind in an instant. This would not be just another sex romp. He had to show her how he felt. He thought that maybe, just maybe, he was starting to snap out of the malaise he had been feeling since 2001.

Jack pulled out the phone book and looked for the closest florist. He would surprise her with some roses. And for Josh, he would pick up a book about Border collies from the pet shop. Yes, a nice surprise, rather than just phoning her with the cliché, "I had a nice time last night."

For the first time in a long time, Jack believed he was ready for a real relationship again.

*****

Heather was fixing Josh his breakfast and had just put a bowl down for Buster. She was thinking what a wonderful gift Buster was to her little family. Josh had never seemed happier, and Buster was probably exactly what he needed—a living being of his own to focus his attention on and care for. No better therapy.

And she thought of Jack.

She hadn't planned last night to unfold the way it did. It had just seemed right, and the wine had no doubt helped her make the move. Being with Jack in that way had been very nice. He was so gentle and seemed sincere. She felt a closeness that she hadn't felt since her husband. Perhaps it was the way Jack related to Josh? Or the genuine interest he had shown in their lives? He was also darn handsome and charismatic. She admitted to herself that it was hard to keep her hands off him, and had secretly wanted to be intimate with him for quite some time. She had finally found the right moment, and the courage to make it happen.

Well, now it was done. She had made the first move and she hoped that Jack didn't think less of her because of that. It was a concern to her that he might think she was easy, or slept around.

She pondered whether or not she should call him, and quickly decided against it. It was up to him. She was afraid to go too far out on a limb and scare him off. And she really didn't want to put herself too far out there only to be hurt. If he didn't call, then it had just been a pleasant evening between two adults and she would have to look at it that way.

Josh came out of his room for breakfast. He was not a morning person, and Heather always made an extra effort to be cheerful in the mornings to snap him awake. But since Buster had joined the family, he seemed to perk up much faster. Down he dropped to the floor for his morning wrestle with Buster, covering his clothes with dog hair.

"What's for breakfast, mom?" Josh asked eagerly.

"Pancakes and bacon. Does that meet with your approval?"

"Great! Can Buster have some of the bacon?"

"Only a wee bit. We have to be sure not to make him sick, and bacon is so greasy."

"Okay, Mom, just a wee bit. Do you hear that, boy? You're going to get a treat!"

Buster came bounding over to the kitchen table as Josh sat down, knowing that his master would come through for him.

Heather pulled up a chair and served out the pancakes and bacon, and of course a big jug of syrup. Some of the syrup spilled onto her jeans, and Buster put his tongue to work. Heather wasn't worried. This was her day off and she was glad that she wasn't wearing one of her work outfits. Buster could lick away.

"Mom, it was sure nice having Jack over last night. Can we do it again soon?"

"Well, that's up to Jack, I guess. He has his own life. He can't be over here all the time. But I agree, it was nice having him for dinner."

"He stayed for a while after I went to bed, didn't he?"

Heather gulped at this question, wondering how long Josh had been awake. "For a while, yes."

"Did you guys kiss?"

"Now, Josh, that's getting a bit personal, don't you think?"

"You're my mother, so it's not so personal. You'd want to know if I kissed a girl, wouldn't you?"

"That's different. You're just a boy, and you need guidance."

"Don't mothers need guidance too?"

Heather laughed and choked at the same time. The things that kids say.

"Yup, I suppose we do sometimes, Josh."

"Are you going to marry Jack?"

"Josh!" Heather exclaimed. "We hardly know each other!"

"Wouldn't that be fun though?" Josh gushed. "We would have two Border collies in the family, and I'd have a dad again, and, oh yeah, you'd have a husband!"

Heather got up and gave her son a hug, crying as she did. She wondered how often Josh thought about things like this, and for him to spout them out to her was heartwarming. A little boy's concept of a family was short and simple, and pretty nice.

"Sure Josh, it would be fun to be that way again, but life has a way of being more complicated than that sometimes. In the meantime, it's just you and me, kid."

"And Buster!" Josh added.

"And Buster."

*****

Jack stopped at the florist and bought a couple dozen beautiful roses, a mixed variety of white, yellow, and red. The florist suggested adding some feathery green ferns and delicate Baby's Breath, to give it that romantic touch. Jack agreed, not really having a clue, but figuring this woman knew what she was talking about. Heather would love these, he thought. Beautiful flowers for a beautiful lady. He pictured her putting these roses in a vase, her short black hair curling around her chin as she leaned over the vase, her lips lifting in that special smile she had with dimples blazing, looking up at him with affection. He longed to see that today. It was very important he see that today after last night. And very important that he be the first one to initiate contact again, rather than her. He wanted her to know how special last night was, and that he was not going to brush her off.

His next stop was the pet shop. Jack bought a nice glossy book about Border collies and how to care for them. Josh would appreciate this and, knowing Josh, he would probably get through it the same day. It had lots of neat pictures too and Jack knew that kids needed plenty of visuals to keep their attention. He recalled how eagerly Josh always skimmed through the Calgary Flames game-day programs, stopping at the pages with photos of the players.

Jack knew that today was Heather's day off, and Josh did not have to go to school due to the teachers' convention. Maybe they could all spend the day together.

*****

"So what are we going to do with ourselves today, Josh? We're both free as birds."

"How about the zoo? We haven't done that in a long time. And then maybe when we get back we can take Buster for a long hike in Fish Creek Park?"

"That sounds like a great plan. The park may still be a bit soggy though. Spring's just around the corner, but there's still a lot of snow and slush down in that valley."

"We can wear boots, and Buster doesn't care, he's a dog."

"All right then." Heather laughed. "Let's get dressed and get to the zoo. Maybe we can beat the crowds."

Heather went to her bedroom to put on a change of clothes, something warmer for the zoo. As she was rustling through her closet, she heard a knock at the door. "Josh, could you get the door please?"

She heard the door open and then heard a man's voice. She hoped it was Jack. Josh called out, "Mom!"

Heather rushed out to the hall and saw two men, both dressed in suits and ties. One had brown hair and was carrying a briefcase, and the other, a blonde, had a duffle-bag slung over his shoulder. With her observant woman's eye, it occurred to her that each appeared to have some makeup on around the eyes and nose. "Hello, ma'am, sorry to disturb you. We're with the property management firm that manages the rentals in this house and others in the city," said the brown-haired man.

"Oh, hello. I'm all paid up in my rent."

"No, don't worry about that, Ms. McIntosh. You're always on time with your payments. We're here about another matter. We understand you now have a dog, and I can see him for myself now that I'm here." Buster was sitting at the man's feet, wagging his tail. The man bent over and petted him on the head. "Nice boy."

"We just got him a few days ago."

"Is he yours, or are you caring for him for a friend?"

"He's our dog. My son's actually."

The man reached into his briefcase, and brought out a sheet of paper. "This is a copy of page ten from your lease, which states quite clearly that dogs are not allowed in this building; in fact, no pets at all." He showed Heather the page.

She put on her reading glasses and studied it closely. "I don't recall this clause being in my lease. I'm a legal secretary, so I read and prepare contracts for a living. Having a small boy who loves animals, I wouldn't have signed a lease that had a clause like this."

"Well, this is a page from the standard lease we use with all tenants," the man replied. "Perhaps you didn't read it as thoroughly as you thought."

"I'm flabbergasted," Heather exclaimed. " I'm usually not that careless. I need to read my actual signed lease, but unfortunately it's at my office downtown. Can we talk about this another day after I've had a chance to look at it?"

"I'm afraid not, ma'am. This clause in the lease gives us the power to act without delay." The brown-haired man shrugged, raised his arms and opened his palms as if to indicate that he had no choice in the matter. The blonde man nodded in agreement.

"Act? In what manner?" Heather asked. "This is my home, and surely you can wait a day for me to check my lease."

Josh was kneeling on the floor, petting Buster, but Heather could tell that he was playing close attention to the conversation.

"There's no need for you to check your lease, this is a page from your lease. What reason would we have to lie to you?"

Heather ignored his question and persisted. "How did you find out about our dog?"

"We had a complaint from the other tenants on the floor above you. They said your dog had been barking."

"Well, maybe Buster has barked a couple of times, but not loud enough to disturb anyone."

"That's not the opinion of your neighbors, Ms. McIntosh."

Heather looked down at Josh again, and could see fright in his eyes now. He was looking up at her, confused. She could tell he knew his dog was in trouble.

She looked back up at the brown-haired man. "What can I do to fix this? Can't I just pay a penalty to the lease for having a dog? Or a higher damage deposit?"

"No, the dog must go, or you must go. This clause I've shown you, which you claim you never saw, gives us the power to either take the dog or evict you immediately."

"That's nonsense!" Heather yelled. "The law cannot possibly allow for immediate eviction or taking possession of a dog. That may be what your clause says, but I doubt it's legal."

"You signed it ma'am; that makes it legal." He stuffed the page back into his briefcase and snapped it shut, signaling finality.

Heather wasn't finished yet. If he thought she would just hand over her son's dog, he had another think coming. "Not necessarily. If the clause is in violation of statute, it doesn't matter if I signed it or not. Statute takes precedence," Heather said defiantly. "I want to phone a friend of mine and have him talk to you, if you don't mind. I'm sure you can wait a few minutes before throwing us out in the street? If you can't wait for that, I'm calling the police."

The man just shrugged, and moved into the living room with his companion close behind. While Heather went over to the phone, the blonde man locked the front door. Heather dialed Jack at his home. No answer. Then she tried his cell phone and left a message. "Jack, please call me right away if you can. I need help with something that has just come up." Heather would have phoned her office to talk to one of the lawyers, but she knew they were all either in court today, or away at settlement conferences.

She turned around to face the two men. She felt a bit sorry for them. They were only doing their jobs, and they were actually quite polite. She had been giving them a hard time, but she needed them to be patient to help her sort this out.

She lowered her tone. "My friend will probably call me back in a few minutes. Can I make you both some coffee while we wait?"

"Sure, Ms. McIntosh. We can wait a few minutes, and coffee would be fine." She noticed that the brown-haired guy was still doing all the talking, and blondie just kind of glared right through her. He gave her the chills. She guessed that the darker guy was the boss.

Heather went into the kitchen, and Josh followed. "Mom, what's going on? Are they going to take Buster?"

"No, dear, don't you worry. I won't let them do that." Josh smiled back, reassured by his mother's confidence.

She put on the coffee, then picked up the phone in the kitchen and dialed another number. "Hello, Joyce? It's Heather downstairs. I have a question for you. Did you or Charlie make a complaint about our dog? No? Okay, thanks. No, I'll tell you about it later."

Heather put down the phone, puzzled, and was just about to head back to the living room to confront the men about their lie when she felt an arm around her neck and a wet cloth against her mouth and nose. In the back recesses of her mind she heard screams, but they weren't hers. Instant alarm and panic flooded her brain. She started to struggle but then found that she became weaker, and weaker…

Josh screamed as soon as he saw the blonde man grab his mother from behind. She collapsed to the floor in the man's arms. Josh ran over to her but the other man picked him up and put a cloth to his face. Josh kicked for a few seconds, then lost his strength. The man gently laid Josh on the floor, while the dog came bounding in from the living room. Buster growled and lunged at the man. He swept him away with a big hand, while the blonde man calmly pulled out a gun and fired. The dart went into Buster along his side, and within seconds he was unconscious. The blonde man opened the duffle-bag and pulled out duct tape. He passed it to his partner who expertly bound and gagged both Heather and Josh. He was careful not to make the tape too tight, just enough to keep them immobilized if they awakened.

They both kneeled over Buster, and rolled him onto his side. The blonde man took out a scalpel and a bottle of rubbing alcohol and put them on the floor. Then he took out a wand and flicked a switch. He waved it over the shoulder area of Buster several times, then looked at his partner, shaking his head. The brown haired man gave it a try. Finally, with a puzzled look on his face, he put the wand back in the duffle-bag. The scalpel and alcohol were also put back in the bag, and the dart pulled out of Buster.

They took one last look at Heather and Josh, and checked their pulses.

Satisfied that they were okay, the blonde man walked into the master bedroom and removed Heather's wallet from her purse and deliberately dropped the purse on the floor. He opened her dresser drawers and removed a jewelry box, leaving the drawers open. Both the wallet and jewelry box went into the duffle-bag.

Just before leaving, the brown-haired man dialed 911.

*****

As Jack was driving to Heather's house, he checked the voice mail on his cell. A message from Heather. So much for being the first one to make contact again, Jack thought with chagrin.

He decided not to call back. He was only fifteen minutes away. He'd deal with her problem in person, with roses.

He pulled up in front just as a black van was pulling away. He went up the walkway and knocked on the door. No answer. He called out. Still no answer. He tried the door handle; it was unlocked. Jack walked into the living room and called out. He entered the kitchen and almost collapsed in shock at what he saw.

He ran over to Heather and removed the tape from her mouth. She was unconscious but breathing normally, with a strong pulse. He then removed the tape from Josh's mouth; he was also unconscious. Jack picked up the phone and dialed 911, while thoughts whirled through his head as to what on earth had happened here. The dispatcher said, "Patience please, sir. We're already on our way."

Jack rushed to the sink, got two wet cloths, and rubbed them over their faces. No response. Jack then noticed Buster lying off in a corner of the kitchen. He put his hand in front of the dog's nose and could detect normal breathing. He removed the rest of the tape from Heather and Josh's hands and feet, and put pillows under their heads. He gently picked up Buster and laid him on the couch.

He then sat down and waited for the paramedics, not wishing to do anything else and make a mistake if there happened to be injuries he couldn't see. He found that his own breathing was becoming labored and his heart was beating far too fast. Jack got up and paced, then knelt on the floor again and stroked Heather's hair. He crawled over to Josh and kissed him on the forehead.

Then Jack started to cry. Slightly at first, then uncontrollably.

Chapter 9

Kerrie stood in her downstairs hall and looked up with disgust at the broken staircase railing. She hadn't gotten around to having it fixed yet. This was her souvenir from the fake building inspector's fall down the stairs. Several spindles were cracked and one of the posts was wobbly. She didn't have a clue as to how to fix it, but she figured she'd use the same carpentry firm who had done the renovations originally.

She had given them a call already, but they said they couldn't get out to see her until next week. They'd pop by earlier if work in progress sped up for them. Kerrie hated waiting for anything. Must be the lawyer in her, she thought. She was trained to push and resolve. It broke her heart to see her formerly perfect B&B sitting in this new state of imperfection.

She took a stroll around her main floor, taking second glances at all of the improvements she had made. Then she noticed a notch in her hardwood floor at the bottom of the stairs. She hadn't seen this before, probably because her eyes had been drawn up to the broken railing. She got down on her knees and fingered the notch. Damn, quite deep and noticeable; at least it was noticeable now that she had noticed it! She knew she would always be aware of it now. This must have happened when the idiot fell, she thought. Perhaps he landed on keys in his pocket or something. She was just about to get up when her eyes caught sight of something shiny underneath the couch. She reached under and slid it out. A cell phone, and it wasn't hers.

She flipped it open and pressed the power button, actually in this case the "end" button. Go figure, she thought. How difficult would it be for these phones to have a button that said "on." But where did this phone come from? How long had it been under the couch? It looked fairly new, and she could tell it was the cheap disposable type. Kerrie pushed the menu button and scrolled to "my account," and then down to "name card." No name was shown, but it did show the phone's phone number. She picked up her cordless phone and dialed the cell number. She let it ring to see if voice mail would pick up. No message. Kerrie then dialed the phone company to see if there was a record of this cell phone number. The operator told her it was for a pre-paid phone service, the number was unlisted.

Frustrated, Kerrie pushed the menu button again and scrolled down to "call history." She clicked on "outgoing" and the display showed ten numbers. Starting with the oldest calls at the bottom of the list, she began dialing. Each number rang with no answer, and no voice messaging. Until she got to the most recent number. It rang five times, and then a voice message said one word that sounded like "Otserp," followed by a beep.

Strange. What kind of a message was "Otserp?" Was that a name? With no friendly message to go with it? She dialed it over and over again, and couldn't help feeling that the voice saying "Otserp" was somewhat familiar. However the word was spoken so quickly and harshly, she couldn't be sure, and certainly couldn't identify it.

She went back to "call history" and checked for "received". No numbers showed under that category.

Kerrie put the phone in her pocket and headed upstairs, rubbing her hands over the damaged railing as she went. Suddenly it hit her. Her attacker had left her more than just a broken railing as a souvenir. This cell phone had to be his. What other explanation could there be? She had had no guests yet, and all the floors had been cleaned thoroughly before the furniture was brought in. So it couldn't have been there before she moved in. It must have fallen out of his pocket when he tumbled. And this was the phone he had made that strange call from while she was taped up! The single word "Presto." And that would have been the last call in the call history, the voice message that answered simply "Otserp." Kerrie shivered with the memory of it. And shivered again when she realized she was holding the creep's phone, with the last number he dialed recorded on it. She phoned directory assistance. The "Otserp" number was unlisted. She had expected that. She enquired about the other nine numbers that were listed in the history. All unlisted too.

Kerrie re-dialed that top number over and over again, listening to that single word, unable to shake the feeling that she knew that voice. She went over to her purse to get out her personal recorder.

*****

Kerrie had a restless sleep that night, re-living the experience of being bound and gagged, gagged with her own scarf yet. She recalled the choking feeling in her throat, the sight of the intruder's foot shooting towards her side. The bruise was still there, and it hurt every time she thought about that man's foot slamming into her. And her jaw still ached from his kick to her face, but thankfully it looked a lot worse than it really was.

She finally rolled out of bed around 8:00 a.m. and strolled wearily down to the kitchen to make breakfast. The phone rang, and she answered half-heartedly. But she perked up when the caller identified himself as a contractor with Lake Carpentry in Kalispell. They had an opening and he wanted to come out today to start on her railing. Kerrie was overjoyed. She wanted the house to look perfect again, and real soon. He said he would be out in about an hour. She made a large pot of coffee. She found that if you fed and watered these guys, they did a much more eager job. She pulled out some doughnuts from the freezer so they would be thawed out by the time he arrived.

In exactly one hour, the carpenter pulled up in his pickup truck and sauntered up to the front porch. Kerrie was waiting for him there, having her coffee outside. Spring was almost here and the temperature was actually tolerable enough now to sit outside for brief periods.

He looked pretty capable, she thought. The usual bulky stature of a carpenter, dressed in fresh white coveralls. She didn't recognize him as one of the guys who had worked on her renovation project, but she was sure he was good. Lake Carpentry was a large firm and they only employed the best, from what she had heard. And she was pleased with the job they had done, for sure.

He introduced himself as "Joe," and with no fanfare, walked into the foyer and gazed up at the staircase. "Shit, did you ever do a job on that!" he opined.

"It was an accident," Kerrie said. She didn't want to volunteer what really happened.

"Well, I'll get started. Shouldn't take too long," he assured her.

He put down his heavy tool case, and wandered into the kitchen. It was like a magnet with these guys: coffee and doughnuts. Joe helped himself to a big mug and a couple of jelly doughnuts, and sat himself down at the kitchen table without saying another word.

Kerrie looked at him and said, "You're welcome."

"Oh, yeah, thanks," Joe mumbled, cherry jelly dripping down his chin.

"Okay, I'll just leave you to it," Kerrie said impatiently. "I have things to do."

"Go ahead, don't worry about me," Joe replied in as pleasant a manner as he could muster.

Kerrie could tell Joe was a man of few words, as most tradesmen seemed to be. Social graces were not taught at trade schools.

She went upstairs to do some cleaning in the bedrooms and left Joe to his work. In a few minutes, she could hear the sound of wood being yanked from its attachments. Good, the work had begun. She busied herself for the next hour, until she heard the sound of a loud crash. Kerrie ran out to the upper hall, looked down and saw Joe on his hands and knees picking up tools that had fallen out of his box. They were scattered all over the living room floor, under the tables, chairs and couch.

"Don't worry," Joe panted. "Just an accident. I'll pick them all up. No damage to the floor at all. Just clumsy me."

Kerrie went down the stairs and examined the floor. Joe had his arms stretched out under the couch, pulling out a hammer and a couple of screwdrivers.

"Well, you're lucky," she grumbled. "All I need is more damage to this house."

"Ma'am, speaking of damage, I have to be honest with you. The type of spindles you have are a special order. I can't replace them with what I have in the truck. I need to place an order and come back again."

"Christ, how long will that take?" Kerrie demanded impatiently.

"If I order them today, should be able to install them in about two weeks. In the meantime, you'll have to be real careful going down the stairs. I've pulled out the cracked post and five spindles."

"Shit. Everything takes so damn long."

"I'm sorry, Ms. Joplin. That's the best I can do."

Joe then walked to the other end of the living room, looked up at the staircase, and circled the room slowly, looking down, looking up.

"What are you doing?" Kerrie asked.

"Just looking at the angles, trying to picture what a different type of spindle would look like."

"I'm not switching. Go ahead and order the same ones, and phone me when they're in."

"Okee dokee, ma'am. We'll take care of you."

Joe walked toward the door carrying his tool case, then quickly detoured to the kitchen and grabbed another doughnut to go. He grinned at Kerrie on his way out, displaying a mouthful of chocolate dip.

*****

Kerrie had the phone book in front of her, looking under the "O" section to see if any "Otserps" lived in the area. Not a one, under either Kalispell or Bigfork. Puzzled, she dialed the number again, still getting the vague feeling that she knew the voice. She sipped her coffee, staring at the cheap cell phone in front of her. Then she stared at the word "Otserp" she'd written on a piece of paper. She knew that the phony building inspector had used only one word when he made the call: "Presto." Just one word would indicate a code or a simple command, she thought. It meant something to him and the receiver, but would mean nothing to an eavesdropper.

Then it hit her. "God, am I stupid?" she shouted.

"Otserp" was merely "Presto" spelled backwards!

Kerrie got the chills. Not that these words meant anything to her, but their reverse relationship to each other indicated something sinister and secret. She'd lived with that sort of feeling for most of her life growing up in her dad's home. She was afraid that it had followed her from his grave.

*****

By the time the paramedics arrived, Heather and Josh were awake. A little drowsy but otherwise doing well. Buster was already walking around looking for his food, a little bit unsteady on his feet but no other outward signs of distress. The attendants took blood pressures, pulse rates, and looked carefully in their eyes. They made Heather and Josh walk back and forth across the room until they were sure they had gotten their bearings back. They talked on the phone with Emergency at Foothills Hospital, and gave the vital statistics. All seemed well, and it was felt that there was no need to make a trip to the hospital. Doctors suspected the intruders had used chloroform or ether on Heather and Josh, and a needle or dart on the dog. No lasting effects would be noticed.

EMS called the police and they were on their way.

Jack thanked the paramedics as they left, and stressed how pleased he was at how fast they arrived. One of the paramedics, as he was heading down the walk, said, "We pride ourselves on our quick response time, Mr. Howser. There was no need for you to call twice."

Jack stared after him. Twice? What was that all about?

He went back inside and sat down with Heather and Josh in the living room. Heather was still shaking a bit, but Josh seemed to have bounced back pretty well. He had Buster on his lap and was stroking his fur.

Jack got a sweater out of the closet for Heather, put it around her shoulders and gave her a hug. She started to cry. "Why would they bother with people like us Jack? We don't have much money, and not much of anything to steal," she whimpered. "They took my wallet, and there was only a hundred dollars at the most in it. They took my jewelry box too, but the things in there are more sentimental than valuable. Steven's wedding ring is gone, and that's irreplaceable."

Jack hugged her tighter. He glanced over at Josh, who was now looking very concerned seeing how upset his mother was. Jack rubbed his shoulder and said, "Don't worry, it's over now. The main thing is that you're all okay."

Josh had a bewildered look on his face. "Jack, why would they want to kick us out of here and take our dog?"

"They were just pretending, Josh. You know how you like to pretend?" Josh nodded. Well, these are bad guys who do that to steal things."

"But we don't have much stuff. Why us?"

Jack couldn't answer that, although another idea was going through his head that he didn't want to discuss with either Josh or Heather. It made him sick just to think about it. Too much of a coincidence, once again.

The police arrived, thankfully different cops than the ones Jack had already encountered. They were very gentle and sympathetic to Heather and Josh, who gave them every little detail they could remember. Their descriptions of those two guys sure matched his first two dognappers. Heather's observation that they seemed to be wearing makeup even made sense. They were trying to cover up the damage Jack had done to their faces.

Jack told them about the black van that was pulling out just as he was arriving. Unfortunately, he didn't think to notice the license plate number. The number was probably smeared over anyway, just like the others.

The older officer said to Jack, "Why did you call 911 twice?" This reminded Jack of the strange comment the paramedic had made when he was leaving.

"I didn't. I called only once, right after I discovered them on the floor."

"Well, someone, a man, called about five minutes before the second call, which must have been yours," the officer said. "And from this same home phone number."

"It must have been the intruders," Jack replied, "which is strange."

"Very strange," the officer commented. "I don't recall hearing anything like that happening after a home invasion. A decent thing to do, but weird… and a bit arrogant."

"They obviously never intended to hurt anyone, and didn't want them lying there for days bound and gagged," the younger officer said. "One for the record books for sure, or at least the police academy!"

Heather seemed relieved at hearing this banter, knowing that they never intended to really hurt her or her son had lifted her spirits a bit. Jack could see it in her eyes and her steadier hands. He felt better too. It was a relief to know that these guys seemed to have at least some humanity. And they didn't take Buster, or hurt him. They were careful to use a tranquilizer, when they could have just as easily killed him.

Heather located the phone number for her landlord, and the older officer called the company. No, they had not sent anyone over to talk with Heather about her dog. They pulled out their copy of her lease documents and confirmed that there was no pet clause on page ten or anywhere else in her lease. In fact, there wasn't even a page ten.

The officers acknowledged that this had been the slickest and most civilized home invasion they had ever seen. They chalked it up as a robbery in their report, and promised that they would let Heather know right away if they discovered her wallet or jewelry. But she would have to go through the process right away of canceling her credit cards, and obtaining a replacement driver's license and other identification. Heather groaned.

The police would also alert local media to put out a warning on the news about this strange new modus operandi for home invasions, so that Calgarians could be on guard.

The 6:00 news that evening posted a breaking news headline: "Gentlemen Callers."

*****

Kerrie was enjoying a martini on the porch when the phone rang, disturbing her deep thinking about the cell phone. It was Greg at Lake Carpentry.

"Ms. Joplin, we have good news for you," he said. "We should be able to get a man out to your house next Monday to start on your railing."

"Oh wonderful! The new spindles arrived faster than you thought!"

"New spindles?"

"The ones Joe said he would have to put in a special order for."

"Who's Joe?"

"Your carpenter who was out here a few days ago."

"No one from here has been out to your place yet, ma'am. And we have no one named Joe working here."

Kerrie clasped her hands together, and cracked her knuckles.

"Ma'am, are you still there?"

"Yes, I'm still here," Kerrie replied, in a voice barely heard at the other end.

"Do you still want us to do the work, or are you now dealing with this Joe fellow?"

"No…no, I, uh, must be confused. Sorry. Please do come out as soon as you can."

"We'll be there Monday then, 9:00 a.m. sharp."

Kerrie hung up the phone in a daze, wondering if she had just dreamt it all. She walked tentatively into the front hall, looked up and saw the spindles gone and the gaping opening in the railing—Joe's handiwork. No, she wasn't losing her mind after all, but her peace of mind was another story entirely.

Chapter 10

The news crew pounced as soon as Josh came out the side door with his school bag. An eager reporter ran up the walkway with his cameraman struggling along behind, and thrust the microphone in Josh's face.

"Are you Josh McIntosh?"

"Y-Yes," answered Josh in a shaky voice.

"Can you tell us what it felt like to be attacked in your home and tied up for hours?"

"Well, it wasn't hours—Jack cut us loose—and we weren't tied up, we were taped up."

"Were you scared, Josh?"

"I don't know, I guess I was kinda asleep."

"Who's Jack? The hero in this story?"

"Jack's my friend. My mom might marry him some day."

Heather looked out the front window and almost fell over when she saw the news vans. Then she saw Josh being interviewed by a reporter. Another reporter and camera crew were now running up the walk trying to get in on the interview.

She ran out the door and down the walkway just in time to hear, "We're at the site of the 'Gentlemen Callers' assault, a new fear in the neighborhoods of Calgary. This must be Josh's mother approaching us now. Let's see if she can add some detail to this shocking story for us."

Josh looked back at his mother, puzzled and petrified at the same time. But he knew she'd know what to say.

The reporter gently pushed Josh aside and strode up to Heather as she was heading his way. He thrust the microphone towards her and said, "Ms. McIntosh, can you tell us what it was like to be terrorized inside your own home?"

"I sure can. Kind of like being terrorized in *front* of your own home! Please go away. My son and I have nothing to say to you. It's appalling that you would approach my little boy on his way to school. What's wrong with you people? Please respect our privacy."

Heather grabbed Josh's hand and pulled him back toward the side door. The reporter pushed his way in front of her, frantically waving his cameraman to follow. He stood blocking the entrance, and spoke into the mike once again. "Ms. McIntosh, can you share something about last night that can help residents of this city prepare for their own safety?"

Heather glared at him, then suddenly put both hands on his chest and shoved him into the bushes. "Get out of my way, and leave us alone!" she shouted. Then she turned around to face the man who had recorded the whole thing. He quickly stepped backward down the walkway, and tripped on the step. The camera went flying through the air, smashing down onto the sidewalk.

The competing news crew had been shooting the whole time. While they were probably disappointed not to have conducted the interview they were no doubt excited about the great footage they had of the other station's bumbling bozos.

Heather and Josh quickly darted inside and shut the door. Both were breathing hard, and Buster merely looked up at them with an expectant "take me for a walk" look.

"Not today, Buster, not today," Heather said gently.

"Mom, that was real cool what you did to that guy. I can't wait to see it on the news!"

"Josh, that wasn't cool at all. Don't learn from what I just did. I lost my temper and I'm ashamed of myself. I hope they decide not to show any of it on the news."

"I hope they do! I'll be famous at school! How neat would that be?"

There was no point arguing with him. Kids will be kids, and this sort of incident was exactly the kind of thing that excited them. Of course, she knew that most of the adults in the city would find that camera footage titillating as well. There was nothing she could do about it. If they showed it, they showed it. However, while she would never admit it to Josh, it felt darn good shoving that idiot reporter into the bushes!

"No school for you, Josh. We'll stick together today."

Josh's face lit up like a Christmas tree. "Let's take Buster for a hike!"

"Maybe, once the television crews leave," Heather replied. "By the way, what did you tell those people?" She parted the drapes and took a peek outside. She could see a few of them standing together chatting, while the cameraman was on his knees picking up the broken pieces of his livelihood.

"Not much, just that we were taped up, not tied up, and oh yeah, that I slept through most of it."

"Did you mention me or Jack at all?"

"Well, kinda. I said that Jack cut us loose, and that you might marry him some day."

"Josh!" Heather exclaimed. "How could you! That's not true, and if it were true, it would be private, just between you, me, and Jack!"

"I'm sorry, Mom. I guess I wasn't thinking. I sure wish it were true though."

Heather looked at her little boy, who was starting to tear up in his eyes. She couldn't resist, she gave him a big hug. "It's okay, Josh. We all say things we shouldn't sometimes. I'll have to warn Jack though, in case this shows up on the news."

She picked up the phone and dialed Jack's number. He answered on the first ring. Heather told him what happened, and Jack shared her disgust about the news hounds. Then she told him what Josh said, and he started laughing. "Out of the mouths of babes, eh?" She was glad he was taking it so well. She felt embarrassed just telling him about it.

Heather mentioned that she was keeping Josh at home today, and that they would probably stay inside until the news folks got tired and moved on to the next story.

"I have an idea. Why don't you, Josh, and Buster pack some things and come over to my place. You can stay as long as you want, and you might feel safer being around Mule and I for a while. Plus, I have an alarm system now." He paused. "There will be ample time for you and I to plan the wedding as well," Jack added, chuckling.

"Very funny. You probably won't let me forget this, will you? Especially after you see it on the news tonight!"

"Uh oh, I forgot about that. Well, at least Josh didn't give my last name, so the news trucks will stay away from here. Unless the police leak my name like they must have done yours."

"I'll take you up on your offer. I would feel better if we can escape this place for a little while...as long as we're not imposing on you."

"Not at all, Heather. It will be good to have the company."

Heather hung up, and Josh, who had been listening from his bedroom, came running out with his duffle-bag. "I'm all packed!"

She smiled at her little guy, and smiled to herself too. This was all too unexpected, but nice.

*****

They were sitting in Jack's living room, surfing the evening news channels. Sure enough, the footage appeared, to no one's surprise. The station that did the interview showed only the part with Josh, but nothing of Heather or her encounter with the reporter or the cameraman. But the other station took full advantage—great footage of Heather's frontal thrust against the reporter, and a great shot of her advancing toward the cameraman causing him to fall backwards. The camera smashing into pieces was a particularly dramatic effect.

Jack couldn't stop laughing—and Josh was just beaming.

Heather, on the other hand, was turning multiple shades of red. "I hate for you guys to see me like that. And what are the people at my office going to say?"

"You'll probably get a promotion. There's no love affair between lawyers and the media, I can assure you of that," Jack commented.

"Still, it's embarrassing to lose control like that," Heather said sheepishly.

"You were defending your son and your right to privacy. Nothing wrong with that," Jack retorted. "More people should do exactly what you did. You're a hero in some people's eyes right now, I would bet."

Heather snorted. "Yeah, just what I want to be."

The two dogs were getting along famously. It was touch and go at first when Buster tried to advance on Mule's food dish. This provoked some serious growls from Mule. And when Buster curled up in Mule's bed-basket, a war almost broke out. Buster took note. He must have been testing Mule, because it became quickly apparent who the dominant dog was. Buster learned his rightful place in the pecking order, and they finally started to get along and play with each other in typical doggy fashion.

*****

Over the next few days, they all got into a routine. Heather drove Josh to school each day, and then went on to work from there. Jack looked after both dogs, taking them on hikes, and just marveling at how two Border collies could work in concert with each other when they decided it was time to herd something. Instinct was a powerful thing, and Mule automatically took the lead, seemingly sending signals to Buster as to what his role was. Some pheasants became so petrified, they ended up crowded into a circle together with both dogs standing guard until Jack could get there. What magnificent animals, Jack thought. So similar but also so different; Buster displayed none of the guard dog tendencies that Mule did. He seldom barked if someone came to the door, and he greeted everyone as a friend.

Mule was much more wary, and angry if he didn't like the look of whoever showed up at the front door. Jack was pretty sure that those 'gentlemen callers' would not have advanced very far in their quest if Mule had been on their case. Since they must have thought Buster was Mule, that would explain why they tranquilized him. They weren't going to take any chances since both of them, if they were the same first dognappers, had encountered Mule before. Jack figured that these two thugs weren't too dog savvy. If they knew some basics about dogs, they would have known that if it were Mule he would have remembered them right away, right at the front door, and probably would have attacked them.

Jack was pretty certain what those guys were doing there. They must have seen him and Josh together with Buster, and thought it was Mule. At that point Heather's place became a target. Once they were there, they must have decided, after Heather's resistance, that they would remove the chip on the spot. They then discovered that there was no chip, probably with a scanner—and quickly left. Jack thought of telling Heather all about what he suspected had led up to this, but decided against it. The less people close to him knew about this mystery, the better. He decided to leave her and Josh out of it, but did feel guilty thinking that what they had had to endure was because of him.

Thankfully, however, they were none the worse for wear, except maybe a little more fearful than before. If he told them some of his vague theories, they would probably be even more fearful. Well, at least Heather would. Josh would no doubt be excited.

*****

It was later in the week when the phone call came, one that Jack did not expect. It was Kerrie Joplin from Bigfork, Montana. Jack was surprised, because he figured he would have to be the one to phone her again. He kept meaning to call her, but something was always coming up—between dognappers, police, Mule's drug examination—aside from Jack's new relationship with Heather.

Truth be known though, Jack had just been putting off making the call. But he knew that talking to Kerrie again would have to be the next step in his "investigation."

"Jack, I had been intending to call you for some time now, but a lot of things have been going on that kept getting in the way. I want to apologize for how I behaved the last time we talked. I was pretty nasty," Kerrie said.

"That's okay, Kerrie. I kind of hit you out of the blue with some personal questions, which was very inappropriate of me. I'm the one who should be apologizing. I wanted to call you again too, but I guess I've been wimping out."

"I understand totally, and it would be great if we could start over. I'd really like to see Mule some time, and I want to extend an invitation for you and Mule to be the first guests at my bed and breakfast. I'm not officially open yet. I've put that off for a while because of repairs. But you can come any time you like, and I won't even charge you—just pay for meals and drinks. I have a menu that's reasonable and I'm a great cook!"

Jack was astonished. This was turning out far better than he could have hoped for. He had wanted to visit her to explore this mystery further, but never dreamed he'd actually get an invitation.

"That's very nice of you, Kerrie. You know what, I'm going to take you up on that. The weather's a lot nicer now, and I'd like to talk to you about Mule. That's one of the reasons I wanted to call you again."

"Anything in particular? Something along the lines of what you mentioned before?"

"I'd rather not tell you over the phone Kerrie. It's better done in person. Perhaps I can buy you dinner one night and we can chat?"

"Wonderful. I'd like that. I really do want to see Mule again. And don't worry, I know he's your dog now. I guess I'm just feeling a bit nostalgic. And also, right about now, I could use a dog in the house."

Jack wondered about that last comment, but let it go. He could enquire better in person than over the phone. He couldn't get it out of his head that most likely every word they were saying to each other right now was being listened to by someone else. Who and why were the big questions he needed answers to. And he knew he wouldn't rest until he had them.

"Kerrie, I don't know when I can get away, but if you don't mind, I'll just show up at your door when the time is right for me. It's a short drive down to Montana from here, and if you're not around when I come, I can stay in one of the local hotels."

"You could phone first, Jack."

"No, I can't. I'll tell you why when I get there." Jack didn't want his listeners to know the exact day he was leaving. He feared that he'd be ripe for an ambush along the way, or beforehand.

"Oh, okay. I'll wait with baited breath. Could you do me a favor before you show up? This may sound like a strange request, but believe me, I have my reasons."

"Sure, Kerrie, just name it."

"Email me a photo of yourself."

*****

The man from Montana said, "From the sound of the last conversation, it's apparent that Howser's on to us."

"You think?" came the sarcastic reply from the man on the other end of the secure phone line in Virginia.

"Well, okay, I guess he would have to be pretty stupid not to know by now that we're listening in. But the good thing is, he has no idea who is listening or why."

"Use your head. He has a pretty good idea why—the chip. He just doesn't know why it might be important, and for all we know it may not even be important. He hasn't yet shared over the phone what's on that chip, and god only knows how incompetent our own specialists have been with this simple task," snarled the Virginian. "Christ, we've pulled off assassinations with more finesse than this."

"I know, I know. It's incredible that we've been thwarted three times. But in our defense I have to remind you that we've tried to be as civil as possible with this, relatively speaking, and our third attempt failed only due to a case of mistaken dog identity. We've also been operating in a large Canadian city where life is fairly safe and benign. This isn't Somalia where anything goes. We can't get caught; it would blow up into a huge international incident that would be embarrassing for America let alone the CIA. We don't belong in that city doing what we're doing; you know that. Luckily this guy thinks he's Sherlock Holmes, so he's kept things close to his chest. I think he's actually kind of enjoying this."

The Virginian ignored this excuse. While it was true, he didn't like excuses and felt if he acknowledged them, his agents would just look for more crutches. "We may have to step it up a notch. Now they're going to be in the same area together. We still have two tasks to complete—the chip and the attic. Then we can decide where we go from there. We also still have that small matter of the cell phone. Any luck there?"

"No, none at all. We were covert in our search, but aside from turning the house upside down, we couldn't find it. I think she's already got it under lock and key."

"That can't be left unresolved."

"We'll continue our efforts, and we'll continue to be discreet. We also don't know when Howser is coming to Montana, so we can't plan an interception on the dog. But surveillance may help us know at least at the last minute, which will enable us to try something."

The man from Virginia closed the conversation, growling the most used expression in his job: "Just get me results."

Chapter 11

"...and I'd be willing to bet that very few of us here today, including those actually employed by the oil industry, really believe that one day we will run out of oil. Why? Because we don't feel the danger. We can still fill up our cars, heat our homes, turn on the lights, fly our planes, ship our goods across oceans, and run our factories. We don't feel the pain yet. Oh sure, we did last year when the price per barrel hit $140, but that was a relatively brief span of pain. We haven't really suffered yet.

"There sure were some panic-driven plans to change lifestyles when the pump prices jumped so high. Every day there were articles in the media about the folly of owning a pickup truck or SUV, causing people to dump their vehicles at almost any price. People sure believe what they read and hear on the news, don't they? Now that the cost to fill our tanks has come down so much, there's a sigh of relief. Guess what? While overall vehicle sales are indeed in the dumper, people are out buying gas-guzzling SUVs and pickups again—not in droves, because the overall economy is still weak—but out of the sales that do take place, these vehicles are no longer labeled as pariahs. The sense of urgency is gone...for now.

"We human beings tend to think short-term, and have for centuries. Witness the fall of every prominent civilization in history. Sure, there were specific reasons for each decimation and historians can analyze those ad nauseum. But, keeping it simple so us simpletons can learn from the past, it was short-term thinking that caused these downfalls.

"And we're doing it again."

Jack paused. He looked out over the audience and saw that he was having the desired effect. He was about two-thirds of the way through his speech as the dinner speaker at the World Energy Summit being held at Calgary's largest convention centre. Even though Jack was retired, he had gained a reputation as a popular spokesperson for the Canadian energy industry over the years he'd spent as CEO of one of the major producers. He still accepted the occasional offer to speak, because he had loved his industry and believed in the fundamentals that were gradually being eroded. Jack felt an obligation to still give back when he could, and he basically did it for free. His fee was always donated to a charity choice of the majority of delegates. This act of generosity gave him even more credibility when he spoke—he had no active role to play anymore, and neither did he benefit financially. And he didn't need to benefit financially. Jack was a millionaire several times over, and whatever he did now he did for the satisfaction of doing it.

He had become known over the years as an engaging and controversial speaker. While there were active CEOs who could speak on the same topics as Jack did, he was in more demand than they were—because he was retired, and because he was just a very talented speaker. Audiences lined up for seats at Jack's speeches; no one was ever quite sure what he would say. He was hard-hitting, honest, and fresh, with the occasional "outside the box" provocation that sometimes left people reeling. Jack enjoyed that.

'If any of you do not think that we're running out of conventional energy, think again. It may not be in your lifetime, but I can pretty much guarantee that your kids will see the effects. The debate about 'peak oil' will continue for years, but not too many years, because the underlying pressures are already with us, you just don't feel them yet. Why do you think that so much investment has already been committed to extract unconventional sources of oil such as tar sands, deep sea, polar regions, etc.? Why would any corporation that is committed to its shareholders, justify spending the vast amounts of money that are needed to get to these more difficult to reach sources? The nature of business is to keep expenses down, and revenue streams up. Well, voluntarily developing the tar sands of Alberta would make no sense unless it was seen that eventually resources like that will be all we will have to draw from. In fact, I suggest to you that the peak of regular oil—the cheaply obtained stuff—has already been reached.

'The theory of 'peak oil' means that our consumption of oil will catch, then exceed, our discovery of new reserves, and then resources will begin to deplete. Essentially there is no cheap oil left to find. We're now into the difficult and expensive reserves, such as tar sands and deep ocean. That requires money, honesty, and commitment, from energy companies, investors, and most of all, governments.

'The global economic crash has caused a reprieve from this looming disaster, which, when it inevitably happens, will have devastating consequences for world economies and how all of us live our lives. Like it or not, that's the way it will be. In fact, we might face these consequences just a few short years after the world economies recover from this current crisis.

'The irony here is, the only reason we have a reprieve right now is because the

economy is anemic. Demand for oil has dropped dramatically and reserves have increased in the same proportion. All we can think of is 'get the economy moving again.' But guess what? Once it does get moving again, the reprieve is over. Oil prices will once again soar and the recovery of the economy will be stifled because everything we do, right now at least, depends on oil. Governments around the world are throwing money at the economy, increasing the future tax burden of our children. These stimulus packages will probably over time have the desired effect, but then the irony will show itself. The law of supply and demand will work as it is supposed to. Surplus reserves will be utilized, GDPs will be growing, demand for oil will be huge particularly from China, India, South America, and, last but not least, the good old U.S.A.

"The price per barrel will have no choice but to rise—and stay there. Then we will have a new economic reality to get accustomed to, and inflation will rule the day. This new inflation will be impossible to fight because the core cause will be outside of any government's control. The core cause will be a non-renewable resource called 'oil.'

"So, economic recovery, while necessary, will simply cause a new disaster. Can we really afford to have the economy recover that much? Isn't that a strange question to ask ourselves?"

Jack paused again and looked into a few eyes in the front rows. He noticed that at least no one was sleeping—they looked alarmed. Good, he thought. They need to be alarmed. There were about 1200 people in the audience, delegates from all corners of the globe. He noticed quite a few were wearing earphones, getting a translation of his speech in the language of their choice. He wondered if some of the countries were getting the right translation.

He decided it was time to bring down the hammer to close out his speech. Jack always spoke without notes, which made his speeches more effective. He'd now been speaking for about forty-five minutes, and he could tell that every word he'd spoken had been absorbed. In addition to being a former CEO, he had the added credibility of being a petrochemical engineer. So the audience knew that not only had he been a high-powered executive, he had the technical knowledge of the industry to back up his words. The lack of notes always gave him flexibility as well to change gears, or message, depending on the reaction of the audience. Right now he could tell he had their attention, so it was time for the hammer.

"What do we do? We wake up, that's what we do!

"Oil and gas companies, for starters, should start referring to themselves as 'energy companies,' such as is the theme for this Summit. There is simply no future

in oil, and it's about time we faced that. It is only a short-term gap solution. Even if we developed all of the unconventional oil sources available to us, society and its economies could not absorb the high costs long term. We have to develop renewable sources, and that is what energy companies should be doing as their first priority.

'For executives of energy companies, why should you be bonused more just because the price per barrel went from $70 to $140? What creative initiatives from you caused that to happen? None whatsoever, unless of course you started a war. At $140 a barrel, immense profits are a no-brainer. Your bonuses from now on should be based on strategic development measures and paid gradually over the long term. They should no longer be based on profits from non-renewable resources, but instead based on your progress towards success with renewable resources. And possibly nuclear energy, which for all intents and purposes, is renewable due to the technology today with improved reactors. Executive compensation could even encourage more efficient and clean processes with coal, for which there are reserves estimated to last another 150 years. Sure, right now it's not clean, but we can work on making it clean. If we can spend hundreds of billions on brainless outer space missions, we can make coal clean.

'Natural gas will outlast oil reserves by about twenty years, so it may be worthwhile to research and develop methodologies to make it less expensive to extract, and cleaner to use. And of course wind, solar, and hydroelectric. Bottom line: there is a lot for you all to do to earn bonuses, but you should no longer be financially motivated to focus on oil. Boards of directors should take note and make their executives accountable in a different direction.

'For environmentalists and other similar do-gooders out there—go get a real job and do something constructive to make the world a better place. You can protest all you want, but nothing changes the fact that you used cars or planes to get here, buses or trains to get downtown, will eat your dinners tonight cooked with gas or electricity, and will sleep in your heated hotel rooms. You live on this planet just like the rest of us, and we are all in this dilemma together. While the environment must be respected, your radical ways cannot be. And your irrationality cannot be either. Be honest with the public and the media as to what the real result will be if tar sands projects do not come out of the mothballs created by this recession. Or if refineries cease to operate because emissions are not up to your ridiculous standards. Or if we ignore coal, one of the most dependable and available natural resources. The world cannot be changed overnight. We can work together to develop new resources and cleaner methodologies, but we all need to be patient. It takes time, and we cannot just destroy the economy out of ideology. You protestors will have plenty to protest, I can

promise you, if you can no longer turn on the lights.

"For governments, sure you own the resources and are entitled to a share of the profits, but don't call yourselves 'partners' with energy companies, because you're not. Real partners also share in the losses when times are bad, not just the profits when times are good. I don't see you doing that. You feel you're justified in publicly beating up on the industry when pump prices are high, holding senate subcommittee hearings and all other forms of time-wasters and vote-getters. But after all is said and done, you happily walk off with your royalties from us, and your taxes on the consumer. You're hypocrites, and it isn't helpful to the future. You share in our profits during good times, but wash your hands of us in bad times. What kind of partnership is that? I would suspect you would view it as a similar partnership to what you've had with the tobacco industry for decades—collect your share of the loot, then just punish the industry when it's politically expedient.

"And in closing, I'd like to add a personal comment on a subject that makes me angry and despondent. I lost my wife on that fateful day of Sept. 11, 2001, to the most terrifying act of terrorism this world has ever seen. All of us who suffer loss in life, whether it is from crime, or terrorism, want and expect to see justice served. This helps with closure. I'm sure I'm not the only one, however, who feels that justice somehow got sidetracked here. How on earth did vengeance for the attacks on New York and Washington lead to a war in Iraq? It started off, it seemed, in the right direction when the invasion of Afghanistan began, but then they all took a wrong turn and landed in Iraq. That country had nothing to do with the death of my wife, but suddenly there on the news I'm watching 'Shock and Awe.' It seemed to me at the time that there were far more despicable despots in the world to get rid of than Saddam Hussein. Yet here we were killing Iraq's citizens in the name of revenge for 9/11, and the supposed elimination of weapons of mass destruction. Then when it became clear that Iraq had nothing to do with 9/11, nor had any serious weapons, we declared it was in the name of democracy. Are there not other dictatorships out there worthy of a lobotomy? Why Iraq?

"We know the answer don't we? Oil.

"Iraq had oil—lots of it.

"I'm personally insulted that the death of my wife was used as an excuse to go after another country's oil reserves—and let's not kid ourselves—that is exactly what happened. How dare they.

"The technology has been around for a long time now, to be able to see you and me very clearly from satellites in space, mowing our lawns and picking our noses in our densely populated cities. Yet somehow, with all this technology, they can't catch

even a glimpse of an almost seven foot tall, turbaned, white-cloaked lunatic in a desolate, unpopulated land. And we're supposed to believe this nonsense? Do they think we're that stupid?

"Apparently so and maybe they're right. Until we start asking some serious questions and holding our elected officials accountable for the nonsense they spout and the havoc they wreak, it will happen to us time and time again.

"I don't think they ever really tried that hard to catch this maniac, because justice seems to be the least of their concerns. The fear of 'peak oil' keeps them awake at nights, not some madman in a cave who murdered my wife.

"And ladies and gentlemen, this is the crux of our crisis. We will continue to have manufactured wars on other nations because they have something we want, and we think we're entitled to it more than they are. The bottom line is, the energy crisis is real even if you don't see it yet, and solving this crisis will not only ensure our economic futures and those of our children and grandchildren, but more importantly, and ironically, it will finally allow us to achieve world peace.

"Now isn't that reason enough for us to change?

"Ladies and gentlemen, thank you very much for coming tonight and listening to me speak. It has been my pleasure. I hope that I've given you some food for thought.

"As I always do with my speeches, the fee will be donated to the charity of your majority choice. Please remember to complete the charity indication cards that are at each table.

"Enjoy the Summit, and please also enjoy the beautiful city of Calgary."

Jack went back to his seat at the head table, and the applause became thundering. Then the audience was standing; well, most of them anyway. The American and British congregations were sitting on their hands, as he expected they probably would. Jack didn't care. He was glad they took it personally. He took it personally too, as he had made very clear tonight, but for different reasons than they did. The servers were running around through the convention hall, bringing out desserts and coffee now that the speech was over. Jack received some congratulatory handshakes from other members of the head table, most of whom he knew personally. However, a high-ranking official with the U. S. Department of Energy took a different approach. He got up from his seat and asked Jack if he could join him in the hall for a discussion.

Jack obliged and they walked out together. As they reached the hallway, the expected outburst came. "You have one hell of a nerve sticking it to us like that! What gives you the right to say those things?" growled the American official.

"The microphone," replied Jack calmly.

"You arrogant, ungrateful, son of a bitch! Without us, you Canadians would be nothing! Show us some respect and gratitude!"

"Sure, thanks. You have my respect and gratitude," said Jack. "But please remember, sir, without us, you'd have a ten percent shortfall in oil. Which five states would you choose to have freeze in the dark? Make sure to keep us in the loop on that so that we'll know which refineries *not* to ship our oil to. I'm sure China will buy it from us so we won't suffer, but you most certainly will. Or perhaps more accurately, five of the states who didn't vote for your party will suffer." Jack turned on his heel and went back to his seat at the head table. The U.S. official chose to skip his dessert.

*****

It took a while for Jack to get out of the hall after dinner. There were line-ups of people from the audience who wanted to shake his hand and thank him for his speech. There were others he could see who glowered at him, and then just looked the other way. Sometimes the truth hurts, Jack thought. That's a big part of the problem. No one really wants to hear the truth, and governments and big corporations inherently know that. Some press folks pushed their way towards Jack and shoved their microphones at him.

"Mr. Howser, did you really intend to call the Iraq war 'manufactured'?"

"Do you really believe the war is only about oil?"

"Were the American people duped?"

Jack ignored all of the shouting and just continued along his path out of the hall, head down, blocking out the questions. He kind of expected this. The press covered these world oil conferences heavily, and anything controversial was a lightning rod. He was determined though that they would not have the satisfaction of him commenting away from the relative safety of the podium. The press would do anything to get a sound byte and then use it as much out of context as possible.

Finally he made it to his car and started the drive home. It was now the middle of May, and the weather was unseasonably warm. Some of the largest dumps of snow for Calgary actually came in May with the mountain effect—cold air hitting warm, snow melting off the mountains, moisture shooting into the atmosphere. Luckily, the snow usually melted fast due to the "chinook" weather phenomena. But it sure did make a mess of things for a day or two, just when people were getting used to the idea of spring. But right now it was quite nice. Jack could have actually walked to the convention centre, but he knew that the weather in Alberta could change incredibly fast. At this time of year it was safer to drive.

Once home, he sat back with a glass of rye and thought of his plans for the next month or so. He would leave for Montana tomorrow, and maybe stay at least one night in Whitefish. He planned to stop at that cute vet's office; Meagan was her name, he recalled. Jack had intended for quite some time now to get that troublesome chip removed from Mule's shoulder, but he had been afraid to get it done in Calgary. Probably just paranoid, but he was afraid that Detective Al might have put out an alert to Calgary vet offices to watch out for a guy named Jack Howser who might try to have something surgically removed from his dog. He figured that Al was like a bulldog with a bone. He was probably convinced that Jack was a drug dealer and had concealed something somewhere in the body of his dog. He knew that Al was perplexed as to why two attempts had been made to steal Mule, and he was probably a suspicious and insecure man by nature. So Jack didn't want to take any chances in Calgary. He would attend to it in Montana.

It had been over a month since he had last talked to Kerrie about coming down to Bigfork. He had emailed her his photo—for whatever reason she wanted it—and reminded her that he would just show up one day. Jack still did not feel good about announcing the timing of his trip, either over the phone or by email. He had hoped to go earlier, but he had committed to this speech at the Summit and didn't want to have to rush back for it if his visit to Montana was proving productive. He also discovered that his passport was due to expire in a couple of months, so he didn't want to take any chances on that. He had now just received the new one—good for five years—so he was all set.

Heather, Josh, and Buster had moved back to their apartment. After a couple of weeks, they were both feeling secure again and the media had moved on to other stories. Heather also really wanted to stop imposing on Jack, even though he had protested that that was not the case at all. But he was somewhat happy to have his privacy back. He liked his life, although he did admit to himself that Heather and Josh were two people he could easily fall in love with. It had been nice having them as houseguests, but it was time for them to move back. He wasn't ready yet for any permanent domestic bliss.

He and Heather had become a lot closer during her visit, and Jack felt very comfortable with her. He knew in his heart that this was one relationship he wanted to carry on with, but he was distracted with the microchip mystery and knew that he had to get it behind him before he could really concentrate on romance. When Jack was obsessed about something, there was usually no room for anything else in his brain.

Things had been nice and quiet the last few weeks—no other attempts to steal Mule, no imposters, no "gentlemen callers." Jack was able to relax a bit more, and even kind of half convinced himself that perhaps it was all over. The spooks had given up. Maybe they had decided that it wasn't worth the risk or effort. But despite these attempts he made to calm himself down, a little voice inside of him—the same voice that caused his hair to stand on end at times—told him to be on guard. He either had some kind of sixth sense or was just plain paranoid, but at times he couldn't help but feel he was being watched and followed.

Something just didn't feel right.

Chapter 12

Jack woke up bright and early the next morning, looking forward to his drive to Montana. He took a shower, fed Mule, and started scrambling some eggs. Then the phone rang. And rang again, and again… Each time Jack answered, it was the same thing—reporters asking him to comment on what he had said at the Summit the night before. Each time Jack replied, "no comment," and hung up. One of the reporters had referred to a newspaper headline. Apprehensively, Jack went out to his front porch and picked up his morning paper. The front page read, "Oil Executive Slams Iraq War."

He read on. The story gave all the gory details, quoting excerpts from his speech; of course only the most controversial and sensational ones. And the article went out of its way to mention how many American officials were in attendance, hinting that the speech was intended as a particularly disrespectful "up yours."

The feeling he was left with after reading the article, for a few moments anyway, was that he, Jack, was one rogue loose cannon; a U.S. basher. The editorial pages, however, gave opinions that were supportive: "about time someone stood up for principle," "people need to hear the truth," "Americans need to wake up and face what their government does to them, and to the world," "bullies need to be put in their place," "the world will be a safer place once it's an honest place."

The phone rang again. Jack was going to ignore it, until he noticed by the call display that it was Heather.

"Jack, you're my hero!"

"Don't be too quick. Heroes can turn into goats in an instant, Heather."

"Sure, but we need more people like you who are fed up and courageous enough to tell it like it is."

"I appreciate your nice words. In all honesty, if I hadn't suffered the kind of personal tragedy that I did, I may not have been so courageous at the podium. But, thanks anyway."

"You're welcome. So are you packed for Montana?"

"No, not yet. I think I may wait another day now, in light of all this frenzy. I'm not in the mood anymore for a long drive. Plus I might get lynched at the border!"

"That's probably wise. You don't want to be daydreaming through the Rocky Mountains. Those roads can be pretty scary."

"You're right. And Heather, I don't know how long I'll be gone, but I'll keep in touch, okay?"

"I'll hold you to that promise. But you've been very cagey as to why you're going down there. Should I be jealous?"

"No reason to be jealous, although I'm flattered. I'm actually working on a puzzle, a real life puzzle. I can't tell you about it yet, and it may be nothing at all, but the trail leads me to Montana."

"All right, mystery man. I'll wait for you to let me in on it later. Sounds intriguing. But I hope you're being careful, whatever it is."

"I'll be careful. Say bye to Josh for me—and Buster!"

Jack hung up and sauntered over to the couch. He flopped himself down and closed his eyes. He needed to think. Did he regret what he said in his speech? No, he believed every word of it. He knew in his heart that if it wasn't for the American bullying tactics throughout the world, his Susan would be alive today. And the war in Iraq? It was a sham. What reasonably intelligent person could think otherwise? A bunch of incompetent power-hungry bozos had planned that one. Dangerous men and women who had no idea of what their limitations should be. What angered him most was how citizens were taken for granted, and at times considered just collateral damage to a so-called bigger cause. How could those in power have thought that people would be stupid enough to believe that the war in Iraq was revenge for 9/11? For god's sake, they were the ones who first had declared Bin Laden the villain, then went ahead and fought on another front. Do they think we're brain dead? The arrogance! To think that people would forgive the fact that they never caught the actual villain, that they just went ahead and targeted someone else.

Jack meant every word that he had said, despite the second-guessing that he was doing right now. The power of the podium brought some freedoms, and the beauty of it was there was no censorship. Most people allowed the rage to burn within, but never said anything. Well, not Jack.

His problem was that his rage was personal. Once in a while he would get like this—pensive, angry, regretful—and it was painful. He was alone now, looking for ways to keep his mind occupied, when Susan used to do a lot of that for him. She was intelligent and stimulating, and while they didn't always get along, it didn't change the respect and love they had for one another. She had a brain and wasn't afraid to use it, and was never afraid to challenge Jack. He needed that, and he missed that.

As he lay there on the couch with his eyes closed, he began to remember her, to picture her in his mind. Waterskiing on Lake Muskoka, auburn hair blowing behind her, laughing as she cut across the wake. Barbecues at the cottage, Susan stomping out to the deck telling Jack the steaks were overdone—he protesting—her being right as usual. Christmas time, opening presents together, seeing the smile on her face as she tore off the paper, looking like a little girl. Her tender kisses when they lay in bed at night, the way she giggled when he lightly touched her neck or her side; ticklish beyond belief. Sometimes their love-making turned into a laugh-fest.

Then the serious Susan, the high-powered broker who shoved her sexy nightie aside in the morning and donned her power suit. Her hair pulled back to look business-like, belying the sexy woman underneath. Jack always found that transformation fascinating and strangely erotic, like wanting to have sex with the local librarian when he was a hormone-charged teenager, fantasizing that without those glasses she'd be hot.

His wife was a one-of-a-kind lady who still nicely haunted him at night. He had had many dreams about Susan, but the most vivid was one last year when she seemed to be right in front of his face. He heard her so clearly: "It didn't really hurt at all, Jack. I was gone before I hit the ground. So sleep well, my dear. There was no pain."

He began to think about that terrible morning again—Sept. 11, 2001—and he began to cry. Jack remembered how he felt watching the television and how his heart was aching. His wonderful wife had been going through absolute hell, and he wasn't there with her. He was helpless, and her situation was helpless. The fear she must have felt, the tears that must have been shed—and the incredible courage it must have taken for her to step to the window ledge on the 106th floor of the north tower and jump. It was hard for Jack to think of what must have been going through her mind. Did she think she would actually land on soft ground? Did that matter at 106 stories high? He had heard of skydivers who somehow survived partial openings of their chutes. Did the people who jumped from the twin towers think of those miracle cases? Did they think the good Lord would save them?

What kind of courage does it take to jump from 106 stories? Jack couldn't place himself in that mindset, yet he tried for Susan's sake. Did she think it would hurt? Did she think she'd be alive all the way down? Jack always hoped that people who fell from high places died on the way down. Some small hope that they were spared the horror of those last few seconds and seeing the ground come up to them in a blur. Spared the feeling of the impact.

Then when Susan came to him in his dream last year, it seemed she cleared up the mystery for him. She said she was dead before she hit the ground. Jack felt comforted by that, for at least a little while. He eventually rationalized that it was only his subconscious trying to make him feel better by telling him what he wanted to hear. He wanted to believe that it was really and truly her that had come to visit him, but his rational side would not let him indulge for too long in such supernatural thinking.

He would never know what her death had been like, and the horror of thinking about how she felt in those last few seconds made him shudder.

Jack opened his eyes with a start and jumped to his feet. He started pacing back and forth across the living room, breathing hard, hands shaking. He got like this every time he allowed his mind to wander that deeply. He would always get wrapped up in the same angry feelings that he had more "politely" expressed in his speech. His own private thoughts weren't so polite. He was angry at the waste of life and the lack of justice. He was angry that the whole event of 9/11 was used as an excuse for something else. It was easy to imagine political power brokers cheering at the event, high-fiveing each other: "Hooray! Finally we have a marketable excuse to invade Iraq! Let's strike now while the grief of those naïve fools is fresh!"

He was angry for Susan, and all the other Susans, who had lost their lives that day. Greed and misplaced interference had brought these attacks to American soil, and ironically, greed and misplaced interference were the motivations that turned the horrible tragedy into an opportunity. Over eight years had passed, yet Jack couldn't shake the feeling he had, that those in power were glad it happened, and glad they had this once-in-a-lifetime opportunity to grab the oil of a sovereign nation. The more Jack paced the room, the more he wished he'd said even more in his speech and had been even more brutal than he was. But then again, he knew that if he allowed too much emotion to show through, no one would really listen seriously. So he knew that tack he took was the right one, and he would continue to pursue it at every speech in the future, assuming anyone asked him back. However, he was only one man and there wasn't much any one person could do. He knew that of course, but it still made him feel better to speak out. He was well aware that most people would prefer not to think of these things, would prefer to stick their heads in the sand. And the mainstream media were the worst offenders. Questions that should be asked to keep governments honest were hardly ever asked. It was like they were paid off, or threatened. It was puzzling how they ignored obvious inconsistencies and pure logic. American patriotism was occasionally nauseating; sometimes abused and misplaced, he thought.

Jack was starting to calm down the more he paced and the more anger he allowed himself to vent. His cheeks were soaked with tears, and he knew that crying, even though a bit embarrassing, was one of the best ways to vent. He always felt relieved afterwards, as if a big weight had been lifted off him.

He sat down at his kitchen table and looked once again at his notes about the strange notations from the microchip. He couldn't let this mystery go. He knew that in his gut. There was something about this that was just too odd. The message must have been intended for a certain someone to notice. And meant to be hidden from certain other people. Who were those people? Jack was becoming more and more convinced that they were Mitch's secretive employers. The fact that Mitch had died trying to force the media to telecast something he wanted to say, told Jack logically that Mitch had had a pang of conscience over something. Maybe as a back-up plan, Mitch had buried a clue in Mule's neck. Jack also suspected that "Mule" was not just some name pulled out of a doggie-naming book. It was a very odd name for a dog, and Jack believed that was very deliberate. The name was a clue unto itself. The dog was a mule for sure, carrying something that had a purpose— the microchip. Similar to the mules that were used as beasts of burden, and the human mules used to transport drugs. In both the animal and human worlds, the mules had no control over what they were carrying, and no control over the outcome. They just did a job, period.

This was his theory, and he had to share it with Kerrie because, most importantly, that message on the chip seemed to have been meant for her. He also believed that the slick operators who had tried to steal his dog twice, and had assaulted Heather, Josh, and Buster, were spooks. They were CIA just like Mitch had been, and part of the same group of people who had killed Mitch without one worry for the innocent people in that bank. Those people had just been more collateral damage, if necessary.

Jack knew he had far too much time on his hands, and that his imagination could run wild sometimes. But he also trusted his gut. These things that he had pulled together in his mind so far made real sense to him, and he wasn't afraid to continue in his quest. Since Susan's death, there wasn't much in life he was afraid of anymore. The worst possible thing in life had happened to him, and he knew that unless he kept his mind active with curiosity and purpose, he would just wither up and die.

Jack went to his bedroom and began packing two suitcases. He intended to be prepared in case he was gone for a longer while. He put Mule's supplies in a separate little suitcase, and dragged all three of them out to the car. He wanted to get going at the crack of dawn.

He could still leave today if he wanted to, but he felt too emotional to embark on a road trip. He wanted to settle down from the press queries, and his own thoughts, which today were both sad and angry. Whenever Jack got like this he needed sleep—lots of it.

*****

The dock was a heavy one, and Kerrie was darn glad she had a strong guy like Bob as a neighbor. The two of them were standing in the cold May waters of Flathead Lake, grunting and groaning as they eased each section of dock into its pilings. Bob had his toolbox with him, and he deftly fastened the dock together, section by section. Done.

They both sat down on the shore for a refreshing breather. Kerrie had brought down a cooler of beers and she cracked one open for each of them. They sat there sipping away, satisfied in a job well done. All Kerrie could think about for the moment was that she would have to do this in reverse in the fall. Oh well, that was several months away and she had a warm summer ahead of her to look forward to. Plus, she would hopefully have Bob around to help her again.

"So, Kerrie, what's been going on in your life?" Bob asked.

Kerrie swung her shapely legs up on top of the beer cooler, and sighed. "Nothing much. Been kind of quiet since you saved it."

"That was quite the night wasn't it?" Bob paused. "Do you think about it much?"

All the time. "I try not to, but I break into a cold sweat if I concentrate on it for too long. It seems like a bad dream sometimes, almost unbelievable."

"It was unbelievable. A tough thing to adjust to, an invasion of your space like that, not to mention the physical threat. You're a strong woman Kerrie."

Her cheeks glowed, and she hoped Bob didn't notice. "Not so strong. I was scared out of my mind, but also scared that he might kill you. You were like a sitting duck coming up the stairs like that."

"I got lucky, I guess," Bob said.

"You know what Bob? I had another mysterious caller. A guy named Joe who pretended to be with Lake Carpentry. He came in here, took apart some of my stairway, and said he'd be back with new spindles. Then I got a call from Lake Carpentry a few days later, and they'd never even heard of this guy. What do you make of that?"

Bob pulled himself up from the sand, picked up a couple of flat stones and began skipping them off the water. "That is strange, and a little scary. Did he try to take anything?"

"No, but he seemed anxious to look around the living room. He dropped his tools, probably on purpose the more I think about it, and was crawling on the floor, reaching under the couch. Then he wandered around the room a bit, looking at every corner pretending to be assessing the angles for different spindles."

"Did he hurt you or scare you?" Bob plopped back down on the sand.

"No, not at all. He was a slob, but polite and not the least bit scary. I got a bit jumpy afterwards though when I discovered he was another phony."

"What do you think he was looking for?" Bob asked.

Kerrie cracked open another beer, and tossed one to Bob. "Well, I've been meaning to tell you. I found a cell phone under the couch just the day before this guy showed up, and I think it belonged to that guy you threw down the stairs."

"Really, so you think he sent someone back to look for it, and that someone was Joe?"

"Yes, and pretty slick too, for him to know that I had contacted Lake Carpentry for repair work, and to so easily impersonate them like that."

Bob ran his fingers through his thick black hair. "Yes, that is slick. Do you still have the phone?"

"I do, but it's one of those disposable types where the ownership and phone number can't be traced to an individual; prepaid services I think they call them."

"Yes, it's impossible to know who owns any one of those phones," Bob commented.

Kerrie got down on her knees and started absently digging a trench in the sand.

"But it did have the phone history still intact. Do you remember I told you how that guy phoned a number on his cell right after he tied me up, and said, 'Presto'?"

"Yes, I remember that."

"Well, that last number is in the history, and it has one word as a voice mail message: 'Otserp.'"

"Otserp?"

"And if you reverse that word, it spells 'Presto.'"

"You're right…that kind of gives me the chills," Bob whispered.

"Me too. It seems as if it was some sort of pre-set code these guys had established; a means of identification as well as a command perhaps," Kerrie said.

Bob poured the rest of his beer into Kerrie's sand trench. "Aren't you being a bit too James Bondish here, Kerrie? I mean, do you really think this was that well organized?"

"Yes, I do, and this latest imposter pretending to be a carpenter tells me that cell phone is something they want back—badly. It certainly wasn't my phone, and it couldn't be anyone else's—no one has stayed here yet. So it had to be that phony inspector's, and his partner must be the slob who pretended to be a carpenter."

"Makes sense, I have to agree," Bob said. "So what are you going to do?"

"Right now, nothing. I have a friend coming down here from Canada for a few days or perhaps longer, so for now I'm going to just enjoy doing nothing and seeing my old dog again."

"Your old dog? Did I miss something here?"

"Oh, sorry. This guy in Canada adopted the dog I owned years ago. It was my father's dog and he left him to me—Mule is his name. He ran away over three years ago when I was on a trip to Alberta. I'm looking forward to seeing him again. I hope he remembers me."

"Okay, I get it now. When is your friend coming down here?"

"I don't know exactly. He was being pretty vague about that. Maybe I'll have you over when he's staying here, and we can all have dinner one night. You can meet Mule too—he's a beauty."

"Sounds like fun. Count me in. What's your friend's name?"

"Jack—Jack Howser."

"I'll try to remember it. And Kerrie, do you want me to take a look at that cell phone for you? Maybe I can fool around with it and figure something out."

Kerrie got up and lifted the cooler, which was now much lighter than a couple of hours ago. "Well, okay. I've tried everything I can think of. You're welcome to it."

Chapter 13

Jack sprang out of bed at 5:30 a.m., anxious to hit the road. Before doing anything else, he did what he did every morning—his karate kata. This usually took him about half an hour, performing abbreviated defensive and offensive positions that flowed so smoothly together as to be almost dance-like. These poetic movements betrayed the lethal nature of the skill; if needed in a real-life situation, the results were lightning-fast and potentially deadly. The kata helped with muscle memory and concentration. Jack would always be in the zone when he performed these, bordering on a trance-like state. When he finished, he felt refreshed, awake, and ready to take on the day. He knew he didn't have to break boards every day to keep his karate intact, and he didn't have to lift weights to preserve the strength that karate required. He worked out to keep in shape, but not strenuously. He was naturally well muscled, and it only took a few dozen pushups and sit-ups each day to keep himself that way. The most important parts of his body for karate, Jack well knew, were his brain and his abdomen. All of the strength and impact for karate movements came from the abdomen, shooting outwards to whichever limb was being used. So he worked hard on keeping his abs strong, and his brain sharp. It was the extreme concentration and discipline of the brain that allowed the strength of the abdomen to be coiled like a snake and released like a crossbow.

Mule was lying on the floor watching Jack. This was part of his morning routine too. Mule would wait patiently, but he always knew ahead of time when his master would be finished, because he would get up only when he recognized that the last movement had commenced, and then plod out to the kitchen. Mule knew that when that movement was finished, his breakfast was coming and he wanted to be in the kitchen ready and waiting. Dogs sure loved routine, Jack thought. And they were masters at memorizing it, more so than most humans were capable of. Jack walked to the kitchen, gave Mule his breakfast, and fried some eggs and bacon. Not good for him, he knew, but once in a while he just couldn't resist. Most of the things Jack liked to eat weren't good for him, but he didn't worry about that too much. Life was far too short, he thought. He knew, more than most people, how true that was.

Since he'd put his and Mule's bags in the car the night before, he didn't have much to do this morning before leaving. However, one thing he remembered to do was phone the border crossing at Chief Mountain, to see if it was open yet. This crossing was closed for the most part during the winter, and didn't usually re-open until the beginning of June. With spring coming early to the mountains this year, the crossing might have opened earlier than usual. It was now mid-May and the chances were good that the spectacular Glacier National Park mountain road was also drivable. And then, once he came out of the park just southwest of Lake McDonald, he would have only a short drive to Whitefish.

He was right. The border crossing was open and the "Going-to-the-Sun Road" through Glacier National Park in Montana was also open, albeit with the warning that only fair winter driving conditions existed. Usually the fifty-mile scenic route took two hours, so Jack figured that today it would probably take four, but he didn't care. He loved that Sun road; it was one of the most scenic in the world. And he didn't want to miss it while passing through Montana. "Fair" condition for the Sun road was actually a pretty good rating. Even in the summer that road was really only fair, as it was narrow, twisting, and close to the edge of thousand-foot freefalls. Jack had thought of passing through a different border crossing, the one at Coutts, Alberta, that connected with Sweetgrass, Montana. He had considered this out of fear that if an ambush was waiting for him and Mule, it would be on the route to the most likely, and closer, crossing at Chief Mountain. However, he decided that he was being too paranoid, and he couldn't live his life in fear. If he wanted to experience the Going-to-the-Sun Road, he would experience it and to hell with these spooks.

He turned off the main water supply, made one last check around his house, and locked up. He loaded Mule into the front passenger seat, where he liked to sit so he could see out clearly, and off they went. This first part of the trip to the border, the southernmost reaches of Alberta, was boring and generally flat, until reaching the Waterton area. Waterton Lake straddled the border with Montana, and actually consisted of a chain of three lakes: Lower, Middle, and Upper. The latter stretched itself across the border between Canada and the U.S. The ancient glacier that had carved out Upper Waterton Lake was estimated to have been 2200 ft. thick.

One could actually rent a boat at Waterton in Canada, and paddle or motor south to the end of the lake in the United States. Hikers could also cross over and hike the trails in the U.S., and were expected to be on the honor system. If they had to stay overnight in Montana they had to report to a specific customs/ranger station. Back in 1932, the two countries decided that due to the friendly nature of their relationship and the mere fact that their border was already the longest unfortified border in the world, they should declare this area of land an international park and manage it jointly. Thus was born the Waterton-Glacier International Peace Park, and the first of its kind in the world at the time. Now there were four other parks of this kind straddling Canada and the United States. In 1995, Waterton/Glacier was declared by UNESCO as a World Heritage Site.

Jack thought that this was a perfect example of how countries should be able to get along without borders getting in the way. It was a formula that worked to this day, despite the fact that the two countries weren't as friendly to each other as they used to be. This was primarily due to Canada's opting out of the war in Iraq. The U.S.A. didn't usually forgive or forget which countries disagreed with it.

Jack was pretty certain that agreements like the international peace parks would never be made again, at least not in the current climate, and probably not even in his lifetime. It was a good thing that these parks were formed long ago. One day they might be written about in history books, professing amazement that two countries could actually do such a "reckless" thing as loosen the border and manage a joint territory together.

Since 9/11, the suspicion and anger in the world had become intolerable in Jack's opinion. While some things deserved to be tightened, particularly border and airline security for obvious infractions that had been ignored for too long, he felt most countries had gone too far. Jack wondered what the world would feel like today if America had only spent less money and attention on their military supremacy and foreign adventures, and instead pumped more into health care and financial regulation. Having such a strong presence in faraway lands and being too involved in their political processes at times was bound to eventually have an explosive effect on the psyche of certain fundamentalists. Those cultures and people are so different, and sometimes they are just simply incapable of discerning good intentions from interference. And how would we feel if the roles were reversed? Would we say, *"Sure, bring your troops and stay as long as you want?"*

Fat chance of that.

If the U.S. had paid more attention to their own domestic issues and far less in other backyards, was it possible that there never would have been a

9/11? Was it possible that all Americans would now have affordable health care, and the financial meltdown might never have occurred? Jack was bitter and he knew it. He had been since 2001, and he couldn't help it. Perhaps he just had to blame someone, and he knew this type of thinking was not healthy. There was no point in second-guessing history, but he did it anyway. He hoped over time that his anger would fade, and that there would be some lessons learned from 9/11 so that it didn't happen to the world again. In Jack's mind, the only way another tragedy like that could be avoided was if those in power asked themselves just one question: *"Why did it happen?"* And then answered it honestly.

He cruised along past the beautiful Waterton area, fighting the ferocious winds that came up from the south end of Waterton lake and the Crowsnest Pass. These winds found their way easily out to the highways and you had to hold tight to the steering wheel to avoid being pushed sideways. Jack reached the Chief Mountain border crossing and waited in line behind several cars. The line was moving pretty nicely. This shouldn't take too long. He slid a CD into his dash and hummed along with a country song from a whining songstress who had lost her love in a bar. So sad.

Finally his turn. He pulled up parallel to the booth and held out his passport and Mule's vaccination papers. The officer smiled and asked him where he was going and for how long. Jack answered Bigfork, and that it would be an extended vacation for probably at least a month.

He asked Jack to wait, and he went back into the booth. When he returned, he wasn't smiling any longer.

"Sir, could you pull up over there in that compound and accompany me into the office building, please?"

Jack felt butterflies suddenly flutter around in his stomach. "What's the problem, officer?"

"No real problem, sir. We just have a few more questions to ask you, and a search of your belongings will be needed. We just don't want to hold up the line here."

"Okay, officer." Jack put the Audi in gear, and pulled up over in the compound area on the U.S. side of the border. He got out, hitched up Mule's leash, and started walking over to the small office building.

"Sir, you'll have to leave the dog in the car."

"That's not possible, officer. The sun is out and it's getting hot. My dog won't survive with his heavy fur."

"Open the windows."

Jack frowned. "If I open the windows, he'll jump out."

"Just open them a bit," the officer retorted sharply.

Jack couldn't keep the annoyance out of his voice. "Just a bit won't give him the air he needs. If you want to talk to me, the dog stays with me."

The border guard stared impatiently at Jack, and was silent for a good thirty seconds.

"Okay, let's go," the officer muttered reluctantly.

Jack and Mule followed the guard into the office, and he was motioned to sit in a metal chair up against the wall with about three inches of knee room between the chair and the desk. Jack recognized this as an intimidation tactic, to make him squirm with discomfort. Businesses used this tactic as well, so Jack was ready for it. He turned the chair sideways so he'd have more room, and then asked the guard for a glass of water.

A couple of minutes later, the guard returned with the water and then disappeared. In walked a man in a suit, flashing a card showing "Customs and Immigration," which identified him as James Spalding, assistant deputy director.

This man didn't bother with any pleasantries.

"Mr. Howser, why are you really here?"

"Because your guard asked me to be here."

He grinned in a knowing way. "Mr. Howser, it will not help you in any way to be smart-assed with me. I'll ask you more directly so we can avoid these games. Why, specifically, are you visiting the U.S.A.?"

"Specifically pleasure," Jack replied. He figured the shorter the answers he gave, the better.

Spalding pulled out a Calgary newspaper and held out the front page for Jack to see. "I presume you are the same Jack Howser referred to in this article from yesterday?"

"I sure am. Isn't freedom of speech a wonderful thing?" Jack replied sarcastically.

"Not when you insult your neighbors," Spalding replied.

"The truth is never an insult, sir," Jack retorted. Spalding did not look pleased. Jack's attitude, combined with the heat, had the man tugging away nervously at the starched collar of his white shirt. Mule had been growling under his breath since they sat down, so he clearly wasn't pleased either. And Jack guessed Mule could sense from Jack's tone and body language that this man was not a friend. Jack looked out the window and he could see two men examining his luggage on a table out by his car.

"I'd like to be with those two men as they look through my luggage. I believe that is my right," Jack said bluntly.

"Yes, Mr. Howser. I'm sorry, that is indeed your right. Go on out there and come back in when they're finished."

Jack and Mule headed outside and stood close to the guards examining his stuff. They went through the glove compartment after they finished with the luggage, and then lifted the spare tire out of the trunk and looked for a false bottom. Then they pried off his mag covers with the special Audi tool in the trunk. They were thorough, Jack had to admit. Then for the coup de grace, they brought out a huge Doberman, who went in and around the car, sniffing. Jack was glad he was out here watching in case they tried to plant something. Mule clearly did not like the Doberman, but the dobie didn't seem to even notice that the Border collie was there. That probably really pissed Mule off.

They finished, and pointed him back toward the little office where the suit was waiting.

James Spalding continued. "Are you here to involve yourself in any political work, Mr. Howser?"

"No."

"Are you here to spread similar propaganda to what is referred to in this newspaper article?"

"No." Jack disagreed with the word "propaganda" but decided he was best off just keeping his mouth shut on that point.

"Are you here to make any speeches?"

"No." Jack looked at his watch, trying feebly to look nonchalant.

"Mr. Howser, you should know that a 'travelers alert' has been issued to all U.S. border crossings for your name."

Jack straightened up in his seat, no longer trying to look nonchalant. "What does that mean?"

"It means that you can be detained at the discretion of the border officials, denied entry, or turned around and sent back to Canada."

"Has this alert been issued solely due to my speech in Calgary the other night?"

Spalding looked down at the clipboard on his desk. "Let's see. Okay, it appears that the alert does indeed refer only to that, sir. It notes also that there is suspicion that you may not look kindly on the United States, and could in fact be an enemy of the United States."

Jack was thinking quickly now, suddenly grasping how serious this could really be. His next move would have to be a request to be allowed to phone the Canadian Consulate in Denver. He knew that there was no consulate in Montana but the Denver office serviced four western states, Montana being one of them.

"I am shocked at this, Mr. Spalding. I am a retired executive of the energy industry, and I am asked to speak at countless functions due to my years of experience in the sector. Many speakers are controversial; that's the nature of speeches if you don't want to put your audience to sleep. I do my best to present the facts, but also some opinions." Jack was looking at the man squarely in the eyes, watching for any initial reaction. None. He continued on.

"Does your alert also tell you that I was the CEO of the Canadian operation of a major U.S. energy company? I have traveled to the States for years on business and have been a staunch supporter of American energy needs, and Canada's role as a major supplier of oil to your country. I'm hardly an enemy of the United States."

Spalding stared at Jack and said nothing.

"Sir, I ask that I be allowed to phone our consular general in Denver. I know him personally, and it would be helpful perhaps if he had a chat with your boss to help clear this up."

Finally a reaction. The man shifted in his seat slightly, and the hint of a grimace flashed across his mouth. Jack figured Spalding's boss must be a real prick.

"No, I don't think there will be any need for that Mr. Howser. I can make the decision here, and in my view you are free to go. I'm satisfied with your answers."

"Thank you very much. I appreciate your consideration here," Jack replied, fighting back his own grimace.

"Just remember, Mr. Howser, the 'travelers alert' will remain in place on you for now, at all border crossings. So please be mindful."

"I will indeed be very mindful," Jack replied with feigned respect.

He pulled Mule out from under the chair and strolled out to his car, walking around it to make sure that the mag caps were re-applied. Then he checked his trunk to see if they had put the special tool back in its place. Jack took his time. He walked Mule over to a patch of grass for a leak, and out of the corner of his eye he could see Spalding looking at him through the window, no longer trying to hide his grimace.

As Jack pulled out, heading toward Glacier National Park, he realized that not one of his "neighbors" had yet uttered the words "Welcome to the United States." He had to admit though, that he really hadn't earned a warm welcome with his speech the other night.

Chapter 14

Kerrie sat on her porch looking out over the lake. It was a brilliant sunny day, and it felt like summer. She had decided to push things a bit today, and was decked out in shorts and a bright summer t-shirt. Looking at herself in the mirror she was quite pleased at what she saw. Her figure hadn't suffered at all over the winter, despite her occasional lazy approach to meals. She knew that her metabolism was inherited from her father. He ate on the fly for most of his life, but he retained an incredibly good physique right up until the day he died.

She decided that the only thing missing from her image was a tan; the western sun on her porch this afternoon was a good way to begin to fix that. Kerrie gazed out over the expanse of water, and looked admiringly at her dock. It was great that Bob had been around to give her a hand with this. He was a handy neighbor to have. It would have been impossible for her to get that dock into the lake all by herself. And it looked really good too. Always a sure sign of summer to see docks in the lake. She wandered down to the shore and out to the end of the dock—a long walk in dock-terms. It was long enough to harbor all three of her ski boats, along with at least two or three patio boats that might drop by to visit her guests. And plenty of room for several people to just stretch out and soak up the rays. She had elected not to install a diving board. Too dangerous, she thought. Her insurance rates would have been enormous. She recalled that when she was growing up in New York, a lodge that her parents had taken her to had a terrible accident one summer. A water skier had come cruising in too close to the dock, trying to spray the girls stretched out in their bikinis. He lost his edge and went slamming in at neck level to the protruding diving board. Decapitated.

She shivered at the thought, and vowed never to have a diving board at her little lodge. She wanted to encourage water-skiing but didn't want the dangers associated with the inevitable show-offs.

She strolled off the dock and saw a familiar figure jogging up the beach toward her. "Hi Bob," she called out. "You're making me feel guilty with all that strenuous exercise you're doing!"

"Ah, I'm about ready to stop now anyway. You've given me a good excuse."

Kerrie gave him the once over. He was wearing a bright red track suit, and his brow was soaked with sweat. She figured he would welcome something to drink. "Would you like to hang out with me and have a beer on the porch?"

"That sounds wonderful," Bob replied enthusiastically, wiping his forehead with the sleeve of his pullover. They walked up to the porch together, and Kerrie reached into her cooler for a couple of cold ones.

"Boy, you come prepared," Bob laughed.

"Why exert yourself going back to the fridge, when you can bring the fridge out here!" Kerrie exclaimed.

"I like your style."

They both plunked down in Muskoka chairs, and sipped their beers. Bob sighed, taking in the scenery. Kerrie could tell out of the corner of her eye that he wasn't just looking at the lake. She ignored his subtle glances, kind of liking it, but kind of not also. He was a nice guy. They'd gone out to dinner a couple of times since he'd saved her life from that ugly creep, but it had never gone further than that. And neither had Bob tried. She could tell he liked her, but he was either an old-fashioned gentleman—how many of those were out there anymore—or he was gay. Her vanity wouldn't accept a third reason—that he just wasn't attracted to her. Kerrie had never had that problem before, so it never really entered her mind. To her, it was a given.

Kerrie wasn't really interested right now in a romantic relationship anyway. Bob was charming and attractive, but there was something about him that she couldn't put her finger on—a veil, a cloak, or something like that. Superficial. Despite the conversations they had had, she had the nagging feeling that he knew more about her than she knew about him. Perhaps just a male tendency. Men didn't talk about feelings generally, unless they were gay or over-emotional.

She didn't see Bob as being emotional. He seemed so much in control all the time. And he always seemed as if he was far away when she talked with him.

So unless over time that started to change, she didn't really feel as if they would have a romantic connection. And she wasn't one to have a casual roll in the hay. That wasn't her style—she didn't need it that badly. Sex toys sufficed for now.

"So Kerrie, except for your stairway, you're almost ready to open up?"

"Yes, although I admit I've gotten a bit lazy. These suspicious imposters who have been showing up at my house have thrown me for a bit of a loop. So I'm enjoying just hanging around doing nothing right now."

"Aren't you getting bored?"

"Funny," she replied, "not really. I'm surprised actually, after the hectic life I had in New York. I've mellowed out quite a bit since I moved down here, and I'm not really hurting for money. So, I'll just take things step by step, and I don't want to be in a hurry anymore. After the stairs are finished I'll make a decision as to opening day, but I'm not as obsessed about the date as I was before."

Bob smiled at her approvingly. "Interesting. I guess we could all use a bit of that attitude towards life."

"Yes, I've learned to appreciate more of the simple things living out here in the boonies!" Kerrie chuckled.

Bob moved on to another question. "Tell me, in your quest to renovate this house, have you found anything unusual or surprising? I mean, this is an old place; it couldn't have been easy gutting it and starting over. Usually it's easier to just tear down and rebuild, right?"

Kerrie winced at the memory of the renovation ordeal. "It probably is, in hindsight, but I'm glad I put myself through the nightmare and kept most of the original charm that was in good enough shape to keep. That's what sets a bed and breakfast apart from the normal motels and hotels. People want to experience something unique, something nostalgic, and I believe my inn will give that to them."

"You're right. People can still afford to be choosy these days, despite the economic times," Bob commented. "And they do want things different, memorable."

"I'm only going by instinct," Kerrie said. "So I guess I'll know for sure once I open and start charging my exorbitant prices!" She laughed.

"I just remembered—have you gone up in that attic yet?" Bob asked.

"No, I told you I would wait until you went with me."

"Well, we both have nothing to do today. Do you want to explore it now while I'm here?" Bob asked.

Kerrie folded her arms across her chest and shivered. "I'm a little nervous about it, but, you know, I have to take a look up there eventually. So, let's go. And we'll take our beers. We might need a swig once we see the ghosts!" Kerrie made a spooky gesture with her hands, and laughed.

"Kerrie, if there are ghosts, we may need something stronger than beer!"

They both headed inside and upstairs, past the broken staircase to the upper hallway. Bob reached up and pulled on the handle, bringing the staircase down in one smooth motion.

"So far, so good," he said tentatively. "Ladies first?"

"No, forget protocol for this," Kerrie said. "I'll follow."

"Promise?" said Bob

"Cross my heart."

Bob climbed the staircase and hoisted himself into the attic, brushing away cobwebs as he went. "Now I know why you wanted me to go first!"

"I'm not stupid," Kerrie said. "Remember, I'm a lawyer. We always know which cases to fight and which to plead."

Bob laughed. "I'll remember that. When you start shamelessly begging, I'll know why!"

They were both standing up in the attic now, and were surprised to see how solid the floor was. There was no worry from what they could see, of anyone falling through. And the ceiling was high enough, except along the sides where it angled, that they could stand without crouching. Bob walked over to the wall and hit a light switch.

The entire attic area was now illuminated, and Kerrie was amazed to see how much useable space there was. She was amazed at what else she saw as well.

They both just stared. It was like a small museum. Military uniforms on hangers on the wall at the far end, two frogman outfits complete with hoods, masks, fins, and tanks positioned on a rack. There was also a spear gun hanging from a nail on the wall. A very large steel trunk with a padlock on it, sat on the floor near the uniforms. There was another section of wall which held a cabinet, where several medals were displayed.

"I don't know whether I should genuflect or make the sign of the cross," whispered Kerrie. She didn't know why she was whispering, but it just seemed to be the appropriate thing to do with what she was seeing.

Bob fingered the scuba suits, turned them around and examined them on the back and on the edges. "Was your dad ever a Navy Seal, Kerrie?"

"I don't know. I know he was in Special Forces at one time, whatever that means, and I know he did a lot of underwater demolition work during the Vietnam War."

"Well, I can tell you that these suits are navy issue. I bet he was a Seal at some point in his career," Bob said with reverence in his voice.

"You know this stuff?" Kerrie asked.

"Oh yeah. Remember, I made the rounds in the military myself—Marines—so these things are pretty familiar. You had to be incredibly good to qualify for the Seals though, so your dad must have been quite something in his day."

Kerrie winced. "I guess he probably was, but I wasn't told enough to be able to feel proud of him. It's sad that maybe I can start to be proud of him now—now after he's gone."

"I don't want to make you cry, Kerrie, but these medals here in the cabinet are a pretty impressive haul. Your dad must have done some very brave things to earn these. I can only dream of having achieved that much honor during my military career."

Kerrie felt the tears start to flow. Bob had tried to be nonchalant for her sake, but this was just far too emotional for her to handle.

"I need to leave this attic, Bob. My chest is feeling tight. Let's head back down."

"I understand how you feel, Kerrie, but we should at least open up this trunk and get the full picture. Otherwise, you'll always wonder. There might be something in here for you that he wanted you to have. After all, he did leave you this house."

Kerrie hesitated, inhaled deeply, and summoned up her courage. "Okay, let's just get it done. Then we'll leave right after, okay? I don't feel good about lingering up here. I feel like I'm invading some sacred ground."

Bob pulled out a Swiss army knife, and picked the tool that he wanted. Within seconds of twisting expertly, he had the padlock open. Kerrie was impressed. He lifted the lid, and Kerrie held her breath. It squeaked in an eerie way, and she was almost afraid to look. They both bent over and gazed inside. Kerrie gasped. Bob let out a whistle. Wrapped individually in transparent bubble plastic was the largest array of firepower Kerrie had ever seen. There must have been a couple of dozen weapons of different varieties: pistols, rifles, machine guns, and a couple of weird-looking long barreled guns that Kerrie had never seen before, even in the movies. These didn't look like rifles, and they didn't look like pistols—they were a weird hybrid. But they were menacing. Bob looked up at her, and then just as suddenly looked down, almost embarrassed.

"I'm sorry you had to see this, Kerrie. It must come as a shock to see this part of your dad's life. He was obviously an operative of some kind, which you already knew, and these were his souvenirs. You mentioned some of the aspects of your dad's life—in the CIA, etc.—that night that you were on codeine after the assault. These guns are just evidence of that life, so you shouldn't dwell on it too much."

Kerrie looked at him blankly. She appreciated his words, but still felt uncomfortable with the fact that she had told him so much about her father. That she was apparently so drugged up that night that she didn't even remember telling him these things bothered her even more.

Bob reached down into the trunk, and moved some of the guns around so he could see what was at the bottom. "There's nothing else in the trunk, you'll be glad to know. As for the guns, I'm sure a lot of CIA agents keep weapons after they retire. Kind of just weird souvenirs, I guess, but some agents probably also feel the need for protection. Once they're free of the CIA, they're on their own, and these guys probably made a lot of dangerous enemies along the way. It's not like retiring from an office job."

You're probably right, Bob. Let's just get out of here. I've seen enough for now."

Bob closed the trunk, and led the way down the staircase. When Kerrie was down, he raised it back up again and only the trap door was once again visible. Kerrie was relieved to be back down in the familiar part of her house again.

She led the way to the kitchen and pulled out a bottle of bourbon. She grabbed some ice out of the freezer, and poured herself as stiff a drink as she thought she could handle. She didn't even offer Bob any.

Kerrie tilted her head back and downed it in one swallow. It took her breath away, but she felt oddly better after it settled. She plunked down on a kitchen chair and looked at Bob.

He didn't say anything for a few seconds. Then, "Kerrie, that was your dad's life. Let it go."

"That's easier said than done. After the way he died and what he did at the end—to see those guns just makes it all the more horrifying. The thought that he might have used them in his line of work makes me feel sick to my stomach. Did I tell you that night that I was drugged up, how he died? The bank incident and everything?"

"You did Kerrie. Not too much detail, but I got the gist of it. I understand how you feel, at least I think I do. But that's life, Kerrie, and keep in mind that your dad didn't tell you much about what he did because he wanted to protect you. He was still your dad, and I'm sure his silence was a sign of how much he loved you."

"Thanks." Kerrie sighed. "You always know how to make me feel better. I think I need some time alone right now to absorb all this."

"No problem, I understand. I'll check on you tomorrow." He gave her a quick hug and a light kiss on the cheek. She didn't return the gesture.

Bob was on his way to the front door when Kerrie remembered something she wanted to ask. She called after him. "Oh, Bob, did you have any success with that creep's cell phone?"

"No, none at all Kerrie. I did the same as you, checked the call history and listened to that voice message for that one number, but I couldn't find any other feature that could give more information. Sorry."

"That's all right. Thanks for trying. Just give me the phone back next time you're down this way."

"Sure. By the way, I must have gotten carried away hitting the buttons. I deleted all of the call history by mistake."

"Including the number that had the 'Otserp' voice message?"

"Yes, 'fraid so, Kerrie. I'm clumsy with these things. I seem to be all thumbs when it comes to pressing those tiny buttons. I always hit the wrong ones."

Kerrie just stared at him.

"I really am sorry, Kerrie."

"Just throw the phone away. I have no reason to keep it now," she said tersely. "I wish you had been more careful, but there's nothing we can do about it now. I have no use for it anymore." Kerrie opened the front door, and led Bob out onto the porch.

"Okay, see you tomorrow." Bob walked on down to the beach and headed back towards his house. Kerrie went back inside and plunked down on the couch. She felt like she needed another drink but decided against it. One was enough, and it had taken the edge off. Any more and she'd be asleep, or throw up.

Another day with twists. She knew in her heart that her dad had lived a violent life, but she hadn't really wanted to think about it. The attic now confirmed it visually for her. However, Bob was right. Mitch had largely kept that part of his life from her, so he must have really cared about her. And the apparent dangers that he had had to live with in his job hadn't really affected how he had treated Kerrie or her mom. Sure, he'd been secretive and preoccupied, but he was truly a gentle giant. He was a nice man and had never displayed anything but the utmost kindness to her and her mom. What she resented most, she decided, was that she had never gotten enough of him. Mitch had been the kind of man who was so charismatic that everyone wanted more of him—particularly his little girl. That had been the void in her young life. The man she adored the most just hadn't had the time for her. And ever since his death she had been discovering things about him that had knocked him off his white charger. She couldn't talk to him about these things, she couldn't hear him tell her he was sorry. She desperately wanted to raise him back up on that charger, but she didn't know how. The more she learned about him, the harder it was becoming.

Kerrie started to cry.

What the hell, she thought, one more drink won't hurt. She poured herself a small one and this time just sipped on it.

It really pissed her off that Bob had erased the history on that phone. It was the only real connection she had to the mystery of that awful night when she was attacked by that asshole who wanted to explore her attic, and probably more…

That and of course the recording she had made of that voice mail message, 'Otserp'. At least she still had that sitting on her personal recorder. She hadn't told Bob that. She wanted him to feel at least a wee bit guilty over how careless he'd been.

She laid her head back and wondered when her new Canadian friend and her long lost dog would arrive. Jack certainly had a wonderful voice. She hoped his looks matched his voice. Jack had emailed a photo of himself to her as she had requested; he looked pretty good, if only from the neck up. But photos could be deceiving.

At least she had a reasonable idea now of what he looked like, and felt safer for that. She was growing more and more fearful of anyone she didn't already know showing up on her doorstep.

Chapter 15

Jack had just passed through the gates at Glacier National Park after flashing his park pass. He had always been thrilled whenever he had the chance to drive through Canada's mountain parks, but this particular one in Montana was unbelievable. The scenery was absolutely breathtaking, and one could very easily drive off a cliff if not paying attention to the road. Slow driving was the key in order to enjoy the sights and arrive in one piece.

This Going-to-the-Sun Road was one of the most memorable that Jack had ever driven. There was always plenty of wildlife to see, but the main attractions were the soaring peaks, waterfalls, and plunging cliffs all along the fifty mile stretch. There weren't any breaks at all, unlike other mountain roads, where the dangerous portions were sporadic. It was a thrill driving on such a dangerous roadway. A macabre thought, but still thrilling nonetheless.

Jack knew of a man in Calgary who had been knocked senseless by a falling boulder from the peaks above. It had come hurtling down as he was driving along with his wife in a convertible. He survived but it took many years to function normally again. A large chunk of mountain had also flattened a Japanese tourist's Volkswagen Beetle. He didn't survive.

It was an odd name for a road. Purportedly, or at least as legends recorded it, an Indian spirit ventured down from the sun to share the secrets of the hunt with Blackfoot braves. On his return to the sun, Sour Spirit, as he was called, made arrangements to have his image reproduced on the top of the mountain to inspire the tribes, ergo the name, Going-to-the-Sun.

The road was now about seventy-five years old, and the speed limit was only 40 mph, even slower in parts where reconstruction was underway. The road was being rebuilt in stages due to the sorry state it was in. Age was one factor, but the severe winter weather itself always took a toll.

Today, however, Jack was moving along at a pretty good pace. The road was actually in great shape: very dry and not much traffic. He found his eyeballs starting to ache from constantly rolling them from side to side to see the scenery, concentrating on the road, and watching for wildlife and any loose rock formations. This short stretch of road was always tiring to drive—there was far too much to be aware of, and afraid of. About halfway through the trek, he started longing for the ride to be over and to be able to let the car loose on a nice straight stretch of road again.

Mule was sitting up high in the front seat enjoying the scenery. Every time he saw a group of mountain goats or bighorn sheep, his tongue hung out, he panted, and hunched his shoulders. The little guy just wanted to herd every living creature he saw.

Jack found his mind wandering a bit. The fantastic scenery had distracted him for a while, but now he started thinking back to his experience at the Chief Mountain border crossing. So, a "travellers alert" had been put out on him. That was interesting. What was more interesting was the fact that the border folks did not seem the least bit interested in Mule. It was Jack's speech to the World Energy Summit that caused the alert.

He speculated that perhaps it had nothing to do with his encounters with the spooks trying to steal his dog, however he didn't believe in coincidences. It was more likely that the speech was used as an excuse, but certain parties—most likely the same parties—wanted him harassed and wanted him to be aware that they were watching him. Though, if that were the case, it was clear that the microchip issue was being kept hush-hush. No lowly border employees would be allowed to be privy to that, and it was apparent that they weren't privy to that. Only certain people were probably aware that there was something odd about that microchip, and that fact wasn't going to be shared with officials who didn't have a need to know. Jack's suspicious mind was in overdrive. He could feel the adrenaline pumping as he left Glacier Park and headed due southwest to Whitefish. He loved a good mystery, and this one was getting better every day. He could hardly wait to meet with Kerrie and bring her up to date on what had been happening and what was contained on Mule's chip. But first things first. He had to get that stupid chip out of Mule's shoulder. If one of the bad guys ever came by again with a scanner like they had done at Heather's, they would know that the chip was gone and they would hopefully leave Mule alone.

He pulled in to Whitefish around 2:00 in the afternoon, and headed straight down Central Avenue to the aptly named Central Veterinary Services office. He hadn't made an appointment, but he was hoping that for such a minor procedure Meagan could just do the job for him today. If not, he would come back. Whitefish wasn't that far a drive from Bigfork so he could easily return another day.

Jack parked on the street, clipped Mule to the leash, and led him into the office. There was a teenage girl at the front desk staring at a computer terminal. She looked up as Jack came in, smiled, and asked if she could help. Jack asked for Meagan and the girl requested that he wait a few minutes until she finished a procedure. Jack took a seat in the waiting area. There was one other man sitting there, looking nervous, probably waiting for the patient Meagan was working on.

In about fifteen minutes Meagan came out, carrying a Schnauzer puppy. The man looked relieved. He paid at the counter, took his precious little puppy into his arms, and hurried out. Only then did Meagan notice him.

"We've met before, haven't we?" she asked.

Jack was a little disappointed that she didn't remember his name. Stupid vanity. He stood up and held out his hand. "Yes, Meagan, we have. Jack Howser. I came in last summer with my dog Mule here, and you scanned a microchip for me."

"I remember now, Jack. You're from Canada, right? Calgary, if I recall?"

"Yes, that's right. You have a good memory." Jack felt a bit better now, and also thought she looked better than ever too. Young and fresh, but carried herself with such grace and maturity. And she had that girl-next-door cute factor that he found so appealing. She still had the deep tan, and he marveled again at how strong her wrists looked.

"If I recall, I gave you a freebie and you were supposed to come back and buy me dinner. And, correct me if I'm wrong, but I don't think your dog was named Mule then."

"I'm impressed," Jack said. "No, his name was Ranger then, but the chip you scanned led me to his real name. An odd name, but he seems to love it."

"Well, I'm glad my freebie paid off. So, not to be pushy, but what about that dinner?"

Jack's heart skipped a beat. "Well, here I am. Are you free tonight?"

"Now I've put you on the spot, haven't I? I'm sorry. I'm sure you didn't come all this way just to pay me back with dinner. What else can I do for you?"

"That chip you scanned for me—I want it removed. Can you possibly squeeze that in today?"

"Actually, that would be no problem at all. But can I ask why you want to put your dog through a procedure like that? The chip is harmless where it is. People seldom have to have them removed."

"It isn't so harmless."

"Is there an infection?"

"No, but tell you what. Remove it for me and I'll fill you in on some of the details over dinner. And you didn't put me on the spot at all. I was hoping you'd be free for dinner." Jack lied—he'd actually forgotten all about that.

Jack had decided that he had to tell her at least some of the story, without giving away too much. This was a lady who clearly cared about animals, and he didn't want her thinking he would subject his dog to an unnecessary procedure. He also had to admit that he didn't want her thinking badly of him.

"Okay, that would be lovely. I just wanted to advise you against having it removed because it is a procedure that will require anesthesia, and I don't like to do that unless absolutely necessary. There is always a slight risk with anesthesia."

"I understand that, and I'd like you to understand why I want it removed also. Believe it or not, the risk is greater to Mule if I leave it in. But I'd rather tell you over dinner."

"Bring Mule into the operating room, Jack, and we'll get started," Meagan said pleasantly.

"One more thing: don't throw out the microchip. I'd like to keep it."

She looked at him quizzically for a second, and then just nodded.

Meagan put Mule to sleep within a matter of seconds, and scanned his shoulder area to make sure she knew exactly where the chip was. Then she shaved the area, cleansed it, and had the chip out in no time flat. It was just slightly below the skin so it wasn't too difficult for her to get at, but Mule had to be put to sleep as he would no doubt have reacted to the pain of the cut. She then gently placed the tiny microchip in a small ziplock bag and handed it to Jack. Meagan stitched and bandaged the area on the top of the dog's shoulders, and Jack lifted Mule off the table. Meagan ushered him back to a kennel area of the office, segregated with several cages mounted to the wall. Jack gently placed Mule down on the floor of one of the lower level cages, and closed the gate. There were no other animals there today.

"He'll be asleep for another half hour. When he wakes up, he'll be groggy for a while," Meagan said. "So, this would be a good time for you to take me to dinner. When we come back he should be just fine and wide awake."

"Good, let's go. Do you have a favorite place?" Jack asked, as he followed Meagan out to the front office area.

"Well, there isn't much to choose from in this small town, but there's a good steak place just around the corner." Meagan opened a desk drawer and pulled out her purse. "Do you like steak?"

"Hey, I'm from Alberta. Steak is all we think about!"

Meagan laughed at that and grabbed her coat.

She sent her assistant home for the evening, then put out her "Closed" sign and locked up. She led the way down the street and around the corner to the restaurant. Jack noticed it was pretty nondescript inside, but the smell of garlic was intoxicating. With a smell like that, he knew the meal would be a good one.

They were seated at a nice table by the window and ordered drinks. The menu was easy to choose from: steak, steak, and more steak. Jack pointed out to Meagan that the most expensive steak on the menu, a rib eye, was advertised as Alberta Beef.

"I've had that before Jack, it's excellent. So, you don't have to brag about Alberta Beef—it speaks for itself. Though for a while there a few years ago, we were getting worried. The Mad Cow scare kept most of your beef from coming in to Montana."

"That was a clear overreaction," Jack replied. "Alberta was penalized heavily for being honest."

"That may be true, but you can't deny the fact that it was a pretty scary scenario. Most people believe what they read and the press was pretty sensational down here over that. Of course, a lot of it had to do with the Montana ranchers seeing an opportunity to compete without competition. It doesn't take much for protectionism to take hold these days, and there are a lot of strong lobby groups out there."

"You're absolutely right about that. Sad, but true."

They spent the next two hours enjoying their steaks, which were wonderful, and having some great conversation. Jack found Meagan to be very intelligent and very charming. She was easy to look at too—brunette, well proportioned, not too skinny. Jack disliked skinny women. Her face was full of expression, and her eyes just sparkled when she talked about something that she was passionate about. They shared stories of their educations, careers, where they had lived, even their heartbreaks. After Jack told his story about Susan, Meagan shared about her fiancé who died mountain climbing about two years ago. She hadn't dated since, but it was clear she was looking forward to getting out there again. She had just rejoined the mountaineering club that she had belonged to with her fiancé. Jack finally had an explanation for the sinewy arms.

After telling her story to Jack, she reached down into her purse and pulled out an asthma puffer. She used it and put it back in her purse. "Please excuse me for doing that at the table, Jack. When I get a bit emotional, I need to use it. I've had asthma since I was a kid."

"No problem at all. But I have a question for you—how on earth can you climb mountains if you have asthma?" Jack was astonished at the thought.

"Very carefully," she laughed. "In all seriousness though, I'm always well prepared, take my time, and the puffer is always with me. If I do climbs that are higher than what I'm used to, I take along bottled oxygen. I refuse to let my condition sideline me from what I enjoy doing."

Jack was impressed by her attitude. He liked this girl.

He finally got around to telling her the story about Mule: how he had adopted him, the attempted dognappings that had happened since Meagan had scanned the chip for him, including what had happened to Heather and Josh. He didn't share the background on Kerrie or Mitch, but he said he had someone to see in Montana who might be able to shed some light on this mystery. She seemed intrigued.

"Jack, I don't remember what was on that chip, but it's clear someone wants to know badly. Or they at least want to know what you know."

"I'm glad you don't remember what was on the chip. The fewer people who know the better. It's safer for all concerned that way. And yes, I'm sure whoever is doing this wants to know what I know desperately, and would probably want to follow the same clues. I have no idea what the clues, if that's what they really are, will lead to."

Meagan paused and stared into his eyes, as if trying to read what he was really thinking. "But now that the chip is out of Mule, they're going to want to talk directly to you. Have you thought about that? They can no longer find out by cutting it out of your dog."

Jack looked down at his plate, feeling uncomfortable with her stare. "I have been thinking about that a bit. There is a good possibility that they will confront me at some point, whoever 'they' are."

Jack felt his pocket to make sure he still had that chip. He was amazed at how tiny the thing was, and he had no idea what he was going to do with it. At this point though, he felt he needed to hang onto it for whatever leverage it might bring him.

"You be careful. You don't know who these people are, and it sounds like they are efficient and quite possibly dangerous. You may be out of your league on this."

"I have no doubt I'm out of my league. But I wonder how far they're prepared to go when publicity could be damaging to them. Whatever this is, it must be sensitive. They've been real careful about being sly and discreet. They don't seem to be anxious to stand out, and they also seem to have resources that allow them to be whoever they want to be. They're quite cunning, and in some ways even quite humane. I told you how they phoned 911 before I arrived at Heather's place. They clearly wanted to make sure that she and Josh were going to be okay."

"Yes, that is quite the paradox," Meagan said. "I guess it's just all about the task itself, and thankfully those people don't have the stomach to do what isn't deemed absolutely necessary."

Jack sipped his coffee, and looked out the window at the cars zipping by. "I'm under no illusions that they will continue to be that way. If they become impatient and frustrated, they may resort to tougher tactics. So you're right—I have to be careful."

She reached across the table and softly touched his hand. "Why are you doing this? Why do you need to do this?"

Jack was taken aback by this question. He'd never really asked himself this before. It was so simple, but also so complex. "I just can't answer that. I'm being driven by something. Call it a gut feel perhaps, but I have to see this through. There's something here that is gnawing at me, and I can't shake it. Maybe part of the problem is my personality, or that I'm a bored retiree who got out too soon. I just don't know. But I can't let it go."

"Fair enough. We all have to follow that little voice sometimes, and if we don't we will always wonder. I would expect my fiancé would have given the same vague answer to the question, 'Why do you climb mountains?'"

Jack noticed a tear appear in her eye as she made that last statement. The memory for her was clearly still fresh, and painful.

"Well, Jack, I think your pooch is probably awake by now and raring to go. We should get back. Thanks so much for dinner. It was a real pleasant evening for me."

"It was my pleasure. We'll have to do it again sometime."

"Yes, and maybe by then you will have solved your mystery and you can tell me all about it."

"If I'm lucky enough to figure it out, I will definitely share it with you. It will at least be another excuse to ask you out to dinner."

Meagan smiled coyly at him as he helped her on with her coat.

They made the short walk back to the office in less than two minutes. It was a nice night, warm with a slight fruity-smelling breeze. Spring in Montana—heavenly.

Meagan opened the front door to her office and they walked in. Jack was anxious to see if Mule had awakened and was feeling okay. Meagan led the way to the door to the kennel room. Standing behind the door as she opened it was Mule, wagging his tail looking none the worse for wear.

"Hey, boy, how did you get out of your cage?" Jack knelt down and hugged his dog gently, being careful to stay away from the bandaged area. Mule started to growl, a low throaty one that Jack recognized as his "I'm not sure I like you yet" growl. Jack figured that he hadn't yet accepted Meagan.

"These darn cages," Meagan said. "They're so old. I have to replace them one of these days once business picks up. This has happened a couple of times, where the latches don't catch properly on the cage doors, and all a dog has to do is nudge it with his nose."

"Mule looks pretty good, Meagan—lively and sharp. But he's a little upset, growling a bit."

"Let's take a look at him before you go," Meagan offered. Jack lifted Mule up onto the examining table and Meagan took a close look in his eyes, mouth, and ears. She took his blood pressure and heartbeat. Mule continued to growl, and was now curling his lips up on both sides.

"He looks okay, Jack. I think you're good to go. He's probably either pissed at me because he knows that I'm the reason he's in this state, or he's a little disoriented from the anesthetic. Bring him back to see me tomorrow if he's still not right."

"Uh, could I ask you to do one more thing before I pay up?"

"Sure, what's that?"

"Since we're here, could you squeeze out his anal glands for me? I can't bring myself to do it—it's disgusting—and we won't be at the vets in Calgary for quite a while. Mule has been scooting a lot lately."

"I charge extra for that—a *lot* extra," she laughed. "It's okay. Glad to do it, you big wimp. I'll actually be here for another hour or so finishing some paperwork, so I'm not in a hurry anyway."

She moved her expert fingers down to Mule's rear, and Jack held Mule tight at the head. She gave a squeeze, Mule squealed, and the deed was done. Then he almost immediately resumed his growling, now almost to the point of a snarl. He raised his head and sniffed in different directions around the room. "He probably smells other animals that have been here. His territorial instinct is coming out," Meagan said.

"You're probably right. I'm sure he'll settle down once we're in the car. So how much do I owe you?" Jack asked.

"Give me a hundred, and we'll call it even."

"Do you accept Canadian dollars?"

"You're kidding me, right?"

"Yeah, unfortunately I am. You know, there was a time, back when I was a kid, when it was the other way around? We didn't want your money," Jack said chuckling.

"Well, I'm far too young to remember that."

"Thanks, Meagan, I really needed to hear that!"

Jack pulled out five American twenties, and handed them to her. As he and Mule reached the door, Meagan touched Jack on the shoulder. When he turned around, she gave him a big hug.

"You're a nice man, Jack Howser. Please be careful with what you're getting into."

"I will, Meagan, and I'm already into it so I guess there's no turning back now."

"No, that's not true. There's always the chance to turn back. Always!"

Jack returned the hug, and then picked up Mule. He didn't want him to walk too far too soon after the anesthetic. Meagan cautioned that he might be a bit dizzy, although he sure seemed to have recovered fast. Mule turned his head and looked back at Meagan. He gave one last growl, and then a loud bark.

Meagan laughed. "You won't want to see me any time soon, will you, boy!" she chided.

As he drove away, Jack looked back at her office, wondering if he would ever see her again. Between Heather and Meagan, he was having second thoughts about his single life.

One good thing about long car trips was the opportunity to just think—about everything. Sometimes he thought too much, but it was nice to have the time alone just for himself. He had gotten used to that, but he was also a bit afraid of becoming too used to that.

Mule sat up straight and shook himself, probably trying to shake off the bandage since it was in a place where he couldn't scratch. The sound was different, Jack realized. Mule sounded different with his shaking. What was it? Jack looked over at his dog. Of course, the collar was missing. They had forgotten to put it back on again, and Mule's metal tags always jingled when he shook. He had only driven about five miles so he decided to turn around and get the collar. It would save him a forty-five minute drive back tomorrow from Bigfork.

Jack cruised back to Central Avenue and parked close to the same spot he had before. He left Mule in the car and strolled to Meagan's office door. He noticed the Venetian blinds were now down on the windows and door, but he could tell that the lights were still on inside. Jack knocked and waited a few seconds. No answer. He knocked again. Still no answer. That was strange, he thought. He had just left her and she said she was working late. He knocked again, and this time called out her name. He heard a dull thump from inside, almost like the sound of a rubber ball bouncing once.

Jack walked away from the door and moved along the edge of the window frame. He found what he was looking for; one Venetian blind slat that was sticking up close to the end. These things never truly hung cleanly, so he was glad that was the case here.

It was up just enough for Jack to get his eyes focused on a narrow band of the outer office area. He caught his breath and his mouth went instantly dry. Meagan was lying on her back on the floor, a man straddling her. He had a knife to her throat, and his other hand covered her mouth. The man's pants and underpants were down to his knees. His penis hung like a deadly weapon.

Jack focused on Meagan's face. She had some blood trailing across her lips, and her eyes wore a look of absolute terror. She was still fully clothed, so it looked like the man had only started getting prepared when Jack had disturbed his concentration.

Jack backed away from the window and moved a few feet along the sidewalk. He pulled out his cell phone and dialed 911. A dispatcher answered right away.

"911 service. Is this an emergency?"

"Yes, it is. There is a lady about to get raped in her office here on Central Avenue, at Central Veterinary Services."

"And how do you know this, sir?"

"She's a friend of mine. I knocked on her office door and there was no answer. So I peeked through the window and saw a man on top of her, partially undressed, with a knife to her throat. Please send someone quickly."

"And what is your name, sir?"

"Jack Howser."

"Where are you right now?"

"On the sidewalk in front of her office. The door is locked."

"Just stay there and wait for us, sir. We'll have a car there in less than ten minutes."

"That will be too late. I may have to do something myself."

"Don't do that, sir."

"Hurry up, then."

Jack flipped his phone closed and walked back to the window. He peeked in again, and saw that the man's hand was now on her throat, with the knife hand poised above her heart. Jack couldn't stand there and wait. The scene inside made him sick. The police, when they got there, would just have to pick up the pieces. He rushed back to the door and looked it over. It was thick and reinforced, and he knew it had a secure deadbolt. There was no way he could kick it in. There was only one way in and he had to take it. He took one last look through the blind, and then backed up about eight steps until he was standing on the road.

Then he ran full tilt at the window. At the moment just before impact, he leaped above the windowsill and covered his eyes with his arms. He went through, smashing the glass into thousands of pieces.

Jack landed heavily on the floor inside, with the blind wrapped around his neck. He yanked it off and in the same motion jumped to his feet. Meagan screamed, the man yanked her up into a sitting position onto his lap and moved the knife around in front of her neck again. Jack didn't move. He just stared at the man's face. It was an ugly one, heavily pockmarked, a nose that looked as if it was permanently broken.

"Why don't you just let the lady go, and I'll let you go," Jack said. "I've already called the police, and they'll be here in minutes."

"Who are you? Batman?" the man sneered. "She's going with me, out the back door. So back off, buddy, unless you want to see her dead!"

There was no way Jack was going to let this sleazebag leave with Meagan. He could see that she was breathing heavily, her chest rising up and down. She was having an asthma attack. He could hear her gasping. He had to act now.

Jack pulled out his heavy set of keys from his back pocket, and poised with them in his hand.

The man laughed. "What are you going to do with those, key me to death?" He had a sick kind of cackle that made Jack want blood.

In a lightning move from Jack's right hand, the keys hurtled through the air in a blur, missing Meagan's face by about an inch and slamming directly into the right eye of the assailant. He screamed in pain and brought his hand to his face, lowering the knife hand for just an instant. Meagan was aware enough to grab the opportunity, and she rolled to the side behind a desk. Jack moved forward fast, and when he was only about ten feet away the man's knife hand flashed. Jack felt a sudden burning sensation in his left thigh. He ignored it and kept going.

The sleaze had now struggled to his feet, but Jack could see that the bastard had forgotten he had his pants down. His mobility was non-existent and Jack took advantage of that. He delivered two quick punches to the man's head, taking careful aim with one of them toward his damaged right eye. Then Jack stepped back and delivered a vicious kick to the throat. The man couldn't stay on his feet, particularly with his legs bound together by his dropped drawers, and he went hurtling backwards in the air, crashing to a stop with the back of his head connecting with a metal desk. The sound of the thud was sickening.

The man fell like a sack of cement onto the floor, blood pouring from his right eye and now the back of his head. Jack knew before he even checked his pulse that he was dead. He was pretty sure he had been dead the second his head made contact with the desk.

Jack ran over to where Meagan was and he could tell she was in real distress now. She was gasping and pointing towards a desk at the back. Jack knew what she wanted. He ran to the back of the office, and pulled out the desk drawer that he had seen her take her purse out of before they went to dinner. He frantically opened the purse and pulled out the inhaler. He rushed back to Meagan. He held it to her mouth and squeezed. She reached her hand up and took it from him. He had it upside down. She held it the right way, gave herself several puffs and took some deep breaths. Her color was gradually coming back, and Jack breathed a sigh of relief. She was going to be okay. When she finally caught her breath, she started to talk…slowly.

"He was hiding…in the closet. He…must have gotten in while we…we were at dinner."

"Take it easy, Meagan. The police are coming. You can tell them when they arrive. The rapist is dead, so you can relax now." Jack could hear the sirens coming down the street.

"He…he wasn't a rapist Jack." She struggled to a sitting position.

"What? His pants were down below his knees!"

"That was...just his threat. He...he wanted the chip. Or at least...for me to tell him...what was on the...chip."

Jack's face went pale. He didn't know what to say. What he felt was pure horror. This lovely lady was a victim of his mystery, and she had very little to do with it.

"Jack, I'm...I'm going to just tell the police that he attempted to...to... rape me. I'm going to...just leave it at that."

"I don't know what to say Meagan." He cradled her head in his arm, and gently leaned her up against the back of a sofa. She was breathing much better now. He winced as he realized that the knife was still protruding out of his left leg. Luckily it seemed to be dangling loosely, so it wasn't in too deep.

"Don't say anything...you saved my life. Thanks for coming back. Why..."

"Seems silly now, but I came back for Mule's collar."

Meagan managed a chuckle. "Thank God."

"Come...to my house tonight, Jack...please. I...I don't want to be alone."

"Don't give it another thought. I already decided that I would do that."

The police peeked through the broken window, and then banged on the front door. Jack walked over and let them in. They had quite the scene to absorb. Meagan sitting on the floor, the assailant bleeding profusely, and Jack with a knife hanging from his left thigh.

They were at the office for quite a while. Jack wondered how Mule was doing, but the dog was used to being left alone for long periods of time, so he should be okay. At least it was nighttime and cooler out now. They interviewed Meagan, and she told them that he had threatened to rape her. Jack told his story. While he was doing that, Meagan removed the knife from his thigh, treated the wound and bandaged him. It was only a flesh wound, so Jack was lucky. Then she treated herself. Her lips had been cut badly against her own teeth when the thug hit her and banged her head down on the floor.

Since there was a death on the premises, the detective in charge called in the coroner and the forensic team. He reassured Jack that based on the interviews with him and Meagan, no charges would be laid against him. And it was clear that Jack had used reasonable force. The wound that killed the man appeared to have been an accidental collision with the desk, so it was self-defense on Jack's part and an unforeseeable outcome. The coroner would confirm all of this of course, but the detective did not foresee any problems. Jack gave the address and phone number of where he would be staying in Bigfork, and the officer said he would get in touch if any more questions needed to be answered. The forensic team had almost finished their work when Jack was helping Meagan on with her coat. They were both anxious to get away from the scene and breathe some fresh air.

Before they left for Meagan's house, Jack wandered back to the body. He took one last look at the guy's distorted face. God he was ugly, Jack thought. "I assume you'll check his fingerprints in your database?" Jack asked the lead technician.

"Not in this case."

Jack was alarmed. "Why on earth not?"

The technician stood up and looked Jack in the eye.

"This bird doesn't have any fingerprints. They've been surgically removed."

Chapter 16

Bob Trundle was hauling his groceries in from the car when he paused on the lakeside deck. He couldn't resist taking a few moments to admire the view. The lake was literally sparkling today, and the air was so clear he could see water-skiers across the lake in their wetsuits getting a jump on summer. Fishermen were out too, in pretty large numbers, keeping wary eyes on the skiers. The water looked so inviting, Bob wanted to run along his dock and dive in. But he knew the water was still hovering in the chilly mid-sixties. He was a tough guy, but not that tough.

He thought how nice it would be to own a house like this one day. Maybe in retirement. That seemed a long way off. He was forty-five, in good shape for his age, but working was what his life had become. Could he ever really settle down and relax? With each passing year he thought more and more about dropping out, so perhaps that was a good sign. He'd been living in this house for over four years now, but it was rented so he felt no sense of belonging. And he didn't spend much time here. He traveled on business a lot, and he also had to squeeze in the occasional visit to his home in Los Angeles, or more specifically, the suburb of Glendale. This house here would be the type of house he could certainly get used to though: beautiful surroundings, comfortable and woodsy inside, and a panoramic view of the lake.

He thought about his time with Kerrie a couple of days ago, and their discovery up in the attic. Poor girl. She was living in a dream world not really knowing or understanding the details of her dad's work. That attic sure hit home for her. Well, at least the shock of that discovery might bring her some closure. He knew she was upset with him over that cell phone business; she would get over it. It was a mistake anyone could make, and she would accept that.

There would be no romantic connection between him and Kerrie. He was pretty sure that he had not given her that impression. He'd tried hard not to. He didn't know how she felt about him, but he was confident that if he had worked harder at being intimate with her, she would most likely have fallen victim to his charms. Charms that he had been born with, but also charms that he had been taught.

They'd at least managed to become friends, and if it would have taken more than that to get her trust he knew as a last resort that he would have done what needed to be done. It wouldn't have been the first time he had had to break someone's heart on the job, and betray his own wife in the process for 'love of country.'

Bob put his groceries away, and plunked himself down on the rented couch. He reached for the phone and dialed a number in Washington, D.C. He gave the girl a number in Los Angeles, and he was re-routed instantly on a secure line.

"Hello?"

"Hi, Janice darling, it's me."

"Sam, I was just thinking of you. Where are you calling from?"

"Honey, you're very sneaky. You keep trying to trip me up but you know I can't tell you that. We go through this every time, don't we? I'm in the country though, and that's all I can say."

"Can't blame a girl for trying. I miss you, and so do the kids. When will you be home again?"

"I have to leave the country tomorrow for a few days and then I'll be flying directly back into LAX. So, in a week's time I'll be home for about four days. Okay?"

"I can hardly wait! Let's slide down to San Diego and take the kids to the zoo!"

"That would be wonderful, Jan, but we'll have to keep our eyes out for those Mexican drug cartels. I hear they're shooting innocents in the streets of border cities if they get in the way!"

"You'll protect us. You're the government."

"Thanks for the vote of confidence, dear, but I doubt there's much I could do. I will indeed wear my gun though, just in case."

"You phoned at a bad time. The boys are out playing in the park right now. But if you call back later, I can put them on for you."

"I'll do that. Say, right after dinner, okay?"

"They'll be waiting and I know they'll be excited. You've been gone for two weeks already."

"I know, I'm sorry. I promise that one of these days I'll do something more domestic with my life."

"I understand, and I know you can't talk about what you do, but if you wait too long to leave that job the kids will be in college and they won't really know you."

"Believe me, I think about that a lot lately. At least I spend quality time with them when I am home."

"You're a great father. They just need more of you. I tell the kids all the time how important you are and that's why you're not here most of the time."

"Yeah, so important that I had to refuse to attend Trevor's parent career day."

"Well, Trevor seemed to understand, and actually got kind of excited when you reminded him that your job was secret work for the government. That's an intoxicating notion for a young boy and I do think he was proud of you. He didn't seem to mind that you couldn't make it because your reason was so exciting!"

"Yeah, the imaginations of young boys. He watches James Bond movies and asks me if I do those things. I have to always explain to him that the real thing is never quite as exciting and adventurous as they show on TV."

"The boy is twelve now so his imagination is a big part of his life. Let him enjoy what he wants to think. In four more years Craig will be that age and you'll have to answer his questions too."

"True enough. I love you, you know. You're a wonderful mother to our boys. You make up for me."

"What a nice thing to say! I love you too. And like the boys, I want more of you myself!"

"I know, and again I'm sorry. I'll be able to get a break in a few months and we'll take a trip away, all four of us."

"That would be great. I'll hold you to that. Now, you won't forget to call us again after dinner, right?"

" I'll call."

Bob hung up the phone and laid his head back. He always found it weird being called by his real name. Most of his time was spent being someone else. It was weird, but also comforting to hear his wife call him Sam. His real name was Sam Summerfield: family man and federal government man. His name for this particular job in Montana was Bob Trundle, retired stock trader. His name for his overseas assignments was Fritz Sonenger, freelance travel writer. And he did indeed do travel writing, which he had to, to make his cover legit. His articles appeared regularly in several travel magazines. He never had to pitch anyone. His powerful employer always made sure he got published. His picture never accompanied his articles either, and the magazine folks had never met him despite publishing his writings for the last fifteen years.

His wife, Janice, never knew where he went or what he did. He was forbidden to talk about it to anyone. He knew there were good reasons for the secrecy, those being his own safety and that of his family, but most importantly the safety of the U.S. government.

He had joked on the phone with Jan about the Mexican drug cartels, but she would probably have a heart attack if she knew he was actively involved in covert activities in border areas of that country—organizing operatives to gather intelligence and disrupt the activities of the four major cartels that operated there. The name he went by for his Mexican work was Carlos Perez. His dark looks helped him blend in with the Mexicans, and it didn't hurt that he spoke fluent Spanish as well.

Along with fluent German, French, Arabic, and Russian.

Bob sighed as he got up from the couch. He had to pack a bag for tomorrow's flight out of Helena to Denver, then on directly to Jakarta, Indonesia. A long flight, but he was used to these treks. He would be going as Fritz Sonenger, so he had to make sure he brought the right passport and other identification. He opened the wall-safe, and sifted through the various passports, driver's licenses, birth certificates, and credit cards. They were all organized in packages for each of his four personas. Sometimes when he was over-tired or jet-lagged, he pulled out the wrong ID package. Luckily he always caught himself in time. As Fritz, he would land in Jakarta—a city he knew very well—and spend some time right away in some of the resort areas around Indonesia. Indonesia was a curious country. The religious diversity was distinct by geography, with most of the country being Muslim, and only the Buddhist island of Bali being the exception. Jakarta itself, while referred to as a city was actually a province, but it was recognized as the official capital of Indonesia. It was divided into five separate cities, but the combined metropolis was seen by most as one big city. Within its boundaries lived a mind-boggling twenty-four million people, ranking it as the second largest metropolis in the world. Bob always avoided spending more time than absolutely necessary in Jakarta. The city had a smell to it that at times was overbearing, a combination of pollution and humidity. This humidity was sometimes impossible to live with, and traffic congestion made it worse. He found it tiresome trying to get around so he usually scheduled meetings and meals within a close walk of his hotel.

But Bali was a different world. It was a tropical paradise that was just as humid as Jakarta, but without the pollution. The beaches were gorgeous, and the tropical foliage took his breath away every time he saw it. Bali was one of the country's thirty-three provinces, but also an island so Bob would have to take the short hops back and forth between Jakarta and Bali on a local airline. A little scary as the planes were old, but a few drinks always made it bearable. Bali's tourism still had a bit of a stigma attached to it from the terrorist bombings of 2002, and again in 2005, but had largely recovered its visitor levels again by 2008. As far as tropical paradises were concerned people always seemed to have short memories.

Bob would do some serious writing on hotels and activities in the Bali area, then make his way back to Jakarta a couple of days before he was due to fly home to L.A. He was to attend a pre-arranged meeting with a senior Al Qaeda operative whom the U.S. had cultivated for many years. He knew the man quite well. The U.S. and Al Qaeda had cooperated with each other for about a decade in Indonesia on projects that had benefited both politically. However, intelligence had come in recently revealing that this operative was getting greedy, indiscreet, and boasting that he had the mighty U.S.A. in his pocket. So, a message had to be sent to the Al Qaeda organization as a whole that cooperation meant protection, more power, and prestige for the terrorist organization. A lack of cooperation and respect meant something else entirely. The U.S. was a friend to have on their side, not one they could afford to piss off. Bob's assignment this week was to make America's point. Bob would have a nice dinner with the man and then they would return to a small hotel where a room had been rented in the operative's name, unknown to him of course. The plan was that they would be continuing their discussions there over a bottle of wine.

But in reality, Bob would quietly slit the man's throat within minutes of entering the room. He would then fly home to L.A. to spend some quality time with Jan, Trevor and Craig. He could hardly wait for a few days off to enjoy his family, and maybe visit the San Diego zoo as Janice had suggested.

At present, Bob had three projects on the go: the ongoing strained relationship with Al Qaeda in Indonesia, the drug cartels in Mexico, and Kerrie Joplin. He got exhausted thinking about how many balls he had to juggle. Like all organizations, the CIA had some staffing issues and agents had to do double-duty.

However, the Kerrie project had gotten more interesting over the last few months. Before that it had been monotonous watching her come and go from his rented house down the beach. And Langley listening in on her conversations and passing them along to him to analyze. This Montana job had been squeezed in between his other more pressing assignments. There was very little time. And he detested doing covert work on American soil. That was not where the CIA was supposed to be. They were supposed to be outside America's borders, but a lot of that had changed in the last few years. And who was he to question.

He reported to the assistant director of the National Clandestine Services, which was a major, but relatively secret department of the CIA. The section he worked in under NCS was the Special Activities Division, otherwise known as SAD. While monotonous, he knew his domestic spying was necessary—for what he wasn't quite sure—but he did what he was told. That old house that Mitch Joplin had left to his daughter was the main priority over the last four years. Keeping an eye on the renovation work, having his own people employed as tradesmen from time to time, reporting back to him on what they found in the house, and what they pulled out while working on it. When the work was finished, one important area of the house was still elusive: that damn attic.

So he had one of his operatives pose as an inspector to see if Kerrie would let him gain access voluntarily. When she didn't, they had to move to Plan B and let Bob look like the hero and save her life. Gain her trust so he could see the attic for himself. That had worked, but there was nothing in the attic out of the ordinary for a retired CIA agent to have had in his possession. Guns and uniforms were typical souvenirs for old spooks. He had a few himself that he had already stashed away. So at least that was out of the way, and he had achieved it with a low profile so that Kerrie wasn't alarmed. Then that damn cell phone. His idiot operative didn't have it secured when he did his stunt work falling down the stairs of Kerrie's house. So Bob had had to get that phone back without alarming Kerrie. Done, and destroyed. God, he was slick.

He had ordered his operatives in Canada to get that dog Mule, but they had failed at every turn. That had to be attempted under the radar also, but Jack Howser had proven to be a very determined and talented man. Howser was lucky that they had deliberately not pulled out the stops. It was Canada, after all, and the CIA couldn't afford the risk of being detected operating covertly in that friendly nation. So they had tried to be as low key as possible. Then, this latest attempt by the same operative who had terrorized Kerrie as the phony building inspector, had just terrorized the vet in Whitefish in an attempt to find out what was on the microchip. Bob had ordered him to follow Howser from the border, and get the dog, or the information. Something had happened; he had read about it in the morning paper, and his guy was dead. The paper said a male friend had intervened and defended the vet in her own office. The male friend wasn't named, but Bob deduced that it had to have been Howser. The assault was described in the news as an attempted rape. This didn't surprise Bob. His man was good, but he was a pervert and he loved to use his position of power to take advantage of women wherever and whenever he could. In hindsight, Bob wished he had never recruited him. He was needlessly brutal and clearly a loose cannon. Probably good that he was dead.

Bob knew he would hear from his bosses over this latest mess. The good news was that Howser was on his way to stay at Kerrie's. When she told him he'd be visiting with his dog, Bob couldn't believe his luck. He had received an alert a few weeks ago from Langley about a phone conversation between the two of them, but Howser had been cagey over the phone and didn't mention when he'd be coming. Now he was going to be here soon, and Bob would have both of them in the same place at the same time. In two weeks when he returned from Jakarta and L.A., he could concentrate on wrapping up this little Montana operation, which had already dragged on far too long in his mind. Bob had to try real hard not to be frustrated. His superior had already made it clear that some people are watched forever, all in the cause of national security. Not killed unless necessary, because that always ran the risk of drawing attention and investigations. The CIA wasn't foolproof. Bob knew that to be true, and it always ran the risk of being penetrated by the right person or persons, or someone who was darn lucky.

He also knew that the CIA had gone a bit kill-crazy in the past with other moments in history, when witnesses—dozens of them sometimes—just "accidentally" died within months of the events. Those always drew attention big time, and the conspiracy theorists frothed at the mouth. Books got written, talk-show hosts had a field day, and while the public never saw it, secret senate committees would put the CIA on the hot seat. Someone always had to answer for it, and the CIA would always get its wings clipped afterwards.

That's why divisions like SAD had sprung up. The work still got done, just with less support and more intense focus on deniability. Agents in SAD knew the risks they faced being out on a limb without a harness, but most of them loved the excitement, the power, and of course the money. The money was huge, and it more than compensated for the inconveniences and dangers of being a SAD agent.

Bob thought about how much he had socked away in banks over the last couple of decades. He knew he could retire right now. But he was afraid that he wasn't mentally ready yet. Christ, their house in Glendale, an upscale suburb of

L.A., was now worth over three million alone, and that was after the housing crunch had wreaked its havoc. He had millions more stashed away at several offshore banks. The job had served him and his family well, at least financially.

He knew that Mitch had worked in the SAD division as well, but hadn't known him personally. He reasoned that the CIA had no choice but to take him out, because it was apparent he had cracked. He was going to talk about something. Perhaps they could have manipulated the press into believing he was a nutcase and destroy his credibility. Deny that he was ever in the CIA, etc., etc., make him look "postal." They had certainly done that many times before with others. However, that was a real wild card because Mitch had wanted to go live on TV and they had no idea what he would say or what documentation he might have had to back up his story, whatever that story was. He had apparently given no hint to the CIA beforehand that he might do such a thing—no confrontation, no visit to the psych office.

So from what Bob could tell, he was a righteous kill. And because he was such a puzzle, the decision was made at the highest Agency levels that Mitch's daughter would be a lifetime watch, or at least until they discovered and destroyed what might still be out there.

The thing that Bob was most curious about, was what Mitch had done that had brought him to that point. He knew he shouldn't be curious; in the CIA the old adage "curiosity killed the cat" was a truism. However, he couldn't help but wonder. What had Mitch had in his possession, or in his mind, that had been torturing him? What particular assignment had rekindled his conscience?

The CIA was skilled at killing the conscience and with it the soul. Its operatives had to be detached and at times inhuman to be successful, and to come out alive.

There was a "need to know" philosophy in the CIA, much like in the military. The more agents knew, the greater chance there would be for conscience to be triggered. They were, after all, still only human somewhere deep beneath their brainwashed shells.

Bob had accepted this philosophy for his entire career with the agency. He had no choice. On some assignments agents did know the reasons for what they were doing, such as with his little task this week in Jakarta. But with other jobs, the brass decided to what extent agents would be allowed to know why they were doing something. And they seldom knew what other agents were doing. Most of the time they only knew what their own little piece was and that was it. There was good logic to this: less chance of a leak, less chance of conflict or conscience, and less chance of anyone putting the entire picture together. Bob had always bought into this. However, the older Bob got, the more he wanted to know. This worried him. Something was shaking loose in his head and he knew it was dangerous. He wondered—was his conscience awakening? Or was he cracking up like Mitch?

Chapter 17

Jack woke up on Meagan's couch, wondering where on earth he was. Mule was sleeping at his feet, snoring away without a care in the world. Jack looked around, saw Meagan's white lab jacket hanging on the back of the chair, and it all quickly came back to him. He had killed a man last night.

Jack rolled off the couch, ignoring a disapproving snort from Mule, and staggered into the kitchen. Desperately needing a jolt of java he searched the cupboards until he found what he was looking for. He put on the coffee and while waiting for it to brew, turned on the little TV mounted under a kitchen cabinet. He surfed with the remote until he found the local news. After about five minutes he saw the familiar image of the front of Meagan's office, showing the smashed window with plywood covering the opening. The on-the-spot news reporter was giving the grim details of the purported attempted rape of a local veterinarian, and the heroic measures taken by her unidentified male friend who had thrown himself threw the window. And of course killed the rapist inside.

Boy, the media loved these stories, Jack thought, particularly in a small town like Whitefish where probably not a hell of a lot happened from day to day. He poured his coffee and thought how glad he was that he was known only as the "unidentified male friend." He sat at the kitchen table and contemplated how he felt about killing a man. He had to admit to himself, he didn't feel too much at all. The rage he had felt towards that ugly creep at the moment he killed him was still within. In Jack's mind, the man deserved to be dead. Sure, his little mystery investigation had brought this man into Meagan's life, but that didn't warrant the terror the man had brought onto an innocent young lady. Nor did it justify threatening to rape her, which in Jack's mind was what the man had really wanted more than the chip. Jack touched the pocket of his jeans to make sure he still had the chip.

Part of his mind was telling him this had gone way too far. First Heather and Josh had been terrorized, now Meagan. He was thinking that he should not even speak to another woman until he solved this mystery. Certainly he should re-think visiting with Kerrie. Meagan's lecture to him the other night over dinner did cause him to question himself again. Yes, he was in over his head, and yes, maybe he should just turn over the chip to the authorities and tell them everything he knew. But the nagging doubt that kept coming back into his mind was the question of the "authorities." Would they even bother to investigate this? He suspected that the "authorities" were doing the terrorizing. Who could he turn to? Local police would be in over their heads, just like him. If this was indeed a division of the CIA that was trying to get this chip, could anyone really do anything? They were far too powerful. Which made him ask himself the obvious question: how on earth did he expect to be able to do anything? He couldn't answer that, and at this point it didn't really matter. He wanted more than anything else just to figure out this mystery, not necessarily do anything about it. There may not even be anything that needed doing.

He wasn't trying to be a hero, or right any wrongs. He didn't know if anything was inherently wrong, putting aside of course the tactics these spooks had used so far. He just knew something was very suspicious and that some people wanted that microchip very badly. Just that fact turned him on even more, despite the dangers. He felt he was being driven by some primal need.

So, one part of his brain was asking a lot of questions and challenging him, while the other part said, "to hell with it, press on." This mystery must be important or these things wouldn't be happening. This was way more than just his active imagination at work. These were real people who played for keeps, and who wanted to know what was on that chip desperately enough to take chances and threaten people.

He had to see it through. Would he still feel that way if Heather, Josh, or Meagan had been seriously hurt or killed? Jack couldn't answer that. It was too much of a leap to get to that frame of mind. Perhaps he would be incensed enough to want to pursue it even more. Basically though, he just refused to think about it in those extremes.

All he knew right now, and it surprised him, was that he did not feel an ounce of guilt or remorse over taking a life last night. And he wanted to pursue this mystery more than ever.

He limped over to Mule and petted his head. He was still sleeping soundly but he stirred at Jack's touch and moaned appreciatively. What a trooper, Jack thought. He just takes everything in stride.

Jack pulled down his pants and removed the bandage on his left thigh. When they had arrived at Meagan's house last night, she had taken another look at the knife wound. It was still bleeding, so she decided that it was deep enough that it needed stitches. She would have done it while they were still at her clinic, but she didn't want the officers to see that she was performing a procedure on a human. She could have lost her license, even though she was just as capable as any physician at things like that. So she ushered Jack into the procedure room that she maintained in her house for pet emergencies, and proceeded to stitch him up. The wound looked good, kind of red still, but he could tell it was already starting to heal. He shuffled into Meagan's procedure room, applied some ointment and a fresh bandage, and was ready to take on the day.

He thought it was kind of humorous that both he and Mule had been stitched up by the same vet within the last sixteen hours.

Jack now knew why Mule had been growling last night at Meagan's office. Mule knew that the creep was hiding, and he was trying to tell them that. If Jack hadn't been carrying Mule out of the office, there was a good chance he would have run right to the closet door to alert them. He sat down on the couch and gave Mule a hug. "I'll have to learn to pay attention to your signs more often, boy. Thanks for trying."

Mule popped his head up and started wagging his tale at the sound of a footfall on the stairs. Meagan joined them in the living room, still dressed in her pajamas and robe. Her lips were purple and swollen to twice their size. She smiled gallantly, wincing as she did.

"How are you guys this morning?"

Jack walked over to her and gave her a hug. "Forget about us, how are you doing?"

"Not bad, considering. I know I don't look too good though. That guy hit me harder than I thought and the back of my head still hurts a bit too. Have you checked your own wound this morning, Jack?" Her words were a bit slurred from the swelling in her mouth.

"Yes, it's looking pretty good. Thanks for what you did for me."

"No thanks necessary. It's no more than I would have done for any old dog, cat, or pig."

Jack laughed, and couldn't help but admire her sense of humor despite the incredible stress she must still be feeling. She had had a scary evening, to say the least.

Meagan walked over to Mule and gently removed his bandage. "His stitches look good. You can leave this bandage off now and let the air get at it.

For you though, leave the bandage on for at least one more day. Your wound is a lot deeper than Mule's. And don't do any of that fancy kicking for about a week. Can you restrain yourself?"

"I think I can," Jack said with a wry grin. "I hope I won't have any more reasons to kick anyone."

"The stitches for both you and Mule are self-dissolving. So they should disappear completely in about four weeks; sometimes a little longer depending on the individual's healing power."

"So I don't have an excuse to come back and see you?" Jack complained.

"Come back when you solve your mystery. It may be safer in the meantime if you just stayed away." Meagan laughed.

"I know you're just kidding when you say that."

"No, I'm really not kidding. As I said over dinner, you're involved in something very serious and last night was evidence of that."

Jack looked at her thoughtfully and paused before answering. "You're right. I'm so sorry that you experienced this first hand. I should have known they would have been following and watching me. I should have anticipated that."

"I was terrified, Jack. I was so lucky that you came back, and I shudder to think what would have happened to me if you hadn't. I don't want to sound ungrateful, because I'm not. I owe you my life, but on the other hand if you hadn't brought your Sherlock stuff into my world I never would have had any of this to deal with."

Jack looked down at the floor. He didn't know what to say. She was right, of course, and at that moment he felt very selfish, foolish…and reckless. These were admissions he didn't like to have to make, and qualities he had never seen in himself before.

Meagan sat on the couch and started to cry, and her shoulders began to shake. Jack sat down and put his arm around her. Mule didn't like the crying one bit and promptly climbed up onto her lap and licked her chin. Meagan's crying turned into a combination of sobbing and laughing. Then she said, "Look at you guys. Both of you my patients and you're consoling me! It's supposed to be the other way around!"

Both of them started laughing, and Mule kept licking. It was a nice moment, and Jack started to feel better. Meagan's stress was beginning to ease a bit, and that was a good thing to see.

The phone rang, and Meagan answered on the second ring. All Jack heard was "Okay, that would be fine. We'll be here."

She hung up and turned to Jack. "That was a detective. He's dropping by in half an hour for some final questions."

Jack shuddered. "Okay, I guess we had to expect that."

Exactly half an hour later the detective rang the doorbell. He was a pleasant young guy, about thirty years old, and seemed both friendly and sympathetic. He introduced himself as Hank Flanders and handed them each a card. Jack thought that it was a pleasure to meet a detective who was the exact opposite of his Detective Al in Calgary.

They sat down in the living room and Hank began his questions.

"Where again was he hiding, Ms. Wilson? I know you already told my partner all the details last night, but I'd like to hear for myself if you don't mind." Jack looked over at Meagan. He realized that this was the first time he'd heard her last name. He felt ashamed that he hadn't known it already.

"He came out of the closet shortly after Jack left," Meagan replied.

"And did he say anything to you at all before he assaulted you?"

"No, the first thing he did was punch me across the mouth. Then he pulled down his pants and got on top of me."

"And Mr. Howser, why did you come back?"

"To get my dog's collar. I'd left it at Meagan's office. We had removed it for his procedure."

"And what procedure was that?"

Meagan jumped in and answered before Jack had a chance to think of what to say. "I removed a troublesome mole that Mule had on his shoulder."

"And why didn't you have a vet in Calgary deal with that, Mr. Howser? That is your home, isn't it?" Hank asked.

"Yes, I live in Calgary. I had noticed the mole a while back but decided to ignore it until it got worse. On the trip to Montana I noticed it was bleeding, so I decided to drop in to Meagan's office and get it attended to."

"You knew each other before this, did you not?"

Jack felt a slight lump in his throat. "Yes, I met Meagan about a year ago when I was traveling through Montana."

"And how did you happen to meet a veterinarian in your travels?"

"I was thinking of buying some cottage property on Whitefish Lake, and I wanted to make sure I had a vet to go to if I needed one." Jack thought that was a pretty good answer.

"Did you buy property?" the detective asked.

"No, not yet, but I'm still considering."

"Had you ever seen that man before last night, Mr. Howser?"

"No. I would have remembered that face."

"How about you, Ms. Wilson. Any prior contact with him?"

"No, none at all," Meagan answered.

"Well, I think we're done here," Hank said. "This man picked the wrong place at the wrong time, and we thank God he did. I can tell you that the coroner advises he died of a brain stem injury. Your kick didn't kill him, Mr. Howser, but the head contact with the desk did. I think you already suspected that. Perhaps knowing that makes you feel better?"

"It does make me feel a bit better, Detective," Jack lied.

"We found no identification on his person whatsoever, his fingerprints were surgically removed and his cell phone was one of those disposable types, impossible to trace. All phone calls had been erased also. His car keys were in his pocket, we used the remote opener to locate his car on the street. It was a late model Lincoln, reported stolen in Eureka a couple of weeks ago. We discovered that only by checking the VIN number because the license plate was from a different car entirely."

Jack and Meagan both nodded silently as they absorbed this information.

"All in all he was scum and you were very lucky, Ms. Wilson, to have escaped relatively unharmed."

Meagan nodded and walked Hank to the front door.

Hank turned back before leaving. "And Mr. Howser, all I can say to you is, you have a wonderful sense of timing. It was very lucky for Ms. Wilson that you returned when you did."

"You're right, Detective. Fate works in strange ways, sometimes in our favor," Jack replied.

After he left, they both breathed a sigh of relief. Jack was glad that Meagan was so quick with her answer about the mole on Mule's shoulder rather than opening up a can of worms by admitting she'd removed a microchip. The detective would have wanted to know why, and rightfully so. As Meagan had told Jack, those chips tended not to get removed once they were implanted. It would have been a red flag if the detective had heard that.

They went into the kitchen and Meagan made some lunch for both of them. She looked tired and Jack had the feeling that he shouldn't overstay his welcome. "Perhaps you should see your doctor today. You might need some sedatives to help deal with this for the next few days."

"No, I think I'll be okay. I just need some rest. I'll take a couple of days off work and all should be fine. It will take a few days for them to replace that window anyway and with the publicity this has probably generated around town, I'm better off hiding at home for a while. I'll cancel all my appointments and surgeries. There's nothing urgent this week. All elective stuff which can wait."

"Are you sure? Is there anything I can do for you before I go?"

"No, I think you've done enough already, Jack. I would like you to go. I need to put this all out of my mind, and you being here is making it hard for me to do that. I do appreciate you staying here with me last night, however, and of course I'm in your debt for your bravery in setting me free. I'll never forget that."

"Okay. Thanks for all you've done for me and for kind of understanding what I'm pursuing. You must think I'm crazy for chasing this, and I certainly didn't deserve to have you cover for me like you did with that detective."

"I do think you're crazy, not in the literal sense, but in an obsessive way. I don't know why you need to chase this; maybe it's just a guy thing. After what happened to you and Mule back in Calgary, your lady friend and her son—and now me—I can't believe you still want to follow this path. This is pretty dangerous turf you seem to be stomping on. I fear for you, and for everyone who knows you."

Jack looked down at the floor and contemplated what Meagan had just said. After a moment he replied, "It feels like I have no choice in the matter sometimes. I know that sounds nuts and kind of obsessive, but it's the only way I can describe it. I just can't turn away from this, not yet anyway."

She attempted a frown, but it looked a bit hideous through the swollen lips. "If you're on a suicide mission, promise me, Jack, that you won't take someone you love with you."

"I promise. Trust me, that won't happen," Jack said in a soft voice, almost choking up at her plea.

"You may be nuts, Jack Howser, but I'm pretty sure you're a trustworthy nut."

Meagan stretched up on her tiptoes and gave Jack a kiss on the cheek. Jack returned it. He could see that her lips were puffed up like small balloons. It must have been painful for her to even attempt to kiss him.

An hour later he and Mule were on the road to Bigfork. Jack was glad to have some quiet time to think, and the car was his favorite place to do that. He had a lot to think about, including whether or not Meagan was right.

Was he crazy?

Chapter 18

It was late, the night before his trip to Indonesia, when Bob Trundle picked up the phone and dialed on a secure line to Langley, Virginia. This was a call he wasn't looking forward to making, but it was time to check in and face the music. Before phoning, he had poured himself a tall bourbon and took a long, soothing sip.

"Virginia, it's Montana calling." Even though the line was secure they never used their own names over the phone, or even their aliases.

"Bring me up to date."

"Well, I recovered Kerrie's cell phone, and it's now been destroyed."

"Good. Was there anything on there that could be traced?"

"Only outgoing phone numbers, including my cell number which had a one-word recording on it, a code word."

"Uh oh. Do you think she could recognize your voice?"

"Unlikely. It was just one word said very quickly, and I've had several conversations with her since she heard it. She hasn't shown any inkling of recognition. And I've now destroyed that phone as well."

"Okay, we may have dodged a bullet. What about her attic?"

"I went up into the attic with her and we found a display of the usual operative souvenirs: uniforms, scuba suits, guns."

"That's it? You're sure?"

"That's all there was. I think we're safe on the attic. I think Mitch would have been unlikely to hide anything there anyway; it's too easy a hiding spot."

"That might have been exactly why he would have chosen it. I hope you took a close look at every corner of that attic."

"Don't worry. It's been covered off."

"This man Joplin was incredibly talented. We cannot take him lightly, even from the grave," Virginia commented.

"I won't take him lightly. I never met him but I've heard in certain circles that he was quite the legend."

"You have no idea. The brass wanted him to join headquarters in a teaching role back in 2001 when he retired, but he wanted no part of the Agency any longer. We were disappointed because there was so much knowledge he could have passed on to our young recruits."

"Why did he sour?" Bob asked.

"Probably the same old reasons: burnout, more time with family."

"He never said?"

"Not as far as I know, and we usually never ask. I wasn't in charge when he retired and I only met him once. He made one hell of a good first impression though."

"Tell me, what is the Agency worried about with Mitch? Was there a particularly sensitive assignment that would have caused him to want to hurt us?"

"They're all sensitive assignments, Montana, you know that."

"Well, of course, but you must have been worried that he was going to share something that would have been particularly damaging. Mitch's death, plus the four-year watch we've had on his daughter, and now the concern with this mutt. What am I into here?"

"Do you really expect me to answer that?"

"It might help me to understand the sense of urgency."

"You don't need to understand. And I'm getting a bit concerned by your line of questioning. You know the rule: "need to know." And you don't need to know."

"Sure, I know the rule. But in this case it would be helpful to know how serious this is, so I know how far you want me to go."

"At this point, you continue to do what you're doing. Get the chip, or the information from the chip. And find out what Howser and Joplin know."

"Then what."

"Then you'll do whatever I tell you to do."

"We know that Howser already knows what's on the chip, but chances are it means nothing to him. That's why he's come down here to Montana. He's probably hoping that between him and Kerrie, they can figure it out."

"Yes, but so what if he knows? Chances are that if Mitch was leaving a message of some sort, it's in one of our recognized codes. They won't be able to figure it out if that's the case, and once we know which code it's in, we'll have it cracked quickly. Then we can follow the trail, erase it, and leave those two alone, hopefully forever," Virginia said.

"So, does it matter anymore if we get the actual chip back? Wouldn't it suffice for us to simply obtain what it is Howser knows is on the chip?" Bob asked.

"Aside from torturing the man, how do you propose to do that? It's still simpler to just cut the chip out of the dog."

"It's already out of the dog." Bob braced himself.

"What?"

"My man followed Howser from the border to a vet's office in Whitefish. He watched the office, saw the two of them leave without the dog. He then broke in through the back door, and saw that the dog had been anaesthetized and had a bandage on his shoulder area. He phoned me with this news, so I ordered him to wait until they returned to try to get the vet alone." Bob paused.

"So?"

"All I know is that the newspaper reported there was an attempted rape of the vet, and a male friend broke through the window and saved her. My man is dead."

"Jesus, an attempted rape? What kind of people do you hire?" Virginia exclaimed.

"I understand your disappointment. I share it, and I realize now that it was a mistake to recruit him. He was indeed a liability."

"That kind of stuff brings publicity and investigations—complications we don't need. You know that. This is American soil we're operating on here, and we don't need the FBI interfering in what we do. They would just love the opportunity to point out to the White House that "they told them so." They already resent us being on their turf for certain national problems. They feel they should handle everything on the ground here at home."

"I understand all that. It was unforeseeable." Bob chose to overlook the lie. "But as usual with all task operatives, he can't be traced to the CIA."

"So where does this leave us?"

"Well, it's obvious that Howser wanted to eliminate the risk to his dog, and take it all on himself now. The chip is gone. It's either in the trash, still in the vet's office, or Howser has it."

"What's your best guess?"

"Knowing how resourceful this Howser is, I'm betting he has the chip. Even though he knows what's on it, he probably wants to keep it in case he has to produce it later."

"I agree. Your plan?"

"I already have Kerrie's trust. I propose to remain close to her, meet this

Howser, and try to be a friend and confidante to both of them. This may give me an opportunity. I can probably find out what we need to know without hurting either of them."

"Okay. Have you briefed Colorado for while you're away?"

"Yes. He'll pose as my brother and house-sitter until I get back. He'll keep an eye on them."

"When does he arrive?"

"He'll be here in four days. He's not finished in Chile yet. And he'll brief you every couple of days once he's here."

"Fine, and good luck overseas."

"Thanks. Should be routine."

Bob hung up and took another long sip of his bourbon. He thought that went reasonably well, considering the screw-up in Whitefish. However, he made no progress whatsoever in drawing out his boss on what the fear was with Mitch's message. He hadn't really expected an answer, but he felt enough anxiety that he wanted to try. He hoped he hadn't alarmed his boss too much by his probing.

What had Mitch done at the behest of the CIA? He had heard of rogue agents before, but never an incident like what happened back in 2003. That was way over the top, and he was shocked to hear that an agent of Mitch's caliber had gone over the edge like that. He must have had a death wish, because surely he should have known that he wouldn't be allowed to broadcast national secrets to the media. But maybe he thought he would get away with it. The fact that he was an explosives expert and a bomb of his design had been strapped to a teller, might have been enough self-assurance for him. Mitch had to have been well aware of the cruel capabilities of the Agency, but he probably thought that there was no way they would blow him away and risk the bomb exploding, killing innocent Americans on live TV. Boy, had he underestimated them.

Incidents like that reminded Bob of his own mortality, and how little he really mattered in the large scheme of things. He was fairly certain that they wouldn't hesitate to kill him if he had a pang of conscience. So if he did have one, he knew he would have to keep it secret. He could never share it with anyone, except maybe a priest.

Of course, the Agency had other ways of dealing with that risk. Money was a big one, and the CIA believed that every single person had a price. That's how they did business as well—paying off people around the world for intelligence, knowing that most people would sell out their own mothers for a million dollars. Just the mere passing along of classified material was punishable with a charge of treason. After all, most patriotic Americans would willingly accept the fact that material like that had to be kept secret. There was really no argument there.

But there were other things agents did that the American people wouldn't be able to accept, and no well-crafted press conference could spin those things. The Agency had to rely on their operatives to be team members, take the money, and shut up. And the money was huge; for the most part it worked.

It hadn't worked in Mitch's case, which made Bob wonder why. It had to have been more than just classified material that Mitch was going to disclose. In Bob's mind it had to have been something very damaging to the integrity of the Agency and the government itself.

For damaging and unconscionable acts, the Agency had another tool in their arsenal: "leverage." They probably seldom had to use it, but they kept it in their hip pocket—actually a secure vault—just in case. Bob thought back to his first days in SAD and the leverage he had to agree that they could have on him, in order for him to pass probation. And he agreed, because he wanted this powerful and exciting position so badly. He figured that he would never give them a reason to use the leverage against him, so it was a moot point anyway.

Every SAD agent, and probably those in the regular CIA ranks as well, had to agree to this leverage, and Bob assumed that the same thing had applied to Mitch. But Mitch's concern must have been so serious that he obviously didn't even care about the leverage anymore.

Leverage meant giving the Agency something they could use against you if you ever showed a sign of disloyalty. It was a way of controlling you, holding something over your head to remind you that they owned you and that you had to do as you were told without question. It worked—usually.

It was really just a form of blackmail. Blackmail that would never be relinquished for the rest of an agent's life. Blackmail that would damage an agent beyond repair if ever disclosed.

It meant selling your soul.

Bob's first assignment had nothing to do with national security, or Agency business, or intelligence collection. It had to do with leverage. A convicted pedophile had just been released from prison. Ten children had been molested by this man, and he had been set free on probation after only five years. This sick little man was a perfect candidate for leverage against a new agent. Bob's assignment was to befriend the man at a local bar, entice him by saying he had access to an adolescent ménage a trios, and accompany the man back to his rooming house for some more drinks and fantasizing. An Agency videographer was following Bob's every move that night, with Bob's knowledge and agreement. The small high-tech video camera, ahead of its time in compact design, was hidden under the videographer's coat until just the right moment. Once Bob got back to the pervert's sleazy room, he made sure the door was left unlocked. The despicable little pedophile made drinks, and they sat together on the couch and talked about boys. The man was getting excited and Bob was feeling sick to his stomach.

Then on schedule ten minutes after they had entered the room, in barged the videographer, camera rolling. Bob, on cue, whipped out a roll of duct tape from his jacket pocket. To this day he could still see in his nightmares the shocked look on the little man's face as the camera pointed in his direction and the tape went quickly over his mouth. He had no time to scream, and he was probably too shocked to even register what was going on. Bob reached to his waist and pulled a large hunting knife out of its sheath. Then, trying to ignore the stark fear in the little man's eyes, he cut his throat deeply from ear to ear. All the while being filmed.

Bob had to look at the camera after it was done, and smile in a "who cares" kind of way. It was like being directed in a movie. He had a role to play and so did the pervert. Except that the pervert didn't know that he was starring in his own snuff film. Bob had looked back at the man after smiling for the camera, and he could see that he had cut so deep into the neck that the head was bobbing without support, blood gushing out over his chest. The videographer pulled an extra jacket out of his pack and threw it to Bob. He put it on over his blood soaked windbreaker, and they exited as quickly and as silently as they had come.

This recorded event now went to the CIA confidential archives vault, accessible only by the NCS director and assistant director. Sure, the videographer was a witness, but he too had leverage against himself as well, going back to the time when he had first joined. No one in SAD was exempt.

For leverage, the CIA of today always chose only candidates who were easy to kill, and easy for their agents to accept and live with due to what these people had done in their sick little lives. However, assassinations of political figures were not used as leverage, at least not any more. If incidents like that were ever released to the press to implicate or damage an agent, people might believe the agent's story that he had been ordered to conduct political hits. The average person, deep down inside, did not generally believe that lone nuts killed senators and presidents—despite being told that they should believe that. That was too much for the typical brain to fathom. People weren't that stupid, although they were usually willing to be led and believe most things they were told. But political kills required planning and engineered security failures. They required lots of people, lots of money, and lots of leverage. A film or photo of a political killing would usually not be believed as being the work of a lone psycho, so such films would have limited use. However, it had taken the Agency a couple of decades to learn that. Bob had heard that back in the olden days of the Agency, films of those kinds of hits made all over the world were kept, and indeed used as leverage. But the more modern CIA leadership of today's world was a little smarter and more realistic.

So, the leverage in this day and age had to be with lowlifes; characters who the Agency could show, by anonymous release to the press, that the agent was just a psychopathic killer who hung around with the sleaziest people on earth and even took joy in having his escapades filmed. That type of video would discredit and destroy an agent if he was thinking of spilling his soul. And he would go to jail for the murder displayed on film, so he would only be hurting himself. That was the logic.

Bob had this leverage on his record now for the rest of his life, as most likely had Mitch. Silence was serious business and the Agency went to great lengths to ensure that coups and assassinations were not discussed or confessed to. Killing agents was a last resort and this was made known to new recruits. It had to be a last resort because jobs needed to get done and agents needed to feel that they were safe as long as they towed the line. The Agency could never embark on a crusade of killing their own agents after missions. Despite being a secret organization, the CIA rank and file knew each other and had their own network of communication. The rumor mill, as in any legitimate business, was loud. It wouldn't take long before the Agency saw a flood of resignations and new recruits drying up, if they thought they had to look over their shoulders for the rest of their lives.

It was indeed risky having these operatives running around with knowledge in their heads, but that was one of the reasons why the Agency seldom let anyone be involved in a project from beginning to end. They each had pieces, and tasks, but no complete picture. It was truly "need to know."

Nothing was foolproof, of course, and sometimes agents had to die despite the money, the threatened charges of treason, and the horrible leverage that was held on them. It was rare, but sometimes they had to die.

In Mitch's case, it seemed like he had decided that death didn't matter anymore. Whatever they had paid him didn't matter, being imprisoned for treason didn't matter, and having his leverage broadcast to the media didn't matter. Bob pondered for a moment what Mitch's leverage might have been. Since Mitch was from the old school, his leverage would not be the killing of a pervert like Bob's film footage was. His film would most likely have been of an actual official assignment from long ago in some foreign land.

Bob wondered what could have possibly created such a mind-set in an experienced agent who by all accounts was one of the best the Agency had ever had? Why did Mitch take such a terrible risk? Why would death have been preferable, instead of just living with the knowledge as he had been programmed to do?

Chapter 19

It was a beautiful spring day in Montana, and Jack was enjoying the scenic drive from Whitefish to Bigfork. He knew it should only take him about forty-five minutes to get there, but he deliberately took his time. The Audi was humming along, sunroof open, Led Zeppelin blaring in the CD player. Mule was sitting upright in the front passenger seat, sticking his head up through the sunroof from time to time. He was clearly enjoying the rush of the wind, licking it in, flapping his tongue happily.

Jack loved the feel of the open road, and really enjoyed taking in the scenery and thinking about his life. That was the good part about road trips—the peace and quiet, aside from Led Zeppelin of course, which Jack found curiously soothing. But hitting the open road in a car blocked out the rest of the world and all the distractions of home. There were no newspapers or televisions to punish him with all their bad news, and no responsibilities except to keep his eyes on the road.

He thought that by now he would be feeling a delayed shock to the realization that he had killed someone. But he didn't feel anything. He hoped that didn't say something bad about his humanity, but he convinced himself that instead it was due to the circumstances and the brutality of the man he had killed. He thought about that man—particularly the fact that he had no fingerprints. He wondered how common that was in the underworld, netherworld, or whatever world these outcasts operated in. It couldn't be easy, or cheap, to have fingerprints removed and the tips repaired with plastic surgery. He figured the average criminal would not have the means to get that done.

Jack thought back to the incidents in Calgary with the two dognapping attempts and the brazen assault on Heather and Josh. No fingerprints had been found at any of those scenes and gloves had not been worn. It wasn't much of a stretch for Jack to come to the conclusion that those attackers had had their fingerprints removed as well. It all fit so tightly together. These people were all pros, and were well equipped to confidently do what they did. This last character however did not seem to have the finesse or class of the Calgary crew. His tactics displayed more cruelty and a clear perversion. He didn't fit the mould. He had threatened Meagan, exposed himself, and seemed to enjoy it. He had a mission to be sure, but he seemed to have also decided that he would take something else while he was there—Meagan's self-respect and dignity.

Jack was so thankful that he had come back for Mule's collar. What a stroke of luck that he had left that behind. He shuddered thinking what might have happened to Meagan if he hadn't come back.

He saw the turnoff for Bigfork and left the main highway. Within minutes he was cruising down the main street in town, admiring the quaint storefronts and bistros. What a wonderful place, he thought. It was so captivating, and bustling. The recession didn't seem to be affecting this town at all. Shoppers were out in droves, parking spots were all taken, outdoor patios for the restaurants and bars were packed. For a town that depended on tourism, this was a good sign that the economy hadn't totally tanked. Jack wished the media would spend some time reporting and filming little success stories like this town, instead of always searching for the most depressing stories, like Flint, or Detroit, which, if anyone was being totally honest, had languished even when times were good. But the media did indeed love those shots of boarded up windows and long lines at unemployment offices. Photos like that made people scared, and being scared meant people read and watched, which sold papers and advertising spots.

In addition to the beauty of the town, it was only minutes from the shores of Flathead Lake, where Jack was headed. He was looking for the northeast corner and Bigfork was practically sitting on it. He followed Kerrie's directions and could clearly see the beautiful shimmering waters as he got closer to her inn. What a sight, he thought. He knew the lake was huge and this side of the lake would get some incredible sunsets. He hoped Kerrie had a nice porch for him to sit and enjoy that sight. Jack had a thing for covered porches; the house where he grew up had had one and he fondly remembered the rocking chairs and potted plants.

Soothing.

But this was mid-day, which offered its own nice alternative to sunsets. He could see the sunlight reflecting off the water, sparkling like diamonds. Each part of the day certainly had its own rewards on a lake. The calm still waters of early morning were also a treat to behold.

There it was—Lighthouse Inn—a sign out by the road guided him down a long dirt driveway to the side of the house. Jack couldn't believe his eyes. This house was huge and full of character. It needed some work on the outside, really only cosmetic, and the way it looked right now retained most of that old charm that a house of this age should be boasting. Some things just shouldn't be changed. He wished Calgary had kept more of its pioneer history. Most of the historic old homes had been leveled or moved to century parks.

Jack and Mule got out of the car and walked. Well, Jack walked but Mule ran, down to the lakeshore a few dozen yards from the front of the house. He watched as Mule went crazy, his tail wagging furiously, following his nose to invisible markers on the ground. It was apparent that Mule did remember this place and was picking up familiar scents—possibly those of both Kerrie and Mitch. Jack gazed down the long dock directly in front of the house. Three boats were moored alongside, gently bobbing in the waves created by a passing water-skier. He could see that the skier was a young boy decked out in a shiny black wetsuit. Shrieking with delight at every wave that made him bounce, he was clearly just learning the intricacies of the sport but enjoying every new twist it threw at him. This brought back some vivid memories for Jack: summers at his grandparents' cottage in Haliburton, learning to water-ski himself. He could also picture himself out fishing with his grandfather, sometimes for hours at a time. Jack would always get hungry and want to go back to the cottage, and his grandfather would always say "toughen up." And Jack did, thanks to him. He missed the crotchety old guy. He had some great recollections of the little things the man did that taught Jack life lessons. His grandfather had a tough outer shell, but a heart of gold that he sometimes allowed to show through that shell with a twinkle in his eye.

This lake was a sight to behold. Kerrie Joplin had done well for herself, or at least her father had done well for her. He gazed back at the house from the lake. It was stunning. The old house made quite a statement and he could see along the far side that there was also a three-storey tower section. He walked along the front and admired the tower's circular construction with large windows set in steel frames. The views must be incredible from the top floor, he thought.

She had a large property, he could tell, and he figured with the renovations she had told him about, that this was a very valuable piece of real estate now, particularly being on one of the most beautiful lakes in the country. He walked around the back and noticed an old dilapidated outhouse about thirty yards from the rear of the house. It was covered in old barn-board, and was sagging on one side with the roof partly caved in. He was pretty certain that Kerrie would tear that down as soon as she could. It was an eyesore and obviously wasn't needed anymore. It must have been the original bathroom facility when the house was first built.

He let out a whistle and Mule came running. Together they walked up to the front door. Jack was thrilled to see that the house had a beautiful covered porch, just like he'd wished for. He knocked on the door and held his breath. He had been a bit apprehensive about this first meeting with Kerrie especially after the initial conversation they had had. Luckily the second one had gone well. He wondered how she'd behave towards Mule, and of course towards him too. Judging by Mule's reaction to the smells on the property, he was pretty sure that the dog would remember her even though it had been almost four years since she'd lost him in Alberta.

The door opened and the most beautiful blonde goddess stood there smiling—first at Mule, then at Jack. She held a printed photo in her hand, looked at him, then looked again at the photo. "Well, it does indeed look like you, Mr. Howser. So, you are welcome to come in!"

She dropped quickly to her knees and beckoned to Mule. He looked at her, cocked his head and froze in his position. Jack thought it was very telling that he didn't growl like he did with most strangers. A little bark inside Mule's head was telling him to be happy.

"Mule, you mangy old mutt!" Kerrie cried out. Mule whined and leaped into her arms. He definitely recognized her. The intelligent Border collie brain had long ago locked up the memory of Kerrie Joplin for future retrieval. "I always called him 'mangy old mutt,' even while my dad had him," Kerrie said. "I knew he would remember that."

"It's great that he recognizes you," Jack said. "That must be very heartwarming for you after all these years."

Kerrie didn't reply, but instead kept on hugging and teasing Mule. He clearly loved the attention from this woman who he probably thought was out of his life forever.

She got to her feet, tears falling from her bright green eyes. She quickly wiped them away. He guessed she was a woman who didn't like showing her emotions too easily. And she had had to grow up early because of her mother's death, and her father's constant absence, so it was probably understandable that she had found ways to cope with emotions, or bury them. Her chosen occupation as a lawyer also spoke volumes of how tough she was, at least on the outside. Jack guessed that he'd find out a lot more about Kerrie Joplin in the days and weeks ahead.

"C'mon in, Jack. It's really great to finally meet you. Again, I do hope you forgive me for our first conversation. I was such a bitch!"

"All's forgotten, Kerrie. Trust me, I'm used to people telling me to 'go fuck myself.'"

She laughed, and led the way into the living room. They both sat down, and Kerrie offered Jack a bourbon.

"Do you have any rye whiskey?" Jack asked, knowing that her answer would be a question.

"What's that?" Kerrie asked, clearly puzzled.

"It's a Canadian whiskey, kind of our version of your bourbon. But it's obvious by your question that you don't have any, so I'll take a scotch neat if you have it. I find your bourbon to be a poor substitute for our rye. Too sweet."

"We barely know each other, and you've already taken a shot at a U.S. staple. Bourbon is the drink of drinks, I'll have you know," Kerrie said, grinning.

Jack was captivated by her quick smile. And those green eyes—unreal. A portrait couldn't come close to capturing the sparkles and color that jumped from those eyes. The overall impression she made was quite stunning. He could tell also that she kept herself in shape—tall and slim, but with genuine curves. She could have been a model although her features were probably a bit non-standard for the modeling racket. They would probably try to hide the prominent freckles on her nose, and definitely work on eliminating the cleft chin. Jack, on the other hand, found all of her features joined together to make Kerrie one very attractive lady. Take one feature away and the overall effect would be substantial.

She went to the bar to get some scotch, and was back in a couple of minutes with his drink and a dish of cocktail nuts. They both sat back and sipped their drinks in silence for a few minutes, enjoying the hypnotic view of the lake from the front window.

"I'll bet I'm enjoying my bourbon far better than you're enjoying your scotch." Kerrie broke the silence, laughing.

"You probably are. From the American movies I've seen, I think you folks put bourbon in baby bottles, you're so obsessed with it."

"Well, we're glad that we're able to provide you Canadians with some film entertainment. I sometimes wonder what y'all would do up there without our Hollywood," she teased.

"We keep busy trying to keep our banks in business after the meltdown y'all have caused around the world." Jack got up and grabbed coasters for each of them off the mantle.

"That's a good one, Jack. You're almost as quick as me. I think we're going to have some fun, you and I." Kerrie jumped up and took him by the hand. "Come, I'll take you on a tour."

Mule bounced up from the bear rug and trotted behind Kerrie, not ready to let her out of his sight yet. She knelt down and gave him another big hug. "I'm so happy to see Mule again. It gives me such great joy to know that he's alive and has an owner who obviously takes good care of him. I'm at peace now."

"He's been a joy for me, Kerrie. I needed a constant companion and he's unbeatable."

Kerrie rubbed the fur around Mule's shoulder, and gently stroked her finger down the side of the shaved area. "What happened to his shoulder? I see that it's been shaved and stitched."

Jack knelt down beside her and petted Mule under the chin. "I had that microchip removed. Remember, I told you about that thing?"

"Yes, I remember. Why did you have it taken out?" Mule was now licking her face, and she turned away slightly so he wouldn't get her mouth.

"It's a long story, and I'll tell you all about it once you feel you're ready. We have a lot to talk about actually, if you're up for it."

"We'll see."

She showed him around the main floor first. Jack was mesmerized by the quality of workmanship and finishes. Kerrie obviously had great taste. The original charm of the house had either been retained where possible, or replicated. Jack had considerable experience with renovations himself with his old house in Calgary. But this house put his to shame, he had to admit. They walked along to the south wing of the house, where Kerrie opened a heavy fire door. It opened up to a small passageway connecting the tower section with the main house. Kerrie led Jack down to the foyer of the tower.

"This tower isn't heated, so it's a three-season wing only. Now that summer is basically here, I'll be looking at things I can do to make it more useable. It's a wonderful space, and with the right touches and furniture, it will be glorious."

Jack gazed around, envisioning plants and exotic statues that could be positioned strategically as a welcome point for anyone who ventured into this section.

"I agree. This is a marvelous addition to the house. Very unique."

They climbed the stairs, a twisting iron masterpiece, to the third floor of the tower and gazed out over the lake. The view was amazing, and Jack thought that if he had a room like this, most summer mornings with his coffee and newspaper would be spent up here.

"The room is circular, so a bit difficult to furnish, particularly with the spiral staircase bisecting it," Kerrie commented.

Jack could visualize an office, or studio of some kind. A relaxing place to hide out and work. Even the most boring hobby would be a pleasure up here. "I'm sure you'll figure out just the right touches, Kerrie, judging by what you've done with the rest of the house."

They carefully made their way down the spiral staircase, and back along the passageway to the main house. Jack felt the floor give in one spot, and stopped to take a look.

"This doesn't feel too stable, Kerrie. You may have to rip it up and reinforce the supports. It actually feels a bit hollow when you walk on this part right here." Jack indicated the area by drawing an imaginary outline with his foot.

Kerrie stomped her right foot on the floor where Jack was standing. "I don't think it's unsafe, but it does feel a bit weak. Probably just because it's old hardwood," Kerrie said.

"You may be right, but hardwood back when this house was built was usually thicker than what they use today. So the age of the floor is a plus if you're looking for strength. I think the wood is okay; it probably just needs a new sub-floor."

"Ah, more expense, just what I need, Jack. Thanks a bunch, " Kerrie laughed. They continued on upstairs, passing through the lovely country kitchen along the way. Jack admired the pine cupboards, and the big window over the sink looking out to the lake.

"There are four bedrooms on the bottom floor, and four on the top. Do you prefer top or bottom?"

"I don't really know you well enough yet to answer that question, Kerrie," Jack replied with a wry grin on his face.

She took a second, then laughed. "You are quick. I'll have to keep an eye on you," she said flirtatiously.

Jack was glad that his off-color humor had been well accepted. He could tell that Kerrie was easy-going and fun, and they both seemed instantly comfortable with each other. He hoped she would be just as open when he broached the subjects that he wanted to broach—the main reason for his visit.

The bedrooms were all decorated Victorian style, which Jack thought was very clever for a bed and breakfast. People wanted something different when they stayed at a B&B, and this place certainly fit the bill. Very warm and cozy.

He noticed the attic as they walked down the upper hall. He wanted to ask Kerrie if she had developed it, but she didn't volunteer anything. He didn't at this point want to ask questions about something she didn't volunteer.

At the end of the tour Jack complimented Kerrie on how beautiful the house was. She was modest, claiming professionals had done most of the work, but Jack knew that this outspoken and gregarious woman had had a big impact on the outcome.

They spent the next little while getting Jack settled in. He chose a room on the top floor, even though if truth be told, he was really more of a bottom guy. Mule would sleep with Jack as he usually did, and Kerrie didn't seem to mind despite the shedding. Jack lay back on the bed and closed his eyes. He knew that this would be a pleasant visit. He also had a strong feeling that the mystery he was pursuing would begin to unfold now.

Where it would take him after that, he had no idea.

*****

The next few days were spent getting to know each other and exploring the area with long walks. Kerrie seemed to enjoy the change of pace and Mule was in all his glory having both of his favorite people to hang around with. One day they went out in one of the speedboats and cruised around a large portion of the lake. Jack was amazed at how expansive it was. It would take days to properly explore every bay, cove, and island. It was wonderful to be out on a real lake again, just like summers in Muskoka where he and Susan had owned a cottage. Ontario lakes were pretty special, compared to the fake lakes—really just reservoirs—that Alberta had. To be fair, Alberta did have beautiful natural lakes, but they were in the mountains and were as cold as ice all year long. And of course Calgary did a great job replicating lakes in their subdivisions, but they were man-made and really didn't fool anyone. Nice make-believe touches, but nothing like the real thing. And Flathead Lake was the real thing.

Walking along the shoreline, past all the unique homes, was a favorite pastime for the first few days. The shore went on for miles, uninterrupted. Kerrie pointed out the houses of the neighbors that she knew. Most of the homes were well back from the shore, but with great views. She was particularly enthusiastic about one place four houses down from hers. Owned by a Bob Trundle, she said. They had become good friends, and he had helped with her dock and a few other problems she had encountered. Jack felt a little jealous hearing her talk in such glowing terms about this Bob fellow. Which was silly, of course. He was only just getting to know Kerrie, so he didn't really have the right to be jealous. It must be just his competitive nature, he thought. He told Kerrie he looked forward to meeting this Bob guy.

They were standing in front of her house on the fourth day of his visit when Mule suddenly crouched down and dropped the biggest poop that Jack had ever seen him do. He immediately grabbed the shovel leaning against the house and began digging another hole in an area of ground well away from the lake. He had been using this spot as his poop cemetery all week so far.

Kerrie walked over to Jack and said, "You do an awful lot of unnecessary work for those shit piles. I appreciate your manners but it's okay with me if you just dump them down that old outhouse in the back. Why dig holes if you don't have to?"

Jack looked at her, and thought how logical an idea that was. Why hadn't he thought of it.

"I won't argue with that. It'll save me a lot of work. I'd forgotten all about your outhouse."

"Someone might as well use it. I certainly never have, and I doubt that it has been used in decades. But be careful, Jack. It doesn't look very solid. I wouldn't step in there if I were you. Just reach in with the shovel and dump the shit down the hole."

Jack scooped the huge turd up into the shovel and made his way over to the ramshackle outhouse. He opened the door and braced himself for the smell of decades-old decay. He was pleasantly surprised. No odor at all. He was just about to reach in and lift the toilet seat, when he stopped himself. He laid the shovel down outside, and stepped in. He couldn't believe his eyes. This was no old outhouse; it was just made to look that way on the outside. It was like one of those western movie set structures that you would see at Universal Studios, where the front looks authentic, but the inside isn't.

From inside the outhouse it was clear that this was not an old building at all. The barn-board on the outside was the only thing that was old. But it was just veneer. The structural wood was clearly seen from the inside, and it was only a few years old. Anyone looking at this building from the yard would not want to step foot inside. It was on a slant, and the roof looked caved in—both false fronts. The actual roof and walls were solid wood. Jack wondered why someone would go to so much trouble to create such a deception.

He lifted the seat and looked down into the toilet hole, sniffing. No foul odor, only the smell of damp earth. He was pretty sure no one had ever had a dump in this outhouse. He examined the inside rim of the frame the toilet seat was attached to, and could see the edge of something shiny. He reached under and touched it—it was a clamp. He flipped it up and felt the toilet seat structure loosen on that one corner. He reached around the other corners and felt similar clamps. Jack flipped them all up and then yanked on the seat. It, along with the base it was attached to, folded neatly upward on a hinge. Jack was now looking at a gaping hole large enough for a person to lower into.

He tried hard to focus his eyes in the dim light coming in from the doorway. He blinked a couple of times and stared down into the hole. He blinked and looked again.

His eyes weren't playing tricks on him. He could clearly see a rope ladder extending down from the floor frame of the outhouse. Right to the bottom, about fifteen feet down.

Chapter 20

Jack straightened up and scratched his head. Then he looked down again, not quite believing his eyes. Why on earth would someone install a ladder down an outhouse hole?

"Jack, what's taking you so long? Are you one of those men who reads a newspaper on the toilet?" Kerrie called out. "And you dropped the shovel. I think you forgot what you went in there for." Jack could hear her giggling.

He left the outhouse and walked over to where she and Mule were waiting for him.

"Come back with me Kerrie. I have something to show you." Jack led the way back to the structure and held the door open so Kerrie could go in first. Mule hovered just behind her.

"Okay…so what am I supposed to be looking at?" she asked, eyebrows raised.

"Look at the wood. It's not very old. And look at how strong this building is. It's only meant to look ramshackle from the outside, but it's clearly not from the inside. The outside is just a disguise. That's the only word I can think of to describe this."

Kerrie looked around at the walls and the ceiling. She banged on the wall with her fist. "You're right. It's solid…" Her face suddenly turned white as a sheet.

"Now lean over and sniff," Jack urged.

She looked at him and grimaced.

"Go ahead," he said. "It's bearable, trust me."

Kerrie reluctantly leaned her head over the hole, and sniffed. "Nothing," she said, surprised.

"Exactly! This was never an outhouse."

"But there's a toilet seat!" Kerrie protested.

"Sure there is, because anyone who looks in here is supposed to think it's an outhouse." Jack lifted the toilet seat and frame up on its hinge, and he could see out of the corner of his eye the shock on Kerrie's face. "Now, take a look down the hole and tell me what you see."

She leaned over again and then suddenly stepped back. "Jesus Christ!" she exclaimed. "What the hell is that for?"

Mule barked at her outburst. "Easy boy, easy," Jack said to Mule. He looked at Kerrie.

"Would you like to find out? That hole is the deepest I've ever seen in an outhouse. It must go down at least fifteen feet, although we'll be able to tell better with a flashlight."

"You don't actually want to go down there, do you?" Kerrie was looking at him like he was mad.

"I was hoping you'd go with me. What do you say?"

"Forget it! I'm not going down that hole. Dark, confined spaces scare the shit out of me," Kerrie protested.

"Well, at least you'd be in the right place for it," Jack teased.

"Not funny, Jack, not funny at all."

"Okay, I understand. Do you mind if I go? There might be something at the bottom that you should know about."

"What do you think could be down there?" Kerrie's voice quivered.

"I don't know, but there must be some good reason to have a ladder extended to the bottom."

Kerrie shivered. "I don't even want to think about it. Why don't we just forget we found out about this. I don't like the idea of you going down there. What if something happens to you? I'd have to go down after you."

Jack laughed. "Just phone 911."

"If you're determined to do this, go ahead. But you need to take a flashlight. And you have to promise to communicate with me when you're down there. No joking around, okay?"

"I promise. Oh, I just thought of something. Did you want to take a picture? Me from the neck up sticking out of an outhouse hole? It'd make a great photo for your website."

"How can you joke about this? This is just way too weird!"

"I have a weird sense of humor. Sorry."

Kerrie walked back to the house to get the flashlight, while Jack examined the outhouse structure a little more closely. This was a work of genius, he thought, a masterful deception. He couldn't help but admire it and the skill that it would have taken to build it to look this way. He was getting that familiar adrenaline rush.

Kerrie came back within a couple of minutes with a large industrial flashlight, one with a wide beam. "One of the workers left this behind," she said. "I guess I must have known it would come in handy one of these days, but I never could have imagined a purpose like this. This is one for my diary, that's for sure." Mule was sitting beside Kerrie watching the proceedings with a cocked head.

Jack took the flashlight and climbed up on the edge of the opening, reaching one foot down until it rested on the top rung of the rope ladder. Mule didn't like this strange move, and barked his disagreement.

"You be careful, Jack. And remember, talk to me when you're down there—often," Kerrie demanded, while she tried to calm Mule down with her hand on his head.

Jack smiled, nodded in agreement, and started working his way down the ladder ever so slowly. It swung a bit, but not as bad as he thought it would. About halfway down, he looked up and saw Kerrie's worried face covering part of the opening. He could hear Mule barking. He must have been puzzled seeing Jack disappear down into the ground.

As the natural light got dimmer, he switched on the torch and continued his descent. Finally he touched solid ground. He flashed the torch around the bottom of the shaft. It was just a flat bottom. Nothing was stored here, and the dirt did not appear to have been disturbed by digging. And thankfully, there were no shit piles.

He flashed the beam around the sides. He got his second shock of the day. A tunnel, headed due west towards the house. The opening was only about four feet wide and four feet high, so he'd have to crawl through. He knelt down, flashing his torch down the length. He couldn't see the end, but what he could see was that this tunnel wasn't just a length of dirt. It was reinforced on the sides and the top with two-by-fours, and he could see that the ceiling consisted of sheet metal, supported by wooden cross-members. Jack thought he had just fallen through the looking glass. This was too bizarre to put into words.

"Jack, you promised you'd talk to me! What have you found down there? Are you okay?" Kerrie called down, her voice echoing.

"There's a tunnel down here! I'm going to follow it. Don't worry, it's solid. I'll be safe." Jack could hear Mule barking frantically in response to his voice, which must have sounded distorted to him coming up from the bottom.

"A tunnel? Jack, get back up here! This doesn't sound safe!"

"Kerrie, I'm down here now so I might as well find out the whole story. I'll just be a few minutes, okay?" Jack could feel the excitement rushing through his body, his heart pounding, his arms feeling warm and tingly.

"Jesus, Jack, you're like a little kid! You shouldn't be taking chances like this!"

Silence.

"Jack?"

*****

The man from Colorado posing as Stan Trundle, Bob's brother for this assignment, came in through the back door of Bob's rented house and dropped his bags wearily on the floor. He strolled to the window and looked out over the lake. He yawned, closed the drapes, and plopped down on the couch. Then just as quickly he got up again, unsnapped his belt holster, and dropped it onto the coffee table. Now more comfortable, he stretched back out on the couch and picked up the phone.

"This is Virginia. Talk to me."

"Colorado. I just got in."

"Good. Was Chile successful?"

"Yes."

"Are you all settled there in Montana now?"

"Sure, as settled as I can get."

"You're aware of your assignment?"

"Yeah, Montana filled me in. Doesn't sound too challenging."

"No, just keep an eye on the situation until he returns in about ten days."

"Any longer than that I think I'd die of boredom."

"Well, at least the scenery's nice, isn't it?"

"Like I care."

"The bad news for you is that we need you to stay there a bit longer after Montana returns."

"Why?"

"We'd like you to keep an eye on Montana. He seems to be going through a tough time right now, and his objectivity may be a problem."

"You think he may be going rogue?"

"Not really, at least not in the way you might think. We suspect he may be starting to question his life a bit. Just a few subtle signs from conversations we've had. He's been asking for explanations of some things and he should know better than to do that. Probably just a small mid-life crisis, but we can't be too careful."

"Okay, I'll keep an eye out. For how long?"

"I'll let you know. He can't know you're watching, of course, so be discreet. A house has been rented in your current name, a few blocks away from where you are now. Go there when Montana returns. Do you have a pen and paper?"

"Shoot."

"The address is 207 Lakeland Heights Drive. The door combination is 7020. A complete appearance kit is already in the house for you, so change your look often. You know the routine. Report to me every two days."

"No problem."

*****

Jack crept along the tunnel on all fours, stopping occasionally to sweep the flashlight around in all directions. The floor was just dirt, but the rest of the tunnel was remarkably well constructed. Someone knew what they were doing when they built this thing. Jack was particularly grateful for the stable ceiling. He tried not to think of how many tons of earth was between him and daylight.

It was very damp, however, and he found he had to breathe much harder to get the same oxygen he was used to. The only air source was from the outhouse hole, he assumed, so he had to be mindful not to stay down here too long.

He crawled ahead and thought he could see the end of the tunnel about twenty yards away. The sooner he was out of here, the better.

He stopped and flashed the torch around the sides of the tunnel again. He could see something hanging from the wood members about ten feet ahead. He moved towards it, a little faster, as he felt his breathing getting worse. It was a large leather case, zipped up along one side. Jack took it down from the wall and unzipped it. He held the light over the open case.

Inside, wrapped up in plastic, were two guns. One a strange looking pistol, and the other considerably larger. He recognized them right away. Both of them were Uzi weapons, the guns made famous by the Israeli military. Jack knew very little about guns, but these particular guns he had more knowledge of than the average person. Many years ago, when he had obtained a contract for his company in Bahrain in the Persian Gulf, he sent a team of fifty engineers and support staff to live in a compound there for the full three-year term of the contract. They were doing consulting work for oil exploration and drilling, but needed private security protection on the compound and while traveling to and fro. A condition of the contract was that the Bahrain Defense Force was not responsible for their safety, and that the corporation had to provide security. Even though Bahrain had the most open and successful economy in all of the Middle East, and was the most progressive with respect to women's rights and religious freedoms, Jack's advisors made it very clear that that there was still a danger of attacks by radical fundamentalists and the staff of foreign corporations like his could be at risk.

So Jack hired a U.S. security firm that already had contracts there with several American companies. They gave him the option of choosing which types of weapons their personnel would use in protecting Jack's staff. After lengthy consultation, Jack agreed on the Uzi line of weapons which were light, versatile, and deadly. He then had to file his intentions with the Bahrain Defense Force, including the types of weapons his security force would use. Finally he had to sign a "hold harmless" in favor of the Kingdom of Bahrain.

On one of his trips to that island country, Jack was given a demonstration of the Uzi capabilities. He included his senior engineers in this demonstration as well, because he wanted them and their families to feel safe and secure during their tenure in the Middle East. They were all astonished at the power of these guns. They were also given a classroom session on how the security force would protect the staff, and the various features of the Uzi guns. In essence, they had to have some basic idea of how to use the guns if their bodyguards were injured or killed in an attack, and they were forced to pick up the weapons and defend themselves.

So, Jack knew exactly what he was looking at in these plastic wrappings.

He carefully unwrapped the guns and took each one out and examined it. They both looked in mint condition, as if they had never been used. Each had the safety engaged and both had full magazines in the grips. The pistol itself was the latest of the Uzi innovations, introduced in the late nineties. It was semi-automatic only, but very accurate and compact. The larger weapon Jack recognized as the Micro Uzi, the smallest of the Uzi family of sub-machine guns, and could be used as either an automatic or semi-automatic. As an automatic, he remembered that it could fire up to an astounding 1700 rounds per minute.

He looked in the pockets of the leather case and found several replacement magazines for each gun. There was also a small bottle of machine oil. He uncapped it and squirted a few drops into the mechanisms, being careful not to use too much. Afterwards, he wondered why he had done that.

Jack then re-wrapped the guns in the plastic, zipped them into the case, and hung it back on the wall. He sat back and took a deep, labored breath. He realized full well that what he had just been handling had been the property of CIA agent Mitch Joplin, and this tunnel had been his creation. Mitch had obviously been a man who was trained for, and accustomed to, being prepared for the worst.

Jack shook his head to clear it, and continued along on his crawling journey to the end of the tunnel, which was now within easy reach. As he approached the dead end ahead, he noticed that the wall frames had changed to two-by-sixes, and the sheet metal in the ceiling had transitioned to steel deck. There were also several metal posts set in the ground as extra support for the joists in the ceiling. He guessed that he was now under the foundation of the house, and Mitch had used extra strength materials here to avoid a cave-in. Jack shuddered once more at that thought and kept going, maneuvering his way around the posts.

He reached the end and was now looking up at a nearly identical shaft to the one he had descended at the other end. There was a rope ladder secured to this shaft also. He climbed, breathing with some serious difficulty now. He could hardly wait to gulp fresh air again.

At the top, he could see that the shaft had been cut through eight inches of concrete; he was now at floor level with the house. He flashed his torch upward and saw hardwood planks, with strips of wood fastened perpendicular to the direction of the hardwood. These strips kept the planks together as one, but invisible to the floor above. Jack went to the top rung and pushed upward with his left hand. Too heavy. He then bent his head down and put his upper back into it. It moved ever so slowly upward. He noticed, for the first time, that there were under-mounted hinges on one side of the structure. Eight hardwood planks moved up as one, and each had been cut at different lengths so that it would not appear to be an obvious square or rectangle section from above. Great effort had been taken to make this trap door invisible.

Jack pushed himself off the rung and onto the floor of the room above. He took a few moments to breathe—deeply. It felt wonderful. He coughed several times as his lungs began to clear.

He looked around. He recognized it as the passageway that connected the main house to the tower section. He carefully closed the trap door, stood up, and looked down at it.

Now that he knew it existed, he could see the signs that it was a trap door. The fitting of the boards wasn't as tight and even though the boards of the trap door had been cut at different lengths, those lengths weren't consistent with the rest of the floor. And of course, the one thing that he had noticed when he had walked through here with Kerrie a few days ago—this part of the floor had felt a bit hollow. Now he knew why.

There was also a large knothole that he hadn't noticed before. A couple of fingers could use this "handle" to lift the trap door up from floor level. He tried it. Yep, heavy, but it allowed the door to be raised a couple of inches so that an entire hand or two could slip under and raise it the rest of the way.

All in all, the disguise would work if you didn't know what to look for. It had fooled him before when he was up here above the tunnel with Kerrie. Which was exactly the effect that Mitch had been trying to achieve—against whoever.

Jack had the eerie feeling that the group of people that Mitch had been trying to be safe from—perhaps the ones who finally murdered him—were the same ones that he, Mule, and his friends had been terrorized by.

Chapter 21

Kerrie stomped her feet on the kitchen floor. Like a woman possessed, she made a beeline for the hallway and did the same thing; then the living room, dining room, and each bedroom on the main floor. She seemed to be trying to cover virtually every square inch of each plank.

"I think that was the only tunnel," Jack said gently. Since he had reappeared out of the tunnel and shown her the opening from the house, Kerrie had been on a mission. "I don't think you need to worry about any others."

She was pacing back and forth now in the kitchen, while Jack sat sipping his coffee. "Sit down, Kerrie, we need to talk."

She plopped herself down in a chair, and rested her chin on her closed fists. "I don't know if I want to talk about this," Kerrie replied. "This is all just too nuts."

Jack leaned over and soothingly rubbed her shoulder. "I don't want to scare you, but trust me—it gets nuttier."

She shook off his touch, clearly not in the mood for being calmed down. "I haven't even shown you the attic yet. Maybe you'll understand how I feel when you see it."

"Why, what's up in the attic?"

She shoved her chair back and jumped to her feet. "C'mon, I'll show you."

Jack followed Kerrie up to the second floor. She pulled down the staircase from the attic trap door. They both climbed up and Kerrie turned on the light.

Jack was looking at a shrine. In a daze, he walked over and examined the uniforms and the scuba equipment, and stared in awe at the collection of medals hanging in the cabinet on the wall. He touched the spear gun gingerly. A screeching sound disturbed his concentration. He turned around and saw that Kerrie had opened up the lid of a trunk sitting on the floor. She pulled out a few transparent plastic bubble wrappings with guns inside that Jack didn't recognize. In, fact a couple of them were so abstract he wasn't even sure they were guns. But they all indeed looked very deadly to him. Some of them made the Uzi weapons in the tunnel look like water guns in comparison.

Jack leaned over the trunk. Numerous weapons were in the same kind of bubble wrapping. Kerrie dropped the guns back inside and slammed the lid shut. Then without a word, she started back down the stairs. Jack took one last glance around the eerie attic, turned out the light, and followed. Neither of them said anything until they were back in the kitchen.

Kerrie sighed. "See what I mean?"

Jack poured each of them stiff bourbons. Today he figured he could handle one of these.

"What do you make of all this? How do you really feel about it? Be honest with me."

She looked at him thoughtfully, took a swig of her drink, and then another. There was silence for at least a minute as Kerrie stared down at her glass. Then she looked straight into Jack's eyes and said, "I feel like I want to sell this place, that's how I feel right now."

"But you've put so much into it, and it's beautiful."

"It feels like it's not my place. I feel like this is not my life. This is not what I expected to feel after the years I've spent working on this project, but it feels like I could easily walk away from it. In fact, it feels haunted."

"Too many memories here to remind you, Kerrie. You need to get rid of them. All that stuff up in the attic could be put into storage, or returned to the military which would be the safest thing to do. And the tunnel, we can just fill it in at both ends. I can do it for you. Remember I told you I'm an engineer?"

"You're a petrochemical engineer, Jack. What are you going to do, fill the tunnel with oil?"

They both chuckled at that comment. It was good for Jack to see her smile a bit. She was getting over the shock of the tunnel discovery, slowly but surely. Talking about the tunnel and the attic was probably helping her. Someone else was sharing her anxiety.

"Kerrie, can I tell you a few things that have been going on since our first phone conversation?"

"Are you going to tell me you went for counseling after my barrage of foul mouthed insults?"

"I probably should have. Sometimes I think I do need counseling. But seriously, are you okay with me sharing a few things with you—about Mule, and some stuff that has happened? Are you up to it?"

"Let me fill my glass. Something tells me I'm going to need it." She poured some more bourbon in her glass, and then in Jack's.

Jack took a deep breath, a sip of the sweet liquid, then began. He told her everything: the attempted dognappings, the impersonations, the assault on Heather, Josh, and their dog Buster, the police intervention with Mule examining him for drugs, the harassment at the border, the attempted rape of Meagan after the chip was removed, and last but not least, the death of the wannabe rapist.

Kerrie was silent for the full hour that it took Jack to tell his story. She stared at him, spellbound, until the last part.

"I read about that poor vet in the paper. That was you?" she asked him, her eyes wide.

"Yes, but it was accidental. I kicked him, sure, and hard, but he hit his head on the desk. That was what killed him. The coroner and the police were satisfied."

"Thank God you were able to help her. The world is a better place with people like that guy dead." Kerrie rubbed Jack's hand to reassure him.

Jack was relieved. He was afraid she would think of him as some kind of monster.

"And he had no fingerprints? How is that possible?" she exclaimed, as she turned her hands palms up and examined her fingers.

"Surgeons can remove them, and I'm betting all of those Canadian assailants had the same surgical fingertips. No prints were found at any of the scenes."

"Unbelievable. Where is the microchip now?"

"I have it in a safe place with my belongings," Jack replied, as he stretched his legs out and rested them on the chair next to him.

"This is all just too surreal," Kerrie whispered. She got up and started pacing the kitchen again.

"What is beyond the shadow of a doubt, Kerrie, is that all of this started happening after I talked to you the first time over the phone. Your phone must have been tapped, not mine, because I had the alarm company check my entire house. There is no way anyone would have known about the chip in Mule's shoulder unless I told them, or you told them. At first, I actually thought you might be trying to get your dog back. But I quickly discarded that as things began to escalate and seemed to be so brazen and slick."

"They've definitely been listening in on me, Jack, whoever "they" are. Some strange things have been happening to me too, so it looks like I'm the common denominator."

Jack raised his eyebrows and looked at her questioningly. "Tell me."

She told him about the assault by the phony inspector Jim, and her neighbor Bob saving her, "Presto," and the "Otserp" message from the lost cell phone, and Joe the doughnut-loving phony carpenter.

Jack felt his heart pumping as he listened. "And all this happened after my first phone call to you?" Jack asked.

"Yes. So you see, it had to have been my phone. How could that creep have known to pose as a building inspector, and how would the carpenter guy have known that I had phoned Lake Carpentry to have the railing repaired? They must have been listening in."

A thought suddenly occurred to Jack. "Describe these guys to me."

She did, in great detail.

Jack nodded, and clenched his teeth. "That phony building inspector matches the description of the guy who attacked Meagan—almost bang on. You were lucky you had Bob."

Kerrie nodded and asked softly. "What's going on?"

"I don't know, but one thing's certain—it's all about that chip." Jack was silent for a couple of minutes as he pondered the latest shocking information. He and Kerrie had been going through almost the same hell, and didn't know it. He was relieved that they were now friends and could put their heads together on this.

"We know that your dad was CIA, and I'm betting that he was part of a special elite unit called the Special Activities Division, otherwise known as SAD."

He then outlined to Kerrie what he had uncovered in his research on the CIA—that SAD was a special unit that apparently operated without restrictions, and seemingly above the law. He explained how their activities were apparently always covert and probably a lot of times without the knowledge of the top administrative officials in the U.S.A.

"You mean they carried out assassinations and things like that?"

"Yes, I'm betting they did. I'm sure with all good intentions, if such a thing is possible. Perhaps the most fearsome dictators in the world have fallen victims to SAD's talents. And some of the worst, most oppressive governments have probably been put out to pasture from the efforts of these folks, through orchestrated coups. There's a lot that goes on, I'm sure, that we just don't know about. It's easy for us to judge with our own moral virtues, but perhaps the world has been a better place because of brave guys like your dad." Nothing could change how disturbing all of this was, but Jack wanted to do his best to help Kerrie feel better about her father. He put the best spin on it that he could.

Kerrie stared at Jack and seemed to be trying to absorb what he had just said. Then she got up and poured both of them another shot of bourbon. Jack thought the bourbon was starting to taste a lot better, the more he had.

"I'm no longer naïve about my father. I'm beginning to accept what it was he did. The things you're saying just confirm my worst fears. The truth of the matter is, my dad was brutal and obviously had to be. He was also a patriot, I'm sure, and you're right, we're probably all a lot safer because of men like him. I agree with you on that, and that's what I'll keep in my mind for the rest of my life. I'm glad I don't know the specifics of what he did. I'm glad he sheltered me and my mom from that."

"I would expect he didn't have much choice in the matter either," Jack commented.

"Maybe so. Some things are just better not known to the American people, I guess, so we can all sleep at night. I wonder how many times we've been in danger and never knew it, and guys like my dad had to shoulder all of the worry and risk themselves." Kerrie's words were beginning to slur a bit.

"You should continue to think of your dad that way. I'll bet he was a fine man."

Kerrie winced at Jack's words. "He was, but you know, he was very troubled and even more secretive than usual during the last few of years of his life. And that didn't stop when he retired. It seemed to get worse."

"The way he died, he definitely had something on his mind that he wanted to share," Jack said. "Something he felt would only be listened to if he went public."

"Do you think it was some criminal enterprise or terrorist cell he uncovered?"

"I doubt it. In his position, even as a retired agent, he would have relayed that to the proper authorities. He knew the channels better than anyone. I think your dad had a secret that he couldn't live with and he felt he had to force people to listen. He must have felt he had no one to turn to."

"It makes sense," Kerrie said softly. "What could that secret be?"

"I don't know, but I think he had a back-up plan—Mule, his treasured dog. And I don't think the dog's name is an accident. His name is a clue unto itself. He was carrying something—he was a "beast of burden" so to speak—

and typical of a donkey, was just doing a job. And typical of a drug mule, was just carrying something to be recovered later. I think your dad was trying to give you a clue when he named that dog 'Mule' That's what I think."

Kerrie was hanging on to every word Jack spoke. Her mouth was half open and her hands were clasped together tight. He knew he had her attention and he didn't want to lose it. With the number of drinks she had consumed, he knew that might only be a matter of time. Jack took another sip of his drink and continued. "But I think your dad was also being very careful. He knew that if it came to the point that the dog would have to give up its cargo to solve the mystery, he would have already failed and most likely be dead. Mule must have been his contingency plan, and a deliberately vague one."

Kerrie gazed down at Mule sitting by her feet, probably viewing her former pet in a new light now.

"Obviously your dad had no guarantee that you would ever discover the chip. So the secret, whatever it is, could have been sealed forever. He must have figured that he needed something in reserve though, even if it was possible that it might never be discovered. And let's face it—it's a fluke that it was discovered. You lost the dog, I adopted the dog, my natural curiosity caused me to check its history. Pure fluke."

"But why would someone be listening in on me? How would they have known something like this "fluke" could arise?" Kerrie asked as she got to her feet and started pacing again, a little wobbly this time.

"I don't know. I'm just theorizing here with all of this, but maybe because of how your dad died and that he wanted to tell the world something, they figured you were worth watching." Jack reached out from his chair and steadied Kerrie as she wobbled by. "Whoa girl—take it easy. No more bourbon for you." Kerrie pushed his hand away and made a circle motion with her hand, indicating for him to continue talking.

"Okay, perhaps they were worried that you might know something. Maybe they've been listening in on you ever since your father died, just to be safe. Then, lo and behold, I call you out of the blue."

"This is giving me goose bumps." Kerrie shivered, and folded one arm across the other.

"I know. It's kind of overwhelming, isn't it? But it's good that we're talking about it. We've both been going through similar scary experiences, but we would have never known how similar if we hadn't shared with each other."

"I guess we're tied together by our little friend Mule here." Kerrie reached down and petted his head, as he lay sleeping at her feet.

Jack jumped up. "We'd better check your phones."

"Good idea," Kerrie agreed. "Let's do a check of the entire house as well. I don't think we know what to look for, but we should just keep our eyes open for anything that seems out of place."

They both went to work, taking the casings off the phones, examining light fixtures and vent openings, exploring underneath furniture and all over paintings and frames. Jack checked the electrical panel in the basement and the telephone line at its entry point into the house. After a couple of hours they were satisfied that nothing foreign had been placed in the house. And Jack noticed that the activity seemed to have worn off Kerrie's buzz.

"Just for good measure Kerrie, we can always get an alarm company to come in here and scan for bugs. I'm glad I got them to do that at my house."

"All this is good Jack—it's good that we checked—but you know, these days tapping phones can be done remotely by authorities who have access to telecommunications systems. If your theory is right, and it is the CIA harassing us, they have the power and the capability to listen in anywhere, anytime, to anyone—particularly now after 9/11."

"You're right. I think I watch too many movies." Jack laughed. "But I feel better anyway that we checked around."

"So, back to the tunnel, you think it was meant to be an escape hatch?" Kerrie asked.

"Yes. It's a panic tunnel. I think your dad went to a lot of trouble to give himself some options if he needed them. He was obviously afraid for his own safety and, considering what he did for a living, for good reason."

"And the stuff in the attic—nothing relevant?"

"I don't think so. I think those were just souvenirs of his secret life. Your friend Bob was probably right on that point. I think your dad wanted to remember that what he did had some meaning. Those medals alone probably gave him some solace, and should for you too. I saved an incredible pile of stuff from my business career, and I don't know why, or what I'm going to do with it all. But I know I'll never be able to bring myself to throw that stuff out. I guess it just helps remind me that I was important at one time. Sounds vain, doesn't it?"

Kerrie shook her head. "Everyone needs to feel important—nothing wrong with trying to hang on to that feeling. I must admit though, I get spooked when I go up there and look at his things. Feels like I should be saluting when I see those medals. He must have been quite the hero."

They both sat in silence for a few seconds. Then Kerrie asked, "So, what message is on that microchip?"

Jack was glad she asked. She was much calmer after their discussions. Now her own curiosity was driving her. And the bourbon was wearing off. Jack asked her for a pen and paper, and he began to write. He knew the message off by heart after all the times he had stared at it. When he had finished, he shoved the paper over to Kerrie. She read aloud: *"Tell her she has the key to her Soul within her reach. Fifteen, Fifteen, Fourteen."* She flicked the end of her pen up and down in nervous thought. Finally after a couple of minutes she looked up. "I don't see anything in this message that would cause me to question it. It tells me nothing. It's nonsense."

Jack needed her to focus, and he had to try to be patient. "Remember, it's probably written in some kind of code. Your dad wouldn't want to make the message obvious for anyone who came across this chip by mistake, just like I've done."

Kerrie looked at it again. "Jack, maybe he was just leaving me philosophical advice for the future. Perhaps in this one symbolic message, he was telling me I should give up my legal career and open this bed and breakfast for the good of my soul."

"Could be, but I don't think so. Think harder. Is there anything, a word or two, that rings a bell with you?"

"No, nothing at all. I think we've been terrorized over nothing. We should post this message out in the front yard, invite the CIA to look at it to their heart's content, and ask them to just leave us the hell alone!"

Jack ignored her outburst, and pressed further. "What about the numbers, Kerrie? Do they have any meaning at all?"

Kerrie studied them again, and began doodling with her pen. "Nope, they don't mean anything to me."

Jack wouldn't let her off the hook. He persisted some more. "Okay, how about the word 'Soul?' It fits in with the message, but I'm wondering why the first letter is capitalized. That seems to be deliberate. Do you know someone who had the last name 'Soul?'"

Kerrie pulled the paper back toward her and studied it once again. Suddenly her face went white, and both her eyelids started twitching. She put her hands to her face and Jack could hear her breathing heavily through her fingers.

She pulled her hands away and looked into his eyes. She was shaking and her voice trembled with excitement.

"Oh my God, Jack, I think I know what that word is supposed to mean!"

Chapter 22

The CIA headquarters' building in Langley, Virginia, is an impressive structure, brazenly signifying the sheer power of the organization. It is, quite simply, massive. The Agency seal in the floor of the lobby is the quintessential symbol a visitor sees, made more than familiar by countless movies. The seal is granite inlaid, measuring sixteen feet across. Before stepping on that seal, which most would avoid doing anyway out of respect, superstition, or both, a visitor would probably make a visit to the CIA Memorial on the north wall. There are in excess of eighty black stars engraved on that wall, each one representing a member of the CIA who has died in the line of duty. There is also a glass case at this site, containing the Book of Honor. This book contains the same number of black stars but only about fifty names. The missing thirty-plus names are still classified.

The Agency was established in 1947 by the CIA Act. This act made the CIA the successor to the OSS, or Office of Strategic Services, formed during the Second World War. The CIA was given the primary function of collecting and analyzing information for advice to lawmakers. The Act specifically stated that the CIA would have "no police or law enforcement functions either at home or abroad."

"Langley" is often used to refer to the CIA instead of actually saying "CIA," as the two terms have become almost synonomous. Ironically, Langley doesn't even really exist anymore, as it was absorbed long ago into McLean, part of Fairfax County.

Basically, the Langley area is a bedroom community for Washington, D.C., and of course the headquarters for the CIA. There isn't much else, except a high school that stubbornly and proudly kept the Langley name.

Most people would be shocked at the picturesque land that surrounds the CIA Headquarters—parkland and forests, offering pure peace and solitude. They would ponder that such scenery seems to be a total contradiction to the violence and secrecy that the CIA has become notorious for. The paradox is stark, and more than one visitor has probably commented over the years that the surrounding acres of property controlled by the CIA headquarters is a tragic waste of beauty.

The outer structure of the headquarters building contains a copper grid that serves to shield the building against electronic eavesdropping. Once inside, one would observe the curved tunnels connecting various areas of the complex. These curves weren't designed for aesthetic reasons; they further protect the hushed discussions taking place inside from external listening devices.

The construction of the massive complex was substantially completed by 1961, but full occupancy by spies and handlers was delayed a bit due to, ironically and perhaps fittingly, an infestation of rats and mice.

The headquarters of all the divisions of the CIA are housed in this Langley facility, and there are many divisions—so many that they overlap in their duties at times. There are "branches" across the nation, some with the unabashed masthead "Central Intelligence Agency" on the lobby directories. Other branches are a bit more discreet, masquerading as legitimate businesses—the words "importers and exporters" usually being a dead giveaway.

In foreign countries, the CIA generally operates their branches out of embassy or consulate offices. In those facilities, their operatives are usually labeled as "diplomats" or other benign titles, and are afforded diplomatic immunity of which they take full advantage. One of the most powerful and controversial divisions of the CIA is the National Clandestine Service, or NCS. Its most free-spirited and secretive operation, the Special Activities Division, or SAD, has its headquarters on the third floor, down the hall from NCS.

Many meetings take place on this floor, and none of them are the "rally the troops" type that private sector employees would be accustomed to. There aren't any pats on the back, no "Good job Harvey!" Leaders are seldom seen mixing with their staff, and there are no such mantras as "management by wandering around," or "customer relationship management." There are no massive staff meetings updating everyone on quarterly results, or congratulating everyone for a successful year. There really are no successful years on this floor, at least not of the type that can be celebrated. No decent human being would celebrate what this division does.

Human Resource experts spend virtually no time worrying about whether employees are happy in their jobs. That isn't important. What is important is how psychologically fit employees are, and whether or not they are on the verge of nervous collapse. How they talk to each other and what they talk about are also important topics. Consequently, training in discretion, rules of engagement, secrecy, and security are commonplace sessions. It doesn't matter whether a person is a file clerk, secretary, or entry-level agent. All are treated in the same cold, efficient, clinical way. It is rare to see anyone smile on this floor, and rare to see a manager's door open.

All employees understand that the CIA is serious business. If they want morning rah-rah sessions, they could always go work at Walmart. Expectations from CIA staff started off low, and stayed low. This is not the place to work if you want to be molly-coddled, or motivated by recognition and encouragement. Those perks are non-existent.

A meeting was just about to commence on the third floor, and it wasn't going to be a pleasant one. However, none are ever pleasant anyway so it's really just a matter of the degree of unpleasantry.

Jim Wingate, the Assistant Director of NCS and the man in charge of SAD, had just taken a seat in the office of his boss, Grant Baker, the Director of NCS. Both of these men were thirty-year veterans of the CIA and had known each other way back in the military. They were generally cordial to one another, but were also, and had always been, competitors. In short, Jim resented having to report to Grant, and Grant feared that Jim would do anything to get his job. There was always tension, but particularly today.

"Do you want a coffee or anything?" Grant asked.

"Just a bottled water if you have some," Jim replied tersely.

Grant reached behind his desk and opened the small bar fridge. He threw Jim a bottle, then rolled his chair back and put his hands behind his head. Grant Baker was a big guy, around 6'2", and weighing well over 250 lbs. He was all muscle and very few people had the nerve to cross him. If he had a drawback, it was delegation. He did too much of it.

Jim Wingate was small, but most were small compared to Grant. At 5'8", Jim was underwhelming. And he weighed only 160 lbs. soaking wet, but that didn't mean he couldn't handle himself. He was more than capable of out-foxing Grant if it came down to a hand-to-hand confrontation. He was about the same age, but much faster and more agile.

"So, what's the status on that little surveillance project you're overseeing in Montana?" Grant asked.

"Didn't you read my last report?" Jim retorted.

"Yeah, I did. Give me your appraisal of where we are in ten words or less."

"We're in good shape. Only a couple of loose ends left."

"Really?" Grant challenged.

"Yes, really. Why are you asking?"

Grant leaned forward over his desk and glared at Jim. "We have a major security breach, and I mean major," Grant said through gritted teeth.

Jim swallowed hard and sat up straight in his chair. "I'm not following you," Jim managed to bravely spit out.

"Well, follow this then. Agent Mitch Joplin's vault box contains nothing but garbage."

"Garbage?"

"Yes, garbage. Joke assignment documentation, fake film. Are you aware that Agent Joplin once investigated a spitting incident at Central High? Or that he had to bring in Mickey Mouse for questioning in a suspected assassination plot against Goofy? And that his leverage film shows him riding the carousel at Disney World and then hoisting the attendant up over his shoulders?"

"You're joking, right?" Jim was trying hard to remain calm and in control.

Grant slammed the palm of his hand down on his desk. "No, I'm not joking, but Mitch certainly was along with whoever helped him."

"You and I are the only ones who can grant access to those vaults," Jim said.

"Yes, isn't that interesting? When was the last time you checked Mitch's vault box?"

"I've never checked it."

Grant raised his eyebrows. "Never?"

"No, he retired in December of 2001, if I recall, and I didn't take over this position until late 2002. So I would have had no reason to check—he was long gone. The last access to the vault box would have been by my predecessor on the day Mitch retired. Protocol is clear: the last item in the box is supposed to be the signed confidentiality letter that is obtained on the final day of service."

"Don't talk to me about protocol, you little weasel. I created most of it!" Grant yelled.

Jim's face turned beet red, and he folded his arms over his chest. "My point is there was no need to check his vault box again. And I wasn't even in charge when he retired," Jim clarified in as calm a tone as he could muster.

"Did you not think to check his box after we had to take him out? Did that not trigger a red flag of caution?"

"No, why would it? We eliminated him. The vault boxes are as secure as Fort Knox. Why would I bother to check the box of a dead agent?"

"You make me sick, you little weasel. A little initiative on your part would have gone a long way. And obviously the boxes were not as secure as you thought."

"Don't call me 'weasel.' I'm asking you politely. And you of all people, with all the years we've known each other, should be well aware that initiative has never been a problem for me. Do I need to walk you down memory lane?"

"Save your whining for someone who cares. Take it home to your wife."

Jim took a deep breath. "How did you happen to look in Mitch's box before it was burned?"

Grant clenched his fists. "As you know, we purge dead agents' boxes every year at this same time."

"Yes, I'm aware of that. Six full years after an agent's death, the box is removed and the contents incinerated."

"Correct. And I personally oversee the purge to ensure that the agent assigned to do the job does not look through any of the contents," Grant added.

"Yes. So?"

"Yesterday was purge day. There were three agents who died in early 2003, and those boxes were removed under my supervision. They were loaded onto a cart and the clumsy prick smashed the cart into the doorframe of the vault room. The contents of all three agents spilled onto the floor. I ordered him out of the room while I picked up the mess. That's when I discovered the joke data that was in Mitch's box."

"Holy shit! Lucky for us the guy was clumsy!"

"We don't have much luck going for us here. However, you're right. It's better we know than not know. The way I see it, somehow the box was emptied and replaced with this crap. Once it was burned, no one would have been the wiser. This clumsy little accident with the cart changed all that."

"Mitch went to a lot of trouble to give us phony data, when just a bunch of paper and a blank video would have done the trick," Jim said.

"Sure, well if you had known Mitch personally, you wouldn't be surprised by that. He always planned for contingencies. He must have figured that in the slight chance the contents were read before burning, deception discovered, he could give us the finger and have a good laugh from the grave."

Jim nodded. "So, our problem is twofold. First, how did Mitch gain access to the vault room, and the answer to that will tell us if we have a serious security problem going forward. Second, where are the contents of the box?"

"Exactly. This is very serious indeed. I don't have to tell you what was contained in that box. You were briefed on the most recent assignments that Mitch had been attached to, and particularly his last one. Certain documentation for those assignments was in that box."

Grant took a deep breath and continued. "In addition, his old leverage video is earth-shattering footage to say the least. Mitch's leverage was done while he was young and officially still in the military, but in reality an agent with the CIA undercover as military. In fact, SAD hadn't even been born at that time, but we still obtained leverage for important operatives. Mitch was identified early in his military career as an incredibly intelligent and resourceful candidate, so he was recruited. Christ, it was so long ago his leverage footage was filmed on eight millimeter and converted later to VHS. I can't tell you what was on that video. It's 'need to know' only. But trust me, even though it's old, it's explosive," Grant emphasized, banging his fist into his palm.

"How would you like to proceed on this?" Jim asked respectfully.

"We have to get the contents of that vault box at any cost, and find out who knows about those contents. Also, we need to know how access was gained. You're SAD, you don't need instructions from me nor do I have to spell out the rules of engagement. Do what you and your team do best. This is a crisis if ever there was one. And we'll keep this between you and me for now. I'm not kicking it upstairs just yet; it will cause a panic. Let's just clean it."

Jim nodded and got up from his chair. Nothing else needed to be said. Before Jim opened the office door to leave, Grant did add one last thing. "Jim, I'm sorry for calling you a weasel."

Jim nodded and managed a thin smile. "And I'm sorry for wanting to rip your throat out."

Chapter 23

Jack felt the adrenaline surging through his veins. The look on Kerrie's face was one he hadn't seen before—awareness, almost an awakening. He looked at her, waiting patiently for her to explain what she meant.

"I need some water."

Jack got up quickly and got her some ice and a glass of filtered water. Water was a good idea, he thought. They'd each had too much bourbon, but particularly Kerrie, and he needed her to be sharp.

"Okay, Kerrie, what do you think that word means?"

She took a deep breath, and exhaled slowly. "I can't be sure, but I think it pertains to a little inside joke my dad and I had. That's what occurred to me as soon as you suggested that it could be someone's name."

"Do you know someone named 'Soul'?"

"No, not exactly. I know someone who *looks* like someone named 'Soul.'"

"Okay, I'm listening. Take your time."

"Do you remember that old T.V. series, 'Starsky and Hutch?'"

"For sure. I used to watch it all the time. It was great. I remember that hot Ford Torino they zoomed around in."

"Well, it was in re-runs when I watched it. I must have been about twelve or thirteen, so in the eighties anyway. I had such a crush on the actor who played Hutch. His name was David Soul. The other guy was cute too, but I didn't care for him too much. But David Soul, oh my God, I used to dream about him. I swear that's the only reason I watched the show. My dad got such a kick out of it, he teased me about it all the time."

"I don't see the connection," Jack said impatiently.

"Bear with me. Dad had a colleague and good friend who would come around once in a while. He had a daughter about my age, and we'd play together outside while my dad and him visited inside. His name was Noah Hendridge, and I almost fainted when I first met him. Even though he was a bit older, he was the spitting image of David Soul. He even sounded like him. I don't think I was too good at hiding my swooning. My dad thought it was so funny, and I think Noah did too. His daughter thought I was nuts; she didn't see the resemblance at all, or pretended not to. I think she thought it was weird that I was swooning over her dad."

Jack looked at her thoughtfully, and began processing what this might mean.

"He was a very clever man, and very charming. He would spend a lot of time talking with me after he and dad were finished their business, and I always appreciated that. I needed the extra support because my mom died in '85 and it was a tough time for me. My dad was never quite sure how to support me, but Noah had the compassionate touch. I think my dad knew that and he encouraged Noah to talk with me. We became close. I looked to him as an uncle. And I idolized him because he looked like David Soul!"

Jack was finding it hard to hide his excitement. This revelation gave the first real meaning to the clue. He took a big gulp of his water. "I'm astonished Kerrie. The fact that your dad might have remembered that as something only you, he and Noah would know about. Using that as a clue would keep it from anyone else."

"Well, I'm only speculating here. That's the only significance I can think of."

"So, is Noah still alive?"

"As far as I know. The last time I saw him was at dad's funeral. He looked good then, but he has to be in his early seventies now if he's still alive."

"Did he work for the CIA too?"

"After what I now know about dad's work, I'm guessing that he must have. I know that they traveled together on business sometimes, and they consulted with each other quite a bit. It would be naïve to think that Noah wasn't a part of all that."

"Does anything else in the phrase seem clearer now that you might know what that word means?" Jack asked.

Kerrie looked at the piece of paper again, and shook her head.

"No, the rest of it is a blank to me. I don't think I have any other choice but to phone Noah."

"Be careful. We don't want to share too much about this with anyone. Your dad intended this for you. I don't know who we can really trust."

"I will only tell him there's a strange phrase and some numbers, and a clue that triggered my call to him. However, don't you think that if my dad deliberately left a clue that would lead me to Noah, he would have been signaling for me to trust him?"

"Okay, good point. But no details. We can't trust the phones any longer. We should actually use a phone booth, but his phone could be tapped at his end so even that's not safe…I sound paranoid, don't I?"

"Yes, you do, but I don't blame you. We'll use a phone booth and decide what to do after that."

"You sound better, Kerrie; not as upset."

"I'm not upset anymore. I feel energized now. Perhaps it's the bourbon, but I feel empowered, after feeling I had no control before. I think there's something we need to find out, and this message from the chip somehow makes me feel closer to my father. Strange, huh? But I still don't want to go crawling around in tunnels though!"

"I won't make you do that." Jack chuckled. "Not yet anyway. Do you have Noah's phone number?"

"I'm sure it's in with some of my dad's records. I'll find it. At least I know where he lived, so I can try to track him down that way too. I hope he's still alive." Kerrie started writing some notes to herself on a pad.

"Did he live in New York?"

She looked up. "Yes, at the funeral he told me he had an apartment in that building where John Lennon was killed, the Dakota if I recall?"

Jack felt another surge of adrenaline. "Are you serious? Christ, it costs millions to buy into that place! And I read once that the residents have a committee that approves any buyers, so no one can get in there without a majority of them agreeing. A lot of famous people live there. How was he able to swing that?"

"God, I don't know. After the surprises I've had in the last few years and months, I don't think anything would shock me anymore. Maybe the residents felt safer knowing that a retired government agent was moving in?"

"But the money!" Jack started cracking his knuckles, a nasty habit whenever he got overly excited. He had noticed that Kerrie did the same thing once in a while.

"I know, I know—it's mind-boggling. Maybe he received an inheritance?"

Jack went to the fridge for some more water. His mouth and throat were dry from getting worked up over this latest bit of information. He was astounded. It was hard to believe that government agents could be paid enough to afford a place like that. But Mitch himself didn't seem to have that kind of wealth. Sure, he left quite a bit to Kerrie and that teller at the bank, but that paled in comparison to the multi-millions it would take to buy into the Dakota.

"Let's find that phone number, Kerrie."

*****

Jim Wingate, Assistant Director of NCS, was relaxing in the back seat of his chauffeur-driven, bulletproof Lincoln Town Car, admiring the scenery as the car wound its way through the tree-lined streets of Fredricksburg, Virginia. He thought it was a very pretty town and it was little wonder that people retired here. He was only a few minutes away from meeting with his predecessor, Kevin Prentice, and he was psyching himself up for what he had to do. He was ready. His bodyguard/chauffeur was also ready.

Kevin had retired to this quaint little place in 2002, after which Jim was promoted to his position. Jim had inherited a well-run SAD division; projects were controlled properly and there were no holdover problems that weren't attended to. He was therefore very surprised when Grant told him about the possible security breach with Mitch's vault box. That was totally unexpected with an efficient guy like Kevin. Jim was going to get some answers today.

Kevin was a dedicated family man, now about seventy years of age, with a wife who still doted over him and four grown children who adored him. As if that wasn't enough for any man, Kevin also had eight grandchildren who held him up on a pedestal.

The Town Car pulled up in front of a beautiful colonial home, with a matching guest house about 100 feet from the main building. The grounds were immaculate, and it looked like Kevin had been busy in his retirement doing the things he probably had always wanted to do. Or, he paid someone to do the things he had always wanted to do. Jim knew that he could certainly afford it.

Jim and his bodyguard, Clint, got out and walked to the front door. It opened before he could even ring the bell. Kevin had obviously been watching for them.

Kevin was beaming. "Hello, Jim. It's so good to see you. This is such a nice surprise."

Jim shook his hand. "Hi, Kevin, it's nice to travel out this way. I don't usually have the time to enjoy the Virginia countryside. You remember what it's like in the trenches."

Kevin made a face. "Oh, I sure do. The best thing I ever did was to retire from that hectic pace. C'mon inside. Mary will be just thrilled to see you again."

Jim introduced Clint, and they stepped inside. Clint was a man of few words. A veteran SAD agent who thrived more on brawn than brains. He, and several others like him, served valuable roles—no longer making decisions in the field, but instead guarding those who did.

Kevin's house was like a designer's showcase—expensive furnishings and impeccable decorating. And Kevin looked good too, good for his age. Still a tough looking guy, but dressed to the nines and he actually looked younger than when he had worked at the CIA. Jim could have sworn also that the man was wearing makeup. The dark circles under his eyes that had become his trademark, had disappeared completely.

Kevin's wife Mary came running into the foyer and gave Jim a big hug. "It's been so long," she said. "You have to visit more often. Kevin was so thrilled when he got your phone call. I think he's convinced you need his help with something, and that has put a real spring in his step today!"

Jim hugged her back. He had always liked Mary, such a warm person. Kevin was a lucky man to have a wife like her. "It's good to see you too, Mary. And Kevin's right, we could use his help today. His expertise is hard to let go of." Jim's compliment put a smile on Kevin's face.

"Can I get you boys some tea?" Mary asked.

Jim shook his head. Clint stood motionless, almost at attention. "No, we'll pass on the tea, Mary. I wish this was purely a social visit, but we need to talk to Kevin privately."

Mary smiled in a knowing way. "I understand. I still remember what it was like. You boys go ahead and do your important stuff. I'll stay out of your way."

"Actually, we'd like to use the guest house. Is that okay with you, Mary?" Jim asked.

"Sure, we don't have any guests right now, so go ahead," Mary replied in her sweet singsong tone. "If you need anything, just let me know."

Jim, Clint, and Kevin headed back out the front door and strolled over to the guest house, a cute little place with its own garden and deck.

"Do you want to sit out on the deck?" Kevin asked enthusiastically. "It's such a nice day. I could get us some beers, which I'm sure you'd enjoy more than Mary's tea!"

"No, we'll go inside if that's okay with you."

"No problem." Kevin unlocked the door, and the trio walked inside.

As if on cue as soon as the door closed behind them, Clint spun Kevin around and slammed him in the gut with his closed fist. Kevin collapsed to the floor and the look on his face was one of pure shock.

Jim rammed the heel of his foot into Kevin's Adam's Apple and kept it there. "Kevin, we're going to make this real quick," he growled. "No bullshit. Clint here is my lie detector test. Every time you crap out on one of my questions, you're going to get gut-punched. And I don't have to tell you what damage that will do with each successive punch. We will leave no marks on your face, but your abdomen will feel like mush." He paused for effect. "So, are you ready for my first question?"

Kevin blustered something unintelligible. Jim knew he was ready.

"Kevin, did you help Mitch Joplin gain access to his vault box?" Jim removed his foot from Kevin's throat to allow him to answer.

Kevin put his hand up to his neck and coughed a couple of times before he answered. He looked up at Jim with a puzzled expression. "Of...course not...that's classified."

Clint grabbed Kevin under the arms and yanked him to his feet, for just a second. The next punch knocked him right back down again. Now Kevin was spitting up blood, and the sight of it made him start to sob.

"Cowboy-up, Kevin," Jim said. "We're far from finished here. Take another stab at answering my question." Jim took a casual glance at his wristwatch.

"I would...never do...such a thing." Kevin was struggling with his words while trying to catch his breath. He was laying on his side, clutching at his stomach, blood still trickling down his chin.

Clint pulled him up again. Kevin covered up his stomach area with his hands, but Clint grabbed his crotch instead and squeezed as hard as he could. Kevin gasped. Clint let go and kicked him in the groin with a force so massive Kevin was airborne for a fraction of a second. He went down once again, and this time he started to cry like a little child.

"Are you ready to tell me the truth, Kevin? We have all day," Jim rasped through clenched teeth.

"Okay...okay. I had to do it. Mitch...made me."

"You were his boss, how could he make you!" Jim put his heel back on Kevin's throat, and pushed down hard.

"He...found out...something," Kevin wheezed.

"What did he find out?" Jim shouted.

"He...had videos...of me in Thailand. With boys. He threatened...to...send them to...Mary and the kids."

Jim looked down at Kevin with disgust, and felt like he was going to puke.

"So you gave him the contents of his vault?"

"Y...yes. I had no choice." Kevin put his hands up to Jim's heel and tried to release the pressure on his throat. Jim pressed down harder.

"And you replaced the contents with that phony stuff we found in there?"

"Yes." Kevin closed his eyes, and Jim could see tears continuing to flow from under his eyelids.

"Did this happen with anyone else?"

"No…just Mitch."

"Do you realize what you've done? Have you thought at all about what was in that box? You were privy to virtually everything, so you must have been thinking something in that useless head of yours!" Jim removed his foot from Kevin's throat. "If I find out you lied to me and that you did this for anyone else, I'll come back here and kill you with my bare hands!"

"I didn't think he would do anything with it…he said he just wanted it for his own protection," whined Kevin. He began rubbing his throat, and coughed up some more blood. Jim thought he sounded relieved, probably because he heard that he wasn't going to be dying today.

"For a smart man, you're pretty stupid, Kevin," Jim said.

"I'm…sorry, Jim. I was…afraid for…for my family."

"Shut the fuck up, you self-centered pervert! You were afraid for yourself! You make me sick, you pathetic piece of shit. You took an oath. You were trusted!" Jim was in a rage now as he looked down at the man who used to be his friend, who he saw now as no more than just another disgusting pedophile.

"I know, I know. What can I do to help?" Kevin cried, with blood smearing on his shirt. He was still drooling small amounts from the gut punches.

"Nothing, nothing at all. But I've changed my mind about not leaving marks on your face. So brace yourself while Clint makes sure that no little boy, especially your own grandsons, will ever want to look at you again," Jim snarled as he motioned to Clint.

All Kevin could do was symbolically protect his face with his hands, as Clint loomed over him larger than life.

Chapter 24

Noah Hendridge called out to his bodyguard to answer the phone. His 4th floor apartment in New York's Dakota building was about 3,000 square feet, and he was no longer willing or able to run to answer doors or phones. In addition, he had decided long ago that it was probably safer for him not to. In this case, even though one of the phones was just a long reach away, he couldn't be bothered. That's what hired help was for.

Also, he was lounging on the couch in the den watching the Mets. He loved baseball, especially his Mets, and hated to have his games interrupted by anything.

"Sir, it's a Kerrie Joplin on the phone," his guard called from the kitchen. "Would you like me to take a message?"

Noah struggled upright on the couch and reached out for the cordless. "No, that's a call I'll take."

"Kerrie? Is that really you?" Noah asked excitedly.

"It's me, Noah. It's been so long. How have you been?"

"I'm wonderful, Kerrie, especially now hearing your voice. You've been missing in action for the last few years. Where are you calling from?"

"I'm in Montana. I've been working on a house dad left me, and I should be ready to open it up as a bed and breakfast in a few weeks."

"You've dropped out of law completely?"

"I have, Noah. I was pretty much blackballed after dad died, so work dried up for me in New York. I like my new life. It's nice to be my own boss and be living in a less hectic place."

"Like father, like daughter. You inherited your dad's independent streak."

"I probably did, which I guess can be either a good thing or a bad thing."

"Overall, it's a good thing, Kerrie. Don't be too hard on yourself, or your dad. We are who we are, right?"

"I guess you're right. By the way, who was that who answered the phone?"

"Oh, that's my man-servant, Carl. He's been with me for many years now. I'm an old man now, Kerrie, so I need help with some things."

"I'll bet you're still that dashingly handsome man I remember," Kerrie flirted. "We don't get older, Noah, we just get better."

"Tell that to my chiropractor, but thanks for the compliment. At my age a man doesn't hear those things too much anymore. So, to what do I owe the honor of your phone call, dear lady?"

"I need to ask you a couple of questions."

"Oh, Kerrie, I'm sorry. I have a call coming in on another line. Can I call you right back?"

"Sure. Sure, no problem. When will that be? I'm calling you from a phone booth and I can't stand here and fend off the hordes for too long."

"I'll get rid of whoever it is and call you right back. Give me the number, dear." Noah wrote it down and hung up.

He then leaned on Carl's arm as he pulled himself up from the couch. "I'm going to use the secure phone in the drawing room, Carl. Could you bring me some tea, please?"

"No problem, sir. Remember to use your cane." Carl went off to the kitchen, adjusting his shoulder holster as he went. He was an athletic-looking man, fifty-five years old, well paid, and loyal. Noah knew that the man would do anything to protect him. He also knew that Carl felt he owed him his life from an event many years ago when Noah had rescued him from a torture chamber in Libya. Carl had gotten his life back, but the torture had damaged his social perspective. He lived with Noah and that's all he seemed to want out of life now—to protect the man who had orchestrated his miraculous rescue.

Noah shuffled off to the drawing room with the help of his custom made, ivory-tipped cane. His right leg didn't move very well anymore. It hadn't been the same since his kneecap was crushed by the butt of a rifle when he was being interrogated in Cambodia. That was way back in 1971, and for quite a few years afterward the knee had still held up okay. Age and osteo were his new enemies. And his left foot only had one toe. Thank god it was the big one. The rest were hacked off by thugs from the Medellin drug cartel in Colombia back in the eighties. He could have sworn that Pablo Escobar himself had been hiding underneath one of the sinister black hoods, wielding a hatchet.

Luckily, some of his lady friends thought that lone toe was kind of kinky. Whenever he had an erection problem, which unfortunately was more often than not, he now had a built-in dildo; worn in a different spot than one would expect. And for that he was fortunate, or rather they were fortunate, that he had an unusually large toe.

As he hobbled towards the drawing room, he passed by his portable dialysis machine; it was a necessary part of his life now due to kidney damage in the late eighties. He painfully remembered how Noriega's Panamanian lieutenants had doubled over with laughter as they force-fed bunker fuel down his throat.

He went over to his antique 18th century colonial desk and located a key. He unlocked a cabinet in the corner of the office and pulled out a roller shelf. There was only one item secured to this shelf, a red phone. He always wanted his secure phone to be a red one, just like the purported hot line phones that connected the White House to the Kremlin. He chuckled, knowing that most times when those phones were used, the political clowns at each end really had no idea what was going on. They never really did. They were just egotistical puppets, and sadly, most of them had egos so big that they could never acknowledge, even to themselves, that they were puppets.

He had been excited to hear from Kerrie. He always looked upon Kerrie as a second daughter. He was glad that she was settled now, and she did indeed sound happy. He only wished his own daughter would pick up the phone once in a while and let him know how she was doing.

Noah knew full well how his daughter was doing, but Sheila didn't know that he knew. She also had no idea that Noah was paying half the outrageous salary she was making at a San Francisco newspaper, or how she had even landed that plum job in the first place. She couldn't know that the ridiculously cheap price she had paid for her downtown brownstone had been made possible by Noah secretly subsidizing the real price with the vendor. Or that the lottery she had won at her son's private school—three years free tuition—was really her father pulling strings with the dean, an "old friend." Noah would always watch out for his daughter. He felt it was the least he could do, since he had done virtually nothing for her for most of her childhood years. He enjoyed a faint feeling of redemption from doing these things—very faint.

Noah still hadn't met his twelve-year-old grandson, although he did have photos of him taken by his contacts. He reasoned that photos would have to suffice for now, and sadly maybe even forever.

Noah picked up the phone and dialed the phone booth number that Kerrie had given him. He didn't ponder why she was using a phone booth. He didn't have to. She obviously had something sensitive to ask him, and was smart enough to do it away from her house, and definitely smart enough not to use a cell.

He hadn't wanted her to say anything more than what she had already said. He and Carl had gone to great lengths to ensure that this apartment and its phones were bug-free, but remote tapping was still possible, and there was no way they could detect that. But, this little red phone, and the lines around the world it was routed through, was as secure as it was expensive. Worth it for the occasional peace of mind that it brought.

"Hello?"

"Hi again, Kerrie. Sorry about that. I lied, there was no other call. I didn't want you saying anything more on my regular phone, so I'm phoning you back on a safe one."

"How did you know you needed to do that? You couldn't have known what I'm about to ask you."

" I'm just a cautious man, Kerrie. Old, but still with good instincts."

"I'll say. You must also have ESP, because I do have a strange question for you."

"Go ahead Kerrie. I'll help you in any way I can."

"My dad left a coded message. At least I think it's a coded message, and it contains the word 'Soul' with the 'S' capitalized. It reminded me almost right away of that crush I had on you when I was young, because you looked like David Soul from the T.V. show, 'Starsky and Hutch.' Do you remember that?"

"How could I forget? I thought you needed glasses badly, but I was certainly flattered."

"So, since that was one prominent word in the message, my first thought was that my dad was trying to tell me to get in touch with you for help."

"I can tell you that he most definitely was, Kerrie. That's typical of a little code we used between us. If a word is capitalized like a name, then it is supposed to be a name, meaning you should first look to that name in order to go further. In this case, your dad was smart enough to know that the word 'Soul' would trigger your memory and only mean something to you, thus keeping the code safe."

"But why would he leave me this?"

"There has to be something that he wanted you to pursue. I know you probably feel that you must track this down, but my advice to you is to just leave it alone. With all due respect to your father, who I loved dearly as my best friend, he shouldn't have placed you in this position."

"Do you know of something that he wanted to tell me, Noah?"

"I have no idea, except that it's probably not something nice or he wouldn't have used a coded message."

"I feel I have an obligation now, and some strange things have been happening that perhaps I should tell you about."

"No, Kerrie. I don't want to know. You discovered in the most shocking way imaginable that your dad was a CIA agent. I'm guessing you know now that I was too, correct?"

"Yes, Noah, I did suspect that."

"Well, trust me then when I say that what your dad was trying to do on the last day of his life was wrong. I don't know what he wanted to share with the world, but he shouldn't have tried. Some things are best left alone, and in his job, with all the secrets that he knew from the years he was with the Agency, he should have respected the secrecy that he was trusted to work under. There, you have my opinion, and for your own safety, drop it."

"I can't, Noah. It's gone too far already, and I feel that the only way I can remain safe is to find out what it is. I've already been in danger a couple of times, and I feel now that I'm at the point of no return."

"Don't say anything more. I don't want details and it's better for your own safety that I not know any details. No matter how strong or experienced a person is they can always be made to talk. Don't say anything else to me that pertains to this so-called coded message. Okay?"

"Okay. But can you at least give me some advice on how to crack it?"

Noah sighed. "Yes. Reluctantly, I'll do that, only because it's you." He paused for a few moments. Then he took a deep breath and continued. "Your dad and I sometimes needed our own little secret dialogues. We ignored the standardized CIA codes because they could easily be broken by our analysts. Our own little code was incredibly simple—so simple that the code nerds at CIA were never able to crack it. We knew they would be looking for difficulty that didn't exist, and we were right."

"So what was it?" Kerrie asked impatiently.

"I'm getting there—bear with me. We called it the '2-2-2' code. The first '2' is that two words side by side are meant to be lumped together to create one new word, perhaps spelled differently, but run together by the tongue they would sound as one word. The second '2' is simply the next two words in the three-word main message. Those next two words can be found anywhere in the entire coded message, however, they are always separated from each other by at least one useless word. The actual message would only be three words long. The rest of the words are useless. Except for the last '2,' which are two important words that have something to do with the main three-word message; not part of the message, but they relate to the message. These two words are not necessarily side by side in the code phrase. They could be separated, but meaningful only when put together."

"I've been writing this down, Noah. I hope I've got it all. I'm going to read it back to you, okay?" She read from her notes and Noah confirmed that she hadn't missed anything. "There are also three numbers, Noah, each separated by a side slash."

"When you see numbers, think alpha. Then when you get the alpha, think numbers again," advised Noah.

"Noah, I don't know how to thank you."

"Yes you do, Kerrie. Forget everything I've told you, and just drop the whole thing. Go live your life. Let sleeping dogs lie."

"No, I can't forget about it. I'm committed to this now, and I feel strangely closer to my father now than I ever was before. He trusted me enough to give me a message. He's confiding in me, something he never did when he was alive. I have to follow it through, whatever this is. It's kind of like an obligation—hard to explain, I guess."

"You're just as stubborn as your father was. An endearing quality most times, but right now I fear for you. I don't think your dad would have wanted you to die unlocking this code."

"I'll be okay, Noah. I have a friend helping me with this, so I'm not alone. We've both been drawn into this separately, and it's gone too far already for either of us to back out now."

"You know that I've always loved you like my own daughter, Kerrie, and I'll pray for your safety. If you get into trouble and you need my help, contact me. But please be careful."

"I will, Noah, and thank you. I love you too, and I miss our chats. Maybe we can meet for lunch sometime when I'm next in New York?"

"Yes, but put this behind you first. We can't be seen together while this thing you're pursuing is going on. It would only make matters more dangerous for you, and for me too."

Noah hung up the phone, pushed in the roller shelf, and locked the cabinet. He ran his stiff fingers through his thick head of hair, and sighed with a heavy heart. He was very worried about Kerrie, and he also felt conflicted. But...he had to force himself not to get involved. He was trying so hard to be retired, and it wasn't easy at the best of times.

Carl came in with a pot of tea just as Noah was struggling back to his feet again.

"I'll have that tea out on the terrace, Carl. It's a nice day. And why don't you bring a bottle of brandy out there and join me. We can spice that tea up just the way we like it."

"That's a fine idea, sir. But let me take a peek around the perimeter first, and you make sure to strap your vest on before you go out there."

Noah looked at him wearily. "I will, Carl, I will."

*****

After Kerrie hung up the phone, she pondered Noah's last comment. She knew he wanted to help, but he also seemed to think that he could hurt matters and put them both in danger. He also seemed very concerned for her welfare, which made her start to second guess herself a bit. If a former CIA agent was concerned, how could she not pay attention to that? However, Noah also had paternal feelings towards Kerrie, so that could be the main reason for his warnings to her.

Kerrie walked back to Jack's car. He had been waiting for her in a parking lot near the phone booth. "Well?" Jack asked tentatively.

"I have something for us to work with now. He was quite helpful, although very reluctant. He sure did his best to try to talk me out of this. He was quite worried about me. And by the way, he did confirm that he had been CIA too."

"No real surprise there," Jack muttered. "I'll bet the only people close to your dad were CIA. Perhaps it's true—'misery loves company.'"

Jack drove the car out of the parking lot, and made his way to the main highway out of Kalispell. They had decided to use a phone booth here instead of Bigfork, so as not to be too close to home.

"So, was he glad to hear from you?"

"He was, but he was very cautious. Before I could tell him anything, he stopped me and called me back on what he described as a more secure phone line."

"So, he still has the tools at his fingertips by the sounds of it."

"It sounds like it, and he had some interesting tips for me about my dad's message. We'll have to sit down and try to make some sense of it when we get back home. I'm really anxious to take a stab at this."

"We'll figure it out, Kerrie. Between the two of us, I'm confident we'll come up with something that will either put us at ease once and for all, or give us some sleepless nights."

"I'm betting on the sleepless nights." Kerrie said with worry in her voice. "I don't have a good feeling about this, especially after Noah's warnings. But, like you, I certainly can't leave it alone either. I'm now probably just as obsessed as you are."

They both sat in silence for the rest of the ride back to Bigfork. Kerrie was picturing in her mind this frail old man who had once looked like a television star, a man who now lived in a multi-million dollar apartment, with a butler. If her dad had lived, is that what his world would have become? She had a hard time picturing it.

Chapter 25

Mule started growling even before the doorbell rang. He went down into his familiar hunch and crept into the hallway, expressing his disapproval as he went. "Mule, settle down, boy," Jack commanded. "It's just a visitor."

He opened the door. A short, stocky, balding man stood on the porch. "Can I help you?" Jack asked with a friendly smile.

"Is Kerrie home?" the man asked bluntly, without returning the smile.

"She is, can I tell her who's asking?"

"Yeah, just tell her it's Bob's brother. She'll know who I mean."

Jack walked back into the kitchen without inviting the man past the front screen door. Kerrie was sitting at the table organizing her notes from the conversation with Noah. Jack also had his own notes spread out all over the table. "Kerrie, you have a visitor. He says he's Bob's brother. Does that mean anything to you?"

"Oh, yes. Bob's that neighbor down the beach I told you about. He told me his brother would be house-sitting while he was away."

"Oh, that Bob. I didn't let him in yet. I suggest you talk to him on the porch, while I hide all of this stuff in case he wants to use the bathroom or something."

Kerrie walked into the front hall and nearly tripped over her own feet upon seeing the man standing on the porch. A far cry from Bob. This guy was only about 5'7", about 200 lbs., balding, and brutish looking. He appeared to be slouching sideways a bit, as if he was about to fall over. She opened the door and stepped out onto the porch.

"Hi, I'm Kerrie," she said, holding out her hand. "You're Bob Trundle's brother?"

The man shook her hand, and Kerrie could feel that the grip was exceptionally strong. Most men softened their grips when they shook hands with women, but not this guy.

"Yes, ma'am, Stan's my name. Pleased to meet you. I'm just staying down at Bob's house until he gets back. He's supposed to be home by tomorrow, so

I'll be gone after that. I should have checked on you earlier, but I've just been so busy. Sorry about that."

"No problem, Stan. It was nice of Bob to ask you to check up on me, but he worries too much. I'm doing just fine. I have a friend staying with me for a while, so that makes it much better for me."

"Well, that's good. Bob mentioned that you've had a couple of bad encounters with strangers, so he wanted me to just keep a watch out. I did keep an eye on your house as I walked the beach every day."

Kerrie thought that was a bit odd. She had never seen him, so if he had been walking the beach he must have done it at night. He didn't look like much of a walker.

"How long have you been there, Stan?"

"About ten days. That's enough peace and quiet for me. Time to get back to the big city."

"And where's that?" Kerrie asked, while her mind wandered. She was thinking about how Stan said he was too busy to check on her, but apparently wasn't too busy to walk the beach every day.

"Seattle." Stan shifted his feet nervously. He seemed uncomfortable chatting.

"That's a fair ways from here. Did you drive?"

"Yes, but I broke up the trip a bit. Paid a visit to our parents in Sandpoint along the way, so that made the drive a bit easier to take." Stan shoved his hands in his pockets, and glanced out towards the lake.

"That's a beautiful area of Idaho," Kerrie commented. "They must enjoy it there."

"Yes they do, but they're retired and it's nice and quiet for them. They nag Bob and I to visit more often, so it must get pretty boring for them. Not the life for me, that's for sure." Stan laughed, but Kerrie thought it sounded unnatural, hoarse.

She lost her attention again for a few seconds, only half listening to him go on some more about how boring retirement life must be. She didn't know what it was, but there was something strange about Stan, aside from how he looked, and it was really nagging at her. She couldn't put her finger on it. Some distant memory, almost the reverse of déjà vu. Not the feeling of something she had done before, but more like something in the deep recesses of her mind trying to claw its way out. She shook her head to clear it. Probably just thinking of too many things at once.

"...and I consult on large construction projects in Seattle as well," Stan finished.

"That's interesting," Kerrie recovered, not recalling a thing that he'd said.

"Well, if you're okay, I'll be on my way. Here's my cell phone number in case you want to get in touch. I'm not using Bob's house phone while I'm here. I don't want him bogged down with a lot of phone messages that aren't for him after I leave."

"That's okay. I have Bob's number. I might just leave a message for him to call me when he returns."

"Nice meeting you, Kerrie." Stan shook her hand, again with far too much strength, and with a slight smile that seemed almost painful to him. Kerrie thought that whatever charm there had been in that family, it was inherited by only one of the sons.

She watched him as he walked down the porch steps and along the beach towards Bob's house. She noticed that he had an unusual gait, and realized this was the reason why he seemed to slouch to one side. It was almost as if one leg was shorter than the other, and he compensated for that with each step. Probably not that noticeable to most people, but Kerrie noticed these things. She had become a student of body language during her lawyer days.

She went back inside and locked the door. Mule had been growling under his breath in the hallway the entire time she was chatting with Stan. And he hadn't stopped yet. Kerrie knelt down and gave Mule a fluffing on his head. He seemed to smile in return. "It's okay, boy. I didn't like him either. I'm not surprised you're growling."

Back in the kitchen, Jack was bringing all of their stuff out of the cupboard and spreading it out on the table again.

"So how do you like your neighbor's brother?" he asked her.

"I don't like him at all. Talk about a cold fish. Getting a smile out of him or just a pleasant look, was like pulling teeth. And those eyes! They just bore into you and he doesn't even blink! It's hard to believe the two of them are brothers. Wait until you meet Bob and you'll see what I mean. They're total opposites."

"I can hardly wait," Jack said. "So, shall we get started on this message? The coffee's made, and my brain is on full throttle!"

"First, I promised to let you hear the voice message from that cell phone. I'm sure glad I recorded it." Kerrie pulled the personal recorder out of her purse and clicked 'play.'

"Otserp" came the message. She turned up the volume and played it again.

Jack shook his head. "Strange. It does sound like a code of some sort, or command."

Kerrie put the recorder aside. "It has to mean something. And the voice. It seems familiar, but I just can't place it."

"That's worrisome. I'm sure it will come to you eventually if it is someone you know. Let's hope that part is just your imagination."

They both sat down and went to work on the message from the microchip. Jack put blank paper and pens on the table, and placed the original message front and center.

"Let's first summarize from your notes what Noah told you about the code."

Kerrie read out the major points of the 2-2-2 code:

"(1) three sets of two words.

"(2) the core message consists of only three words.

"(3) the last set of two words does not comprise part of the core message, but relates to it. These words may be separated from each other in the original message, but are meaningful only when put side by side."

She pushed her hair behind her ears, deep in thought now. She continued reading the summary:

"(4) the first two sets of two words comprise the core message.

"(5) the first word of the core message is made up of two words, that are shown side by side, and are to be lumped together. The spelling may change once they are together—the sound of them together is what matters.

"(6) the next two words of the total three words are words that are elsewhere in the original message. They are separated in the original message by at least one useless word.

"(7) think alpha for the numbers, and then think numbers again."

"Whatever that means," Kerrie said with a final sigh. They each stared at Noah's points. Jack doodled on his sheet as he concentrated.

"Let's focus on the message right now, and the numbers later."

"Okay," Kerrie agreed. "And let's rewrite the message each time we solve something. Whatever we solve gets written in capital letters. We've already solved 'Soul.'"

Jack re-wrote the message: *"Tell her she has the key to her SOUL within her reach. 15/15/14"*

When he finished writing, he said, "Let's start with your fifth point." He tapped her notes with his pen. "Two words that sound like something different if they are lumped together. This should be the easy part if they're supposed to be side by side."

They both began making the sounds as they ran each side-by-side word together. Kerrie made the first suggestion. "'Her' and 'the' run together sound like 'hearth.'"

"Yes, you're right. A fireplace hearth perhaps? Right here in the house maybe?"

They stared at their papers for a few more minutes.

Kerrie jumped in again. "'To' and 'her' put together sound like 'tour,'" she said with excitement in her voice.

Jack started making a list of the possibilities.

Suddenly Kerrie shouted, "Christ, it's staring right at us! The first two words: 'Tell' and 'her' sound like 'Teller!'"

Jack's head snapped up. "Jesus, that fits! That poor teller in the bank!"

Kerrie squeezed her arms together across her chest. "I'm getting goose-bumps and I never get goose-bumps!"

"Me too! But I think that's the right combination. '*Teller* she has the key to her Soul within her reach,'" Jack said quickly. He wrote down the new word "Teller" in capital letters at the beginning of the message.

"Wait," Jack said. "If that is the intended combination, then your dad planned this for quite some time. Mule's chip was implanted in late 2002, and your dad died in February, 2003. So he knew that a teller would be involved at the time he implanted Mule, which means your dad's actions that day were not done on impulse."

Kerrie nodded and Jack could see her eyes were getting wet. "We need two more words that make up the core message of three words. According to your notes here, the next two words will be separated by at least one useless word," Jack summarized.

Kerrie stared at the page.

After a few minutes Jack jumped up from his chair. "'Has' and 'key!' No other two words make sense. Kerrie, I think the core message is 'Teller has key.'"

Kerrie's eyes seemed to expand to about twice their size. "Shit, Jack, I think you're right. He must have given her a key at some point and he's trying to tell us that."

"He's trying to tell *you* that Kerrie. No one else was supposed to be involved. All along I've assumed the message on the chip was directed at you, the 'Tell her' part. But he wasn't referring to you as the 'her,' because he assumed you would still have Mule. I should have realized that the 'Tell her' part made no sense since Mule was supposed to still be with you. He wasn't directing words of wisdom at you, because if that were the case he would have used 'You' or 'Kerrie' in the message, not 'Tell her.' I feel so stupid now."

"Hey, I didn't see it either," Kerrie consoled.

"Sure, but I've been sitting on this message for months. For you it's only been a short time," Jack whined.

"On second thought, you're right. You should feel stupid!" Kerrie laughed.

Jack went over to her and gave her a big hug. "We're making progress. Don't you feel the rush?"

"I do, but we're not finished yet."

"You're right. Let's go back to it." Jack sat down again and caught his breath. He was feeling the adrenaline and it felt darn good. It reminded him of how he felt when he concluded large business deals, or reported a successful quarter to the board of directors. God, he missed that rush.

He picked up his pen and wrote: "TELLER she HAS the KEY to her SOUL within her reach."

Kerrie flicked her pen in thought. "All we need now are the two words that relate to the core message. They're not supposed to be part of the message, but are important to the message. They are not necessarily side by side, but meaningful when put together…"

Jack jumped in. "There are only seven words left. If we remove those supporting words of no real import such as 'she,' 'the,' 'to,' 'her,' and 'her,' we're left with two words that might have some kind of meaning: 'within' and 'reach.' I think those are the two words we need to focus on. Put together, we could have 'within reach' or 'reach within.' Any thoughts Kerrie?"

Kerrie nodded. "They have to be the two words. How they fit in, I just don't know. Nothing is jumping out at me."

"Could it mean that the teller has the key 'within reach,' or does she have to 'reach within' something to get the key?" Jack pondered.

"Maybe, but if the teller has the key, wouldn't she know it? Seems redundant."

"True, makes sense. These words must have some other meaning."

They stared at the page for a few more minutes, and now both of them were furiously clicking their pens.

"Let's leave those last words for now, Kerrie. Why don't we take a stab at the numbers."

"Okay, maybe something will come to us later." She looked at her summary. "Let's see, Noah said to think alpha when we see numbers, and then when we get the alpha, think numbers. I don't know if I understand that. It seems contradictory, like we'd just be going around in circles. Numbers to alpha, alpha to numbers."

Jack started counting on his fingers while reciting the alphabet. "The letter 'N' is the fourteenth letter, and 'O' is the fifteenth." He wrote down O/O/N.

"What on earth does this tell us? Then revert back to 15/15/14? I don't get it."

Jack knelt down on the floor and wrestled with Mule for a few minutes. "Okay, boy, you've brought us this far. Can you take us any further?" Mule responded by grabbing his arm lightly in his mouth as he usually did, challenging Jack to give up.

Jack suddenly jumped to his feet and announced, "I think I've got it!" Kerrie clasped her hands together in anticipation.

"We shouldn't be thinking the numerical numbers, we should be thinking the alpha version of the numbers. In other words, what number's spelling begins with 'O'?"

"'One!'" Kerrie nearly shouted. "I see where you're going. And 'N' would be 'Nine.' So instead of 15/15/14 or O/O/N, we would have 1/1/9."

"Exactly," Jack replied.

Kerrie started prancing around the kitchen. She was clearly excited. "Jack, we may have solved this! We may have actually done it!" She gave Jack a big kiss on the cheek, which he promptly returned.

"Don't get too excited, Kerrie. 'O' could also mean 'One Hundred' or 'One Hundred and Three,' etc. 'N' could stand for 'Ninety', and so on, and so on."

"Thanks a lot, Mr. Wet Blanket. I was just starting to feel like we'd really accomplished something here." Kerrie sighed.

"I think we have. I'm just playing devil's advocate. Logically those would be the numbers. Remember, Noah said the code they used between them was a simple one. The logical choice would be the first ones in the numerical scale. Anything higher I think would require a different code, because the combinations would be enormous. I think the numbers Mitch wanted you to know are 1/1/9. So let's agree on that for now, okay?"

"I like the way you think, Jack. You know, after I talked with Noah I thought right away that I might have a chance at solving all of this with a smart guy like you in my corner. I was right."

"No need to thank me. We've been thrown into this together, so we'll see it through together."

Kerrie smiled warmly at him, then just as quickly changed to a grimace. "Now that we may know the real numbers, what good are they? What the hell do they mean? I guess we shouldn't be rejoicing too fast here."

"We also don't know what those last two words mean either," Jack reminded her.

"There's still work to be done and serious thinking to do." Jack continued on. "You know, my first thought on those numbers would be that instead of being separated by slashes, they are actually one number: '119,' which could be the number to a safety deposit box. Ties in nicely with the teller holding a key. Could be a box right in that same bank."

"We won't know until we talk to that teller." Kerrie suddenly slapped herself on the side of her head. "Jack, we don't even know which teller dad meant. There were two tellers he used that day in the bank—one as a hostage wearing the bomb vest, and the other one he used to deliver a note outside to the police."

"Think calmly, Kerrie. He was your dad and you know his heart. Which girl do you think he would have entrusted a key to?"

"Thanks, Jack. You're being logical again. I like that. Yes, he would definitely use the one who wore the bomb vest. He had known her for several months and according to the teller, they chatted all the time and had become close. And I told you how he left her $200,000 in his will. Yes, she's the logical one, and the obvious one."

"What's her name?"

Kerrie looked at him blankly. "I don't recall, but I know where I can lay my hands on it real quick."

Kerrie ran over to the file cabinet kept in a corner of the kitchen. She yanked out the will documents and scanned down the pages using her finger as a guide.

"Connie Reynolds. And I also have her phone number and New York address." Kerrie looked over at Jack and couldn't help feeling swept away by his confident smile. "Okay, smarty pants, where do we go from here?" she asked with a girlish grin on her face.

"We go to New York."

Chapter 26

The alarm clock went off shaking her out of a deep, dreamless sleep. She rolled out of bed and fumbled to turn it off, checking the time as she did. It was 3:00 in the afternoon, and her room was as dark as night. She had purchased blackout blinds a couple of years ago and they worked wonders.

She dragged herself to the bathroom and splashed water on her face, fearfully taking a peek in the mirror. Disappointed as usual, she opened a can of face cream and rubbed it carefully under her eyes. No matter how much cream she used, those dark rings wouldn't disappear. Her complexion had taken on a pasty look—no color, no life. Her hair, which used to be perfectly coiffed, was a mess. It was clean, of course, as she showered daily, but it had lost its glow. There was no longer any style to it. It just kind of hung there, without purpose other than to cover her scalp. It used to frame her face and bounce as she walked. She remembered that. And small gray hairs were struggling to make their debut amongst the auburn strands. Not good, she thought—at twenty-nine years old she shouldn't be seeing these.

She took solace in her figure. She worked out at home, as she had plenty of time on her hands. She found that the exercise really helped to relieve the stress as well as cope with her demons. At least during the time that she was huffing and puffing.

She walked over to the window and opened one of the blinds. Outside she could see children playing ball in the street, and her neighbor across the way had a barbecue going. She knew that if she went outside she would smell it, but that probably wasn't going to happen—not today. Maybe tomorrow or the next day, but not today. She needed a few days in advance to prepare herself for that kind of adventure. Connie realized that she hadn't been outside for a week now. For most people that thought would be abhorrent, but for Connie Reynolds a single week was somewhat of a triumph. She had actually come a long way, in her mind. Her longest stretch without stepping outside had been four months, and she had gradually been getting better over the years. At least she thought so anyway. Her brother John didn't agree, and neither did her shrink.

But she had to do this on her own time. Only she knew how she felt. She knew it wasn't rational, but neither were the events that had made her this way.

She put on a gray and black jogging suit, and headed down the hall to the kitchen. Too early for dinner, she thought, despite the barbecue guy across the street who seemed to think differently. Instead she popped some bread into the toaster. Connie was glad she had cleaned the house this morning. She didn't have the energy now, and never really did later in the day, which was the reverse of when she had worked at the NY State Security Bank. She had always enjoyed the afternoon and evening shifts. That was when her adrenaline seemed to be at its highest. Not anymore. Even in the mornings she had to drag herself. Now she was tired all day, but worse after lunch.

Connie's day generally meant sleeping in until 9:00, doing some stuff around the house, eating lunch, going to sleep again until 3:00, working on the computer for a few hours, eating dinner, watching some T.V., then going to bed around 11:00. It would start all over again the next day—waking up in the morning feeling exhausted and not being able to remember one single dream, which in Connie's view meant she hadn't dreamed anything. Her shrink disagreed with this too. He said she wasn't allowing those dreams to rise to the surface. They were locked deep in her subconscious, and one day they would unlock and she would start to feel a whole lot better. What a load of crap, she thought.

He also told her that crying was good, at least at first. Now he seemed to be losing patience with her, because she had to admit to him that she cried every day. Never at the same time of the day; only when her thoughts got the better of her. It could be at night, over breakfast, when she was watching T.V. There was no rhyme or reason. She just cried. Which perhaps helped to explain the dark circles and puffiness under her eyes, she figured.

Connie sat down at her computer and went to work. This was the perfect job for her: web design. She had studied a couple of years ago, online of course, and had obtained her diploma. She had five clients now. Not an onerous amount of work, but enough to keep her busy and pay most of the bills. Most importantly though, this job allowed her to work from home. Three of her clients she hadn't even met yet, which suited her just fine.

She installed an alarm system in the house about five years ago after she had returned from the "home" as she referred to it—really a nut house. She had spent almost a year there, having voluntarily checked herself in after suffering a nervous breakdown. The alarm gave her a sense of security that she desperately needed. She had even thought about buying a dog, but then she would have to take it out for a walk every day. Not possible.

When she was released from the home, far from cured, her shrink gave her a diagnosis of severe depression compounded by agoraphobia. In essence, she was sad most of the time for reasons she thought she knew, and she had an extreme fear of being outside in areas unfamiliar or in areas where she had little control. Social interaction was tough for her, and being in wide open spaces was frightening. Being in crowds of people made her feel like she was suffocating. Her shrink had stressed to her that the depression and agoraphobia were side effect mental illnesses resulting from an overall umbrella ailment of PTSD, or Post Traumatic Stress Disorder. He felt quite confident that that condition had triggered the other two, and if not dealt with once and for all, it would trigger more.

She popped two pills daily: Lexapro for depression; and another whose name she could never pronounce, to be taken at moments of extreme anxiety, which meant basically every day. That pill worked very fast and served to calm down her heartbeat, a heartbeat that would race so fast it seemed it would jump right through her chest. The trouble was that these meds, in her mind at least, had become a crutch. Instead of naturally fighting the feelings that overcame her from time to time, she was so afraid of the fear that she would pop the pill before it got that bad. She hated those feelings when they did come: dry mouth, racing heartbeat, dizzy, a fog covering her eyes, and weak limbs, almost to the point of collapse. Her shrink said this was her Sympathetic Nerve System acting to protect her from a perceived fear. She had asked him to explain how on earth those bodily reactions could possibly be protecting her when they seemed to be destroying her. His response was that they originated from the subconscious and both the subconscious and the Sympathetic Nerve System were irrational. She was caught in a vicious circle.

She looked up from her computer and gave her eyes a rest. Gazing around the living room, she couldn't help but feel comforted. This was, after all, the home that she and John had been raised in—her safe haven. Everything was familiar. She wished that John still lived with her. She had bought out his share of the house a couple of years ago, allowing him to buy a little condo in Queens. She knew he had to move on with his own life, and living with a basket case like her would be a downer. She understood, but she missed him terribly.

She was proud of her little brother—actually not so little anymore at twenty-two. He had moved on from the shocking death of their parents, and had truly become a man. And a decent one at that. He had graduated from the fire academy two years ago, and was now a proud member of the FDNY. He told her that he had made his mind up to join the fire department way back when he was seventeen years old. Not only was it an excellent profession, but John told Connie that this was his way of dealing with the death of their parents. He was so proud of the hero firefighters and police officers who had marched up the dozens of flights of stairs, each carrying about sixty pounds of equipment, to save complete strangers in the World Trade Center. Only to be thanklessly crushed. He thought that those men and women were the ultimate heroes. So that was John's way of giving back. Connie was proud of him, but at the same time ashamed of herself. What was she doing to "give back?" Crying every day, that's what she was doing. And hiding. But she couldn't help it. Much as she wanted to, she couldn't.

Connie had always thought that she was tougher than this. What had happened to her mind? Why did she break down, unable to deal? The brain was a very sophisticated organ, her shrink had told her, and sometimes it defied logic. She would have to be patient. It would sort itself out in its own good time, and sometimes in a very irrational way in response to something very innocuous. Those thoughts gave Connie a shred of hope at least. She certainly didn't want to be this way, despite the doubts of some friends who couldn't understand why she didn't just "shake it off." She couldn't just shake it off. She didn't know what to shake. It was too complex. Sure, there were clearly events in her life that had piled up on her to the point where it had become overwhelming. A human being could only take so much.

The 9/11 passing of her parents was the first shock to her system, and her ideals of what life was supposed to be like and who was supposed to be in it. Then the bank incident with Mitch—the event that pushed her over the cliff. There wasn't a day that went by when Connie didn't think of the violent deaths her parents had experienced, and the bizarre end of Mitch's life. She knew this wasn't healthy and her shrink told her it wasn't healthy, but she just couldn't control her thoughts. They always popped back up again despite her best efforts to distract herself.

For a while, she thought she had been handling the deaths of her parents pretty well. She had gone to counseling and no longer felt that terrible anger that had been eating her up. She still couldn't shake the horrible image of her parents tumbling down 1200 ft. along with the collapsing walls and floors of the World Trade Center. But at least she had reached the point where she no longer wished for public hangings of a mostly innocent and decent Arab population. Then came that day at the bank, and Mitch's death.

She knew she had loved Mitch. Her shrink told her it was a replacement love for the loss of her father. Connie didn't care what it was—she knew she had loved him.

That's what made it so bad. Why had he chosen her to help him end his life? Why not scare the bejesus out of some other teller? And why did he have to die? Why did he bring himself to that point? What was so important that he had to say on live television, that was worth risking his life for?

She could still see in her mind's eye the almost perfect circle in Mitch's forehead, and the death stare in his eyes. She could still see that red button pop up, and worse than that, hear it. Then nothing. She had braced herself to be blown to smithereens, but nothing. Then to find out that the bomb was a dud, and the gun was unloaded. She was convinced he had committed "suicide by police." She only found out that day by watching the live feed on the closed circuit monitors in the bank that Mitch had been CIA. She had asked him months before what he had done for a living, but he had never answered her. Well, on February 13, 2003, she finally got her answer.

Despite the extreme shock of that day, as the years went by and especially after she was released from the home, the day itself had become blurry. She only remembered certain things about it, mainly images from towards the end of the ordeal. The most shocking parts, she surmised. Her shrink had another explanation for that, but it was just more mumbo-jumbo, more crap.

Just as strange, even though she felt strong affection for Mitch, whether as a father figure or something else, she couldn't remember everything about their relationship. It had only lasted a few months and he had made a huge impact on her, but her memory was a bit vague. She thought this was weird. She felt the fond feelings and strong bond like it was yesterday, but some specifics had faded.

Her shrink asked her to compare this to how many things she could actually remember about her life before she was four years old. He asked her if she could remember the day she started remembering things as a child. Well, of course she couldn't, no one could. But he made the good point that despite that, she still loved her parents as a child, so some serious bonding had taken place when she was very young even though her mind wouldn't allow her to remember specifics.

The same thing had occurred with Mitch. They had bonded. She felt it.

For some reason that only her brain knew, she wasn't able to retrieve some of those memories.

Connie started to cry. A typical day for her, she thought. Round and round in circles, and getting nowhere. She forced herself to head on down to her dusty unfinished basement to get some blank CDs to burn for a client.

At the bottom of the stairs her head turned automatically toward the old wardrobe in the corner, as it did every time she came down here. She knew there was only one set of garments stored in that wardrobe, and she hadn't opened those cupboard doors in six years. Her shrink told her that some day she would, and that day would be a pivotal day in her recovery. Even more pivotal for her if she burned those clothes. That would mean closure and a new beginning.

The clothes she had worn the day of the bank incident were zipped up in a plastic garment bag and hanging in that old cupboard. She had put them there when she got home from the police station that day, February 13, 2003. She hadn't looked at them since. And she couldn't bring herself to destroy them either. Why, she had no idea. It seemed silly to her, and for those clothes it was a state of limbo. Her shrink said they were a symbol. Whatever. And worse than keeping them all these years, she hadn't even laundered them, as one thing she did remember vividly was emptying her bladder right there in the bank lobby in front of Mitch and everyone.

She carried her blank CDs upstairs and was about to insert one in her computer when there was a knock at the door. She cautiously approached and looked through the peephole. There on the porch was the one person she always wanted to see, her little brother John.

She opened the door and the two of them hugged as if they hadn't seen each other in a year. "Sis, I've really missed you. How are you feeling today?"

"Johnny, you saw me a couple of days ago. How could you miss me that much?" Connie beamed. "And I'm feeling just fine, thank you." She lied, as usual.

"Well, I've still missed you."

Connie ruffled his hair like she had always done when he was a boy. And just like back then, John quickly smoothed it back down again.

"C'mon in," Connie said. "We can enjoy a glass of wine together."

"Love to, but I go on duty in about an hour so I can't stay long. I just stopped by to make sure you're okay, and, oh yeah, to make a proposition to you."

"Johnny, you can't marry me, I'm your sister!"

"Very funny. How would you like to double-date with me and Heidi this Saturday?"

"Who is it this time?" Connie asked warily.

John playfully tapped his index finger on the tip of Connie's nose. "A cousin of Heidi's. I've met him. He's a great guy: handsome, friendly, has a great sense of humor," John said eagerly.

Connie turned her back on John and walked into the kitchen. "He'd have to have a great sense of humor to go out with me. One look at me and he would probably die laughing," she called out behind her.

John didn't let her walk away. He followed her into the kitchen. "That's not true and you know it. You're still hot in my opinion. You just need a little sprucing up here and there."

Connie turned back to John and made a face. "A little? More like I would need a total makeover like they do on those T.V. shows."

"Well, maybe this guy could arrange that for you. He's a television producer."

"Always trying to make the sale, aren't you?" Connie replied with a grim look on her face. "I'm starting to feel dizzy just thinking about going on a date, John. I'm not ready yet."

"Sis, I've introduced you to some real nice men over the years. The last time you went on a date was my graduation from Fire College. I matched you up then too with a real nice guy, and you barely looked at him the whole night. That was two long years ago. You really need to treat yourself to some fun outside of this house. And this cousin of Heidi's is a great talker, so you wouldn't even really need to talk all that much."

Connie looked at John with eyes that betrayed her sadness. She loved her little brother so much, and they had been through such tragedies together. She could actually feel the twinkle in her eyes every time she gazed into his. He came over several times a week to see her, and she always made roast beef and Yorkshire pudding for him every Sunday. He was the only person in her life, aside from her shrink, and without her brother she knew her life would probably just end. She stretched up on her tiptoes and gave her strong young brother a kiss on the cheek. He looked at her hopefully, waiting for the answer he so desperately wanted to hear.

"No," Connie said sadly, dropping her gaze to the floor.

Chapter 27

It had been a couple of days since the brainstorming session, and their emotions were running high. Excitement and curiosity were building to a fever pitch.

Today was Tuesday, and Jack suggested to Kerrie that they try to get flights out on Monday. Kerrie wanted to leave earlier than that, but Jack convinced her they needed more time. They had to get in touch with that bank teller Connie Reynolds first, and make sure she was open to their visit. She might not be, and then what would they do.

Secondly, they had to make sure that Mule would be cared for by the right person while they were gone. If they couldn't find anyone, they would need to search out a kennel. So Kerrie relented, reluctantly. Monday it was.

This morning they would drive into Kalispell once again and make their phone calls. First to Connie, then to the airline. They did not want to make either of those calls from the house. Kerrie also insisted that they do a bit of shopping while there. She needed a new outfit if she was going to New York.

They arrived at their favorite phone booth before noon, one of the only phone booths in town. Jack produced his phone card but he suggested that she do the talking. At least Kerrie had met Connie before, and there was a connection there from the past that Connie might warm up to. But he urged her to keep it short, simple, and non-threatening. Something like, "I'd like to visit with you while I'm in New York." Not a good idea to say that she was going to New York specifically to visit her. Kerrie agreed. They couldn't take a chance on alarming Connie in any way, and blow an opportunity to meet with her face to face.

Kerrie put in the codes from Jack's calling card and dialed the number she had found in her legal file. Jack went back to the car and waited for her.

"Hello?"

"Hi, is this Connie Reynolds?"

"Yes."

"Connie, you might not remember me. My name is Kerrie Joplin. We met about six years ago at my dad's funeral and again at the reading of the will."

There was a pause. Then finally, "Yes, I remember you very clearly. You were kind to me. How could I forget?"

"That's nice of you to say, Connie. How have you been?"

"I've been okay, thanks."

"Are you still working at the bank?"

"No."

"Oh, you made a career change?"

"Sort of. I work from my home now."

"That must be nice and relaxing."

"Yes, it can be."

Kerrie was reaching for words to say. Connie was speaking in a monotone and didn't seem all that eager to talk. Kerrie felt like she was talking to an electronic message.

"Connie, I live in Montana now, but I'm going to be in New York next Monday for a few days. I'll be traveling with a friend of mine who wants to see the big city sights. Would you care to join us for dinner one night?"

Connie answered quickly. "No, not really, but thanks for asking."

Kerrie didn't expect this. She figured a nice dinner would be an non-threatening social setting that Connie would easily agree to.

"How about getting together for a coffee? Just to chat?"

"No, I don't think that would be a good idea."

Kerrie was running out of options, so she decided to just put her on the spot like she used to do with witnesses in the courtroom. She knew Jack wouldn't approve, but she had to take a chance.

"Connie, I need to see you. It's a matter of great importance. Something my father left for both of us to talk about."

The line went completely silent. Then Kerrie could hear breathing, lightly at first, then heavier and heavier.

"Connie, are you okay?"

She could hear a clunking noise as if the phone had been dropped. Then footsteps. Kerrie waited, perplexed. She looked out to the car where Jack was watching her. She raised her arms up in a helpless gesture. "Connie? Are you there? Talk to me, please." Silence at the other end. Kerrie could see that Jack had left the car and was on his way over to the booth. She wasn't looking forward to explaining to him how she had scared the phone out of Connie's hand.

Kerrie waited on the phone for about a minute before she began to hear sounds again. Once more, breathing, but shallow and rapid this time. "I'm... back. S-sorry about that. I...started g-gagging on something I ate. Had to... run and, and...get some water." Connie was having trouble getting her words out, and stuttering. This was odd.

"Are you okay now?" Kerrie asked, real concern in her voice.

"Yes, I...think so."

"Are you sure? Do you want to rest while I call for help?"

"No, no. I'll be j-just f-fine."

"Good." Kerrie paused for a second, unsure about whether or not she wanted to continue pursuing this. Jack was standing in the open door of the booth now, gesturing for her to push it along.

Despite her misgivings, she decided to continue. "So what do you say, Connie? Could I perhaps come by your house for a quick visit if you can't get out to meet me? I know that working from home must tie you to the house sometimes, so I understand if you can't leave."

"Oh, okay then. Do you have...the, the...address?"

"Are you still living at the same address as 6 years ago?" Kerrie gave Jack the thumbs-up sign.

"Yes...I am."

"Great, then I already have the address. Would 2:00 Wednesday afternoon work for you?" Kerrie decided it would be better for them if they met her on Wednesday, due to jet lag and the long trip on Monday. Tuesday would be a good day to relax, get their game plan together and collect their thoughts a bit.

"No, no...you'll have to make it 3:30 if...you...you don't mind. I'm b-busy in the early afternoons."

"Okay, 3:30 it is, Connie. I look forward to seeing you then. And thanks very much for..." Kerrie heard a click as the phone at the other end was disconnected. No goodbye from Connie. After hanging up, Kerrie let out a deep breath.

"So are we in?" Jack asked with a worried look on his face.

"I think we are. She'll see us on Wednesday afternoon. But it was tough going. She didn't want to join us for dinner or even coffee. Connie's working from home now. She left the bank." Kerrie ran her fingers through her long hair. She felt drained after that phone call. And a bit bewildered.

"Did she say if it was due to what happened to her in 2003?"

"She didn't say and I wasn't about to pry," Kerrie said. "Jack, at first, this girl sounded stoned. There was no expression in her voice, kind of robotic. Then she seemed to clam up when I mentioned my father, and it sounded like she was having trouble breathing. She dropped the phone and then just disappeared for a couple of minutes. When she came back, the breathing was a bit better but she started stuttering. I hope she's okay."

"Maybe you just caught her at a bad time, or it might also be a bittersweet surprise for her to hear from you after all these years. She's probably been trying to forget the shock of watching Mitch die right in front of her eyes, and then here you are on the phone, his daughter, out of the blue."

Kerrie frowned, and pulled her coat up around her neck. She felt oddly chilled after that conversation with Connie, "Could be, but my women's intuition tells me it's more than that."

"I think you women put far too much faith in that intuition stuff," Jack teased, as he made an abracadabra motion with his hands.

"And you guys put far too much faith in gut feel. Say what you want, I'll take my intuition any day over your macho gut feel shit," Kerrie retorted, a grin on her face.

"Well," Jack said, laughing, while rubbing his tummy. "Right now my gut feel tells me it's lunchtime. What do you say to that? My treat."

"As I meant to say, gut feel is a good thing!" Kerrie laughed back.

They walked up to the intersection of Main and E. Idaho in the downtown area, and crossed over to a large barbecue restaurant. Jack felt like having a good old western burger, and Kerrie had a hankering for some ribs. A lot of other people had the same idea, as the place was crowded. Luckily the hostess was able to find them a table, but at the very back. That suited them just fine. It gave them a bit more privacy. They were only seated for about a minute when Jack could see Kerrie's eyes light up as she looked past him. He turned around and saw a tall dark-haired guy heading right toward their table.

"Kerrie, what a nice surprise to see you here!"

"Bob, welcome back! What brings you to the big city?" She jumped up and gave him a hug. Jack noticed that he returned it eagerly.

"Well, when I got back from my trip, I noticed that my cupboards were pretty empty. I needed to do some major re-stocking and Bigfork is far too expensive for that! I decided it was far cheaper to drive a little further."

"You got that right. Bob, I'd like you to meet my friend from Canada. Jack Howser, this is Bob Trundle. I've told you a lot about him."

Jack got up and shook his hand. He noticed that Bob had a grip of iron, or perhaps he was just being a bit territorial and trying to send Jack a message. He could see that Bob was beaming pretty brightly around Kerrie. "Sit down, Bob, join us," Jack said in the most neighborly voice he could muster.

"No, I can't. I just finished my lunch as a matter of fact. Try the cedar plank salmon. It's great."

"Bob, we met your brother Stan. He came by to check on me. That was awfully nice of you to ask him to do that," Kerrie said, rubbing his shoulder affectionately.

"No problem. I was worried about you after all that you'd gone through. I assume you've filled Jack in on your ordeals?" He nodded briefly towards Jack, but Jack could tell he was doing it only to be polite. Bob's eyes were boring into Kerrie, and he certainly hadn't moved his arm when she was rubbing his shoulder.

"Oh yes, and I told him all about your heroics as well." She smiled coyly at him.

Bob lowered his eyes to the floor. "Well, that was nothing. I was just in the right place at the right time."

"You're far too modest, Bob. In any event, nice to have you back."

Jack thought he was going to throw up.

"Nice to be back, and get caught up on my sleep. It's been a busy two weeks."

"Bob, I was going to ask you something when we got back home, so I'll do it now instead. Would you be able to look after Jack's dog Mule for us for about a week? We're going to New York on Monday, and you look like someone who would get along well with dogs. He would be good company for you too."

"Why are you going to New York?" Bob asked.

"Do some sightseeing. Jack has only been there a couple of times before, and of course it's my hometown. So I can show him around a bit."

"Great time of the year to go. The weather should be nice there right now," Bob commented. "But Kerrie, I'll have to say no to the dog-sitting. I'm going to be busy with some short trips myself, overnight stuff, over the next few weeks."

"Oh, that's too bad. Well, we'll find someone else. You were my first choice though," Kerrie said. Jack could tell she was disappointed.

"I'm flattered. Maybe next time. Look, I have to run. Nice meeting you, Jack." He leaned over the table and shook Jack's hand again. Jack noticed that the iron grip hadn't lost any of its potency during the last five minutes.

"Maybe the three of us can have a beer on that lovely porch of yours, Kerrie, before you guys fly east?" Bob asked eagerly.

"Sounds great. We'll try to squeeze that in." Kerrie gave him a big hug.

Even bigger than her first one, Jack noticed with chagrin.

As Bob made his way toward the front exit, Kerrie looked at Jack expectantly. "Well?"

"Well what?"

"Do you like him?"

"Hard to tell by two shakes of the hand, but he does seem like a nice guy. Although I hear that tall, dark, and handsome stuff is getting to be a bit passé these days." Jack said with a sly grin on his face.

Kerrie playfully punched him on the shoulder. "Does that mean women shouldn't bother looking at you anymore, Jack?"

"Flattery will get you everywhere," Jack replied, laughing.

"Too bad he can't look after Mule. I'll ask one of my other neighbors, Sarah. She already has a dog, but I'm sure she wouldn't mind another one for a little while. She just loves animals."

"I'd like to meet her. Let's arrange that when we get back." Jack took a sip of his coffee and then looked up at Kerrie. She had a puzzled expression on her face as she stared towards the door that Bob had just exited a few minutes ago.

"Penny for your thoughts?"

Kerrie suddenly snapped out of her trance and smiled at Jack. "No real earth-shattering thoughts going on here, Jack. I was watching a guy who just left the restaurant. It was kind of weird—he walked with the same kind of gait that Bob's brother had. You know, kind of leaning to one side and a shuffling kind of movement with his one leg?"

"Maybe it was Bob's brother. Maybe the two of them were having lunch together."

"No, no. This guy left a couple of minutes after Bob and he didn't look like Stan. He was short and stocky, but had long blonde hair underneath a cowboy hat. Stan was bald."

Their orders came—as planned, a burger for Jack and ribs for Kerrie. Neither of them felt like taking Bob up on his salmon recommendation. They ate in silence. Jack thought about their trip to New York and where it might lead them.

Jack was also thinking about how he would feel when he saw Ground Zero again. He had mixed feelings about that. It would be nice to see it looking civilized compared to the last time he had been there. He had flown down for a memorial service for the known victims a few weeks after 9/11, after things cooled down, and the site looked nightmarish. It had been heart-wrenching for him to see the devastation and know that Susan had perished there. He had even summoned up the courage to accompany the memorial organizers down close to the promenade area where her body had been found. He would always remember that moment. There were other families there with him as well. All of them, like him, had lost someone who had jumped and this spot on the promenade was an emotional one for all of them. They couldn't get very close due to the debris field, but they could see and feel the spot, and that was enough.

If he would see the site this weekend, cleaned up and getting ready for the public to enjoy again, he suspected that it would probably leave him empty. How could anyone find peace and joy at such a place?

They made one more visit to the phone booth, this time to book their flights. They managed to get the last two seats on Northwest out of Helena, leaving at 8:20 a.m. on Monday. It would be a long trip, as the plane would make a stop at Minneapolis/St. Paul. Jack didn't care. This ordeal was already several months long, so what were a few more hours to get some answers, finally, hopefully.

Before heading back to the car, Kerrie made good on her promise to buy a new outfit—a nice black pantsuit which Jack thought looked stunning with her long blonde hair. That done, they started their drive back to Bigfork, feeling relieved that most of the important details were out of the way. Now to meet the neighbor, Sarah, who might be looking after Mule. Jack wanted to make sure that she was good with animals. He sort of trusted Kerrie's women's intuition, but he did indeed put a lot of faith in his own gut feelings. Mule was special in ways that Jack couldn't even put into words, and he needed to know that his buddy would be happy while he was at the other end of the country.

*****

The next day Jack and Kerrie walked down to Sarah's house. They took the road instead of the beach, as she lived on a street that branched off perpendicular to and back from the lake. Mule came along for the visit. Jack wanted to see how he would relate to Sarah and the other dog in the house. As they walked along close to the back of Bob's house, they could see a gardener hard at work clearing brush from the side of the road. He was loading the branches up and throwing them into the back of a pickup truck. Mule started to growl, a growl that got louder the closer they got to the man. The man nodded to them as they passed, and it took all of Jack's strength to hold on to the leash. Mule was tugging and puffing, trying to get at the guy. "Sorry about that. He's a little ornery today," Jack said to the man.

The gardener just grinned and continued his work. He looked hot in a green lumber jacket, straw hat, and sweaty black hair tied into a ponytail. He had a scraggly beard that hung down past his Adam's apple. It was 80 degrees outside. Jack started sweating just looking at him.

Their visit with Sarah was very pleasant. A widow for several years, she had a large German shepherd as her live-in. Jack figured anyone who could handle a shepherd could handle a Border collie. She immediately bonded with Mule and he took to her right away. She had a nice home, with lots of fenced space in the backyard. It was perfect for Mule. And the shepherd was very friendly. The two dogs seemed to have no problem with each other. By the time they left, Jack was sold. Sarah would be the perfect dog-sitter.

As they made their way down the road, they could see up ahead that the gardener was just finishing up. Mule began his growling again. The man had his back to them and was walking toward his truck. Kerrie suddenly put her hand up to her mouth and gasped.

Jack looked at her, puzzled. By now he was quite familiar with that expression of hers, which was kind of cute, but it also usually meant something was very wrong.

"What's the matter, did you forget something?"

Kerrie was staring at the man up ahead as they walked. She shook her head.

"This is crazy, and I'm being silly I'm sure. I'll tell you when we get home."

Minutes later they were sitting together on the front porch. Jack clasped his hand gently over Kerrie's knee. "Okay, we're home. What did you want to tell me?"

"Promise you won't laugh. Remember that man I saw at the restaurant in Kalispell, who I thought had the same gait as Stan Trundle?"

"Yes."

"Well, I just saw another man with the same gait. Now I've seen three men with the same unusual lean and walking style in the last few days. That gardener was bang on, exactly the way Stan had walked. "

"C'mon, it's just your imagination. I didn't notice anything unusual about the way that gardener walked. He was a little on the short and heavy side, and people like that tend to waddle a bit anyway, so maybe that's what you were noticing."

"Jack, body language is what I know best next to the law. I studied it, took courses in it, and I used that skill for jury selections. It's something I always take time to observe in people. You and most people may not notice certain things that I would see right away. I'm telling you, all three walking styles were identical. Each of them walked as if one leg was a bit shorter than the other."

"Okay, I'll test you. What does my body language tell you about me?" He sat up straight, striking his best Adonis pose.

Kerrie made a display of studying him, from head to toe. "Well, that's hardly a fair test. I've gotten to know you quite well over the last few weeks. But, trying to be objective, you walk with a confident posture, not exaggerated, just slight. Enough to convey to anyone who sees you that there is very little you're afraid of. And you're probably always striving to be first, the best. You don't like to lose, and aren't accustomed to it. And you look like someone who is mischievous enough to get into trouble from time to time. How's that?"

"Well, who wouldn't want a reading like that? Of course I'm going to agree with you!"

"Quit being the devil's advocate. I know what I saw!"

"Okay, I believe you believe that. Again, I didn't notice anything but I'll defer to your powers of observation which are probably far better than mine."

"Thank you, Jack. It could be just a strange coincidence, but with what has happened to you and me separately over the last few months, and the imposters in particular that we have both come up against, the word "coincidence" doesn't sit well with me anymore. My instincts right now tell me that all three men were the same person. Why and how that could be, I couldn't hazard a guess. It's nuts to even think about."

"Women's intuition?" Jack asked, with a tease in his eyes.

"Yes, smart-ass."

Chapter 28

It was Sunday, and a picture perfect day to spend on the porch overlooking Flathead Lake. Summer visitors had now flooded the area, with water-skiers and swimmers alike taking full advantage of the hot weather. Cottagers were lounging on their docks, probably remembering how long it had taken for winter to leave. This past winter season had been one of the worst in memory for the western United States.

Jack, Kerrie, and Bob were stretched out on chaise loungers on Kerrie's covered porch, her ever-dependable cooler of beer between them. Kerrie chuckled as she listened to Jack and Bob banter back and forth about the relative merits of American beer versus Canadian beer. Jack was asserting that Canadian beer had so much more flavor and that American beer was too watered down. Bob's only argument was basically that drinking anything other than American beer was treasonous. Jack had to gently remind him that Canada did indeed have its own government and citizens were not required by law to be patriotic to the United States of America. It was all tongue-in-cheek, and both were playing it up as guys liked to do to each other. Trash talk.

Kerrie was glad to see they were hitting it off. They talked passionately to each other about baseball and football—Jack arguing how the Blue Jays of the "twofer" World Series years were the best teams ever seen; Bob making the case that the Yankees were the champs of all time, with history on their side—Babe Ruth to name just one example.

The more beer they drank, the more animated their discussions became. Mule seemed just as amused as Kerrie. Every time Jack's voice raised a notch, Mule barked as if joining in to try to make Jack's point. Every time Bob's voice raised, Mule released a muted growl. It was like he was participating in the discussion, and there was no doubt as to who's side he was on. Kerrie just sat back and listened. She knew very little about sports, but loved to hear old jocks argue. Both of them started citing their own sports achievements—Kerrie knew it was a man's civilized way of comparing penis sizes. Having a woman around probably made them want to brag even more about their athletic triumphs, events that no one could dispute of course, and guaranteed to get more distorted and exaggerated with each additional beer.

The good thing was, they teased each other and laughed about it. At their ages, although Bob was at least a decade younger than Jack, that's the way it should be. No point in their taking themselves too seriously any more.

"Kerrie, do you have any of those hotdogs left over that we could throw on the barbecue?" Jack asked with a slight slur.

Suddenly Kerrie felt hungry at the mention of hot dogs. "Yes, let me run in and get them. Are we okay for beer?"

"There's plenty in that cooler for me, but I don't know what Jack's going to drink!" Bob teased.

Jack drained the remainder of the bottle in his hand. "Well, as far as I'm concerned, any Yankee fan should have as much beer as he wants. He'll need it to get through the season!" Jack laughed mockingly. Mule barked.

"My father used to say that a Yankee fan is the only true baseball fan—because a Yankee fan stays true to the team no matter what. Look at you Blue Jays fans—the Jays win back-to-back World Series in the early nineties, then have a few losing seasons and your expensive domed stadium practically empties. Now they're winning again and the seats are filling up. What a bunch of fickle fans you Canadians are." Bob's voice rose a full octave. Mule growled.

Kerrie laughed as she made her way to the kitchen. Men loved to spar like this. She guessed it was their way of showing affection or camaraderie. As opposed to women, who loved to share how they felt about things, deeper things. Men would usually only allow their casual conversations with other men to be superficial and non-threatening. Bob talking about his father was a perfect example. Only in the context of a baseball discussion would his father even get mentioned. The 'Yankees' was about as sentimental a topic as Bob would allow, as far as his father was concerned.

As she was putting the hotdogs and buns onto a platter, she suddenly stopped what she was doing and thrust her hand over her mouth. "Oh my God," she said out loud. All of a sudden it came to her. She knew what it was that had been bothering her when she was chatting with Bob's brother. Hearing Bob mention his father brought it back to her in a rush of memory. She went into the bathroom, splashed water on her face, and noticed that her hands were shaking. "Okay," she said out loud. "Don't overreact. There's probably a good explanation." Kerrie went over in her mind that conversation with Bob from way back in January, when she had caught him walking off with her firewood. They were having coffee and doughnuts in her kitchen after she gave him a tour of the house, and he had asked her how her father had died. Kerrie remembered feeling a bit violated by that question, and he apologized and told her that his parents had died in a car accident a few years ago. He expressed empathy.

Then Kerrie fast-forwarded in her mind to the conversation she had with Stan almost two weeks ago. He told her that he had visited their parents in Sandpoint, Idaho, on the way to Montana. He even mentioned how their parents urged him and Bob to visit more often, and commented on how boring retirement must be. There had to be some mistake here, she thought. Perhaps she wasn't remembering those conversations correctly. No, that would be unusual if not impossible for her. She did recall that she had been troubled during her conversation with Stan, and just hadn't been able to put her finger on why. Now she knew. Her subconscious had been sending her smoke signals that there was a disconnect between her memory and what she was hearing from Stan.

Trivial bits of data get locked away in the brain ready for retrieval if necessary, and most of the time that stuff just sits on the shelf. However occasionally the marvelous organ called the brain quickly collates and computes what it has and what it is hearing, and lets us know if they don't match. Or if a solution exists to a problem that we just can't seem to grasp, yet the solution is sitting there dormant ready to be accessed. So many times, Kerrie remembered, she had awakened in the middle of the night with answers to troublesome courtroom questions right at the forefront of her consciousness. Yet during waking hours those answers remained elusive no matter how hard she concentrated.

Now today, her brain was giving her a rare daytime heads-up. She was determined to listen to it.

Kerrie went back to the porch with the hotdogs, buns, and beers, and turned on the barbecue. While the hotdogs were cooking, she handed out the beers. The three of them continued to chat.

During their lunch, Bob gave them tips on what to see in New York, some places of interest that Kerrie had never visited while she lived there. His favorite that he urged them to see was a haunted house in Brooklyn, apparently the spot where a group of men had conspired to overthrow the U.S. government in the 1800s. An urban legend, he told them, but perhaps it was true. All four men who had attended the meeting perished in a fire while they were drunk and asleep. The building was saved and opened up as a museum ten years ago. Spooky noises and moving objects were guaranteed to be seen by any visitor, any day of the week.

Kerrie got shivers up her back as she listened to this story, and vowed to herself not to visit that place. Jack, true to form, was clearly excited and wanted to check it out.

They all sat quietly for a good fifteen minutes, mesmerized by the shimmering lake and observing the various water activities being enjoyed by the neighboring cottagers. Jack had finally had enough watching. He suddenly jumped up and announced that he was going for a swim. He stripped off his shirt, jumped off the porch, and went running down the length of the dock, executing a perfect dive into the lake. Mule didn't let Jack enjoy this moment on his own. He was right behind him, launching himself in a dive that beat Jack's in distance by a good foot.

Kerrie thought this was the perfect time to lay the question on Bob, while Jack was not there to intervene, or more correctly, interfere with what she wanted to say. She really liked and trusted Jack, but sometimes he was a bit overbearing about which tactics they should employ. She guessed it was because he was so used to being a take-charge guy most of his life.

"Bob, when I was talking to Stan, he mentioned that your parents live in Sandpoint, Idaho. I thought you said they had been killed in a car accident."

Bob looked at her thoughtfully. She thought she saw surprise on his face for a fleeting moment. Then he gazed out at the lake, as calm as could be. It took him a few seconds to reply.

"Yes, Kerrie, our parents do live in Sandpoint. It's a long story, but the truth of the matter is I really don't think of them as my parents. I was raised by an aunt and uncle in Denver, and I came to call them Mom and Dad over the years. They were the ones who died in the car accident that I mentioned to you."

"Were you adopted by your aunt and uncle?"

"No, not legally, but they raised me nonetheless and I really didn't connect again with my real parents until after my aunt and uncle died. We're trying to have a real relationship now after all these years, but in reality it's too late. It's just polite and that's about it."

"I understand. Do you want to talk about it?"

"No, not really. It's too painful."

"Okay. Thanks for clarifying. I'm sorry to have put you on the spot like that."

"That's okay. I don't blame you for being confused. Stan was raised by our real parents, and sometimes he forgets that I don't view them the same way he does."

Kerrie was starting to feel better. Her stomach had been in her throat until she asked the question, but now it was starting to ease. She felt kind of bad now for being suspicious. Bob had clearly been distressed by her question, and was honest enough to give her a straight answer. She appreciated that, and she suddenly felt a lot closer to Bob than she had felt before. He had obviously had a troubled relationship with his biological parents, one that was difficult for him to talk about. And because of that, he and Stan had probably been estranged during their childhood years as well.

But despite feeling more at ease, something in her brain made her continue to pry. "Stan seems to have a bit of a limp when he walks. Is that my imagination?"

"No, you're not imagining things. He had polio when he was a child."

"That would have been unusual for his generation. I thought that disease was pretty much eradicated by then."

"It was, but Stan didn't get the polio vaccine. He was left exposed when he was young."

Kerrie detected some irritation from Bob at this latest question. Something in his tone. A tone she had never heard from him before. Impatience perhaps? Or maybe he didn't like prying questions the same way she didn't like them? She persisted anyway. "It's hard to believe you two are brothers. You don't look anything alike."

Bob turned his head slowly toward her. "We're half-brothers, Kerrie."

"Oh, I guess that would explain it."

Jack and Mule came up from the dock and Jack grabbed a towel off the railing. "That was wonderful. You guys should take a dip."

"I'd love to, Jack, but I have to get going. I have some errands to run in town. But this has been wonderful. I'll have you guys over to my place when you get back from New York." All of a sudden Bob seemed anxious to leave.

"That would be great. I've never even seen your place on the inside despite the many months I've known you," Kerrie responded.

"Well, I definitely have to rectify that. I hope you guys have a great trip to New York. Ciao." Bob started down the stairs.

Kerrie almost didn't want to ask her last question. She had saved it until the end, and was tempted to just put it on the shelf. She wasn't sure she wanted to hear his answer. The responses Bob had given her to the other questions were fine, and she told herself she should be satisfied. But she wasn't, not completely. The emotional side of her wanted to leave it alone, but the lawyer side of her wanted to lay on the proverbial trick question to the witness. The lawyer side won out.

She called after him. "Oh Bob, I was sorry to hear that your dad is in a wheelchair now—rheumatoid arthritis, Stan said. Is there any hope he'll improve?"

Bob looked back at her, and Kerrie noticed irritation showing again on his face. Very slight, but she saw it. She was trained to notice such things.

"No, I'm afraid he'll be in that chair for the rest of his life, Kerrie. But thanks for asking."

Bob turned and walked slowly down the beach toward his house.

*****

Jack and Kerrie both finished packing later that afternoon. Their flight was at 8:20 the next morning, and the drive to Helena was about three hours. So, allowing for delays and check-in time, they would have to leave the house around 4:00 a.m.

Jack had already taken Mule over to Sarah's, so he was nicely settled in. He seemed to like the new surroundings, particularly the fenced backyard where he could run to his heart's content. He had given Mule a big hug before he left, and received an affectionate lick on the face in return. He knew they would miss each other, not having been apart very long at all in the years they had been together.

Jack carried his suitcase down from the second floor, along with a sleek mountain knapsack which he used as his carry-on. He was glad that he no longer had to bring a stupid briefcase with him wherever he went. Those days were over.

He noticed that Kerrie had been very quiet since Bob left, and when he came into the kitchen he saw that she was sitting at the table with her head resting in her hands. She seemed troubled.

"Are you nervous about the trip?" Jack asked.

"No, not the trip. There's something else that is really bothering me, and I think I'm in denial. I want to tell you about it, but I want to make sure I'm thinking straight here first. I keep going over it and over it in my mind, but I can't get past it."

Jack sat down beside her, and held her hand. "What is it Kerrie?"

She pulled her hand free. "Give me a few minutes, Jack. I need to make a phone call first, to give someone the benefit of the doubt."

She looked up a number in her book, picked up the phone, and dialed. After a few seconds, she quickly hung up without saying a word. She looked back at Jack and made the now familiar gesture of putting her hand over her mouth. That combined with the stricken look on her face convinced Jack that something was terribly wrong.

"Kerrie, talk to me."

She ignored him and ran to her purse, pulled out her personal recorder, then ran back to the phone. She punched the re-dial button. Kerrie put her ear up to the receiver for a few seconds, then pulled her head back and put the recorder up against the phone. She hung up and sat down beside Jack.

"You just won't believe this. I've been so stupid. Listen to this." He leaned over the table as she pressed "play" on the recorder. They both listened to the first message: "Otserp." Then, the second message: "Hi, this is Bob. Leave your name and number and I'll get back to you."

Kerrie looked up at Jack and pressed "rewind." She played both messages again.

Jack started cracking his knuckles, and shifting in his chair. This was quite the surprise, one that they could both do without. "Those voices are the same."

"I'm not imagining it, am I? It is unmistakable, isn't it? I knew the voice saying 'Otserp' was familiar, but I just couldn't place it. And I still couldn't until I heard Bob's voice message just now over the phone. So, the 'Otserp' voice message must have been on his cell phone. In person, voices sound so different than they do over the phone. I had never heard Bob's voice message on his phone before until just a few minutes ago. Then I knew." Kerrie covered her eyes with her hands and started to sob.

Jack got up from his chair, went behind her and began rubbing her back. "It's okay. I didn't connect that 'Otserp' message to Bob's voice until you played his phone message either. But what possessed you to make the comparison?"

"It was purely accidental. I was actually phoning to ask him something, to get something clarified that he told me this afternoon. I didn't expect to get his voice mail."

"What were you phoning to ask him?"

"I had asked him a couple of questions today while you were swimming. It suddenly came back to me this afternoon that Bob had told me his parents had been killed in a car accident. He told me that about six months ago and I had totally forgotten it. Then when I was chatting with Stan, he said their parents were retired in Sandpoint. The contradiction didn't occur to me until today when Bob was talking to you about baseball and his father. That triggered the memory. I was shocked by the two different stories."

"Understandable. So what did you ask him?" Jack probed.

"I simply stated to him what Stan had said, and reminded him of what he himself had said. He answered fairly quickly, and in a self-assured kind of way, to the effect that he had been raised by his aunt and uncle and he always referred to them as Mom and Dad. He said they were the ones who were killed. And when I pointed out how different he and Stan looked, he said they half-brothers."

Jack nodded and encouraged her to continue. She took a deep breath.

"I was relieved by those answers, thinking I was making something out of nothing. Getting paranoid, like you. I actually felt a bit guilty. But a little voice was telling me to press on. That's when I decided I would indeed ask that final question about his dad being in a wheelchair."

"I was back from swimming when he answered that one. So what was the problem with his answer?" Jack asked, puzzled.

"That was a trick question. Stan had never said any such thing to me about his father, but of course Bob had no way of knowing that. At that point, he must have been trying to play along with whatever he thought Stan had told me. I must admit, Bob is pretty quick on his feet. He lies like a pro."

Jack could feel sweat starting to form on his brow. "So what were you phoning him back about a few minutes ago?"

"I started second-guessing myself. I actually started thinking that maybe my trick question had actually hit the truth. Maybe his dad really is in a wheelchair. I just wanted to talk to Bob again and hopefully make myself feel better. I know I just didn't want to believe what I had figured out. As I said, I was clearly in denial. Not anymore."

All of a sudden, Jack started feeling chest pains, little sharp ones jabbing at him. He knew it was stress. He used to get these on the job as well. He got up and paced around the kitchen until they settled down. This new information was clearly unsettling and ominous, and they were both feeling it. He could see it in Kerrie's face as well. She had clearly developed some affection for Bob, and trusted him. But he had been lying to her, playing her for the longest time and he lived only four houses away. She had just tripped him up. How much danger did that leave them in?

Kerrie continued. "I should have clued in a long time ago that there was something not right about Bob. The way he engineered us bumping into each other, the way he probed about my father as well as his interest from the outset in my attic. I can see it all so clearly now. The attack on me by the phony building inspector; it was all about the attic. When that creep said 'Presto,' he was really saying something like: 'Time for the next plan. She won't let me see the attic, so it's time for you, Bob, to come in and play hero.' It was all a ruse to get my trust so I would tell Bob everything and let him up in the attic."

Kerrie stood up and started pacing the floor. "The whole thing was staged, just for me to see. Which means that Bob is responsible for me being attacked by that inspector guy, and scared out of my wits. The only thing they didn't plan on was having the cell phone fall out of the guy's pocket during his stunt fall down my stairs. God, if that hadn't happened, I would never have clued in. Bob did a good job explaining the contradiction between his statement and Stan's about their parents, but he would never in a million years be able to explain why his voice is saying 'Otserp.'"

"Calm down. At least now we know," Jack said soothingly.

"I can't calm down. I'm thinking back over every little detail now. It's all so clear." She wouldn't listen. She was on a roll now and she had to talk it through. "Then he was so smooth, so subtle, in helping me decide not to report the assault to the police. And I had wondered at the time how Bob was able to get in the house to save me. I always lock the door—he said it was open. I should have clued in later when I saw how easily he popped the lock on the trunk up in the attic. That's how he must have gotten in the front door when I was being attacked. He just expertly picked the lock."

She continued, only stopping for a sip of water. "Then he conveniently erased the history off the cell phone I found. He must have been the one who sent that phony carpenter in to hunt for the cell phone before I stupidly just handed it over to him. God, am I trusting or what!"

"Cut yourself some slack, Kerrie. You had no reason to be suspicious of him. Anyone would have been fooled by all of this. These guys are slick."

"So this must mean that that Stan guy is not his brother. He's just another imposter partner of Bob's. It also probably means I was right in thinking that those other two guys I saw limping along were in fact Stan in disguise, which begs the question: What is he doing slinking around, disguised three different ways and apparently following Bob?"

"Yeah, you were bang on in your observations about those guys—er, that guy. I'm sorry for doubting you. Too much of a coincidence. I couldn't even hazard a guess as to what's going on between those two, and why the gimpy one seems to be watching Bob. Stan left that house when Bob got back from his trip, but he must have stuck around the area. This is just too strange—Bob keeping an eye on you, and Stan keeping an eye on Bob. If this wasn't so serious, it would be funny!" Jack got up and looked out the window towards the beach.

"Jack, what are we going to do about this? Once Bob talks to Stan, if they talk, he'll know that I tricked him with that last question. He'll know that I know he's a phony. I'm scared thinking what he might do once he figures that out!"

Jack started pacing the kitchen as he talked. "Well, if Stan has some higher-authority reason to be following Bob right now, chances are they won't be talking to each other. So, perhaps we have some time before Bob catches on."

"Do you think these guys are CIA?" Kerrie was wringing her hands together, a nervous habit that usually resulted in such chapped skin that she had to lather on the hand cream.

"I think that's a certainty. Everything that has happened to the two of us over the last few months has probably been orchestrated from here, by Bob. Also the things that happened to my friends in Calgary and in Whitefish. Bob's probably the puppet master, but perhaps he's fallen out of favor with his bosses due to the lack of results. Maybe his superiors are having him watched now because of those failures."

Jack grew silent. Kerrie looked at him and asked apprehensively, "So, what are you thinking about?"

He looked up at her with a pensive frown on his face. "How long has Bob lived here?"

"He said about four years."

"That's about as long as you've lived here Kerrie, at least here in Bigfork. You said you first lived in Kalispell for a time before you began your renovations here?" Jack asked.

"That's right."

"So, resign yourself to the fact that you've probably been watched and listened to the entire time you've lived here. It was pretty quiet for you, until my phone call back in January. Then things started to happen to you and to me. My phone call triggered all of this. They were listening and up until I phoned, nothing earth-shattering caught their attention. Once they heard there was a chip with a message, maybe they assumed that the message might lead to the attic."

Jack saw the look of awareness come over Kerrie. Her personal life had not been a private life for several years now, and she was just beginning to realize that.

Jack continued. "They took a two-pronged approach: one, to try and capture Mule to find out what the message was, and two, to try and gain access to your attic. And they wanted to accomplish both things without too many alarm bells going off. And I think it's safe to assume that Bob doesn't really live four houses down the lake. That has probably been an on and off posting for him for the last four years, his temporary headquarters just for you."

Kerrie bit her lip while still wringing her hands. "It's an eerie feeling thinking that for the last few years my private life has not been my own. And Bob was someone I considered a friend. I feel betrayed and used by a man I trusted and could have actually found myself getting involved with romantically. And the way I've been gushing over him for saving my life! God, I feel like such a fool!"

Jack walked over to Kerrie and gave her a comforting hug. She rested her head on his shoulder, clearly exhausted from the shocking revelations.

He leaned back, cupped her face in his hands and said, "We've got to get out of Dodge. Now!"

Chapter 29

"I beg your pardon?" Jack asked.

"I said I can't issue boarding passes to you or Ms. Joplin. You both show up on my screen as being on the TSA 'No Fly' list," the attendant at the airline check-in counter replied.

"That's ridiculous. We bought our tickets over the phone just a few days ago and the agent didn't say anything at all to us," Jack said through gritted teeth.

"Sir, please keep your voice down. I can't have you upsetting our passengers waiting to check in."

"We're your passengers too, because you sold us tickets. You have no right to refuse to give us boarding passes. Are you saying we're suspected of being terrorists?"

The attendant gave him a steely stare, and lowered her voice. "Sir, it's against the law to use words like that in an airport. I'll warn you only once. If you say alarming words like that again, I'll have you arrested."

Jack leaned forward and whispered, "How about 'fuck off.' Can you have me arrested for that?"

She motioned to a man standing behind her and he disappeared behind the baggage loading area.

"Sir, in situations like this, I'm obligated to summon a security representative from TSA. He will discuss this matter with you. In the meantime, could you please move your bags over to the side there, and you and Ms. Joplin can kindly wait until he arrives? It should only be a couple of minutes."

Jack grunted something he was lucky she didn't hear. Grabbing their bags, they both moved off to the side to make room for the next passenger.

Kerrie patted Jack on the back. "Calm down. There's nothing we can do but wait. I'm sure there's been some mistake. It happens all the time I hear."

"You're right. I'll calm down. This reminds me of my detainment at the border with their so-called 'traveler's alert.' Now they're catching you in their net too!"

Kerrie tried to lighten things up. "You know, I heard on one of those investigative news shows a few months ago, that it took one couple eighteen months to have their toddler removed from the 'No Fly' list. And in the same news segment, they mentioned that someone's dog was on it, 'Puddles.'"

"It's just ridiculous," Jack said. "The way your elected officials here in the States overreact to virtually everything. Innocent people get caught up in the government's rush to restrict freedoms. They make mistakes all the time with their regulatory gobblygoop, and there's absolutely no logic applied when they try to find ways to correct them. And right here right now, I know and you know, that they're abusing this stupid list by using it as a weapon against us!"

Kerrie ignored his tirade. "Jack, what is the TSA? I know I should know this."

"That's the Transportation Safety Administration. They were formed a year or two after 9/11. I think they report in to Homeland Security. No wonder it's so fucked up."

Jack was pissed, probably because he was also tired. He and Kerrie had made the mad dash out of Bigfork in the middle of the night, long before they had planned to leave.

They did the three-hour drive south to Helena, arriving there at the ridiculous hour of 2:00 a.m. They were glad to get out of that house, with Bob Trundle, or whatever his name was, being only about a block away. They didn't feel the least bit safe hanging around.

They parked the car at the Helena airport, reclined the seats of the Audi to the prone position and went to sleep. They awoke to honking horns in the parkade at 6:00 a.m., went into the airport and had some breakfast, then tried to check in. The first red flag they should have clued into was the automated check-in kiosk. It rejected their attempts to print boarding passes, so they had to line up instead. But Jack was accustomed to those airport machines not working; they broke down all the time and it always seemed to be when he was in a hurry. He did notice, however, that they were the only ones who seemed to be having problems. Usually when the computers went down, they all went down together. He had shrugged it off and accepted that it was probably just the usual automation pretzel logic.

By the time they had waited their way through the long line-up, only to be told that they were on the infamous 'No Fly' list, he'd pretty much had it. Jack had a temper to begin with; sometimes it didn't take much to set him off. So something as serious as this really got his back up. He was getting more agitated as the minutes slipped by. Their flight was due to leave in an hour, and they still had to sit through a grilling with this TSA representative, if he or she ever arrived.

Finally after waiting another fifteen minutes, a youngish man in a suit and wearing a TSA identification badge came up behind them and introduced himself. He then directed them back to an office behind the ticketing counters.

Once they were seated, in cheap metal chairs in front of his desk with the mandatory absence of legroom, he asked if they would like some water.

"No, we'd just like some explanation for all of this. Our flight is about to leave and we're sitting here talking to you," Jack asserted.

"Mr. Howser, I doubt very much that you'll be getting on that plane. Tell me, have you ever encountered the 'No Fly' list before in your travels?"

"No, and what do you mean we won't be getting on this flight? Surely we can sort this out. There's no reason for us to be on that list." He turned his chair slightly to the side to give more legroom. Kerrie copied him.

"There must be a reason or you wouldn't be on it. There are only about four thousand people on that list. But first let's make sure you are the right people and that there has been no mistake. Please, both of you, write down on this piece of paper your birth dates and places of birth, your middle names if you have any, and where you are currently residing." He shoved paper and a pen across his desk.

Jack and Kerrie did as they were asked, and waited for him to compare the information with what he had on his computer screen.

"Yes, you're the same people that the list has targeted," the security officer said.

Jack rose from his chair, placed his hands on the desk and stared down at the TSA officer. "Why weren't we told this at the time we booked our tickets over the phone? Why wait until the last minute when we'd traveled all this way to the airport in the middle of the night? What is wrong with you people?" Jack raised his voice at the end of his rant. The officer got up and closed the door.

He remained standing, seemingly determined to show Jack that he couldn't be intimidated. "Passengers are never told they are on the list until they actually check in for their boarding passes. Their status could change between when they book and when they travel, so it wouldn't be fair to deny them a ticket," the officer replied politely.

Kerrie couldn't resist. "What are you saying, that a toddler might eventually mature to kindergarten age and no longer be a threat?"

The officer chuckled. “So, you saw that news segment too, huh? Yes, we have certainly had some bad publicity so far.”

“Why are we on this list?” Kerrie demanded. She stood up herself to join the two men.

“The list never expands to a reason. I have no idea why. My job is to ensure that there hasn’t been what is termed a ‘false positive,’ and to enforce the list.”

Jack was suddenly hopeful. “Could ours be a false positive?”

“No, because your identification matches what is on the list. That toddler on the news was an example of a false positive. The program also has another category, ‘Selectees,’ where certain people are deemed to require extra security checks before they board. Neither of you are ‘Selectees.’ You’re simply deemed ‘No Fly.’”

“I’m delighted to hear that we kept things simple for you.” Jack sneered at the officer. “So what do we do now? And whom do we have to talk to, to find out why we’re on this stupid list, and how we get off it?” Jack asked.

“Well, for now, you could just drive to your destination.”

Jack looked at him, mouth wide open, dumbfounded. “We’re going to New York—are you serious?”

The officer hardened his tone. “Not my problem, sir. Go to the Homeland Security website, under ‘No Fly Disputes.’ Enter all of the information that is asked and await a ruling. If that fails, you can hire a lawyer to represent you in your case to get removed from the list.”

“That’s it? We have to go through a website for something this serious? There’s no real live person we can talk to?” asked Kerrie, exasperated.

“That’s it.”

They both grabbed their bags, skipping the niceties of goodbyes, and headed out to the concourse area. Jack went to the ticket counter to make sure that refunds were going to be processed for their useless tickets. It was the principle more than the money.

A few minutes later, sitting together having coffee, Jack leaned forward with that determined look that Kerrie had become so familiar with and said, “We’re still going to New York.”

“How? Neither of us wants to drive that far!” Kerrie exclaimed.

“We’re going to fly.”

She looked at him, puzzled. “Weren’t you present for the same discussion I was just involved in? Didn’t you hear what he said?”

“We’re going to charter a plane,” Jack replied.

Kerrie’s eyes lit up. “Aren’t they under the same regulations?”

"No, not quite. At my company we purchased two corporate jets for air travel because of the security nonsense after 9/11, and things like the SARS epidemic. We traveled all the time, all over the world, and we needed a secure and dependable way to do that within at least North and South America. They weren't large enough for our transatlantic travel though.

"The existing rules require any charter jets over 100,000 lbs. to be treated the same as if they are scheduled airlines. For example, certain items passengers can't bring onto the plane, vetting through the 'No Fly' list, etc. Any plane smaller than that is not subject to the 'No Fly' list," Jack explained.

He took a sip of his coffee and continued. "The rules are due to change again very shortly, but they haven't gone through yet. The TSA has had a lot of opposition from private pilots across the U.S. The TSA wants to bring within the regulations, which they call 'Large Aircraft' regulations, all private and charter planes over 12,500 lbs. So we have a window of opportunity until the rules change."

"So, we have to charter a plane less than 100,000 lbs.?" asked Kerrie, feeling excited again.

"Yes, which is actually how we made the purchase decision at my firm. We deliberately negotiated for two corporate jets in that size range so we could escape the red tape nonsense. What we bought was actually in the mid-size range, around 40,000 lbs.—the Falcon 50—which is made by an excellent French firm called Dussault. Very safe, very comfortable, and state of the art. It has three engines: two behind the wings and one at the rear on top of the fuselage. It seats about nine people so we'll have plenty of room to stretch out. A very safe plane and most charter companies have them in their fleets."

"Can it get us all the way to New York?" Kerrie asked.

"It sure can. It has a range of about 4000 miles, probably even more than that with just the two of us on board. So we'll have about 2000 miles to spare."

"Can we afford this? It must be very expensive."

"It is expensive, but don't worry. I'll take care of it. We're not going to let these bastards tie our hands," Jack said. "Let's just hope a plane is available on such short notice."

Kerrie looked down at her half empty cup of coffee, and was silent for a few moments. Then she looked up, worry lines on her face.

"Jack, what you said before—about them using this list as a weapon against us. Do you believe that, or could this just be some kind of mistake?"

"It's no mistake. Just another intimidation tactic to make us drop this whole thing and contain us to where they can best keep track of us. Just like when I got hassled at the border. I no longer believe in coincidences, and I know that you don't either. We've been specifically targeted here for a reason that they will never admit to."

Kerrie nodded. She opened her purse, pulled out some hand cream and rubbed it on thick. Her hand-wringing had caused the usual side effect.

"Okay, if you're finished your coffee, let's go," Jack insisted. "There's an airline charter office at the other end of the terminal. I noticed the sign when we were coming in." He slung his knapsack over his shoulder, picked up both bags and led the way.

*****

There was a three-way call taking place between the man called Virginia, the man called Montana, and the man called Colorado. Colorado was still in Montana, two blocks away from Montana. But Montana didn't know that.

"Things have gotten a lot more serious. We have discovered that there was a security breach years ago. Agent Joplin's vault box contents are on the loose," Virginia informed the others. "Including documentation on all of his assignments right up until he retired, his last assignment being of monumental concern to us. It's a matter of national security."

"What was Mitch's last assignment?" Montana asked.

"If I wanted you to know that, I would have told you already," Virginia replied. "Suffice to say, it can't be made public. In addition, the old videotape of Mitch's leverage assignment is missing. Trust me, another huge concern."

"So you must think the information from that box was what Mitch was planning to unleash at his bank press conference?" Montana asked.

"Obviously. It went missing from his vault for a reason, and that microchip in the dog was probably his contingency plan. However, we can't confirm that until we know what's on that damn chip. If I'm right about the chip, whatever clues he has provided on it are going to lead to the documents and the video. We have to assume that, in light of this security breach, the message on the chip is not just some pathetic love note to his daughter," Virginia explained.

"Speaking of his daughter, I have to say that I almost got tripped up with Kerrie the other day. Colorado, when you were filling in for me as my brother you put me in a bad spot when you told her our parents lived in Sandpoint. What possessed you to say that? I had told her my parents died in a car accident. You could have at least called me to tell me what you said to her so that I was prepared," Montana complained.

"I'm sorry. We were chatting and I just filled in some detail for realism. Obviously I wasn't thinking. Did you squeeze out of it okay?" Colorado asked, not sounding the least bit apologetic.

"Yes, I did, thank God. But that business about our dad being in a wheelchair threw me for a loop. I didn't think I would recover from that one."

"I didn't say anything about a wheelchair."

"What?"

"I never mentioned a wheelchair. She was playing you."

"Christ, she's on to me then."

Virginia had been following this conversation with increasing concern. "Okay, you've been blown. You'll have to make contact with her now, as well as this Howser fellow."

"I can't this week, they're on their way to New York today. I've got scouts watching for them at La Guardia, JFK, and Newark, and they'll pick up the tail from there. Would you prefer that they just grab them instead?" Montana asked.

"I doubt they'll be going anywhere by air this week, or the rest of this year. We put them on the 'No Fly' list a couple of weeks ago as a precaution. So I expect you'll see them back in Bigfork very shortly. You work out a plan of action with Colorado, and he can assist you," Virginia instructed.

"Time is running out. We need to know what they know, we need to know what is on that chip, we need to recover those documents and video, and we need to destroy that chip. I don't care anymore how you get the information out of them, just do it." Virginia was clearly losing his patience. "The time for civility is over. This is a national security issue with the documents that we now know are out there."

"What if they have already recovered the documents and have seen them?" Montana asked tentatively.

"You know the answer to that one." The phone clicked off in the great state of Virginia.

*****

"You want to fly…today?" The charter airline representative asked, incredulous.

"Yes, as soon as you can get off the ground. We can't get seats on the regular scheduled flights, and we have a family emergency in New York. We would appreciate whatever stops you can pull out for us," Jack pleaded.

"Well, we aim to please, but this is really unusual to do a charter on such short notice. Let me take a look and see what we have available."

Jack and Kerrie waited with baited breath.

"There's just the two of you?"

"Yes, just us."

"Well, you're lucky the economy is so bad, but the unlucky part is that the planes we have available right now are way too big for the two of you. We have a Gulfstream, Lear, Hawker, and Falcon. All of our smaller jets are out right now."

"We'll take the Falcon. Is that the 50 model?"

"Yes, the 50EX is already out on charter, but the 50 is a beautiful plane. I know you'd like it, but I warn you, it's big and of course expensive. Not as big as the Gulfstream or Hawker, but still a bit on the large side for two people."

"I'm sure it will suit us just fine. How soon can you be ready to go?"

"Well, the standard is six hours. We need to do catering and beverages, as well as fueling, pre-flight checks, and a flight plan."

"How soon if you skip the catering and beverages?"

The agent looked at Jack as if he was crazy. "You don't want to eat? It's a long flight."

"How soon if we skip that?" Jack repeated.

"We can have you off the ground in four hours tops."

"Let's do it then."

"Sir, how do you wish to pay?"

"We'll do a bank transfer. I'll make a trip to your bank in town and arrange for a deposit from my bank in Canada. Should only take a few minutes, but you'll need to give authorization to your bank manager for me."

"No problem, Mr. Howser. For a one-way trip to New York, count on $50,000 minimum. Are you okay with that?"

Kerrie gulped and looked over at Jack.

"That's no problem. In fact we'll make it $150,000 round trip paid in advance, if you'll have the plane stick around and wait for us for six days."

The agent once again looked at him as if he was daft. "Are you serious?"

"Yes, I want the plane to wait for us until Sunday and be available on demand. We might be okay to return on, say, Thursday, but let's say Sunday to be safe. Hopefully the extra money on deposit will be an incentive to wait for us?"

"Absolutely, sir. Same rules coming back. Give us four hours' notice if no catering needed. And don't be concerned—the plane will be reserved for your exclusive use until Sunday."

The attendant made some notes, and then continued, more excited now.

"We usually avoid the three large international airports in the New York area due to congestion. We prefer to use two smaller airports that pander well to charters—one being Teterboro in New Jersey, and the other is Long Island Macarthur Airport in New York. Any preference?"

"Yes, use Long Island."

"Okay, LI it is. The pilots will then be staying at the Marriott Islandia, close to the airport. You can ring them there when you want to come home. I'll give you their cell numbers too."

"Wonderful. Let's get the banking done then and get this show on the road," Jack said, clearly relieved

Kerrie looked at Jack with admiration. He clearly had a very quick mind, and was a man who obviously didn't worry about problems as much as he worried about solutions. She was very impressed with his decisiveness, and thought to herself that he would have made an excellent lawyer. What started out as doom and gloom an hour ago had now turned around in their favor. She felt a sense of triumph, as the goons who had tried to lock them down in Montana were now going to fail. The money Jack had just committed blew her mind. She didn't have the luxury to even think of liquid funds in that sum.

They took a cab to downtown Helena and went to the bank branch used by the charter company. Jack phoned his personal banker in Calgary and the money was transferred in U.S. funds to the airline company's bank account in a matter of minutes. He also asked his bank to transfer an additional 20,000 dollars that he took out in cash.

Kerrie saw him counting the pocket money. "What do you need that for? That's too large an amount to be carrying around with you."

"It's not all going to be with me," he said as he handed her half. "As of now, we no longer use credit cards. Cash is king for the next few days."

"Why?"

"If we use our cards we'll be sitting ducks. They'll trace every movement we make."

"Yes, of course. You're right. What about hotels and rental cars though? They won't accept cash."

"We'll stay at a small hotel and throw enough cash at them to make them look the other way. They always do. As for rental cars, forget it. We're just going to have to cab it wherever we go. Cabs will accept cash, in fact they prefer it."

Kerrie looked at him admiringly again. He had it all worked out, and she started feeling a little intimidated around this lightning quick brain. But at the same time, comforted and protected.

They killed time downtown until a few minutes before their scheduled 2:00 p.m. departure. Then, back to the airport and right on time they boarded the sleek jet. They were welcomed on board by both the pilot and co-pilot and ushered back into the luscious cabin. Kerrie was amazed at how comfortable it was, albeit a little tight on headroom. The seating was all beige leather, with a couple of couches, and chairs that swiveled into conference position facing each other over a worktable. One of the couches even transformed itself into a bed, and Kerrie thought that she might just make use of that. Since there would be no catering on this flight, an attendant wouldn't be along for the ride. But they did have a self-service fridge with water and pop, along with a few snacks. Jack seemed right at home on this jet, and Kerrie remembered that he said his company had owned a couple of these during the time he was CEO. So she guessed this plane brought back some memories for him of his high-flying executive days.

They strapped themselves in, laid their heads back on the generous headrests, and watched out the window as the confident Falcon taxied down the runway, its three Honeywell turbofan engines humming as smooth as silk. As the jet reached skyward, both of them were hoping that Wednesday would be the day they would finally get some answers.

Chapter 30

Jack awoke to the co-pilot gently shaking his shoulders. "Sir, we'll be starting our descent into New York City and the Long Island Airport in about an hour. Would you be interested in having us fly over the WTC site? If so, we need to file our approach plan in advance."

"Oh yes, absolutely. Get as close as the controllers will allow you." Jack was groggy, but just the mention of the WTC site shocked him awake. He appreciated the courtesy of the co-pilot asking him. The pilots had no idea of course that he had lost a loved one on 9/11, but it was probably a fairly common thing for charters to ask their clients if they would like to see the infamous site.

Jack had decided against visiting Ground Zero again. It didn't feel right to him. The site was now a construction zone with all traces of the attacks now basically eliminated. He knew no one would forget what had happened that day, but it did hurt him to know how quickly it was being transformed into several shiny new skyscrapers. Flying over the site would suffice for him. He had done his grieving long ago. He was more bitter and angry now, than grief-stricken.

He had kept up to date on how the site was being re-developed. The whole thing had turned into a political football over the years, and the insensitivity of it began right at the process of hauling away all of the debris. The city coroner had verified to authorities that any debris hauled away to landfill sites would most definitely contain human remains—lots of human remains. The debris field was so massive, and the task to uncover any further remains would be Herculean. However, the cruel irony of it all was that they chose a landfill site on Staten Island, which had the incredibly macabre name of 'Fresh Kills Landfill,' which refers to its location along the banks of the 'Fresh Kills Estuary.' Jack couldn't believe the poor judgment that went into that decision. He shuddered to think of family members whose relatives' remains were never found, having to live with the fact that their loved ones' bones could possibly be resting at a place going by the name 'Fresh Kills.' How stupid and insensitive could they be?

That particular landfill site was opened in 1948 and had grown to become the largest of its type in the world, taking up a full twelve square kilometers. It was actually closed down early in 2001, but then re-opened again after the WTC attacks just to handle the debris. After it was all hauled there, it was decided that the landfill site would be closed once again and turned into a park and memorial. To be fair, Jack acknowledged that perhaps that landfill site was the only one in the New York area that could handle the huge volume of debris, but the name of the place was an incredibly horrible coincidence. He wondered if they had considered alternatives. Couldn't barges have hauled the debris out to the deep Atlantic and dumped it? Of course whale-huggers would have had a field day with that. So perhaps the government really had no choice.

Well, 'Fresh Kills' now had a more appropriate reason for its name than just an estuary. Then the lobbyists and money-grubbing visionaries got in on the act. In 2002, a contest for New York architects and designers was launched, then quickly withdrawn. Then a local architect was summarily selected, only to have his six designs rejected. A couple of months later, a press release announced that seven semi-finalists were selected to compete to be the master design architects for the WTC site. Then it was down to two, then a winner was announced, but they had to work with another architect who was chosen by a developer to be in on the deal anyway, even without competing. Jack guessed that the money, being divided up into so many tasty little pies, must be enormous. The New York Port Authority had turned tragedy into one massive business opportunity, and it was now the main money game in town. Nice.

Five new skyscrapers were to be erected, along with the tower known as 7 World Trade Center, which Jack understood had already been completed and opened in 2006. This tower replaced the third tower that collapsed on Sept. 11, 2001, the tower that wasn't even hit by a plane but somehow managed to collapse just perfectly anyway. Jack always wondered about that one.

One of the new towers, to be known as 1 World Trade Center, would be the centerpiece of the complex. It would rise to 1362 ft., the exact height of the original WTC South, the first tower that had been hit. However, in typical U.S.A. symbolism, this tower would have an antenna at the top that would shoot up another 414 feet to bring the total height of the structure to 1776 ft. This will signify, in a patriotic salute, the year in which the Declaration of Independence was signed. Jack thought that he could have used these marketing geniuses when he was in business. All for show, ceremony, and might, but don't dare ask them about the 'Fresh Kills' landfill site.

The new WTC area will also have the usual mandatory memorial, to be called "Reflecting Absence." And in glossy theatric fashion, it will have a field of trees broken by the footprints of the twin towers. These footprints will be filled with water, and a wall will contain the names of all of the victims. Susan's name would be there.

There will also be a new train station, a museum, and a performing arts center. The site will be a magnet for tourists, no doubt. And it will be spectacular. And a lot of people will make a lot of money building it and operating it.

Jack knew he had been getting more and more cynical over the years since 9/11, but despite trying his hardest to be to the contrary, he just couldn't help it. All this symbolism, pageantry, and blind patriotism didn't pay proper tribute, in his mind, to the horror of that day, and gave absolutely no acknowledgement of what really caused that day to happen in the first place. A little less blind patriotism and "go get 'em boys!" attitude, and a lot more attention to holding politicians accountable for their actions, would go a long way.

Jack pushed his seat button and pulled himself out of the recline position. He looked to the back of the cabin and saw that Kerrie was still asleep. The first thing she had done when the plane reached cruising altitude was to pull out one of the couches into its bed position. She was lying under a blanket looking as if she didn't have a care in the world. They both knew otherwise, of course, but she was clearly enjoying the moment.

He walked down the length of the cabin and used the washroom. On his way back, he carefully stirred Kerrie awake. "We'll be landing soon, sleeping beauty. You might want to freshen up?"

Kerrie smiled back in a lazy kind of way, and stretched her arms out in front of her.

"Now I understand why you were an executive for so long. I could get used to this."

"Trust me, it was no picnic most of the time. After the novelty wore off, we looked at our planes as just utilities," Jack commented.

He went back to his seat, and within minutes the captain advised them over the intercom to fasten their seatbelts as they were beginning their approach to New York center. Looking out the window, he could now see the skyscrapers of the city off in the distance. It never failed to astonish him as to how big and powerful New York really was. An incredible city, with a spirit and energy that kept on ticking, no matter what. He had to give it credit for resilience.

The captain announced that they were now flying over the Ground Zero site. Jack gazed down. While construction of the structures was well under way, it was still easy to discern the huge empty chasm carved into the center of downtown New York by the terrorists. He could see the completed WTC 7, and the foundations and substructures for the other five towers were already in the ground. Jack knew that this project would take until 2013 to be completed, and he was confident that it would become a world landmark even more famous than the original. While cynical as to motives, he was not insensitive to the need for New York to get closure and be beautiful again—not just physically but in its soul also. For that, he was glad. This great city deserved it.

The Falcon soared over the site and gave them a great view. Jack was intrigued to at least see the progress they were making down there, but didn't regret his decision to not go in person. His Susan was buried in Toronto, not in the rubble of Ground Zero….or Fresh Kills landfill.

They continued their descent as they approached Long Island Macarthur Airport. Jack had chosen that airport over Teterboro because it was within about thirty minutes of Connie Reynolds' house by his estimate. Avoiding New York traffic when possible was a must for savvy travelers to this area of the world. If he were a tourist, he would choose to stay at a hotel right smack in the middle of the city near Times Square. But this trip would not afford them the luxury of sightseeing. They just wanted to get in and get out, quickly.

The jet gave them the smoothest landing either of them had ever experienced, and made a short taxi over to the charter terminal wing. They were out of the plane and hailing a taxi within minutes. Before leaving, Jack reiterated to the pilots his instructions to remain on standby until Sunday.

Before they got into the taxi, Jack pulled Kerrie aside. "Let me do the talking and please don't get insulted or angry at what you hear me say to the driver, okay?" Kerrie looked at him, a little bit alarmed but also intrigued. She nodded.

The driver put their bags in the trunk while Jack and Kerrie hopped into the back seat.

"Where to, folks?"

"I'm hoping you can help me with that. We want a little hotel or motel, very discreet, and one that will take cash. I'm on a little getaway with my lady friend here, and I don't want any possibility of being tracked, you get my drift?"

The driver smiled into the rear mirror. "No problem, sir. I know just the place, not too far from here. I know the owners and they like cash. They really like cash."

The next thing Jack felt was a kick to his ankle. He turned his head and looked at Kerrie, wincing as he did. She looked embarrassed, but she also looked like she was stifling a laugh.

About ten minutes from the airport, the cab pulled up to a small four-storey hotel called the Lamplighter Hideaway. It actually looked quite charming. Jack was expecting some sleazy-looking dive. The driver turned around and gave them his instructions. "Ask for Chuck when you arrive at the front desk. He's one of the owners. Tell him Larry sent you. I get a kickback, of course. Chuck will take care of you."

"Thanks, Larry," Jack said. He handed over a twenty dollar bill, which Larry quickly pocketed.

"No problem," Larry called out as they were walking away from the cab. "Nice doing business with you. Have one for me!"

Kerrie glared back at the cab driver and then punched Jack on the shoulder.

"Kerrie, I'm sure he meant for me to have a drink for him," Jack pleaded feebly. "He didn't mean what you're thinking."

"Yeah right. You men are all so predictable!"

They went up to the front desk, and were pleasantly surprised to see that this hotel actually looked as charming on the inside as on the outside. It had stained glass windows, stylish Tiffany lamps, large leather couches in the lobby, and a huge fireplace. Adjoining the lobby was a lounge, and they could hear the mellow sounds of jazz over the din of voices and laughing. It didn't look like the kind of place that would accept cash.

True to Larry's recommendation, Chuck was more than accommodating and his eyes lit up when Jack paid him $2,500 cash up front for a six night stay, for a room that had a nightly rate of $150. Jack also teased him with the promise of a bonus for the day they checked out. If Chuck was discreet and disclosed to no one of their stay there including anyone enquiring by phone, he would get another $2,500 on the day they left. Jack also told him that they would not be giving their names for his register. Chuck eagerly acquiesced and winked knowingly. He was obviously used to this.

Two anonymous people were staying in room 207, which actually consisted of two rooms that adjoined. Out of respect for Kerrie's privacy, Jack had requested that type of accommodation. And the rooms were just as charming as the lobby. The décor oozed that instant feeling of relaxation, and as soon as the two travelers dropped their bags they threw themselves onto their beds and just soaked it up. Nice to be in New York and nice to be feeling safe.

Kerrie got changed into her pyjamas and robe and sat down on Jack's bed. "They probably know that we're here by now, don't you think?"

"Well, at best we're a few hours ahead of them. We can assume Bob knows by now that you're on to him. They're also well aware that we weren't able to get on that Northwest flight. And they know we didn't return to Bigfork. So they're figuring by now that we either started our drive to New York, or chartered a plane. Let's hope they think we drove, because it would take four days to do that and they would think they still had plenty of time."

"They would easily be able to track a charter and a large bank transfer in your name," Kerrie commented.

"True, but I didn't do either of those things in my name. I own a shell company in Canada mainly for tax purposes, so I did the transfer out of that account instead of my own personal account and I put the air charter contract in that company name as well. So, if they have an electronic alert out for my name, nothing will pop up. They would need to search further to find a money transfer and charter contract for an Alberta company, which will buy us a bit more time but it won't stop them from eventually finding out what we did. The only question is how soon they'll find out."

"So before too long they will know we flew to New York, and which airport we landed at," Kerrie observed.

"Yes. We can't kid ourselves into thinking we've duped them. As I said, we've bought a few hours head start at the very best," Jack said. "But they don't know where we're staying or who we're visiting while we're here. So for now I think we're relatively safe. We're not using credit cards, and you can bet they will have electronic trackers out for those. They're going to start getting pretty frustrated once they start looking."

"Okay, I feel better now." Kerrie became silent and they both got lost in their own thoughts for a few minutes.

Jack allowed his eyes to wander. She was sitting close to him on the bed and he had to admit that she was an intoxicating beauty. However, he had no urge to take it beyond the friendship they had developed. He thought to himself how amazing that was—how many men would kill right now to be lying on a bed with someone sitting within kissing distance, who looked as incredible as Kerrie did. Something had happened to him, and he knew it was Heather back home. He had already called her about a dozen times since he left Calgary, and despite the free-wheeling lifestyle that had been his trademark for the last few years he found himself now thinking only of her. This was a good thing, he thought.

And the other good thing was that Kerrie seemed very comfortable with him and did not act as if she was afraid she would be pounced on sitting beside him on the bed dressed in her robe. She obviously trusted him, and Jack felt good about that. He was a bit puzzled, however, over the little pangs of jealousy he had felt about Bob, but he wrote that off as just typical male rivalry. At least he hoped that's all it was. It would be too complicated thinking seriously about two women at the same time.

"Kerrie, what are you thinking about? You seem lost in thought."

Kerrie sighed and lowered her head. "Well, I have to confess that I still feel so stupid for trusting Bob as much as I did. And the worst part of it is, I really liked him. I believed in him and felt so sure he was looking out for me and my safety. As I told you, for a while there I even thought we might actually become involved in a romantic way. Thank God I didn't let that happen; I would really feel like an idiot."

Jack sat up, and put his arm around her shoulders. "Don't feel like that. By now you know the sophistication of the group we're dealing with. These people lie for a living, and they do it very well. Give yourself a break. Okay?"

She looked back at him affectionately. "Okay." She gave him a kiss on the cheek and went back to her room. Jack could hear the bedsprings creak as she got under the covers. He noticed that she hadn't bothered to close the adjoining door.

*****

The village of Northport resided in Suffolk County on the north shore of Long Island. Long Island was big, and home to some of the most picturesque towns and villages in the New York City metropolis. People who lived in Northport had the benefit of living in an old world community, but as penance they had to suffer through an hour's commute to downtown. So be it, as the benefits were substantial.

The village was right out of a Norman Rockwell painting, with old-fashioned ice cream parlors, antique stores, and even a village green that would host concerts on hot summer evenings. Its main street still had trolley rails embedded in the asphalt, reminiscent of the days when streetcars ruled. To thrill tourists, the village had adopted a new version of the trolley, ironically more primitive than the original. The twenty-first century version was horse-drawn, and ran on rubber tires rather than metal wheels on the rails. The visitors to Northport didn't care that it wasn't authentic. This was far better than the original, at least for photo ops.

The population in Northport now was about 8,000, and half would commute daily into downtown New York. The other half probably worked at the Northport Power Station, the largest oil-fired electric generating station on the entire east coast of the United States. The four enormous stacks, each 600 ft. tall, could be seen as far away as Connecticut, and appeared in the nightmares of environmentalists as far away as Portland.

The cab turned down Main Street. Kerrie instructed the driver to turn right at Ocean Avenue, all the way up to Sea Cove Road, then another right. It was Wednesday afternoon, and they were arriving at the home of Connie Reynolds at exactly 3:30 as she had requested. She had been pretty adamant about that time, so Kerrie didn't want to push things and get there any earlier than that.

They could see that Connie's house was a cute craftsman style, one and a half storey, with a large covered porch. The color of the house had been sky blue at one time, but now looked faded and tired. The grass was sparse and burnt out from lack of watering, and the bushes under the front window had been dead for quite some time. There were no flowers in sight. This house at one time must have been splendid. Not anymore. The condition of the exterior of the house gave them a clue as to what they might have to brace themselves for on the inside.

They walked up to the front porch and rang the doorbell. Within just a few seconds, the inner door opened and a once-pretty face peered out at them. "Connie?"

"Yes, I'm Connie."

"Hello again, Connie. Do you remember me? Kerrie Joplin?"

"Yes, I do. I remembered you were coming and I've put on some coffee. Who's he?"

"This is Jack Howser, that friend of mine I told you about. Do you mind if he visits with us?"

A slight pause. "No, I don't mind."

They stared through the screen door at each other for a few more seconds. Finally Kerrie said, "Connie, could you unlock the screen door so we can come in? Would that be okay?"

"Oh, yes…sorry."

She unlocked the door and they walked into the hallway. Kerrie and Jack looked around. The house was incredibly dark. All the blinds were down, and it was the middle of the afternoon. Strange. In stark contrast to the bleakness of the house exterior though, the inside was spotless. The furnishings were dated, but everything seemed to be perfectly in its place and the décor was tasteful.

Connie led them into the kitchen and pointed to the chairs around the table. They sat down as Connie fussed with the coffee and poured three cups. Jack could see that at one time, probably not too long ago, this girl had been a looker. She had auburn hair just like his Susan had, but it wasn't cared for. Her face was pale, but he could tell that her features were attractive. She wore no makeup, but her face structure didn't seem to need it. She just needed color, natural color. And those dark rings underneath her eyes. She looked like she hadn't slept in weeks.

He noticed that her movements were forced, almost weary. However, her figure was excellent. She was very shapely. Connie seemed, in Jack's view, to be somewhat of a paradox.

Jack and Kerrie looked at each other, puzzled. So far Connie had been, at the very best, robotic. Jack remembered Kerrie's comment, that when she had talked with her on the phone she had seemed stoned. Jack thought that perhaps she was stoned right now also. There were no niceties, no expressions, no smiles. Connie sat down and joined them at the table. They each sipped their coffees.

Then she suddenly raised her head and put down her cup. Tears were rolling down her cheeks as she looked directly at Kerrie.

"I loved your father. I really did."

Chapter 31

"They haven't returned here to Bigfork." Sam Summerfield, aka Bob Trundle, was speaking on the phone with his superior in Langley, Virginia. "Gone—no doubt about it."

"They're most certainly in New York, despite our best efforts. We double-checked with the FAA, and they were definitely not on board the Northwest flight. We also checked FAA records on charter flights: one out of Helena filed a flight plan for New York and departed at 2:00 p.m. Monday," Jim Wingate, assistant director of NCS and head of SAD, reported.

"What was the charter booked under?" Sam asked.

"It wasn't in either of their names; it was booked under a corporate entity. And there was a bank transfer from that company on Monday, to the charter company's account in Helena." Jim replied. "But get this, we traced the company to its headquarters in Calgary, Alberta. Just a post office box."

"A dummy corporation most likely. Howser is from Alberta, so that's too much of a coincidence." Sam commented.

"Yes, it's a strong probability that they were on that charter. Though do you think they could have driven?" Jim asked.

"Doubtful, Virginia, unless they rented a car. We found Howser's Audi parked at the airport," Sam replied.

"Well, these two are resourceful. They've shown that right from the start. The 'No Fly' list did not discourage them in the least, and we obviously never thought that chartering an aircraft was within their financial means. We should have checked Howser's financial background a long time ago. I think they were definitely on that charter. Its flight plan took it to Long Island Macarthur Airport," Jim mused. "And we've had tracers out on their credit cards. No transactions recorded yet at all. If they are there, they're being mighty careful to use cash only. No surprise, since the Joplin lady is now on to you."

"What do you want me to do? Stay or go," Sam asked.

"You need to get to New York. You're the lead agent on this case, Montana, and I don't want to have to bring any more agents in on this problem than I have to. You'll see this through to the end. We'll have Colorado camp out at your house in Bigfork again in case they return," Jim instructed. "We'll have four agents meet you at Long Island. They'll know nothing about this case other than the basics and what you brief them on. Use them for surveillance and assistance, but no details other than who we want to grab and their photos."

"Okay, do we have any of our planes out this way right now?" Sam asked.

"Yes, we have one on hold for you at Great Falls, fueled and ready as we speak. I've also just sent you an email, with two attachments. The first contains the names and addresses of all of Mitch's old contacts and friends in New York. It's not long—he was a loner. The second lists the closest contacts that his daughter had when she lived there. Rotate your men on these people and we might find them making contact. New York is a big place, but we have to start somewhere."

"Virginia, we don't know why they're in New York, but why would we grab them before we let them lead us to something, or someone. I strongly suggest that if we do locate them, we just watch them for now," Sam advised. "Otherwise, we'll have nothing. We should manage the problem, and let it work for us."

Jim paused, thinking over Sam's suggestion. "Yeah, I think that's wise. Follow your own good judgment. But I *do not*, repeat *do not*, want these two turning into loose cannons. Do you read me?"

"Loud and clear."

*****

Kerrie got up from her chair and walked over to Connie's. She put her arms around her and gave her a gentle embrace, while at the same time giving Jack a subtle motion with her hand for him to leave the room. Jack got up quietly and went into the adjoining dining room.

Kerrie knelt down and looked straight into Connie's eyes. The poor girl was sobbing and shaking, and her eyes were bloodshot. She looked back at her in a way that Kerrie sensed was a plea for help. At that moment Kerrie felt overwhelming compassion for Connie Reynolds.

Connie laid her head on Kerrie's shoulder. "I don't understand what's wrong with me. I can't continue like this."

"Connie," Kerrie said softly, "it's okay for you to have loved my dad. I loved him too. He was just that kind of guy. He had that effect on people."

"But I don't know why he did this to me. We were so close, even though we always had a bank counter between us, but we shared things, you know? I must sound crazy because he was sixty-five and I was only twenty-three."

"You're not crazy, and age has nothing to do with these things. Sometimes people we meet only briefly in life make a huge impact. There must be a bigger, perhaps more spiritual reason that you and I will never understand," Kerrie soothed. She gently wiped Connie's eyes, and handed her a tissue to blow her nose.

"Kerrie, I've only met you once before, but I feel close to you. Probably because you remind me so much of your father."

Kerrie smiled at the touching comment. "That's nice. My dad would probably be happy that you and I are spending some time together."

"I told him things about myself, things that I wouldn't tell a stranger. He knew that I had been through a terrible time after my parents' deaths. He gave me advice and seemed to really understand. He was always concerned about me." Connie reached for another tissue.

"That sounds like my father—not telling anyone too much about himself, but always concerned about others."

"He knew I was angry after the World Trade Center attacks and he helped me deal with that. I don't know how I would have handled it without his shoulder to cry on."

Kerrie came more alert at this last statement. Did Connie have a personal story about 9/11 just like Jack? She noticed that Jack hadn't missed this either, as he peeked around the corner from the dining room. She shooed him back with her hand.

"You know, I blamed every goddamned Arab I saw on the streets. As far as I was concerned, they were all guilty of killing my parents. Mitch helped me handle that anger. Despite what he did to me at the end I'll always be grateful for his compassion. I truly loved him for that."

Despite Kerrie's attempts to keep him out of the room, Jack obviously couldn't resist any longer. He came back into the kitchen, sat in one of the old wooden chairs and pulled it beside Connie on the other side of where Kerrie was kneeling. He took her hand in his.

"Connie, you don't know me, but you and I have something tragic in common. I heard what you just said about your parents. I lost my wife in the World Trade Center. Kerrie and I had no idea that your parents died there too."

Connie reached over with both hands and framed them around Jack's face. Tears were streaming down her cheeks. "My God, you poor man. You know what I've been going through, then. It never goes away, does it?"

Connie's hands wrapping around his face brought back an instant poignant memory to Jack of his loving mother and how she used to console him. It felt so comforting. "No it doesn't. To lose someone that way is so graphic and so public. Every year in September during those tedious memorial services and with every stupid, insensitive news organization that has to show it to us all over again, we victims have to *live* through it all over again."

Connie nodded quickly, as if Jack were speaking her own thoughts.

Jack continued. "Most people aren't forced to relive the deaths of their loved ones in that fashion. So go easy on yourself. Your parents and my Susan were the ultimate victims of that terrorist attack, but you and I were victims too. It's okay for us to feel like victims, but we have to try our best to feel other things too. We can't let it consume us or control our lives."

Connie was staring down at the table and wiped her tears away. Then she looked up, wincing as if she were in physical pain.

"I was starting to recover from it quite nicely, I really was. It's true what you say and I was able to re-focus on other things. And Mitch helped me deal with the anger. But then he did what he did that day in the bank and I fell apart. I can't seem to bounce back. Maybe because I was in love with him—my own little secret—and couldn't explain in my mind why he would do that to me. I felt betrayed. And then he just died. And I never found out why he terrified me like that. I know he wanted to broadcast something, but why did he choose me to be his hostage and make me wear that horrible bomb vest? I thought he cared about me."

"Have you sought out some professional help, Connie?" Kerrie asked. She still had her arms around her shoulders, and Jack had taken hold of her hand again. She had stopped shaking. It was evident from her willingness to talk about her tragedies, and cry so openly, that human contact was helping. That and the common horror she shared with Jack, were helping her to open up. She no longer sounded like the zombie Kerrie had heard over the phone, or even looked like the person who had opened the front door just an hour ago. She actually now had color in her cheeks, and instead of being aloof she actually seemed to have warmed up to the interaction with the two of them.

"Oh sure, lots of talk and clinical crap. And pills, tons of them. For depression, anxiety, and agoraphobia. The agoraphobia means that I can't let myself go outside that often, or be with strangers, or be in strange places. Panic attacks can happen at the drop of a hat, and they're bad when they come—chest pains, can't breathe. Just horrible."

"We're basically strangers, Connie, and you're talking with us just fine," Kerrie said.

Connie smiled as if this was a revelation that she hadn't been aware of. "Yes, you're right. That's unusual for me. It feels kind of nice, believe me."

For the next several hours, the three of them chatted. Connie seemed to have cast her shell aside, and was freely opening up to the two of them. The connection between her and Jack was real. It was clear she was glad to have someone to talk to who had gone through exactly what she had gone through eight years ago. And she was very warm towards Kerrie; the fact that she was Mitch's daughter seemed to have opened up a channel.

It was getting late in the evening and they had all forgotten to eat. Jack suggested ordering a pizza. Connie and Kerrie were all for it, but to Jack's chagrin they both loved anchovies.

As they sat in the dining room eating pizza, which Jack thought was the best he had eaten in a long time despite the anchovies, Kerrie started probing a bit more about her father. "Connie, do you remember much about my dad? You mentioned earlier that some memories over the last few years had become a bit fuzzy."

"I know we shared things between us, and I remember some, but there should be more. It feels as if I was very close to your father, and I can't stand this void. Almost like back in my college days when I sometimes had too much to drink, and then the next morning struggled to remember. It's kind of like that, like I've been drunk the last few years. And I should clarify, I'm not much of a drinker." Connie chuckled.

Kerrie leaned across the table and gently rubbed Connie's hand. "Can you remember if my father ever gave you anything?"

Connie ran her fingers through her hair. "I only remember one thing he gave me: a locket necklace. He suggested I put my parents' photos in there and keep them close to my heart." She patted her left chest.

"Would you be able to show that to us?" Jack asked, excitement building.

"Sure, glad to."

Connie went off to her bedroom and came back a few minutes later with the necklace. It was beautiful, white gold, the locket encrusted with diamonds around the edges, and in the shape of an abstract heart. Connie opened the locket to reveal two miniature photos of her parents, one on each side of the shell. They were smiling and looked like such nice people. Connie started to cry again. Kerrie examined it, to see if there was a key perhaps hidden behind one of the photos. She looked at Jack, shook her head, and closed the locket.

Then she went behind Connie and helped her put the necklace on. It looked beautiful on her.

They had all sat in silence for a few minutes when Jack asked, "Do you recall if he ever gave you a key?"

"A key? No, I don't recall that at all. He did give me a poinsettia that last Christmas before he died. That's the only other thing he gave me that I can recall. Why did you ask about a key?"

Jack told her about the message on the chip and how they thought they had figured out the clues, which brought them to her doorstep. He didn't share with her any of the misadventures they had had. Connie didn't need anything else to be stressed about.

"We're just curious if he left you something he was keeping secret through this coded message."

"I wish I could remember, I really do. I wish the last few years would open up for me. If he did leave me something else to pass along to you, I would want to know." She paused. "I'm worried now that I may be letting him down." She started rubbing her eyes. The crying had left them bloodshot.

"No, don't think that way. We're probably just grasping at straws here anyway. Perhaps we misinterpreted the clues that he gave. Perhaps he even meant the other teller that he used that day, the Hispanic girl?" Kerrie said.

"Conchita passed away about a year ago. Breast cancer." Connie said softly. Silence again. That was the kind of statement that would usually throw a wet cloth on any conversation.

"That was sure one good pizza," Jack blurted out awkwardly. Connie started giggling first, then Kerrie, and Jack finally joined in. He hadn't intended it that way, but the pizza turned out to be a good icebreaker.

Connie looked at both of them once the laughing had stopped. "Be honest with me. Do you think Mitch's message may be about something serious?"

Jack answered. "Yes, but we don't want to alarm you. That's not what we came here to do. You've asked for honesty, so you deserve to hear how we feel. We do believe it's serious. We think it may have something to do with what he did that day in the bank and why he did it. And there are other people who are trying to find out what that message means also; people who aren't too nice. The things those people have done to us have convinced us the message involves something troubling."

Connie stood up, and looked down at them with an almost defiant look in her eyes. "Then I want to help you. I need to help you. If he was referring to a teller in the message, he had to have meant me. He didn't know Conchita at all, so there has to be something that I'm just not remembering."

Kerrie stood up and squeezed Connie's shoulder. "Don't feel obligated. If you don't remember anything about a key, then there's not much we can do. But I'll leave you our hotel room's phone number if you remember something after we leave." Kerrie took a pen and some paper out of her purse, wrote down the number and handed it to Connie. "Don't hesitate to call us, anytime day or night, okay? We're staying at the Lamplighter Hideaway near the airport. This number will connect you right to our room, so you don't have to phone the front desk."

"Okay. I'll think very hard tonight, I promise."

They hugged at the door and said their goodbyes. Connie seemed much more human now, more alive. Smiles had come easier to her in the last couple of hours. The talking had done her some real good, and the connection with Jack over 9/11 appeared to have been a godsend for her.

They hopped into their cab and rode in silence for the first few minutes on the way back to the hotel.

Then Jack said, "You know, what Connie needs is some group therapy with other relatives of victims. I think it would do her a world of good. Look at how she changed over the course of the evening as we talked and talked. She actually had some color in her cheeks when we left."

"Yes, but the agoraphobia is probably holding her back from things like that. She said that she only sees her therapist once every couple of weeks, and he has to come to her house," Kerrie replied.

"Before we go, I'd like us to visit her again. Not for any talk about the key but just to see her. I don't think she will remember anything else that Mitch might have given her. I think that's a dead end. But I believe she could use our help. Perhaps one more chat with her might do a lot of good. What do you think?"

Kerrie looked at Jack and held onto his hand. "So kind of you to suggest that. You must have read my mind."

*****

Jack and Kerrie were enjoying breakfast in their rooms the next morning. Both of them were emotionally exhausted from the hours they had spent with Connie the day before, and weren't in the mood to sit in a restaurant. They chatted about her and what a difficult turn her life had taken. Kerrie was feeling responsible because it was her own father who had done this to her.

That thought had been nagging her all night, and her sleep had been poor. She couldn't stop thinking about that sad little soul hiding in her house to keep safe.

Both of them realized that this dead end left them with nothing to pursue. There was no other lead they could follow. The concept of a key had given them a purpose, a major clue that could have led to something else.

Jack wasn't about to give up though. He pulled out his notes. He was sure they had missed something. Kerrie had suggested they just fly back to Bigfork, but Jack was insistent that they spend at least one more day going over the code before they left, trying other combinations of words.

Then the phone rang. They both jumped, and Kerrie shot her hand to her mouth. They were startled as Connie was the only one who knew their hotel and their direct line phone number. "Hello?" Kerrie answered in a tentative voice.

"Kerrie, is that you? It's Connie."

"Connie, so good to hear from you! I hope we didn't keep you up too late last night" She wondered if Connie could detect the relief in her voice.

"Oh no. It was wonderful that you and Jack came over. I feel very good today."

"That's great to hear. We enjoyed it as well, and we know of course that Jack just loved the pizza! So did you remember something, is that why you're calling?"

"No, sorry, but I would like to be hypnotized."

This took Kerrie by surprise. She was at a loss for words.

"Did you hear me?"

"Yes, sorry. Would that be safe? Would your doctor agree to that?"

"He recommended it several times to me. He said it would unlock my brain and relax me. He said something about closure."

"Okay, can he do it on short notice?"

"I don't want him to do it. That's why I never agreed. I've never felt comfortable with him, and I certainly don't want to be under the spell of any man again, so to speak. But I need this fog to go away. I want to do this for your sake, but mainly for mine."

Kerrie heard Connie take a deep breath. She knew this was a huge step for her to take, and it was exhilarating for Kerrie to witness this brave new person emerging.

Connie continued. "I was hoping that you might know someone who could do it, someone with patience. A woman."

A light went off in Kerrie's brain. Of course she knew someone—Belinda McIntyre, one of her best friends when she had practiced law in New York. Belinda was a psychiatrist as well as being one of the best hypnotherapists in the city, if not the entire country. Kerrie had used her many times as an expert witness, and they had become close. Unfortunately, over the years they had only talked a couple of times by phone. They kept saying they would visit each other but promises like that usually never came to fruition. Sad but true. When you moved away from a city, you moved away from the lives in that city as well.

"I do know someone—a woman, and one of the best hypnotherapists around. I'll call her and see if she can fit us in."

"Oh, what a relief. I hope she'll agree."

"I'll try my best to convince her. You just sit tight, okay?"

"I will. As you now know, I'm not likely to go very far." Connie chuckled, and then added, "Please tell her that I want the fog to disappear, forever. You and Jack in just one visit have given me new hope. I'm indebted to you for that, and I've decided I can't live like this anymore. I know that deep down inside I'm strong enough to do this, and it's up to me to take this step."

Kerrie could hear the determination in Connie's voice, and it warmed her heart. "I believe you are strong enough, Connie, and I believe my dad knew that too."

Chapter 32

Dr. Belinda McIntyre pulled on her coat, grabbed her keys and headed out the door. It had been another marathon day, and sometimes she didn't know where she found the energy or the stamina. Between her professorial duties at NYU where she was tenured, her private psychiatry practice, and regular visits to Washington D.C. to serve on the Surgeon General's Mental Health Council, she barely had time to eat and sometimes just plain forgot to. But she enjoyed every minute of her life. And getting a surprise call out of the blue from her old friend Kerrie Joplin had made her day, if not her year.

Belinda had met Kerrie back in 1997. The nineties were a blur for Belinda—she had graduated from Harvard Medical School, completed her residency, and had opened her private practice. Kerrie was practicing law in New York at that time, and they bumped into each other at a political rally. They became fast friends, and Belinda eventually did some testifying for Kerrie at several trials requiring an expert witness in mental health matters.

Belinda was young to have accomplished so much, but she had always been young. She had graduated from high school at fifteen, finished her undergraduate degree at eighteen, and her medical degree and residency by the age of twenty-three. She knew she had a genius I.Q. but she never talked about that. It tended to intimidate people and made them act weird around her. Except for Kerrie, who had always just teased her about it.

Belinda was one of the youngest ever to serve on a White House committee. Her work with the Surgeon General was fascinating, and she was so proud to have been appointed to such a prestigious committee. The posting had also allowed her to make several visits to the White House and meet all of the senior officials, including the big guy himself; in fact, both big guys due to the government changing hands halfway through her committee term. She was humbly aware that she was now well connected, which could only help her career in the future. The prestige of the appointment also led to other interesting venues: parties, receptions, foreign embassy affairs, junkets to consult in other countries. Life was good.

When Kerrie had phoned her this morning and asked for her help, she didn't have to ask what it was for before saying yes. Friends didn't question; they just went. Now here she was, on her way to Northport, Long Island, from her Manhattan condo. Kerrie had only mentioned that there was a friend, a young lady named Connie Reynolds, who needed and wanted hypnotherapy and she couldn't leave the house due to agoraphobia. She also had severe depression and the last few years of her life had been in a "fog." She wanted the fog lifted.

Belinda knew how to lift fog. She was a recognized international expert now in hypnotherapy and in particular her specialty, hypnoanalysis. She realized that most people never distinguished between hypnotherapists and hypnotists. Hypnotists never went too deep. They were the ones who put on the shows at state fairs and purportedly put dozens of people into instant trances. When asked to do therapy one-on-one, they would also handle it generally through direct or indirect suggestions—like suggesting to a person that smoking is dirty and that they didn't want to have a dirty habit, or that anxiety is an irrational reaction and that one should feel calm instead of anxious. Sometimes suggestions worked, but more often than not the problems in a person's mind went much deeper and needed to be uncovered. That was hypnotherapy.

And hypnoanalysis was a sophisticated technique of hypnotherapy, involving recollection of moments from the past to confront and release locked-in emotions and fears. Belinda agreed to visit with Kerrie's friend and do it pro-bono. Years ago, Kerrie had represented her in her own divorce, free of charge, and Belinda had never forgotten how instrumental Kerrie had been in getting her through the most difficult time in her life. She was glad she could do this little thing to reciprocate, and perhaps be of some help to a lost soul at the same time.

They hadn't chatted for long on the phone. Belinda had been late for her first class of the day, and had several patients to see afterwards. But they agreed to meet at Connie's house on Long Island at around 5:00 p.m., visit with Connie, and then maybe grab dinner together if it wasn't too late.

Unfortunately, now she had to deal with rush hour traffic, so it would probably take at least two hours to get there whereas in the middle of the day it would only take an hour. Northport was on the northwest section of Long Island, and Manhattan was a separate island entirely. Bridges connecting the islands were a major part of the problem in rush hour. She would have to go due northeast from Manhattan as the crow flies, but in reality she would have to go in several different directions because of convoluted bridges and expressways.

She had been so happy to hear Kerrie's voice again. It had been several years since they'd seen each other, although they had chatted on the phone a few times. But when Kerrie moved to Montana, Belinda knew that the friendship would begin to fade. Distance did that, despite the cliché to the contrary.

Belinda handed her keys to the valet, who went to fetch her silver BMW 750i sedan from the underground garage. She shuddered looking at the traffic whizzing by her as she waited. Oh well, that's the price of living in the most exciting city in the world, she thought cheerfully.

The car was delivered to her in less than two minutes. She slipped into the front seat and enjoyed a whiff of the nice new leather smell. She slipped the gearshift into "drive" and was on her way, weaving in and out of traffic with her sleek machine. To be fair, New York wasn't so bad to get around in, she thought, once you knew the streets to take to get to the freeways. And sometimes she enjoyed taking longer to get someplace—her Bimmer had a nice cabin to be stuck in.

She tuned in her Bose twelve-speaker stereo to her favorite jazz station and began to unwind. She would get there when she got there, she resigned herself. A similar thought was probably going through the heads of the two SAD agents who were following a discreet distance behind her in a black Lincoln MKZ, as Belinda turned onto the Williamsburg Bridge on her way towards the Brooklyn/Queens Expressway.

*****

Jack and Kerrie were excited at the prospect of Connie undergoing hypnosis. They figured that this was their last chance to find out if there was any basis to the clue they thought they had pinned down.

They admitted to each other that this was selfish thinking, but Dr. McIntyre might also be able to help Connie with her demons. That was important and they wanted to see that happen, but what was foremost on their minds right now was getting what they came to New York for. Connie needed help and she would hopefully get it, but they needed help too. If they were lucky, two goals could be achieved tonight.

They had both been in danger, along with Heather, Josh, and Meagan, and that was not going to end until they solved this mystery. To quit now was not an option. They were in too deep, and who could they turn to for help when the government itself was after them? Even though they really knew nothing at all yet, the CIA probably thought they did. Which put them in just as much danger as if they did know something. So, at the very least, they needed some kind of bartering chip to stay alive.

Belinda wasn't going to be able to meet them there until around 5:00 p.m., so they were going over to hang out with Connie at around 3:30. They had actually wanted to go earlier, but Connie was again insistent that it had to be 3:30 or later. That seemed to be her earliest slot for visitors.

They rang her doorbell right at the prescribed time, and Connie let them in quickly. No hesitation at the door today. She gave them each a hug and led them into the living room.

Connie had her family photos out on the coffee table. They couldn't resist having a peek, and she was more than pleased to tell stories about each photo. Her brother John was in more photos than they could count. All the current ones of him had been taken in her house. She told them about John, how he was now a fireman with the FDNY, and how he had his own condo and a lovely girlfriend, Heidi. They could tell that Connie really loved her brother, and was proud of him. She told them how she had had to raise John during his teen years, as their parents died when John was only fourteen. He was twenty-two now, and she was pleased that he had turned into such a wonderful young man. They could tell also that she knew in her heart that her love and caring over the years had something to do with that. She was proud and she wore that pride whenever she mentioned him. Perhaps that was really the only thing she was proud of anymore. At least she had that, which was a nice place to start.

Kerrie took some of her own photos out of her purse—one of her parents on their wedding day, and another one of her dad and mom just a year or two before she had died of cancer. Then she had one more to show, that of her dad in his early twenties, in his military uniform. Jack could see that Mitch had been a strikingly handsome man with a physique that movie producers would have killed for to have on screen.

Jack pulled out of his wallet a wedding photo of him and Susan from 1976, when they were both only twenty-two years old. He hadn't looked at this photo in quite some time. He stared at it for a full minute, then wiped his eyes and passed it around.

Saved by the bell, Jack thought. The doorbell was ringing and he knew that the next phase of their visit was about to begin. He was feeling apprehensive about this, having never witnessed hypnotism before, and also a little worried that Connie may not be strong enough to endure it. He hoped they, and she, were not pushing things too fast.

After Kerrie and Belinda had finished their hugs, which were numerous, Kerrie introduced her doctor friend to Connie and Jack. The two friends were beaming, delighted to be together again. They didn't waste time catching up however. After the greetings, Belinda got down to business.

Jack could see that this lady not only acted like a pro, but dressed like one. Her clothes appeared to be right out of a Saks 5th Avenue catalogue, and her hair was short and fashionable. She didn't have the hard features that Jack had imagined a stereotypical seasoned psychiatrist would have; they were soft and attractive, but with a seriousness in her eyes that hinted at the busy life she had.

She sat down beside Connie on the couch and told her all about herself first—her background, education, and specialties. She then asked Connie to outline the events that she thought had brought her to this point. Connie was honest—just as honest as she had been with Jack and Kerrie the night before. She didn't hold anything back. Belinda learned all about the WTC deaths of her parents, the incident with Mitch in the bank, Connie's love for her parents and brother. Then she blurted out that she had loved Mitch too. If Belinda was surprised by this revelation, her expression did not betray it. She was as calm and nonplussed as could be.

Belinda didn't take any notes during this conversation. Jack was impressed to see that she had given Connie her undivided attention, nodding where appropriate, asking some open probing questions when she needed more information, but otherwise totally focused on everything Connie had to say.

Belinda then told Connie all about the hypnotherapy approach, and hypnoanalysis in particular.

"How will you know if I'm under?" Connie asked.

"That's a very common question. Let me correct one word there: "under." That's a common misconception. In hypnosis you are never really "under." Some people are indeed trance-like, but you are still aware of everything around you when you are hypnotized. You will hear voices, the phone ring, a dog's bark. It's sort of like daydreaming, but a little less conscious than that," Belinda answered. "And contrary to what people think," she continued, "you will remember our conversation afterwards."

"So how does it work? I've always thought of hypnosis as falling into a trance and just talking uncontrollably," Connie asked.

Belinda crossed her legs and leaned towards Connie. "Like me, you probably watch too many movies. They always like to show the dramatic trance-image of hypnosis, but it's really not like that for most people," Belinda explained. "You will be in a very relaxed state—an unusually relaxed state. That's what hypnosis is in a nutshell. In that kind of state, with the proper probing, I am able to reach your subconscious mind, which is one powerful machine. If we can reach that section, which most people only experience in their REM sleep, we can unlock some hidden information and images." Belinda paused to make sure she was making sense. Connie nodded, indicating to her to continue. Jack looked on, impressed with how Belinda was explaining it to Connie. He found that he was learning a lot himself too. But he was most impressed with how alert Connie seemed to be, how interested and inquisitive she was.

Belinda continued explaining. "The information that the subconscious mind may be hiding from the conscious mind, either for reasons of competition or protection—we don't know which for sure—can cause stress, anxiety, depression, and amnesia. Because even though these are two separate sections of the brain, they do need each other to function properly. The subconscious mind needs the conscious mind to express what it wants to express, and the conscious mind needs the subconscious mind to draw its information from, for day-to-day normal functioning. If one mind shuts down and refuses to cooperate, the other mind gets frustrated. And that frustration can manifest itself through human phobias and depression."

Belinda stopped talking and looked around at the three of them. They were sitting transfixed. She snapped her fingers and laughed. "Sorry folks, sometimes I explain more than everyone needs to know."

"I'm fascinated by what you're saying. Thanks so much for going into such detail and in a way that's easy to understand," Connie said.

Belinda smiled in appreciation, and held Connie's hand. "One really important point that I want to make is that the subconscious mind is totally irrational and illogical, whereas the conscious mind is *very* rational and logical. They're inherently in conflict with each other, and if they don't find a way to work in harmony, trouble results. In other words, shit happens." They all laughed, glad to see that Belinda was able to show some everyman humor with such a serious subject. And just the way she was able to simplify a complex subject, made it seem less ominous.

Belinda nodded. "Well, Connie, are you ready to begin?"

"Yes, should I lie down like in the movies?"

Belinda chuckled. "That part they do get right. So yes, by all means lie down and get comfortable. But if you're more comfortable sitting up, that's okay too."

*****

"Virginia, this is Brooklyn and Harlem. We were assigned by Montana to tail a Belinda McIntyre. We've followed her to a house located at 15879 Sea Cove Road in Northport, on Long Island. He said to check in with you for detail."

"Hold on, Brooklyn. Let me call it up." They could hear the tapping of Jim Wingate's fingers on the keyboard at the other end of the phone.

"Okay, we have the house registered to a Connie Reynolds. Her record shows that she's been a recipient of monies from the Victims of 9/11 Fund. She was in a mental institution for a year, released in 2004, and she's self-employed. Her previous work record shows that she worked at the…NY State Security Bank until…2003. She left after a tragedy that involved…okay, this may be important. I want you to contact Montana right away and let him know the details I've just told you—and follow his instructions. Tell him you were talking with me."

"Understood. And what about this McIntyre lady?" They could hear Jim's fingers tapping again on the keyboard in Virginia.

"All right, listen up. This woman's a prominent psychiatrist with strong connections in Washington. There's a 'no touch' flag on her file. Make no contact whatsoever," Jim cautioned. "I repeat, make no contact with her."

"Roger, Virginia. Out."

Brooklyn phoned Sam Summerfield, aka Bob Trundle, and outlined his conversation with Virginia. He gave him the information on Connie Reynolds and Belinda McIntyre.

"You're sure she went into Reynolds' house alone? No sign of anyone else there?" Sam asked.

"Well we're sure the Reynolds' woman is there, but we didn't see anyone else enter, though they could have been there already before we arrived," Brooklyn answered.

"Okay. The doctor is our best lead for now, being that she was a close friend of Joplin's. After she leaves, follow her until she arrives at her condo in Manhattan. I want to know if she makes any other stops along the way. If she goes straight home, then head back to Northport and make contact with Ms. Reynolds." Sam heard a sigh at the other end of the phone. "I wish I had more men at my disposal so you wouldn't have to backtrack, but I don't. Talk to Ms. Reynolds seriously about our two subjects, and see if she knows where they are. This sudden visit by the good doctor might mean something is happening. Our subjects may have already made contact or are about to. I can tell you only that Joplin's life has intersected with both Reynolds and McIntyre in the past, so this is significant. But do not hurt Ms. Reynolds, do you read? *Do not hurt her!*"

"Roger, Montana. Out."

*****

Within minutes Belinda had Connie so relaxed, Jack and Kerrie thought she was asleep. She was stretched out on the couch, a pillow under head, hands folded across her tummy. All Belinda had done was talk to her in soothing tones, with repetitive words. No swinging medallion, no ticking metronome, just words in a voice that seemed totally different than the Belinda they had heard talking only a few minutes before. She was good, no doubt about it. She asked Connie some control questions, and she answered them in a very calm, dreamy voice. Then she took her back to the day her parents had died. She asked her to express some words that described that day.

"Shock, despair, falling, crashing, alone, fire, explosion, planes, nothingness, anger, heartbreak," Connie rhymed off without hesitation.

Then she asked her to use short phrases to describe her attempts at dealing with the disaster.

"Went to counseling, looked after my brother, looked after our finances, remembered my parents, talked about my parents, went to work."

Belinda then asked her to outline which friends were helpful to her. Connie smiled widely and openly.

"Oh, only one: Mitch. He came into the bank one day and my heart jumped. He waited to see me, just me. It was like he knew me. We talked every day when he came in, and he only came to me. I told him my situation, and he talked with me all the time about it, to make sure I was dealing with it okay. He advised me to get counseling, and I did."

"What did you like about Mitch?" Belinda asked in a whisper voice.

"His eyes. They looked right through me, into my soul. And his swagger, he was so in control. I felt so protected around him. His nature. He was caring, understanding, unselfish, and he was only interested in me; he didn't care about telling me about himself. I knew I loved him, but I was frustrated that I knew nothing about him."

Connie was alert, so confident and relaxed. There were no signs that she was in a trance, and no resemblance at all to the fearful, insecure Connie who had greeted them at the door only the day before.

"Did anything change in your relationship with Mitch?" Belinda continued in her soothing tone.

"On February 13, 2003, everything changed. He died and I don't know why, and I don't know why he made me help him." Connie was starting to cry now.

Belinda ignored the tears. "Tell me more, Connie."

"He came into the bank, and he was different. He was actually *indifferent.* He seemed to be looking into space. When he talked to me that day at the counter, those wonderful eyes tore right through me, past my soul. I was scared. He told me not to be but I was anyway. I thought he was holding up the bank, but he told me to push the alarm button. I couldn't do it. I was scared and I fell down. He jumped over the counter and helped me back up. He pressed the button himself."

Connie stopped and took a deep breath. Belinda waited a few seconds, then gently urged her to continue.

"His arms felt so strong around me. He held me up like I was a paper doll. I felt good again for a second because he was holding me up, not wanting me to get hurt if I fainted."

She stopped again. Belinda said, "That's a nice memory, Connie."

"He…put something…in the pocket…of my…suit. Yes, he slipped…his hand into my pocket. The sound of paper crackling. I didn't know what it was."

"Continue on, Connie. You're doing very well."

Jack and Kerrie looked at each other, and Jack shifted restlessly in his chair. Something in her pocket?

"He put the vest on me. I knew it was a bomb vest. I'd seen them enough times on the news. He led me out to the lobby area and we waited. Forever we waited. He winked at me, as if to make me feel better."

"I was terrified. I had never been so scared in my life. And heartbroken; he didn't care about me after all. He was just using me. And he wasn't the man I thought he was. He was a monster. I had never seen that monster before." She was speaking rapidly now, her voice more frantic. Jack was spellbound by the tale he was hearing, and he wondered how long she could keep this up. As if reading his mind, Belinda stole a glance at her watch.

"I had to pee, real bad. I held it as long as I could. Finally I couldn't take it anymore and I just let it go. I could feel the warmth trickling down my pant legs. The pain was gone, and I was surprised that I wasn't embarrassed. I looked back at Mitch and he just looked sad. He looked like he pitied me." Connie's voice had risen to a higher pitch, still rapid but she gave no indication that she wanted to stop talking. Belinda moved closer to her and it seemed to Jack as if she was observing Connie's throat. "They came in wearing those awful suits. You could see their eyes, but not much else. An older man was carrying the video camera—I could tell he was older by his eyes, eyes like Mitch's. For a second it looked like Mitch recognized him. The room seemed to stand still for an eternity, then a flash from the camera. They shot him, they killed him, the bullet whizzed right past me, I could hear it."

Connie gasped and seemed to stop breathing, her body began to tremble. Jack stood up and started walking over to the couch. Belinda simply held her hand about two inches above Connie's nose for a few seconds, while waving Jack off. She was being careful not to touch Connie in any way.

Connie began talking again. "I turned around and saw Mitch falling. I was horrified. His finger came off the button and I leaped to grab it, but I was too late. Just before I closed my eyes to brace for the blast I saw the hole in Mitch's forehead. His marvelous eyes had lost their life."

She went silent. Belinda leaned forward again. "Connie, I'm going to count backwards from ten, and I want you to count with me. When we get to one, you will sit up and feel totally relaxed. You will remember everything you told me, and will not feel sad or anxious about your memories today. Do you understand?"

"Yes."

They counted down together.

At the bottom of the countdown Connie sat up and exclaimed triumphantly. "Apparently, there's something in my pocket!"

Chapter 33

They were all standing in Connie's large front foyer. Belinda gave Kerrie a hug and a kiss on the cheek. "It's too late for dinner now, Kerrie. I have an early class tomorrow and it's at least an hour's drive back to Manhattan."

"Oh, I understand. I remember the hectic life in New York. I don't miss it one bit. We'll do dinner another time."

"When are you and Jack flying back home? Can we do it on the weekend?"

"Well, we're scheduled to fly back Sunday, but it's a charter so we can head back earlier if we finish up here. We'll see. I'll give you a call if it looks possible. I can't believe it's Thursday already; we're running out of time."

"Okay, I don't know what it is you two are doing here, but if helping this young lady is part of the objective, your trip has been worthwhile." Belinda smiled and paused expectantly. Kerrie didn't respond. "Well, we'll try to do dinner the next time you're in town if this weekend doesn't work. And bring that handsome Canadian with you!" Belinda smiled coyly at Jack.

"Go get your own man, girlfriend! There are enough of them in New York to choose from!" Kerrie joked, while playfully punching Belinda on the shoulder.

"Sure, but they don't have that funny way of talking that Jack has, 'eh'?"

"Hey, don't mock us Canadians! You Americans are the ones who speak funny, not us!" Jack laughed.

Belinda walked over to Connie, reached out for both hands, and squeezed them warmly.

"I hope tonight's session was helpful for you Connie. It was just a short one, so really just a good start. We need to do a few follow-up sessions. There's no doubt in my mind that you're suffering from Post Traumatic Stress Disorder. I'm sure your doctor has mentioned that to you already."

"Yes, he did tell me that."

"So, would you like me to visit you again and we can do some more of what we did tonight?"

"Dr. McIntyre, I can't afford you. You can see for yourself, look around."

Connie waved her hand around the room.

"It won't cost you a cent. You're a friend of Kerrie's so you have me for free."

Connie put her hands up to her face as she started to cry. Belinda put her arms around her and gently rubbed her back. "There, there, sweetie. You're going to be just fine. I'm going to make sure of that."

Belinda kissed Connie on the forehead, and laid her business card on the telephone table.

"Please call me when you feel you're up to another session. I recommend that you don't wait too long though; it's important that sessions be fairly close together. And until you're ready to leave the house on a regular basis, I can come here. Okay?"

"I don't know what to say, Dr. McIntyre. You've made me feel hopeful that maybe I can be normal again. I can hardly wait to give Johnny the news. He'll be so proud of me!" Connie's face burst into a smile as she mentioned her brother.

"You are normal, Connie. Life has just beaten you up a bit. Remember: 'whatever doesn't kill us makes us stronger.' It's true, believe me," Belinda said in a confident voice.

"Thank you Doctor. I'll definitely be in touch. I already feel so much better, like some of the fog is gone." Connie pulled Belinda's coat from the front closet and helped her on with it.

"There's still a lot of that fog left though, my dear, so you and I have to work on that together."

Belinda gave each of them a kiss, and headed out the door to her car. Jack peeked out the front window and thought she might be headed for the Lincoln parked further up the street, but was pleased to see her get into the BMW. Good choice, he thought. Good taste in cars.

*****

Brooklyn started up the Lincoln a couple of minutes after Belinda had rounded the corner at the end of the street. He gave a voice command to the hands-free phone.

When it connected, he said without expression, "Okay, Montana, it's 9:00 p.m. and we've resumed following Dr. McIntyre. We'll see where it takes us and once she's snug at home in Manhattan we'll be heading back here to Northport as ordered."

"Roger, Brooklyn."

*****

Connie sat down with Jack and Kerrie in the dining room, and started talking to them in a whisper. "As you heard, Mitch might have put something in my pocket."

"It sounds like he did. You never found anything after the incident?" Kerrie asked.

"No, I never checked." A sheepish look came over Connie's face.

Jack was feeling discouraged now. That was six years ago. The clothes had either been laundered several times since then, or more likely had been thrown out.

"I completely forgot about what he did with his hand until tonight. So I never had a reason to look in the pocket."

"Do you still have the clothes, Connie?" Kerrie asked hopefully.

Connie smiled, a sly smile that they hadn't yet seen her use. "Yes, I do still have them, and even better than that, they've been zipped up in plastic and closed away in a cupboard ever since that day six years ago." Connie's voice was tinged with excitement.

Jack jumped to his feet. "Let's go check out that cupboard!"

Connie's eyes grew wide. "Uh, I'd like Kerrie to come with me, alone."

Jack looked at her, concerned. Had he scared her with his gregarious outburst?

"Sorry Jack," she said. "I have *unmentionables* hanging up to dry, and…" she trailed off.

Jack quickly sat down again, and started squirming uncomfortably in his chair, his complexion now a bit splotchy red. He lowered his eyes. "Oh…no problem. I understand totally. Uh, you girls just go ahead then and I'll wait here."

Connie led Kerrie to the stairs, then turned back to her. "Remember that I peed in my clothes that day in the bank? Well, they've never been laundered and they're going to stink something awful. I didn't want a man to be down here when I open the cupboard."

Kerrie's smile was warm and comforting. "I completely understand."

They came to the basement and entered a modest sized storage room. Connie approached the antique wardrobe but didn't touch the knob. "My shrink told me that this would be a big step in my recovery—just opening this door and burning these clothes."

Kerrie walked over and stood beside her. "He's probably right. Go ahead, you can do it."

Connie stepped aside. "Why don't you do it, Kerrie? I don't mind."

"No. You need to do this yourself," Kerrie said softly. "And I'm sure that Dr. McIntyre would agree with me on that."

Connie hesitated, trying to summon up the courage. "Okay," she said. "Hold your nose."

"Don't be embarrassed," Kerrie said. "But, just in case…" she added, pinching her nose tightly.

Connie held onto the knob for a few seconds. She took a deep breath, squeezed her nose with her other hand, and yanked the cupboard open. She jumped back a bit, almost as if she were afraid something was going to leap out at her.

There, secure in the cupboard, was a plastic garment bag. Connie reached in and quickly unzipped the bag. "Oh boy," Connie said, turning her head away. The odor wafted out at the two of them, and even with their noses plugged, it was rank. Years of urine fermenting, and who knows how many types of bacteria growing happily in there, created an odor that defied description. Connie reached down into the garment bag and thrust her hand inside one of the pockets. She pulled out a small envelope, zipped up the bag, and slammed the door shut.

They ran up the stairs from the basement, going right to the dining room where Jack was waiting. He couldn't fathom why both of them were doubled over and gasping for breath.

"Are you girls okay? What's wrong?"

"Just a little musty down there," Kerrie quipped.

Connie took the tiny envelope over to a table lamp and turned it on. She peered down at it, and could feel something solid inside. There was writing on the envelope and she recognized it as Mitch's, from all of the deposit slips he had passed her over the time she had known him. Just a handful of words were written: *"Connie, keep this in a safe place. Love, Mitch."* Connie closed her eyes for a few moments, and tears began to escape from under her eyelids.

She passed the envelope to Kerrie and plopped down into a chair. Kerrie sat down beside Jack and they looked at the words on the envelope together. Kerrie opened it. Inside, just as they had deciphered from Mitch's coded message, was indeed a single key. "Teller has key," they whispered in unison.

Jack just stared at it, realizing that this might just open a "pandora's box." He was relieved and triumphant that their perseverance had gotten them this far, but at the same time, apprehensive. What would this key open?

Jack walked over to Connie and showed her the key. "Can we assume this is a key to a safety deposit box at NY State Security Bank?"

Connie looked at it carefully. "No, that's not one of our keys. It's too large. You know, it looks like a padlock key."

Jack sighed heavily. Another dead end.

*****

It was 10:30 p.m. by the time Jack and Kerrie said their goodbyes to Connie and got into their cab. One of the last things Connie said to them was that she was excited that her brother was going to drop by after his shift at the fire hall, around midnight or so. She was going to wait up for him and tell him about the session with Belinda.

They were glad that Connie held some hope for the future. But as far as the key went, they had no idea how to figure out what lock it would open. They had naively pinned all of their hopes on the obvious—a safety deposit box at the very bank where it had all happened. Now that idea was crushed.

It then occurred to Jack that even if it were a key to a safety deposit box, how would they have gained access? They would have needed to be signatory to the box. He guessed that Kerrie would be able to get a court order to open her father's box, but not if the box had been registered under an alias. They rode back to their hotel in silence, both exhausted by the rollercoaster of emotions.

*****

The SAD agents parked their Lincoln on the street a few houses down from Connie's house. They had followed Belinda McIntyre back to her Manhattan condo and then turned right around and came back to Northport as ordered. They each gulped down their third cup of coffee, trying desperately to stay awake and alert. It had been a long day of doing nothing.

They got out of the car, walked up to the house and rang the doorbell. It was 11:15 p.m.

*****

Connie heard the bell and ran to the door, expecting John. She peered through the peephole and was startled to see two men in suits standing on her front porch. She called through the door to them. "Yes, what do you want?"

"Ma'am, we're with the NYPD. We've had reports of a prowler around your house and we just want to make sure you're okay and ask you a few questions."

Connie didn't like this intrusion. And what prowler? Wouldn't her neighbors have phoned to warn her before reporting it to the police?

"I'm just fine, thank you. I'm sorry, I can't let you in."

"Ma'am, we won't be more than just a few minutes."

"Go away. I have an alarm system and I'm going to press it."

*****

Brooklyn looked at Harlem contemplatively, and whispered, "We can't cut the line because she probably has line security on the alarm. The alarm company will respond instantly."

"We'll pop the lock," Harlem whispered back.

"How long will that take? She might push the panic button."

Harlem nodded as he bent over and examined the lock. "Two seconds tops." He pulled a tool out of his pocket.

*****

Connie figured they had gone. They hadn't called to her through the door again and there was no sound from the front porch. She started to feel better, but she was afraid to move back to the peephole to look out. As she started walking back to the kitchen she heard a metallic noise against the door lock. She dashed back to the foyer and frantically stretched her hand toward the alarm panel. Just as she was about to push the panic button the door burst open, knocking her to the floor.

Two men came in. One grabbed her under the arms and yanked her to her feet. She tried to scream but no sounds would come through the rough palm that was covering her mouth. The other one pulled out a gun with what looked like a long cylinder attached to the barrel. He shoved it up against her head, and she could feel the cold steel pressed into her temple.

"Be smart. What's the 'all clear' code? Now!"

Connie blurted it out: 46987. The man with the gun quickly closed the front door and punched the number in to the alarm panel keypad. The red flashing light instantly turned to steady green. They dragged Connie over to a kitchen chair. One of them continued to hold his hand over her mouth and the other pulled out a roll of duct tape. They quickly wrapped her arms and legs to the chair.

Before removing his hand from her mouth, the one man said, "If you scream, we'll kill you. Just a couple of questions and we'll be gone. Can I take my hand from your mouth? Are you going to be a good little girl?"

Connie nodded her head. The man took his hand away slowly and growled at her. "Don't make me regret this."

He didn't waste any time. "Do you know a Kerrie Joplin or a Jack Howser?"

Connie shook her head. She felt her jaw starting to hurt.

The man squeezed her throat, and asked the question again. Connie quickly nodded her head in response.

"Good, now we're getting somewhere," the man said. "Have they contacted you?"

Connie shook her head again. Her neck was getting stiff now as well as her jaw, and a sharp jabbing pain had started in her left shoulder and arm.

The man nodded at his partner, who pulled out a small drill-like instrument. He pushed a button and it started to whir. The one man held her head steady, while the guy with the drill started bringing it down toward her left eyeball. Connie trembled and closed her eyes so tightly her eyelids hurt. The man pried them open, and she screamed. He slapped her hard across the face. The man with the drill raised his arm again and aimed the instrument down toward her eye. Connie started wiggling in her chair, rocking it, trying to avoid the menace from above. She could see it coming. She panicked and yelled out, "Yes!"

The first man smiled and said, "See, this isn't so hard. Now, where are they staying?"

"I...don't know." She was finding it hard to breathe now. She started gasping for breath, and pleaded with them to help her. "I need...a pill... they're in the bathroom." They just smiled, while the one man turned the drill on again. The other one concentrated on holding her head still and her left eyelid open.

It came down fast, no teasing this time, and she convulsed from the sudden shock as the drill sliced into her eyeball. She let out a silent scream—she couldn't find any sound. It was like a bad dream where you try to scream to wake up, but you can't. The pain was excruciating; she had never experienced anything like it before in her life. It partially masked the crushing feeling she was now aware of in her chest. She started to cry, but the tears only came out of her right eye. She looked up but there was only blackness on her left side. She knew she was now half-blind.

The first man asked again, "Where are they staying? Your other eye will be next."

Connie couldn't hold up any longer. "The Lamplighter!" she screamed, from a throat that was choking her.

Just then she could make out through her one good eye the image of another figure in the doorway, rushing in a blur toward the man who was holding her head. John!

Through that one eye, she watched as her brother knocked the man to the floor, watched as he picked up a chair and smashed it into the face of the other. She felt relief in her soul for a few seconds. The pain in her eye was now radiating outward to her entire face. It was a burning sensation that was unrelenting, and Connie thought she was going to pass out. But she couldn't let herself do that because John was here and she told herself she would be okay now.

She watched as her brother rushed over to her and started scratching hopelessly with his fingers at the duct tape, tears streaming down his cheeks. "Connie, hold on. I'll get you out of here," he sobbed. She wanted to kiss his kind face, but she couldn't. She wanted to hug him but her chest was squeezing the life out of her. She knew she had something wonderful to tell him about, but she couldn't remember what it was. She wanted to say something, anything, to him but the words wouldn't come. Connie watched through her right eye as one of the men put the gun with the cylinder up against John's forehead. She heard a gentle spitting noise. In slow motion, she saw a perfect hole form in John's forehead—or was that Mitch's forehead? She saw him lurching backwards, but he wasn't holding his finger on a red button. It really was John, she now knew for sure. And her heart broke for the third time in her young life. Connie sighed and slumped down in her chair as far as the tape would allow, being crushed by what felt like a sack of cement sitting on her chest. She watched for a few seconds more as everything turned to black. And she sighed one last time.

Chapter 34

Brooklyn had never had an occasion to use this special phone number before. He scrolled down the electronic directory in his listing of CIA departments, and found the one he was looking for under the heading "Housekeeping." He recited the number and the call went through.

"Your identification please?" A woman's voice.

"Brooklyn, 478 Bravo, Charlie, Augustus."

"Verified, go ahead."

"Housekeeping needed at 15879 Sea Cove Road, Northport, Long Island."

"House or apartment?"

"House."

"How many rooms to clean?"

"Two."

"Is there an alarm system?"

"Yes."

"Code, please?"

"Just one second." He quickly scanned his notes. Brooklyn had an instant recall memory, but sometimes he liked to double-check just to make sure. "46987," he replied.

"Remain in your car at the premises until a scout arrives. Thirty minutes."

The call disconnected. Brooklyn and Harlem reclined their seats and closed their eyes. They had half an hour to catch up on some sleep.

*****

It was still Thursday, close to midnight, and Jack couldn't sleep. He had his notes spread out in front of him on the bed, and he kept going over things in his mind that he had already gone over a hundred times before. He could hear Kerrie tossing and turning in the next room. She must be having the same problem, he thought, but at least she was trying to go to sleep. More than he could say for himself.

They had arrived back at the hotel from Connie's house about an hour ago, and both had mixed feelings. They had the key, but where did it belong? That was the overwhelming mystery now. Jack knew there was an answer, somewhere. He knew in his curious soul that it was probably right there in front of them.

He was looking at the remaining parts of the code that they had not yet solved.

There were the numbers—15/15/14—that they had already translated down to 1/1/9. There were also the two remaining material words—*"within"* and *"reach"*—that would be important to the three-word main message but not part of the message itself.

The main message that they had already deciphered, and had turned out to be correct, was *"Teller has Key."* The remaining two orphan words *"within"* and *"reach"* were important to that main message. And the numbers played a role as well, though they could no longer be a safety deposit box number. He had been counting on that when he was thinking that the key would fit a box.

A locker at a bus depot or train station perhaps? No, couldn't be. Not secure enough and it would have been cleaned out long ago. Mitch wouldn't have taken a chance on a short-term rental. He would have picked a facility that could be prepaid in advance and for as long as he wanted…as long as he wanted…

Jack jumped up and went into Kerrie's room. He gently shook her awake.

"Jack, what's the matter? Is something wrong?" She asked wearily.

"Don't pretend you were in a deep sleep. I heard you thrashing around in here," Jack teased.

"I was just starting to doze off, a teeny bit anyway. You might think of doing the same thing."

"Get up, Kerrie We have work to do on the internet."

"I can't plug in my laptop. There could be tracers out."

"No, I mean down in the hotel's business center. It's open 24/7. We can access the internet there. I think I know what we have to narrow in on Kerrie, and I won't be able to sleep until I know for sure. I don't want to leave you here alone."

*****

A black SUV pulled into the driveway at 15879 Sea Cove Road exactly thirty minutes after the call. A man stepped out of the car and walked down to the bottom of the driveway, and looked directly at the black Lincoln. He made a 'time-out' sign with his hands, then turned around and walked up the front porch and in through the unlocked door. He turned on the lights and punched in the alarm code.

The Lincoln pulled away from the curb and headed back to the city.

The man walked into the kitchen and pulled out a camera from his duffle bag. He took photos of the two bodies from every corner of the room. He took some close-ups as well. Then he went into the other rooms on the main floor and took photos of those, every nook and cranny.

Then he reached into his duffle bag again, and pulled out an air-purifying machine. He plugged it into a kitchen socket, and turned it to full power. He didn't worry about leaving fingerprints; he had none to leave.

He began his exit fifteen minutes after he had arrived. He opened the door, punched in the alarm code again, shut the door and secured the lock with a tool from his pocket.

*****

They had the business centre all to themselves. No surprise; it was 1:00 a.m. on Friday morning. Who in their right mind would be surfing the internet in a hotel at that time?

As they sat at the cubicle, Jack showed Kerrie his new notes on the remaining puzzles. She listened intently as he explained his rationale. "I'm certain this key is to a storage facility. You know, one of those self-serve types where you pay for a unit and put your own lock on it?"

"Hmm, that's a viable option." Kerrie said, still slightly groggy from being shaken awake from a very light sleep.

"Okay, here goes nothing." Jack searched the word "Storage."

They looked as thousands of choices popped up in the search result. Jack clicked on a directory of storage facilities in the New York environs.

The screen jumped and the display listed facilities alphabetically. "Brace yourself, here's the moment of truth."

He scrolled down to the W's. They stared at the screen. Kerrie shivered and crossed her arms. Jack almost jumped out of his skin.

There were nine locations in New York and New Jersey for "Within Reach Storage." Their motto was: "Keep Your Possessions Within Reach."

Kerrie grabbed Jack's head, turned him towards her, and planted a big smacker on his lips. "You're an absolute genius!"

Jack blushed, but kissed her back. "Now, to figure out which location it is."

Kerrie sighed. "You're right, give me that kiss back."

"I already did. I'm surprised you didn't notice." Jack grinned.

They stared intently at the list of franchise locations: Syracuse, Buffalo, Albany, Bernardsville, Newark, New York City, Painted Post, Tonawanda, White Plains.

Kerrie suddenly put her hand up to her mouth and gasped. "The location we want is Bernardsville. Dad used Bernardsville," Kerrie uttered in a hushed tone.

"Why do you think that?"

"Because his middle name was Bernard."

*****

Sam Summerfield sat back in his leather office chair and rubbed his eyes. It was late and he knew he should head back to his hotel for some zzz's, but he just didn't feel like it. He thought of calling his wife, Jan, but it was far too late, even back in L.A. He didn't want to rouse her out of bed and make her worry needlessly.

Agents Brooklyn and Harlem had just called. He thought about that poor Reynolds girl, and wondered what part of *"Do not hurt her"* those two cowboys didn't understand. He felt like sending a cleaning crew to *their* homes. At least they found out where Jack and Kerrie were staying, but their brutal actions against the Reynolds siblings made him halt, for now, the task of moving in on the Lamplighter.

He was developing a headache and he guessed it was from lack of sleep, or maybe something else. He pictured Kerrie in his mind—beautiful, funny, naïve Kerry—and worried about her. What had she gotten herself into? Sam still didn't know. Jim Wingate knew what it was, he was sure of that, but there was no way he was going to get it out of him. Sam was just a robot. If he got promoted in the future, he would get to see full scenarios. But for now, just little pieces.

He didn't know anymore whether he wanted to move up higher. He was already a senior CIA agent, with serious power within the SAD division. Did he really want more? Did he really want to know entire scenarios? Could he sleep at night if he knew? He had a tough enough time as it was. He rubbed his eyes some more. He just wanted to go home to Glendale, to Jan, Trevor, and Craig. He longed to be a normal person again. But he couldn't recall what that was even like anymore. The idea of retirement had picked up momentum in his mind over the last few weeks. He didn't need the money, so why did he still do it? Well, aside from the excitement, probably the only reason that made sense was "patriotism." He, like others, was convinced—or brainwashed—that he was serving a higher, nobler cause. Service of country, protection of the innocent, bravery under fire, and staring in the faces of enemies of the American way of life.

Yeah, he thought soberly, tell that to Connie Reynolds.

He shook his head to try to clear it. "Snap out of it," he commanded himself, "these are a dead man's thoughts."

*****

It was a beautiful, sunny, Friday morning in Northport, Long Island. The birds were chirping, the butterflies were flitting from flower to flower, and a large white van with the signage "Benson Renovations" pulled into the driveway of 15879 Sea Cove Road.

Four men got out, wearing authentic-looking company coveralls. Two of them set up shop on the front porch. Over the next four hours, they would completely dismantle the porch and then just methodically put it back together again. They would also restrict access by any means required.

The other two men popped the lock, went inside and punched in the alarm code. They were carrying several large duffle bags, which they promptly dropped to the floor and started unloading, quickly and efficiently—and without a word between them. One of them went back to the van and dragged into the house a thickly folded plastic contraption.

They spread out large thick plastic sheets over the living room floor. Several bottles of cleaning chemicals—a type that could never be purchased at the local hardware store—were carefully placed on the kitchen floor. They each pulled on rubber seamless suits that covered them from their necks to their toes. Next came goggles, filtered masks, and gloves. They moved both bodies carefully from the kitchen over to the plastic sheets in the living room. Then they unfolded the plastic contraption, which transformed quickly into a completely enclosed tent, which sealed itself to the sheets on the floor.

Last but not least, two muffler-equipped handsaws were pulled from a duffle bag.

One of the men got up and switched on the homeowner's little pink radio, tuning in to his favorite hard rock station. An AC/DC tune was playing, and he cranked it up loud, very loud.

One man said to the other, "Which one do you want—boy or girl?"

The other man shrugged. "Doesn't matter, but let's get a move on. I have a softball game at 4:00."

One man unzipped a wall of the tent surrounding the bodies, and they both entered, zipping back up again before they knelt down on the plastic floor.

They turned on their powerful battery-operated saws and commenced the quality work that Benson Renovations was renowned for. After a minute or two their heads started jerking in rhythm to the banshee screaming of AC/DC's "Highway to Hell."

*****

Jack and Kerrie were up at 5:30 a.m., had a quick continental breakfast and were waiting for the cab in front of their hotel by 7:00. They had only managed to get a couple of hours sleep, but it didn't matter. They were both pumped today. Last night's internet revelations had them very excited, and they each felt that this day was going to be a momentous one. At the same time, they had no idea what they would find, but they were fairly confident that the key would fit a lock at Within Reach Storage in Bernardsville.

They instructed the cab driver as to where they wanted to go. The cabbie was excited too. This would be a big fare. Bernardsville was in the Somerset Hills of New Jersey, and about ninety miles from their hotel. The storage location was right on US-202, just outside of the town center.

They were both deep in thought as the cab made its way along the Long Island Expressway, then the Cross Island Parkway, merging onto I-295, then I-95 into New Jersey, along the New Jersey Turnpike. They barely noticed that they were now in the "Garden State." The taxi merged onto I-80, then I-287, and finally US-202. The scenery along the way was captivating, but neither of them noticed. The Somerset Hills area was gorgeous but not to be admired today; it was like they were in a trance. The lack of sleep plus a myriad of thoughts had achieved a state of near anesthesia.

They came out of it only when the cabbie said, "We're here." Just over two hours had gone by, yet both of them felt as if they had just left.

Jack paid the driver, and they stood on the sidewalk looking at the Within Reach Storage facility. It was just like any other self-storage—units clustered together in pods, dull exteriors, fenced compound. This particular facility looked brand new, and Jack hoped that they weren't wrong in their guess. As he and Kerrie walked up to the little office, he said to her, "The numbers we deciphered must be the unit number." Kerrie nodded in agreement. Jack noticed that her face seemed to have drained of its usual color.

"Are you okay?"

"Yes, but I'm feeling very nervous. I guess it's a fear of the unknown. Now that we're here, I'm scared to death about what we might find in there."

They opened the office door and walked in. An elderly woman greeted them with a welcoming smile.

"Hello, how can I help you two?"

"Hi. I want to access a unit that my father rented here. His name was Mitch Joplin, and the unit number should be 119. We have the key." Kerrie shifted nervously from foot to foot as the woman clicked away on her computer.

She looked up from her monitor. "No Mitch Joplin on our records, dear. Close, but no cigar." She chuckled at her little joke.

Suddenly Kerrie had a thought. "Try Bernard Joplin please. Sometimes my dad went by his middle name." She waited, biting her lip.

"Well, you're in luck. Here we are. But the unit number is not 119. You're close again though. You had it reversed. It's 911—building 9, unit 11."

Jack and Kerrie quickly exchanged glances, seeing the same astonishment in each other's eyes at the mention of 911.

"I remember your father very well. A nice man. The record shows here that he was one of our first customers when we opened up back in 2002. He had his pick of units, and that's the one he picked, by George! I recall he was quite insistent on that. I'm one of the owners here by the way. Name's Millie."

They shook hands, and Jack had the sneaky feeling that Millie would talk to them all day if they let her.

"I never saw your dad again after he reserved his unit. I was quite surprised by that. And you know what? He is the only customer who has ever paid us for more than a year in advance. He bought twenty years of storage! My word, that's a lot of money, but I remember he didn't seem the least bit concerned. He said he wanted it for twenty years and just paid us in full. He didn't even ask for installments." Millie shook her head in astonishment. Clearly the memory was still fresh in her mind.

"Millie, can you point the way to Building 9?" Jack asked as politely and patiently as he could muster.

"Oh sure, go straight down the middle aisle then hang a left after four buildings. It will be clearly marked. You can go into the compound directly through the back of my office here. Will save you from having to use the combination on the fence gate."

The walk to the unit was a short one. They found Building 9 and walked to the end unit #11. Jack stood in front of the door and held the key in his hand. Kerrie was standing behind him. "Would you like to do the honors, Kerrie?"

"No, you go ahead. I'm just going to stand here with my fingers crossed."

Jack knelt down on the ground. The door was a rolling overhead type with the lock secured to two embedded rings in the cement driveway. He slipped the key into the padlock and tried to turn it. It wouldn't move. He looked back at Kerrie, grimacing. She stepped forward and gently took the key out of his hand. Kneeling down, she spit on the key and slipped it in herself, jiggling it around a few times in the lock. It turned smoothly, the padlock popped open, and the steel overhead door began to slide up ominously on its runners. Jack and Kerrie stood on the threshold, frozen in place. Neither of them said a word.

Chapter 35

It was 8:55 a.m. on Friday, and Sam Summerfield sat in his office in downtown New York City, awaiting the arrival of the agents code-named Brooklyn and Harlem.

Where he was sitting was still only temporary, until suitable permanent offices were decided upon in New York center. This temporary situation had existed since September 11, 2001, when the CIA Clandestine offices were destroyed in the collapse of WTC building 7, a full seven hours after the Twin Towers had come down.

Sam was hoping that a good location was found soon. He never liked temporary. It was hard to justify expenses for necessary upgrades to work stations and infrastructure, when there was always a possibility that they would be moving. They needed to be downtown due to the undercover work his division did with corporations, the United Nations, and the foreign visitors who came to New York every day.

Sam had lost track of how many times he and fellow agents had portrayed wealthy businessmen, looking to make deals at any cost. They were all slick enough to pull off such deceptions, and it was amazing how easy those deceptions were when money was no object. And with the CIA, money was never an object. They had trapped countless corporate executives in payoff schemes over the years, enabling the CIA to use them going forward as information-gatherers and manipulators. And of course, for insider trading. Congress never gave the CIA all the money it needed to do its work, so other methods of revenue were necessary. A separate team of specialized agents handled the sophisticated work of day trading and stock manipulation. The drug trade was another lucrative revenue stream for the CIA. While the four prominent drug cartels in Mexico got all the publicity for their violent ways, there was a fifth cartel that operated with no publicity—and a little less violence.

Insider trading and drug dealing aside, blackmail was the easiest of crimes and useful as hell. If only the American taxpayers knew how many Fortune 500 companies they had invested their hard-earned money in that were basically beholden to the CIA, they would have thought twice before buying stocks. But the good thing for the CIA was, the American people generally believed whatever they were told to believe, and the mainstream press cooperated with the government quite nicely to make sure that happened. Sam thought it was pathetic how citizens in supposedly free nations like the United States loved to brag about how glad they were to live in a country where their government and media told them the truth, as opposed to communist countries. Yes, they were sure proud to have a free press, with free speech, and that they had a government that respected their right to know. Yeah, right. If they only knew. Most of the mainstream press was in the CIA's pockets, again through blackmail. The CIA pulled the strings, and if they wanted stories thrown in a different direction, all they had to do was ask. Editorial control, in essence, was in the hands of the CIA. Of course from time to time they had to allow some controversies to be reported, and some criticisms of government policies. This was necessary to add credibility to the real serious stuff they manipulated. They had to throw them a bone once in a while.

It was merely a matter of content control, and the CIA had an entire division that did that and nothing else. It was a full time job. They arranged for the juicy blackmail information, or if none existed, created it. They communicated the blackmail, they groomed the next-in-line rungs of editorial talent, and they made the threats. The system was slick and it worked. And sometimes when threats failed, the balls were handed off to SAD to execute the threats.

The CIA was officially in the business of information *collection*. Unofficially they were in the business of *controlling* information. But oftentimes if it didn't exist in the manner they liked, they were also in the business of *creating* it out of thin air.

Hell, even when major news stories like Watergate hit the front pages citizens who applauded their "independent media" didn't have a clue that Watergate was simply allowed to happen. It was one of those stories that the CIA reported. Watergate was merely a bloodless coup.

Most people were unaware that the CIA had undercover offices in the WTC Building 7, along with the mayor's Office of Emergency Management, and the Securities and Exchange Commission. Many other tenants had been in that building as well, but they were hardly as important.

Well, until more permanent offices were established, Sam would just have to try to make himself at home here on Barkley Street whenever he was in

New York. His comfortable office was always here for his exclusive use, and of course when he was at this office he was a "coffee importer," as were all the other CIA employees at this location.

Sam swung his chair around, put his feet up on the credenza, and stared out the window. From his eighth floor vantage point he had a good view of the WTC site and the extensive preparations being made to make it into a world-class facility again. He chewed on the end of his pen as he thought in amazement about the incredible damage the terrorists had caused. It made him sick to think that America actually cooperated with those maniacs in other parts of the world when it was politically expedient. And he was one of the facilitators. Well, he just did what he was told. If he had his way…

That was one horrible day eight years ago, and one that made him glad that organizations like his existed. Even though disillusionment had set in for him lately, he was proud of what he and many others like him did every day to help keep America safe. In his lifetime he never wanted to witness another attack like that. It was scary, to say the least, and he was a man who wasn't accustomed to being scared. He couldn't even imagine the horror ordinary civilians had felt when they watched their television sets that day.

Suddenly his thoughts were interrupted. His secretary's voice came over the intercom advising him that his guests had just arrived. "Send them right in."

Brooklyn and Harlem were escorted into his office, and his secretary closed the door behind her. Sam didn't bother to stand or shake their hands. He asked them to sit. Neither of them showed any signs of being nervous. That would change.

"I'll get right to the point," Sam said as he leaned over his desk. "What you did last night was a travesty."

"We got the information, didn't we?" Brooklyn asked sarcastically.

"Yes, you did, but you were ordered specifically not to hurt her."

"She died of a heart attack," Harlem jumped in. He stretched his arms out behind the back of his chair, and yawned.

"And you did nothing to prompt that heart attack?" Sam probed, trying to keep his anger in check.

"No, just tied her up and scared her a bit," Brooklyn answered, while brushing some lint off the shoulders of his Armani suit.

Sam clenched both of his fists. "Have you ever had to call in our cleaning service before?"

"No, first time."

"I guess you're not aware then that the scouts take photos?" Sam asked through clenched teeth.

Silence. They both shifted in their seats.

"I saw the photos early this morning." Sam said sadly. "You tortured her."

"Well, okay, we did a little."

"You drilled out her eyeball, you fucking asshole!"

Silence again.

"And why did you have to kill her brother?"

"Is that who he was?" Brooklyn asked nonchalantly.

"Answer my question."

"He was compromising the situation. We had no choice."

"You are trained in lethal martial arts. You know plenty of methods of subduing a man, short of putting a bullet through his head," Sam retorted.

The young agents nodded, both of them now sitting stiff in their chairs. Harlem leaned forward slightly. "Could I have some water?"

Sam reached behind his desk and grabbed a bottled water off his credenza. He got up and walked around his desk to where Harlem was sitting. Harlem reached out his hand. "Thanks, much appreciated."

In a lightning move, Sam slapped the bottle into Harlem's open hand, while at the same instant Sam's other hand grabbed the man's wrist from the back. Both of Sam's hands worked in unison to produce a loud snap. Harlem gasped as his hand bent backwards well beyond ninety degrees. The plastic water bottle fell to the floor from a hand that could no longer even hold a pencil.

Brooklyn jumped to his feet, thinking he was next. He was right. Sam delivered a fast kick to his solar plexus sending the agent flying backwards over the coffee table.

Sam's secretary opened the door and came rushing in at the sound. Sam held up his hand in the "Stop" symbol, and she immediately turned on her heel and left, closing the door again.

Sam used his significant presence to dominate the two cowards—one of them sitting in a chair holding onto a dangling, useless hand; the other still lying on the floor holding his stomach, gasping for breath.

"Stand up! You're both suspended, pending an investigation. Give me your weapons and your identification, including your magnetic entry cards. You don't deserve to call yourselves agents. You're not agents—you're just hollow dime-a-dozen killers." Sam paused for effect to let his order sink in, and continued. "If it were my call, I'd put you in front of a firing squad right now. You're a disgrace to the CIA and to this country. Those two good citizens were not the enemy. We just wanted information and you were trained to use other ways to get it."

The two agents were now standing, with their eyes aimed down to the floor. Their arrogance was gone.

"Two innocent American lives, decent lives, were needlessly wasted because of you heartless clowns," he added as he motioned for them to hand over their guns. Sam was well aware that some people might be justified in calling him heartless as well, but he consoled himself by thinking that he knew where to draw the line. Some people deserved to die, had to die—and others simply didn't. Agents had to be careful not to completely lose their sense of humanity. He also knew that it was easier said than done with the power trip that the CIA vested in its agents.

Brooklyn and Harlem quietly took out their side-arms and identification, laying them on Sam's desk. Sam punched the intercom to his secretary. "Let them in now, please."

His door opened and two uniformed guards appeared. "Show them out of the building," Sam ordered, voice dripping with disgust.

*****

They began walking into the storage room, slowly. The unit was only 10' by 20' but appeared cavernous. There was only one item in the room. Right smack in the center, looking almost like an altar, was a wooden pallet with one metal box sitting on it. Kerrie moved over to the pallet while Jack flicked the light switch and closed the overhead door. Then he joined her. They both looked down at the box, realizing that their madcap search had led to this—whatever it was.

Jack knelt down and looked at the box. It wasn't locked—it sat there just begging to be opened. He looked up at Kerrie. "Whenever you're ready."

She knelt down beside him, took a deep breath, and opened the box. On top of the other contents inside, was an envelope with her name on it. She picked it up, stood, and walked over to a corner of the room. Jack watched her as she opened the envelope and withdrew several pages.

"It's a letter. Addressed to me."

"Go ahead and read it, to yourself. This is a private moment for you. Don't think of me."

As she read the long letter, tears began to flow, her eyes became wide, and she clutched at her chest. Jack forced his eyes away from her and let her have her moment. He looked down and began rummaging through the rest of the contents. The next item he found was an old photo with Mitch, Kerrie, and her mother. Kerrie was about five years old, and they looked like the typical happy family. On the back was written, "Kerrie, for a time, we were happy. Love, Dad."

Underneath the photo were a couple of layers of plastic sheeting, and beneath that a videotape, and a miniature cassette tape. That was it. Nothing else was in the box. He looked at the videotape—the cardboard case was old, faded, and bore the CIA seal on the front. There were no labels and nothing else to indicate what was contained on the tape.

Jack looked up at Kerrie. She was still reading through the letter, and was now crying uncontrollably, her tears dropping onto the pages. He didn't want to disturb her. Jack opened his knapsack and stuffed the videotape into an inside hidden pocket. He would tell her about it later. She had enough to deal with right now. If she had the courage to watch it, he would hold her hand as they watched it together. He slid the tiny cassette tape into the side pocket of his jeans; he knew Kerrie had her personal recorder with her, so they could listen to that together as well if she wanted to.

Kerrie slid down the wall and onto the floor, letting the pages fall from her hands as a gasp escaped from her mouth. She just sat there and looked down at the cement floor, wiping her eyes with the sleeve of her jacket. "Kerrie, are you all right?"

She looked up at him and smiled thinly. "I don't know. I don't think so."

Jack sat down on the floor as well, to be eye level with Kerrie. But he kept his distance. "Is there anything you want to share with me? I'll understand if you don't want to."

"I can share it all with you, Jack. You can read for yourself."

She picked up the scattered pages, crawled over and placed them in Jack's hands. "God help us all," she whispered.

Jack slowly took the pages while his eyes fixated on the dead look on Kerrie's face. A little voice in his head told him not to do it, but he ignored that voice and forced himself to read:

Dearest Kerrie,

If you're reading this letter, then I am dead. If the wrong people are reading this, then I have clearly failed at the last two things I tried to do with my life.

I loved you with all my heart, and I hope you know that. I am aware that I was a horrible father. I just wasn't there for you or your dear mother. My life was out of control, and it shoved everything else out of the way. Also, the things I did left very little of my soul left to share. I felt like a hypocrite, daring to set an example of love and compassion when the things I had done had already sucked me dry.

This is not intended to be a goodbye letter, because I expect my departure is old news by now. It is intended to be a confession. There are a lot of things I could confess to, but there is nothing more horrible than what I was a part of shortly before I left the CIA. I'm sure by now you know that being one of their agents is how I wasted my life.

I won't bore you with too many technical details, just enough for you to understand. There is further documentation that will provide all of that to you and others, if you indeed choose to involve others—and if you're successful in locating that other documentation.

A little bit of history—some of this you may know. I joined the military right after high school and was trained in the skill of sharp-shooting. I was a sniper. I was recruited while still in the military to join the CIA. I wore both caps for several years. They discovered early on that I had an affinity for math and science, so I was targeted for an education within the military for a degree in structural engineering and explosives demolition. I eventually graduated with a Masters degree.

The military—Special Forces—first used my explosives skills in Vietnam with underwater demolition work: bridges, dams, fortifications, etc. At the same time I was on the payroll for the CIA. I became an expert in the early technology of Thermate, and a less potent version called Thermite. These are pyrotechnic compositions that are capable of generating short bursts of extremely high temperature, burning through steel and other alloys with ease, quickly and without explosion. Thermate had valuable military uses, and because it was able to burn without an external source of oxygen—it actually generates its own oxygen— it was very useful for underwater work.

Over the years with the CIA, I was involved in countless projects around the world, using Thermate or other more conventional explosives. You might have read about some of these events in the news, but of course they were always attributed to some other group, or country. Unfortunately, I became the CIA's foremost expert in structural engineering and explosives. It was a reputation that they made full use of.

In the year 2000, I was approached by my superiors with an unusual request. They wanted me to prepare schematics and recommendations for implosion destruction of the World Trade Center twin towers. This was unusual for the obvious reasons, but also for the mere fact that we were to be involved in a project on American turf.

I was alarmed. I asked what this was for, and I refused to do any work on it until they told me. We were not usually given reasons for most projects. However, in this case I demanded one.

I believed them when they told me that this was merely preventative caution, that if a terrorist attack were to occur, by missiles, jetliners or van-laden bombs such as the 1993 attempt on the WTC, the authorities would be in a position to topple the buildings safely if they became too dangerous for occupancy, or too dangerous to remain standing.

In other words, they wanted these towers and others like them throughout the United States to be prepared in advance for demolition if the need arose. The analogy they used in their explanation was that it was similar to avalanche control. Bring the tons of snow down when it was safe to do so, rather than allowing it to happen when it wasn't safe. To solidify their point, they code-named the project "Operation Avalanche." The World Trade Center was the first to be considered for Operation Avalanche, and after that would follow other similar tall structures in major cities. This was to be a long-term CIA project, to prepare and rig in advance all the most obvious terrorist targets. Their theory was that once a building was damaged by an attack, it was too late to rig it properly for demolition. So, doing it in advance would be safer and more expedient. As an engineer I couldn't disagree with them. It actually made good sense to me, for the safety of our major cities. I realized, sad to say, that this was the first project I would ever work on that would directly save lives, rather than directly take them.

I agreed only on the condition that any eventual demolitions would be to vacant buildings; occupants would have to be evacuated well in advance and that the demolition would be announced and the sites secured beforehand. I asked for such assurances in writing and that they were to be placed in my vault at Langley headquarters. I insisted on having the right also to inspect my vault box every three months to ensure that this documentation was still there. They agreed to these demands. I prepared the specifications. My recommendation was that we would use a more powerful variant of Thermate—being TH3. The beauty of Thermate is that it can simply be sprayed on a surface and can sit safely for years, basically unnoticed. It is stable and does not pose any danger until a high heat source is applied—a very high heat source, otherwise a Thermate reaction will not be achieved. My recommendation was that we would use Magnesium fuses, magnesium being one of the few substances capable of such a high ignition temperature. Also, my specifications outlined that the Thermate TH3 would be sprayed onto internal support column surfaces, accessed from elevator shafts, and basement or underground parking levels. Also, at strategic points higher up in the structures. Some internal finishes would have to be pulled away to gain access.

Such work would be done under the guise of fireproofing work to sections of the buildings, and ongoing maintenance. The radio-receiver magnesium fuses would be implanted into the sprayed-on surfaces, and would be computer/ radio frequency controlled with respect to the detonation itself and the timing of it.

The most basic premise of any demolition is to allow gravity to do most of the work. Removing resistance is the key. And removing resistance as far down in the building as possible is crucial, to allow the massive weight of the structure above to finish the job. The explosive fuses can be programmed to detonate in any sequence, from top to bottom of the building, or bottom to top—or any variation in between. It's all in the computer program itself. Once the tiny fuses achieve their basically invisible explosion, the Thermate TH3 does its work, burning quickly and furiously through the metal.

After my plans were approved—documentation that was also required to be in my vault—I was asked to actually rig one building as a test example to demonstrate to other CIA engineers how it would be done on the Twin Towers if they ever decided to enact the plan. I was also asked to train the engineers in the intricacies of the computer program itself, so that I wouldn't be needed to oversee any future riggings after my retirement.

The building they chose was Tower 7 of the World Trade Center, the 47- storey tower that also coincidentally housed an undercover CIA operation. I agreed to the demonstration.

In the early months of 2001, I was in Tower 7 non-stop with a team of engineers, purportedly to do additional fireproofing to the bowels of the building. We sprayed the Thermate TH3 to all of the sections that my engineering indicated would permit total implosion of the building. We implanted the magnesium fuses and I designed and demonstrated the computer program that would be needed to generate the unique radio frequencies and detonations.

Then on September 11, I was shocked and horrified along with the rest of the world when the planes struck the twin towers. I was glued to the television like everyone else and watched as both towers imploded exactly the way a controlled demolition would take them down. There is no way those buildings could have collapsed with impact by airplanes alone, and especially so soon after the impacts, and the fact that the planes hit the upper floors. All those deaths—I was sick. I knew in my soul that they had gone ahead with other engineers to enact the plan I had designed for the twin towers, and it made me sick to my stomach. They had used me, and deceived me, and I felt responsible.

Then, while I was in front of the television, I received an urgent phone call on a secure line, half an hour after the North tower had collapsed. I'm not going to name names, as all the names are in the documentation. But names aren't important anyway.

The caller demanded I unlock the computer program to detonate Tower 7, the tower that I had done the engineering demonstration on. You see, I hadn't really trusted completely the promises they made to me, so I built in a back door virus to the computer program for Tower 7. They had apparently tried to implode that building at the same time the North tower was detonated, but it failed due to my lock. Even though Tower 7 had not even been hit by a plane, they wanted it to come down within the dust and panic of the North Tower. Everyone would assume that debris from the North Tower had brought # 7 down as well. You see, it had to come down as the entire scheme had been hatched and controlled within that building, on the CIA Clandestine floors. Everyone in Building 7 had already been evacuated after the South Tower had collapsed, in preparation for the planned collapse of # 7 simultaneous with the North Tower.

They were no doubt shocked when it wouldn't detonate, so in a panic they contacted me. I refused to give them the solution to the virus lock. I was enraged that this 9/11 devastation was a CIA job and disgusted that I had designed it.

In the meantime, while they were trying to convince me over several phone calls and several hours to change my mind, they were getting increasingly paranoid of the evidence that would be left in that building on hard drives, top secret files, etc., if they weren't able to convince me to allow them to detonate. So they sent two operatives into that building to start fires on two floors—crucial floors. There were already a couple of other fires raging in that building from the debris hits, but those were on different floors than these crucial ones. They were caught in the act by a Secret Service Agent, who for some reason had entered the building. No one knows why he was there. His body was the only one that was discovered in the rubble of Tower 7 when it finally did come down. He was murdered when he discovered the arson that was taking place on the two floors. His death hasn't been reported widely, but you'll see reference to him in some 9/11 reports. It was never investigated. My own theory about that death was that the White House became suspicious about some aspects of the so-called "attack," and sent at least one Secret Service Agent to Tower 7 to sniff around. It made sense that one or more of them would pay a visit to Tower 7 because that was where the CIA undercover office was. They probably suspected CIA involvement.

My superiors contacted me numerous times after the collapse of the twin towers, trying to convince me to give up the program codes. I refused, until they finally gave me an ultimatum.

Either I allowed them to detonate, or you, Kerrie, would disappear.

My resolve obviously withered and I gave up the codes. Building # 7 went down, seven hours after the collapse of the North Tower. Very few people can understand to this day how that building collapsed. It was not hit by planes, and the fires were confined to only a few floors. Yet it fell just like the twin towers—straight down, no lean. I know how it went down, and so do a few others. Now you know too.

Most people have accepted the official government theory that the towers collapsed due to the planes and the subsequent fires. On some level they've accepted that, even though that is not what happened, and is actually scientifically impossible for those buildings to come down like they did without some major implosion help. However, the spectacular and violent images of jumbo jets slicing through the towers created an illusion in the minds of most; they could truly believe that is what brought them down. Just like a magic act by David Copperfield—this was all an illusion. I know how the twin towers fell and I know how Tower 7 fell.

I also know that the planes were just for dramatic effect, and that this entire project was a strategic alliance between the CIA and Bin Laden. To placate me after the disaster, I was told about the entire plan. I guess they were hoping that if they brought me in on the picture, I would see the merits of what they felt they had to do, and feel better about how I was used. Operation Avalanche was, if I can believe what I was told, a rogue mission. The administration did not have a clue. They did not approve it. There are a lot of conspiracy theories suggesting that elected officials planned this or allowed it to happen. But that just doesn't appear to be true. That's not to say of course that they didn't go along with covering it up after the fact—who knows, and the American people will probably never know the entire story.

Those same American people would actually be shocked if they knew how much power the CIA has. Their ability to pull off major operations without any elected officials knowing, is mind-boggling. It is dangerous beyond belief.

I'm actually quite surprised they didn't just kill me earlier than they finally did. But they are, if nothing else, realists. They know they can't kill everybody. I also played along, pretending to be a patriotic supporter after they told me. Inside, I was dying.

Most people aren't aware that Bin Laden and his organization were created by the CIA during the Soviet/Afghanistan war way back in the eighties. He was our man. He needed us, and we needed him. This 9/11 disaster benefited both partners. He even had his own code name within the CIA—Tim Osman. He visited the U.S. and even the White House during the eighties, arranging arms for the Afghan resistance, which the U.S. eagerly provided. Any help we could give to the

Mujahadeen in repelling the Soviets was a joyful gift. I digress—the deal was that the U.S.A. would have an excuse to go after Iraq after trumping up a connection between Hussein and Bin Laden. Bin Laden actually hated Hussein, so he was okay with that. Oil was the prize. And Bin Laden volunteered the suicide fighters to take over the planes to make it all look like an authentic terrorist attack. He would be made the celebrated villain for the disaster.

The hijackers were duped as well—they thought that this was a legitimate jihad. In fact a couple of them held down in Guantanamo Bay are still bragging about how they were the masterminds, with Bin Laden's blessing. They still want to die as martyrs. Bin Laden is smart—he was counting on that, and counting on the fact that he would have countless volunteers to be in those planes. Of course, Bin Laden would then gain the notoriety that he longed for and had never really gained before, attract more recruits, and be a counter-balance in the Middle East to help the U.S.A. keep Israel in line. In return, the USA promised to abandon its search for him in Afghanistan early, and never really try to find him. Not seriously anyway. They intended to just go through the motions to fire up the American people. Their big chance to grab him was at Torah Borah, but that was an unexpected accident, and the CIA had no choice then but to sabotage their own mission. They had to hold up their end of the bargain. The military was left confused and scratching their heads over that one. The American people bought in to the Torah Borah story. They were made to believe that the Special Forces were incompetent. They weren't. From this one act of terrorism, Bin Laden would become the poster boy for decades as the outlet for American hate, and that was good for America and good for Bin Laden's cause. A win/win for everyone involved. It gave the U.S.A. an excuse to go to war, and have a military presence in Iraq and Afghanistan for decades to come. Excellent news for defense-spending advocates, and phenomenal news for oil companies. The folly of it though, in the long run, was the creation of a Frankenstein who would probably one day no longer be singing the same song as the U.S.A. Getting into bed with that guy could only invite real terrorism down the road. But the immediate need was a war for oil, so I guess they saw it as crossing one bridge at a time.

However, and here's an even more horrifying kicker, my own theory is that those two wars are just a side show. The "war on terrorism" is the main event. This is a war that has been created by deception and fake attacks. Most Americans are not aware that the office of the President is basically powerless unless the country is in a "state of war." When that happens the President's powers under the United States Constitution are almost limitless. When we allowed war to be declared on terrorism, it basically meant that we are in a war that will never end. And if things settle down and people think the war is over, all that has to be done is fake another terrorist attack to keep Congress and the American people in a state of fear. I believe we are now in an era of perpetual war, and an era when the President's powers to limit civil rights, expand detentions and torture, wiretaps on citizens, and attack whoever he pleases, are out of control because of the wording of the Constitution. And the President doesn't even have to agree. Foreign policy in reality is dictated by intelligence services and the military—the President really has no say. If he disagrees with a course of action, he can easily be coerced or threatened. If he still won't tow the line…well, trust me on this, things can happen.

Kerrie, I know this is a shock to you as it will be to the world if it is ever disclosed. However, this is just a letter—anyone can write a letter. The documentation on Operation Avalanche is elsewhere and you may never discover it; maybe by now you don't want to. Or it will just bubble up one day and you will have it. Then you can decide what to do with it.

I also have more money than my will ever disclosed. Hopefully, you'll discover where it's hidden.

I could not afford to take the chance to have everything hidden in one spot. I had to scatter it. I have also left a mini cassette tape of those conversations with my superiors on Sept. 11, wherein they attempted to convince me to unlock the program and then threatened your life. As well, there is an old video located in the box. It has nothing to do with the subject of this letter, so it will not help you find the documentation. I have included it only as a throw-in. You can view it one day after you have recovered from this shock, if you want to. You might as well know completely who I really am. Needless to say, it won't matter to me anymore.

I became a tool of destruction and deceit, Kerrie. I'm ashamed of what I've done, and of what I know. Some very powerful people in my beloved country have come to believe that "without destruction, there can be no construction." And sadly, they now also seem convinced that "political power comes from the barrel of a gun."

Give my love to Connie Reynolds. I used her in my stunt only for symbolic reasons, because of what happened to her parents on 9/11.

I'm sorry for who I was, and I'm sorry for everything I did over the course of my life—with the exception of marrying your mother and bringing you into this world. I hope that God shows a bit of mercy for my soul, although I can't think of a single reason why he should.

All my love, Kerrie. Look out for yourself.

Dad

Chapter 36

Jack smacked the pages down on the cement floor, then got up and started pacing the little storage room. He suddenly felt pains in his chest, and was finding it hard to breathe.

He rolled up the overhead door to let in some fresh air. That was better. He walked out of the unit and started pacing the driveway in front. He had to walk this feeling off. He walked faster and faster. Then he felt a gentle arm encircling his shoulders and he turned around. Kerrie was peering into his eyes, and it felt like she was piercing his soul. She didn't have to ask the question. Jack knew what it was from the look in her eyes.

"I always felt like her life had been wasted, Kerrie. But this is like a kick in the gut."

Kerrie snuggled her head into Jack's neck and rubbed his back. She didn't say a word.

"Susan and those thousands of others never saw it coming—neither did the rest of us stupid, naïve, law-abiding citizens. Those poor innocent people just going about their lives, doing their jobs, and they get snuffed out by scum who deemed their lives expendable and worthless. They were all just part of a stage show to fool the world. What is it that expression? 'All the World's a Stage?' It sure was that day, wasn't it? They were all just extras in a play." Jack's voice level was rising with each sentence.

"What helped me cope was the thought that I had maniacal villains to blame. What can anyone do against fundamentalist nutcases who just want to end their own lives? And I always partially blamed the U.S. for creating the situation where the country was hated so badly that these nuts wanted to attack them. But now, to read this! God, I feel sick." He brushed Kerrie off and started pacing again.

"My wife gave her life so the U.S. could fake a war against another country. Susan died so the U.S. could have an adequate supply of oil! Passengers in the planes were slaughtered, workers in the towers were slaughtered, our soldiers in Iraq and Afghanistan have been slaughtered. Not to mention the tens of thousands of innocent citizens in those two countries who have had the shit bombed out of them! For Christ's sake, what kind of fucked-up world is this?" Jack could feel his chest jabbing at him harder. He patted at it with his open palm.

"I can picture her, standing on that window ledge 106 stories above the ground, crying, choking, and screaming, knowing in her heart that there was no way out. She was probably coughing from the smoke, and for a short time she probably even believed that the authorities would come to her rescue. Then finally, she surrendered to the inevitable and let go, jumping, the ground rushing up to her in a blur, watching her loves, wishes, and memories vanish in mid-air." Jack's breaths were being taken in gulps now, and his face was beet red. He didn't care. He ran over to a garbage can and kicked it with all his might. The thing crumpled and rolled end over end down the alleyway.

"What are my dreams going to include now? One extra image—that of a smiling, bearded Uncle Sam draped in the stars and stripes, giving my wife a shove!" Jack was yelling now, with his face looking up to the sky. Then his knees buckled and he collapsed to the ground. He lifted his head up and retched. Kerrie ran over to him and cradled his head in her hands. Jack began struggling to his feet, wiping his mouth against his sleeve. "It's okay, Kerrie. Help me back inside. I need to take a couple pills."

He leaned against her as they walked slowly back into the storage unit. Kerrie eased him to the ground with his back against the wall, and she pulled down the overhead door.

Jack pointed at his knapsack and she brought it over to him. He reached inside and pulled out a container of aspirin, some prescription medication, and a bottle of water. He cracked open the water, and swallowed the pills. His breathing was getting a bit better now that he was sitting down, and in a few minutes the pains in his chest began subsiding.

"Jack, what's wrong? Were those heart pains?"

"No, not really. Stress pains. Sure, emanating from the heart, but my heart's okay. It was actually more of an anxiety attack kind of thing. I used to get them on the job all the time—not so much anymore since I retired. I pop aspirin, and once in a while I have to take an anxiety pill as well. I'll be okay."

Kerrie sat down beside him and laid her head on his chest. She wrapped one arm behind him and laid the other on his lap. They stayed in that position, surrounded by their own separate thoughts. Neither of them wanted to talk any more.

Then they fell asleep, each emotionally wasted.

*****

Two middle-aged agents, code-named Staten and Bronx, were sitting in Sam's office, sipping their coffees.

Sam passed a couple of photos over to them. "These are the people we want: Jack Howser and Kerrie Joplin. Stake out the Lamplighter Hideaway on Long Island and confirm to me once you have them in custody."

"How long do you want us to stay there?" Staten asked.

"Until you get them."

"And after we get them?" Bronx asked.

"Cuff them, and take them to the safe house in Queens. I'll meet you there. And watch out for Howser; he knows martial arts."

The two agents nodded, not looking at all concerned.

"But they are not to be harmed," Sam said emphatically. "Do you hear me? If you hurt them, I'll hurt you." They nodded again, then got up and left the room without another word.

An hour later the two agents arrived at the Lamplighter, and made their way through the lobby to the front desk. A gregarious guy with the nametag "Chuck" was flirting with a couple of ladies who were checking in. The two CIA men waited patiently.

"Can I help you, gentlemen?"

Bronx pulled out the photos and showed them to Chuck. "Are these people staying here?"

Chuck quickly, and nervously, shook his head. "No, I haven't seen them."

Staten pulled out an NYPD gold shield with photo I.D., which looked as authentic as the real thing. He flashed it in front of the jittery hotel man. "Don't fuck with us. Look at these photos again and tell us the truth, or you'll be going downtown with us on a little field trip."

Chuck put on his glasses and took another look. "Oh, yes, now that I have my glasses on, I do remember them." He checked a note he had on the ledge. "Room 207."

"Give us a key, and don't say a word to anyone that we're here," warned Bronx. "Trust me, we'll know if you do, and you won't be a happy man afterwards."

"Yes, sir, no problem at all sir." Chuck gave them the key to room 207, and realized with regret that he probably wouldn't be getting his $2,500 bonus from that nice guy in the photo.

Jack and Kerrie awoke about an hour later, stiff from sleeping against the concrete wall. Kerrie folded the letter, stuffed it back in the envelope and gave it to Jack for safekeeping in his trusty knapsack.

They left the storage unit, closed the door and didn't bother to lock it. No point anymore.

As they made their way out to the street, Kerrie noticed a little motel just down the road. "It's only noon, but I still need to sleep, badly. My head is pounding. I don't know about you, but I just can't handle a two-hour cab ride right now. Why don't we grab a room at that motel for a couple of hours?"

"I agree—let's do that. I need to close my eyes a bit more myself." In fact, the way he felt right now, he thought it might be nice to just close his eyes forever.

They walked down to the motel, and Jack slipped the attendant $500 to bypass the credit card rule.

The room was small but clean, and had two double beds. It would do for a couple of hours. As soon as Jack closed the door, Kerrie stretched out on one of the beds and closed her eyes. He could tell she was exhausted, and he understood. He felt the same way. Not physically exhausted, but mentally and emotionally drained. Dejected, discouraged and depressed. This discovery was ominous, particularly since he and Kerrie now bore the burden of probably being the only civilians in the entire world who knew the ugly truth about the 9/11 slaughter.

In a few minutes Jack could hear Kerrie gently snoring away, and he found himself becoming more and more agitated the longer he stared at the ceiling. He knew this feeling; the longer he thought of going to sleep, the more awake he would become. There was no point in trying any longer.

He got up, sat at the little table in the corner of the room, and turned on a small lamp. Jack glanced over at Kerrie. Good, still asleep. Opening his knapsack, he pulled out Mitch's letter and went through it again, carefully, word by word. His mood had changed. He felt angry and energized now. Jack wore his emotions on his sleeve, and when he expressed them it could be like a tidal wave. It was a release that was always quick and explosive, but characterized by a recovery that was just as quick. Nothing ever kept him down for too long.

Jack was looking for clues. He was certain they were in this letter and he had to find them. In his mind, Mitch's shocking revelations were all the more reason to see this through to the end. He would allow himself to feel the pain when this was all over, but for now, they needed the documentation that Mitch had referred to. They needed it desperately. Jack didn't quite know what they would do with it once they found it, but a little voice was telling him to get it just so they could continue living. He scanned through the early portions of Mitch's letter, and he saw no real signs of any clues. Mitch was providing information and telling his story in that part of the letter. Jack was convinced the clues had to be near the end, after the story part was finished.

He concentrated on things that seemed out of place, commentary or advice statements that didn't quite fit in with the context of the letter. After a couple of hours of reading and re-reading, and trying to concentrate over Kerrie's snoring, he had his answers. He gently shook Kerrie awake and sat down on the bed beside her.

"Kerrie, do you want to push on? If you do, I do."

Kerrie stretched and yawned, then said, with as much conviction as anyone could who was just waking up, "I'm glad to hear you say that. With how upset you were earlier I was worried that you might want to drop the whole thing."

"No, I want this finished more than ever. I don't think we can take the chance of walking away from it. I don't think we'd survive. Our best chance of survival is to get it all."

"Let's do it then," Kerrie said without hesitation. Jack could see the determination in her eyes. He knew she felt the same way he did. "My dad would want us to. He tried to correct the wrongs, but failed. He did some horrible things, but I know he would never have willingly done this Avalanche operation if he knew the true purpose. He was duped."

Jack leaned over and kissed her cheek. He waved the pages of the letter in his hand. "I studied your dad's letter some more, and I think I know what the remaining clues are."

He had her attention. She sat up in bed. "Show me."

Jack turned to the last page. "Notice that your dad has a couple of phrases in quotation marks?"

"Yes, and I recognized those quotes from high school history class. I can't remember who said them though!"

Jack began to explain. "Both quotes are from Mao Tse Tung, or more correctly known by the Chinese as Mao Zedong, the communist leader of China until his death in the mid-seventies. He had what was referred to as 'the little red book,' which was distributed to all the citizens of China. It contained all of his famous quotes over the years, and the book was supposed to be a guide to how the Chinese should live their lives and view their world, his world. At his very best, the man was full of himself. At his worst, he was a butcher.

"He was a brutal leader, revered, but brutal. Millions died under his rule and particularly during his infamous Cultural Revolution. I think your dad quoted him because he's making a comparison between America now, and China during Mao's rule. "The first quote, '*without destruction, there can be no construction,*' I think is a decoy. Your dad may have thought that was appropriate to describe what he came to see as the twisted views of the U.S. government, but I don't think that quote has any meaning for us.

"The second quote, '*political power comes from the barrel of a gun,*' was also meant as a criticism of the government. But I'm convinced that this quote is the real clue, and that he's referring to those guns he had stored up in the attic of your house. I believe that one of those guns has a clue to the documents he's referring to, and I'm betting that whichever gun it is, it's a Chinese weapon."

Kerrie looked up at Jack and nodded quickly. He could see the excitement in her eyes, as the logic of it all sunk in.

"Jack, I think you've got something here; at least I hope you have. There's really nothing else in that letter that jumps out at me as possibly being a clue." She added soberly, "But if that's not it, we have a big dead end."

"There's actually one more clue in the letter which makes me think I'm right. When Mitch referred to you possibly finding the documents, he wrote '*it will just bubble up one day*'"

"Okay, so?" Kerrie questioned, impatiently.

"It's tempting to just think of water when we hear the word 'bubble,' right?"

"Jack, quit talking like a professor. Cut to the chase."

"Okay, sorry. Those guns in the attic are wrapped in plastic—*bubble* wrap plastic."

Chapter 37

Jack reached into his pocket and pulled out the mini cassette tape. "Kerrie, this must be the tape recording of those phone conversations your dad referred to. How do you feel about listening to it?"

They were still in the motel room, preparing to cab it back to their hotel in Long Island.

"Okay, we might as well give it a listen, but if it's too much for me, I may ask you to turn it off."

Kerrie reached into her purse and brought out her personal recorder. She removed the cassette that had the two voice messages of Bob's she'd recorded, and popped in her dad's tape.

There was some static and then Kerrie heard a familiar voice.

"Hello."

"Sniper?"

"Yes. Go ahead, Langley."

"You have to unwrap the parcel."

"Not going to happen."

"You don't want to play with us like this. This is very serious."

"I'm not going to let you drop and break another parcel, you bastard."

"This is bigger than you or I, Sniper. Don't throw it all away now."

"Fuck off."

They heard a click, then silence. The tape started up again.

"Hello again."

"Sniper, we can't access your gift, and time is running out."

"My gift was never intended to be opened that way."

"It's our decision how we use a gift. You don't know what you're doing."

"I know exactly what I'm doing."

"Where are you, Sniper?"

"Yeah, right."

Then click and silence once again. There were two more similar exchanges. The caller trying to convince Sniper—which they figured must have been

Mitch's CIA code name—to unwrap the "parcel," which they now knew meant the detonation program for WTC Tower 7. Each time, Mitch refused in progressively angrier tones. Jack could see that Kerrie was teary-eyed from hearing her father's voice again, but otherwise she was holding up well.

Then came the last exchange; a different voice this time at the Langley end. Harsher, more sinister.

"It's getting late, and we're running out of time and patience."

"Not my problem."

"You have a lovely daughter, Sniper."

Silence.

"Her name is Kerrie, and she's an associate at Faulk, Williams, Ziegler."

Silence.

"You have fifteen minutes to unwrap the parcel. Shortly after that, our window of opportunity will be gone. If you have a change of heart later, it will be too late."

Silence.

"You have fifteen minutes to keep your daughter from going on a sabbatical, Sniper."

There was another pause, then Mitch finally replied. "What time do you have right now?"

"The time is 2:58 p.m."

"Okay, check: 2:58 p.m., nine, eleven, oh-one. We're synchronized. I'll be back to you with my answer at 3:11 p.m."

The tape ended and there were no more exchanges. Jack and Kerrie looked at each other, their eyes wide in shock. Kerrie looked especially horrified after hearing her fate being discussed by a deadly stranger. Jack couldn't believe what they had just heard. Recorded evidence, even though cryptic, of what happened that day and the threatened murder of an innocent young lady.

"Your dad was pretty smart to get that date and time on record at the end."

"Oh, no doubt about it, he was a smart man." Kerrie shook her head and went into the bathroom.

When she came out, Jack said, "There were two more things in that box." He reached into his knapsack, pulled out the photo and handed it to her. Slowly a smile crept over her face as she looked at the photo of her, Mitch, and her mom. Then she turned it over and read the note on the back. She just sighed and put the photo in her purse.

"Here's the last thing." Jack pulled out the old videotape and passed it over to her. Kerrie looked at it closely, noticing the CIA seal on the front of the cover. "This must be the videotape Dad referred to. He said it had nothing to do with the documentation or the story he told us in the letter."

"It may be just a taped message he had for you. We could slip it in the VCR right now if you're up to watching it."

Kerrie thought for a moment then quickly shook her head, frowning. "No more right now. I can't take any more messages from my dad. I've read and heard enough for one day. Just tuck it away in a safe place and we can talk about it again later. Okay?"

"I understand. I think I would probably say the same thing if it were my father. All of this must be hard to take." He stuffed the videotape back into the inside pocket of his knapsack, and popped the cassette out of the recorder and put it back in his pocket.

"Oh, Jack, before we go, I want to phone Connie and see how she's doing after last night's session with Belinda." Kerrie started rummaging through her purse, looking for the number.

"Go ahead. It's probably long distance, but I've given the guy at the front desk more than enough to cover it. Let me phone him first and get him to lift the long distance lock on our phone."

The manager was more than cooperative for his $500. Kerrie dialed Connie's number. No answer. She dialed again, still no answer.

"That's strange. Where would she go? She's afraid to leave the house."

"Maybe today she decided to brave the world a bit. I wouldn't worry too much about it." Jack was stretched out on the bed with his eyes closed. Lack of sleep was causing them to ache something fierce.

"You may be right. She did look and sound a lot braver when we left last night. But I'm going to try Belinda to see if she's talked to her today."

Kerrie phoned Belinda's cell, and Jack listened to her side of the conversation. He could tell by the questions she was asking and the pitch of her voice that she was getting agitated.

She hung up and sat down beside Jack on the bed. "Something's wrong. Belinda was actually on Connie's front porch when I called. She tried to phone her this afternoon and when she didn't get an answer she got concerned too. So she drove over there, knocked on the door, still no answer. She tried the door and it was locked, looked in through the window—the drapes were open. But everything looked clean and tidy inside." Kerrie stopped to take a sip of water. "Then Belinda called the FDNY to track down her brother John's station house. They said he had missed his shift this morning, hadn't called in and wasn't answering his phone. So he seems to be missing too."

Jack slid off the bed and went into the bathroom. He squeezed some drops into his sore eyes, and called back to Kerrie. "Well, maybe with her new-found courage, John and her went away for the weekend. He was supposed to drop by to see her last night, remember?" Jack knew this was a feeble argument but he wanted to try to allay her concerns somehow.

Kerrie wasn't buying it. "It didn't sound to me like John would be the type of person to abandon his shift without telling anyone. I'm worried."

"What did Belinda have to say about it?"

"She's contacted the police, which the FDNY had already done about John. They said there was nothing they could do for forty-eight hours, but after that they'll post a missing person's alert on each of them."

"Okay. We'll have to check back in a day or two. I agree with you, it doesn't sound right. But there could be a logical explanation, and I'm sure they'll both turn up."

"Let's get out of here, Jack. And I mean out of New York. I'm getting a creepy feeling. I think with what we've found, we're pushing our luck staying here any longer."

"Can't argue with that. Let me call our pilots and get the plane fueled up. They need at least four hours notice and it will take at least two hours to get back to our hotel. We'll grab our things and zip to the airport."

*****

In just about two hours on the nose, they arrived back at the Lamplighter on Long Island. Jack paid the fare in cash, including a generous tip, and asked the cabbie to wait for them. Jack and Kerrie made their way through the lobby and up the stairs to their room. Jack opened the door and they walked in.

Almost immediately, they were hit from behind and knocked to the floor.

Two men stood over them. The taller one reached behind his back and produced two sets of handcuffs. "Be good, we're going for a little ride," he said. The other guy grabbed Jack by the collar and dragged him away from Kerrie, roughly shoving him against the wall. The tall guy threw him a pair of handcuffs.

Kerrie's guy pushed her onto her stomach and managed to snap a cuff on one of her wrists. He was just reaching for her other wrist when Jack made his move. In no time flat, Jack's guy was doubled over from a hard and fast foot to the groin. Then, with both hands clasped together while he was rising to his feet, Jack yanked up under the man's chin and sent him flying back against the couch. The guy holding Kerrie's wrist let go and sprinted towards Jack. Jack was on his feet now and moved in a blur. He spun in a 360 degree turn and crunched the man's chin with his foot. Before he had a chance to collapse to the ground, two of Jack's fingers formed a peace sign and jabbed deep into his eyeballs with lightning speed. The man screamed and fell to the floor, hands over his eyes, blood streaming through his fingers. Jack ran to Kerrie and pulled her to her feet. Her eyes were glazed over; Jack knew she was in a state of shock. He slapped her sharply on the cheek, then put his face close to hers. "We have to go—now!" She nodded, and held up her hand with the cuffs dangling from her wrist. "Forget about it!" Jack yelled.

He yanked Kerrie in the direction of the door. Before they could get out, he heard a shout behind them, "Stop!" He knew it was the guy he'd kicked in the balls. The other guy would never be able to see the light of day again, so he wasn't a concern. Jack ignored the command and dove to the floor, pulling Kerrie down with him. A shot rang out just as they both scrambled on their knees out into the hallway. They could hear the bullet smashing into the doorframe just above their heads. They turned in the direction of the stairway to the lobby, but instead of running for it, Jack quickly pulled Kerrie up against the wall beside the door to their room. He did the same, standing as flat as he could, closest to the right hand side of the door. He extended his left arm all the way over to his opposite side, clenched his fist, and waited. Within a fraction of a second, a figure came carelessly rushing out into the hall, and Jack's arm shot across in an arc straight into the man's face. He screamed in pain and went down. Jack pounded down on the guy's bleeding face with the heel of his shoe as if he were stomping on an ant, accompanied by a sickening crunch. The man screamed again. Jack picked up the gun now lying on the floor and stuffed it into his waistband.

Kerrie stared down at the blood-soaked man. Jack grabbed her by the jacket and yelled, "Run!"

They ran down the stairs and through the lobby. Jack could see Chuck at the front desk, eyes wide as he watched them heading toward the lobby door. Jack couldn't resist—he formed his hand into the shape of a pistol, cocked his thumb, and pointed it at the little man as he ran for the exit.

They practically dove into their cab, to the shock of their middle-eastern cabbie. He jerked his head around so fast as they threw themselves into the back seat, Jack thought for sure that his turban would fall off. And the man couldn't take his eyes off the ugly jewelry dangling from Kerrie's wrist.

"Eyes forward! Move this car now!" Jack yelled.

The car burned rubber as it pulled out of the lobby driveway and out into the street.

"Where to?" the cabbie called back with a tremor in his voice.

"Straight ahead for now. I'll let you know."

Kerrie was lying against the side of the door, unmoving. Jack could feel his adrenaline at full throttle. Survival mode had kicked in. His training in martial arts over the years had also honed his mind to be disciplined and think survival against all odds. He'd rarely had to use survival mode; just those two times with Mule a few months ago in Calgary, and of course recently when he had saved Meagan. But the training was imbedded and his mind was as sharp as a razor blade at this very moment.

Jack looked behind him as they put distance between themselves and the hotel. He wasn't surprised to see the man with the bleeding face lurch out of the front lobby door and over to a dark sedan, holding a handkerchief up to his nose. Jack urged the driver to go faster, and the man responded by grumbling something in a language that Jack didn't understand.

"Shouldn't we head to the airport?" Kerrie's voice was shaky.

"We can't now. The plane won't be ready for another two hours, and we sure don't want to lead these people to the airport. With all the armed personnel there, we wouldn't stand a chance. They'd conscript everyone possible to help them by convincing them that we're terrorists or something. No one would believe us over the CIA."

At the word 'terrorists,' the driver immediately started moaning and humming to himself, moving his head up and down. Jack ignored him.

"But maybe they won't be following now after what you did to them," Kerrie protested.

"The one who still has eyes is already in his car, Kerrie. I just saw him. And you can bet there will be reinforcements."

Kerrie covered her face with her hands and started to tremble. Jack rubbed her back, while urging the driver to go faster.

Suddenly their cab turned at the next corner and came to a screeching stop. "Get out! Get out!" The driver yelled. Jack wasn't about to waste time arguing. He pulled Kerrie upright and dragged her out of the car. He pointed up the street towards an alley, and they both began to run as fast as they could. Kerrie's new bracelet was jingling and jangling as she raced.

Jack took mental note of the major intersection before they turned into the alley. He led them down about halfway and stopped at a dumpster. "Get in, now!" She looked at him with a brief question in her eyes and then hoisted herself up, getting stuck halfway. Jack gave her a hard shove and she tumbled in. Then he followed.

They laid there in the stinking mess with the lid partly open, and tried to resist breathing too deeply. For the moment they felt safe, and now just concentrated on blocking out the overpowering smell. Jack slid his knapsack off his back, opened it up and popped a couple of pills.

After a few minutes catching their breath, Kerrie suddenly reached into her purse and pulled out her cell phone. "Jack, the time for caution is over. There aren't any phone booths around here, and we desperately need help—fast."

"Who are you calling?"

"Noah. He said I should call if we got into any trouble; right now we're definitely in deep doo-doo. He'll help us, or at least know someone who can."

"Go ahead. We have no options, and they're on the prowl for us for sure."

Kerrie dialed Noah's phone number at the Dakota. He answered the phone himself this time, and as soon as he heard her voice he said he would call her back on his secure phone. Within a minute Kerrie's phone rang.

"Kerrie, nice to hear from you again. Are you all right?"

"No, I'm not, Noah. My friend and I are in trouble. You said to call if I needed help and I hate to put you on the spot, but we are in real danger. We're being hunted and are on the run. For now we're hidden, but I don't know for how long before we're discovered."

"Oh dear, I warned you about this. But no matter, I'll send Carl. Say no more to me. We'll talk when you get here. And stay hidden until Carl arrives. He's armed so if there is any trouble, he'll take care of it, I promise."

"Noah, I can't thank you enough. I'm so scared."

"Don't be scared, my dear. Just stay hidden. Promise me you'll do that."

"I will."

"Now, where are you exactly, please?"

Kerrie looked over at Jack sitting over in his corner of the dumpster. "Jack, do you know where we are?" He nodded. "Noah, I'll put my friend Jack on. He knows where we are."

Jack took the phone and dispensed with any niceties. "We're in a dumpster in an alley. From what I could see, the only dumpster in the alley. The alley is off Sagebrush Lane, just past Sunflower Lane. Sagebrush connects with Express Drive South, parallel to the Long Island Expressway. Got all that?"

"I've got it, Jack. It'll take my man about an hour. He'll be driving a white Mercedes C350. He'll park beside the dumpster. Don't come out until you hear him call out the code word, 'Mets.' Okay?"

"Understood, Noah. I don't know what to say, except thanks."

"No need for that. I would do anything for Kerrie. Sit tight."

Jack handed the phone back to Kerrie. "He sounds nice, doesn't he?" she asked, pride in her voice.

"Yes, he does. He's going out on quite the limb for you. You're lucky to have a long lost friend who cares about you so much."

Jack laid his head back, cautioning her at the same time with his open palm. "We should talk in whispers from now on."

"You're right." Kerrie lowered her voice. "What was the deal with all of those moves back there? Where on earth did you learn to do all that stuff?"

Jack held his finger up to his lips. "Shh." He stood up quietly in the dumpster, and peeked out the top. All clear. He plunked himself down again amongst the trash.

"I learned karate a long time ago, kind of a hobby. Never thought I'd have to use it."

They both dozed off after a few minutes, now getting used to the foul odor. For the second time in the same day, they were emotionally drained. They awoke suddenly to the sound of a car engine. Jack slid the pistol out of his waistband. They glanced warily at each other, wide-eyed, and Jack braced himself and the gun into position for whoever might peek over the edge of the dumpster.

Instead, all they heard was one word, and a welcome one at that. "Mets".

Chapter 38

Carl didn't like to talk very much, they found that out real quick. From the back seat of the Mercedes, all they could tell about Carl was that his shoulders were broad, his head and neck were thick, and his big hands on the steering wheel looked like baseball mitts. He was a tough-looking guy, and was probably an excellent bodyguard for Noah, Kerrie thought. And he looked straight as an arrow, with a military-style haircut right out of the movie *Full Metal Jacket.*

He was at least gentlemanly enough to get the one handcuff off Kerrie's wrist right after they got into the car. It only took him half a second with a special tool he pulled out of his pocket. Then he noticed the gun in Jack's waistband, and politely asked for it. He explained that while Noah may trust them, he was being paid not to trust anyone. Jack handed over the gun.

After a couple of questions that received grunts for replies, Jack gave up trying. One thing Carl did tell them was to keep their heads low as they drove through streets with stoplights. On the expressway, Carl seemed to be in agreement that they could come up for a breath of air. They knew he was only looking out for their welfare, and they weren't going to complain after being stuck in that dumpster for over an hour. They also knew they stunk to high heaven, and their first clue was Carl's constant sniffing. He couldn't be feeling too happy about how the Mercedes was going to smell after this ride was over. Kerrie, however, had actually started getting used to the odor, so it didn't really bother her as much anymore.

Kerrie felt a huge sense of relief at having Noah and Carl come to their rescue. There was no question that they would have been discovered over the next few hours. They could not have remained undetected in that dumpster for too much longer. She felt a lot calmer now, and was even aware that she was smiling, a smile that had started right after she had called Noah from the dumpster. He had always had a calming effect on her, and she was excited that she was going to see him again. She knew she still had her childhood crush on the man.

Suddenly a thought occurred to her. "Jack, we left all of our stuff back at the hotel!"

"Not all of it. You have your purse with our passports and my car keys, and I have my knapsack with all of the real important stuff. We both have lots of cash, so we're okay. We'll send for the other stuff when we get back to Montana."

"You're right. And why am I worried about such a trivial thing right now anyway?"

"Very simple. It's because you're trying to pretend like everything is normal and that everything is okay. Your brain is trying to give you a break from all those other troubling thoughts."

Kerrie nodded, peering out the window as they took the off-ramp from Henry Hudson Parkway, onto Columbus Ave. She watched Carl turn left onto W. 72nd St. She knew they were very close now. The Dakota was located right across from Central Park itself, down at the very bottom of W. 72nd St. Most of these streets were still familiar to her. New York City still felt like home. It was now close to 7:00 p.m., and she knew that at this time of the year it would stay fairly light out until around 9:00. That's when the city really came alive, she remembered. It dawned on her that they hadn't eaten anything since breakfast. Suddenly she was feeling hungry, as she saw a couple of New York's famous "smokie" stands on the street corner.

Jack disturbed her thoughts with a nudge on her shoulder. "Looks like we're here." He was gazing out of his side window, taking in the impressive edifice known as The Dakota.

Kerrie followed his gaze. She had read a lot about The Dakota over the internet, before they left Montana. She had been curious about this famous building, knowing that Noah lived here. It acquired its fame mainly because John Lennon was shot and killed here back in 1980. His wife, Yoko Ono, still lived here from what she remembered. And she had read that the smallest apartment in the building cost about fourteen million dollars!

The building had been built back in the late 1800s, considered way ahead of its time, and back then was considered remote from the established center of the city. Critics harshly predicted its failure. The building got its name apparently because of the criticism of it being so far away from the action, that it "might as well be in the territory of Dakota." Almost as an "up yours" to its critics, the building has the image of a Native American carved on its façade facing W. 72nd St., symbolic of the Dakota territories back in the 1800s.

In fact, The Dakota was so successful it graciously and proudly allowed history to eventually give it credit for transforming the entire Upper West

Side of New York City, to the standard of sophistication that it is today. The hype of the building attracted celebrities, and just generally very wealthy and connected people. It had developed a reputation that was hard for any other building to replicate.

Kerrie noticed the unique architecture of The Dakota as they pulled up to the front sentry gate. It was a potpourri of styles, described in magazines as German Renaissance, French Colonial, Victorian, and Gothic. The structure had high gables, interrupted by dormers, niches, balconies, and balustrades. In short, it was magnificent, and because of that, the exterior had been used in numerous movies; the most eerie of those being Rosemary's Baby. Kerrie felt that was a good choice, because the design of the building certainly suited the story line.

The Dakota was the quintessential New York City address and nothing else apparently even came close, although Trump might disagree.

Carl pulled the car up to the entrance, which consisted of a sentry box and wrought iron gates that pulled across a narrow passageway to what looked like a courtyard beyond. There were two doormen or, more appropriately, gatemen on duty. They opened the gate as soon as they saw Carl, tipped their hats, and the Mercedes eased its way slowly and carefully through the passageway to the courtyard. It was a good thing this was one of the smaller Benz vehicles—anything wider would never have made it through. As the car entered into the courtyard, Kerrie noticed that the building was actually constructed as a large square surrounding this open central area. The yard had a large fountain, which Carl drove around and then came to a stop in front of one of the four sections of the building.

"Is this where the owners park?" Jack asked in a friendly tone.

"Well, only for brief periods of time. A garage is a couple of blocks away. But most people don't own their own cars here. They walk or have limos pick them up. There's really no need for a car." This was the most Carl had said to them since they had started their journey with him.

Carl led the way to a corner double doorway, and they entered a beautifully adorned lobby with an elevator. Carl explained that there were really four distinct buildings, each with their own lobbies and elevators at the four corners of the courtyard. He swiped his pass card, and pressed the button for the fourth floor.

Once they reached Noah's apartment, Carl swiped his card again and swung the door open. They entered a grand foyer with beautiful travertine floors. They noticed that the ceilings appeared to be at least fourteen feet high, as they peered down through a side hallway. The hallway went the whole length of the apartment, with side doors coming off the hall into the rooms along the way. Peeking around a corner, Kerrie could see that each room also connected to the next through arched doorways. She guessed that servants would take the hallways, and residents and guests could move freely from room to room through the arched openings.

The apartment was enormous and opulent. Jack and Kerrie couldn't help but gaze around, spellbound, as Carl led them into a parlor room. He invited them to have a seat, and then he disappeared down the hall.

In a few minutes they heard a knocking noise on the hardwood floor, and as they looked up, a frail old man came into the parlor leaning heavily on a cane. Upon seeing him again, Kerrie found it easy to recall how as a little girl she was convinced that he was the twin of the actor, David Soul. He looked now how she would have pictured the actor himself to age. He was slim and broad shouldered, but now quite bent over belying his former height which had been well over six feet. His face was strikingly handsome for his age, with piercing blue eyes and a full head of blondish white hair.

Kerrie squealed with joy and jumped to her feet. They hugged each other, but Kerrie was being extra careful not to squeeze too hard. The old guy grunted, "Hey, I'm not made of porcelain, you know! Go ahead and get fresh with me!"

Kerrie laughed and cried at the same time. She kissed him on the lips and Noah's face turned red. "That's better," he said with obvious glee.

He hobbled over to Jack and held out his free hand. "You must be Jack. What on earth have you gotten my little girl into?" He chuckled.

Jack shook it warmly. "Thanks again, sir. We're in your debt."

"Oh, nonsense. There's not much an old man can do for fun anymore. So let me still enjoy some mischief with this cloak and dagger stuff." They all laughed.

Kerrie went up to Noah again, and held his face in her hands. "You dear man, what has happened to you over the last few years? I don't ever remember you relying on a cane before, and you certainly didn't have one at the funeral."

"No, this is something that's developed in the last two years, Kerrie. A few old injuries that suddenly reared their ugly heads just to keep me out of trouble. But it's okay. I still get around, with the help of Carl here." They had forgotten all about Carl, who was standing sentry off in the corner of the parlor.

"Are you two hungry?" Noah asked.

"I'll say we are!" Kerrie exclaimed. Jack nodded in agreement.

"Carl, could you please go rustle up some ham and eggs for us all?" Noah asked nicely, but really it was more like an order.

Carl turned on his heel, and headed down to the kitchen.

"And by the way, you both stink something fierce! I'm going to have to have this place fumigated after you leave!"

Kerrie smiled at Noah. "You're still a barrel of laughs, Noah. A little more crotchety, but you're still my Noah." He smiled back at her and Kerrie could feel that they still had a connection after all these years. It was nice.

"Let me show you where the guest showers and extra clothes are. You can bag those old ones up and stuff them in Jack's knapsack if you want, or we'll dispose of them for you. And yes, Kerrie, I do have some ladies' clothing here. Don't ask!" Noah laughed.

They enjoyed their showers. It was a relief to feel normal again. Noah had an excellent selection of clothes for all sizes, and for both sexes, in a separate dressing room next to one of the three guest bedrooms. Built-in drawers in the room had underwear and socks as well. It felt like a department store. Before Jack tossed aside his contaminated jeans, he made sure to take the mini cassette out of the front pocket and transfer it to his new pants. And it was clear that neither of them wanted to take their old clothes with them, so Noah asked Carl to bag them up for the incinerator.

When they rejoined Noah in the parlor, he said, "So why don't you start telling me the story about what kind of trouble you two are in. Now I'm prepared to listen to you since you seem to have been in some distress."

Jack and Kerrie started telling their story, beginning with the assault that had just happened at their hotel, and then all the way back to Jack's discovery of the microchip in Mule. Noah nodded from time to time, and seemed to be listening intently. He only interrupted when Carl let him know the meal was ready. "Let's head into the dining room, and we can continue talking there as we eat."

Noah led the way, and they entered a room down the hall that was capable of seating at least twenty for dinner. A huge ornate table dominated the room, and the ceiling was inset with a magnificent crystal chandelier hanging regally over the table.

They each took a seat and Carl served them. Then he joined them as well. Jack and Kerrie dove into their food, which was excellent. Kerrie suspected that anything would taste excellent after their scary ordeal, compounded by twelve hours of fasting.

Carl brought out a tray with four glasses already filled with brandy. He served each of them a glass. Jack quickly downed his, while Kerrie chose to sip hers. She never enjoyed the burning feeling of brandy as it worked its way down her throat. They continued telling their story to Noah. He reminded Kerrie that he had asked her to abandon the project. He shook his head wearily when Kerrie described Mitch's storage unit, the details of his shocking letter, and the revealing conversation that was on the cassette.

Kerrie saw Noah's face change to a harder, more serious look. "And where is this letter now, dear?"

"Don't worry, we have it safely tucked away in Jack's knapsack," Kerrie replied.

She looked across at Jack, and she could see he was starting to sway a little and his elbows were slipping further apart on the table. Carl gave him a fresh glass of brandy.

"Jack, be careful, you don't look too well," Kerrie said softly.

"I've only…had…one glass, Kerrie. I'll just…sip this one." He smiled back at her with a silly look on his face. She had never seen him like this before, and certainly not after one drink. Maybe exhaustion was catching up to him, and the one drink was like five.

Kerrie started to get back into her story, when Noah suddenly interrupted her.

"Let's change the subject to a lighter one for a second. Have you phoned home to Montana to see how Mule is doing?" Kerrie noticed an almost imperceptible nod from Noah in Carl's direction as he said the word "Montana." Carl, as if on cue, got up from the table and left the room.

Kerrie talked about Mule for a few minutes and how excited she was to finally see him again. She didn't think Noah was listening to her until he touched her arm gently and said, "He must remind you of your dad, Kerrie. That's nice."

Kerrie was watching Jack, increasingly worried. She noticed him trying to reach for his fresh glass, but was struggling to move his arm. He tried bracing it with his other hand, but both seemed reluctant to move in the direction he wanted.

She noticed he was having trouble following the conversation as well. His head bobbled, and every time he tried to jump in to say something, his tongue seemed to get in the way. Kerrie rubbed his shoulder a few times and asked him if he was okay. He tried, but couldn't answer her—at least not in a way she understood.

Jack suddenly struggled up from his chair and promptly fell over onto the floor. Kerrie knelt down and helped him back up. Jack was muttering and grumbling and she couldn't make out a thing he was saying. Noah suggested they move into the living room where Jack might be more comfortable. "Does he usually drink this much, Kerrie?" Noah asked in an accusing tone.

"He hardly had anything. I don't understand what's wrong with him." Kerrie walked Jack, one baby shuffle at a time, down the hall to the living room and gently eased him onto the couch. Kerrie sat down beside him, and when she looked up she was startled to see Noah's piercing blue eyes appraising both of them, in a way that wasn't friendly. She suddenly felt a shiver of goose bumps on her arms and she didn't know why.

Jack belched, and as Kerrie cradled his head in her hand, she felt it lose its resistance and just flop over to one side. She panicked and quickly checked his pulse and breathing. She let out a sigh of relief—he seemed okay, but just sort of asleep. His eyes were still open though, which made it seem weird.

She looked deep into his eyeballs, and suddenly caught the vague reflection of someone entering the room behind her.

Chapter 39

The handsome man walked into the room, and Kerrie couldn't believe her eyes. She was seeing it but not believing it.

"Hello Sam," said Noah.

Sam just nodded and walked over to where Jack was slumped over on the couch. He pulled out a pair of handcuffs, rolled Jack over, and cuffed his hands behind his back. Jack stirred slightly, and Kerrie could see some drool coming out of the corner of his mouth.

She looked up at the familiar face, the man she had drunk beer with on her porch, the man who had pretended to save her life. "Bob?"

"Sorry about this, Kerrie. And call me Sam."

He motioned for her to put her hands behind her back, and he pulled out another set of cuffs. He snapped them on, and sat down.

Kerrie looked over at Noah, who was sitting calmly across from her in a Victorian wing-backed chair.

"Noah, I don't understand. What's going on here?"

"You should have left it alone, Kerrie. I was hoping I could let you leave, but once you told me what you'd found, I couldn't. I'm sorry. You've left me no choice."

"But this is me—Kerrie!" Her heart felt like it was up in her throat.

"I was hoping and praying that what your dad was trying to lead you to was not that particular subject. I guess it was just wishful thinking on my part," Noah answered soberly.

"You knew about the 9/11 farce? You knew about this Operation Avalanche?"

Noah stared back at her with a stoic look on his cinematic face.

"Answer me! You knew about all this?" Kerrie demanded.

Noah struggled up from his chair, leaned on his cane and motioned for Sam to follow him down the hall. He glanced over at his bodyguard. "Carl, watch these two for a few minutes please?"

*****

"There are some things that I need to tell you, Sam. You're involved now whether you like it or not. And I can't leave it without you being briefed."

Noah explained in detail what Kerrie and Jack had found, and outlined Operation Avalanche to him. He mentioned that there were still more documents to find and that the clues may be in that letter Kerrie had. Sam nodded a few times as the story progressed, devoid of expression. Inside, his stomach was churning. When he finished his briefing, Noah said, "I'll let Wingate know that you're now in the loop on this file. He will want to completely brief you, no doubt, and arrange for the usual confidentiality commitments. You know the score."

"I do indeed. Let Jim know also that I'll be taking them to our safe house in Connecticut. I'll contact him when I get there."

"You know, Sam, very few people have an inkling about any of this. Some may have their suspicions, but they aren't privy to what really happened. So this will now put you into the inner circle. It will help your career. 'Knowledge is Power' as you know. You might even be able to afford to live in a place like this one day." Noah waved his free hand around in a flourish.

"Oh goody," Sam said, as he started for the hallway. Noah frowned at Sam's reply, as he hobbled after him.

*****

Jack was starting to come around. Kerrie was leaning over to him, as best she could with her hands cuffed behind her back. She was talking to him in hushed tones, trying to get him alert again. Carl was still sitting off in one corner, with his unblinking eyes constantly on the alert.

"Don't worry, Kerrie. He'll be okay in a while. We just gave him a little something to keep him under control," Noah reassured her as he came back into the room.

Kerrie turned her head toward him, and she knew she couldn't hide the disgust in her eyes. "I loved you. So did my father. What kind of human being are you?" She seethed.

Kerrie saw a look of instant rage appear on Noah's face. His mouth contorted in a way that made him look like a different person entirely.

"The kind who protects people like you from the boogie man, that's who I am! Judge me if you need to, I quite frankly don't care!"

Kerrie shuddered at his outrage. This was not the man she knew—or thought she knew. "You're supposed to be retired. What are you doing involved in things like this? Why did you call Bob…Sam on us?"

"You don't really retire from a job like this, Kerrie. That's something I'm beginning to understand, and something your father never did." Noah banged his cane hard on the coffee table as he emphasized the word 'father.'

"At least he seemed to have some semblance of a conscience. That's more than I can say for you," Kerrie said. Was this just a bad dream? Was this really the man she grew up loving?

"Your dad was about to commit treason six years ago—don't talk to me about conscience. He had secrets that he was sworn to protect with his life. He chose to ignore his oath and try to expose the United States to unthinkable disaster. I can't begin to tell you how devastating it would have been for the American economy and America's relations around the world, if what really happened on 9/11 became public knowledge. There would be anarchy in our streets—rioting crowds would be massive and uncontrollable. No one would trade with us, and no one would want to be our ally; the only friend in the world we might be able to cultivate would perhaps be a pariah like Venezuela. Oh, and maybe that pansy prostitute of a country your friend there comes from." Noah pointed his cane in Jack's direction.

"So our country sacrificed thousands of its own lives, and for what!" Kerrie was nearly hysterical.

Noah waved his cane in Kerrie's direction, and made a circle in the air with it. "For your freedom, for mine—to preserve our standard of living and our position as the world power!" Noah seemed more agitated with each of Kerrie's challenges.

"Who cares about all that when innocent people have to die!" She shouted.

"Believe me, you would care years from now if your nation was being run by gooks, turbans, or ruskies. You have no idea of the dangers that face this country every day and people like your father, Sam, and I keep you safe. You little people who can never see the big picture, go to sleep at night and feel just fine. Well, it's people like us who give you that good feeling! Understand?" Noah shouted back. He tried to brace himself to stand, but fell back into his chair again. Sam was sitting next to him but just looked on impassively, didn't extend any help to the old man.

Noah continued, a wild look in his eyes. "And do you even have a clue as to how close we are to running out of oil? Do you realize how that would affect your cozy little life?"

He was preaching now, and Kerrie thought to herself that David Soul was actually a madman. She looked to her right and saw that Jack had come around nicely. He seemed alert and had heard the last exchange; she could tell just by the look in his eyes. He still couldn't talk, however. She could see he was trying to, but his tongue was hanging slightly out of the corner of his mouth and he was struggling to form words. Kerrie reminded herself, with relief, that they hadn't gotten around to sharing with Noah the clues they thought they had figured out as to the location of the rest of the documents. That knowledge might keep them alive for a while.

Noah took a sip of his brandy, and seemed to calm down a little. But he continued his rant. "Operation Avalanche was in planning for years. We designed it so that our acceptable casualties would be confined to primarily the people in the planes, and those above the floors that were hit. That's why we designated the target floors to be as high as possible, to keep the deaths low. We're not animals, you know. But the CIA does know what it's doing in the best interests of the American people, which is a lot more than I can say about some of our so-called leaders."

Kerrie was sickened listening to him trying to justify himself. "You people weren't elected by anyone, Noah. None of you have the right to make those kinds of decisions; it's abhorrent to think of even an *elected* person making that kind of call. You're obviously just a power-hungry madman, a Napoleon—you and your merry band of CIA hacks!" Kerrie snorted and shook her head. She couldn't believe how this man was rationalizing such despicable, brutal actions, actually trying to paint the planners as compassionate people. It was pathetic.

But then she realized he had used the word "We" in his lecture. "So you didn't just know about this, you personally had a role in that disaster?"

Silence.

"Your muteness answers my question," Kerrie said to him in disgust. "You say you're not animals, but consider the innocent thousands who died. Do you ever think of those people, or do you just think your silly patriotic memorials make everything okay? And consider the risk your CIA friends took in the bank as well the day my father was killed. That could have been a real bomb, and it could have killed many more. You people just don't stop, do you? You're seriously twisted!"

"We didn't take any risks that day. We could tell the bomb was a fake. No innocent people were going to die that day," Noah retorted indignantly.

"How could you possibly have known? My dad was an expert at that stuff. The CIA was well aware of how deadly his skills were."

Noah shouted back at her, seemingly desperate to make his case. "It was a fake, and I knew it. Mitch always left a clue as to whether or not a bomb was a dud; that was a superstitious habit of his in all his years of explosives work. And he never changed his habits or modus operandi."

Noah reached down, took off his shoe, and massaged his foot. He winced in pain, then continued his diatribe to Kerrie. "For authentic Joplin bombs, he would always attach a small American flag that would be easily visible from the front." Noah took another sip; his voice was starting to become hoarse. "That bomb vest did not have a flag, I can tell you that for a fact. So you see, Kerrie, we weren't willing to sacrifice innocent lives that day—only your dad's." Noah seemed to be pleased with himself.

Kerrie had that gnawing feeling again, the same one she had gotten that day when Stan tripped up talking about his and Bob's parents. Noah's last comment brought back into her memory Connie's words when she was under hypnosis: *"They came in wearing those awful suits. You could see their eyes, but not much else. An older man was carrying the video camera—I could tell he was older by his eyes, eyes like Mitch's. For a second it looked like Mitch recognized him. The room seemed to stand still for an eternity, then a flash from the camera. They shot him, they killed him, the bullet whizzed right past me, I could hear it."* Kerrie put her hand up to her mouth and gasped. The room started spinning around as the blood rushed to her head. She knew she was looking at her dad's murderer.

"You were there that day, weren't you? My God, you were the phony cameraman, you were the shooter," Kerrie said in a whisper, tears streaming down her cheeks. Noah just coldly stared back at her and took another sip of his brandy.

"Answer me! Give me that at least, Noah! Did you kill my father, your best friend?" Kerrie screamed.

Noah struggled up from his chair and hobbled over to where Kerrie was sitting. He looked down at her with a glare as cold as ice, held onto the arm of the couch, and pointed his cane a couple of inches from her nose. "Yes, I did. And I would do it again. Governments can't allow secrets like that to be broadcast to people who are too small-minded to understand. That fundamental is more important than friendship. Your dad had to die."

Noah turned and hobbled toward the hallway. He directed his gaze at Sam, who was still sitting, and said, "You had better get going. It's a long drive to Connecticut. Jack's knapsack is beside the front door. What they've found so far is apparently in there."

"Okay, Noah, I'll handle it from here." Sam grabbed Kerrie roughly by the arm and hoisted her off the couch, then held onto her cuffs from behind and guided her to the door. He nodded at Carl to do the same with Jack. On the way out, Sam picked up Jack's knapsack and Kerrie's purse and slung them over his shoulder. They exited the elevator and the two of them were escorted out to Sam's car parked in the courtyard. He opened the doors to the BMW 535i, and Carl shoved Jack and Kerrie into the rear seat. Sam threw their belongings into the trunk, then nodded to Carl and got into the driver's seat. He turned on the engine and pushed a button that activated a solid pane of thick glass, which slid up to the roof from a panel installed behind the front bucket seats.

Kerrie looked out the window and watched as they crossed the Robert F. Kennedy Bridge, then onto I-278 East. The miles clicked away as they merged onto I-95 north, en route to Connecticut. She called out to Sam through the glass—no reply. She shifted an elbow down to the armrest and tapped the power door lock button, and then the power window button. No luck—she had expected that anyway. She felt her arms cramp up, the handcuffs were taking their toll.

She didn't want to know why they had to go to Connecticut. She just wanted to know if they would have a chance of getting out of this. She knew that it didn't look good right now. She knew also that Jack was probably their only chance, but being handcuffed as well he was pretty impotent. She looked over at him and flashed her best weary smile. She didn't feel like talking, and she could tell that Jack seemed to know that. He made no attempt. He did look a lot better now though, which was a relief to her. She wondered what they had put in his drink.

Kerrie thought back over the last few hours, and about Noah. She had been so proud of that man her whole life, only to have that pride shattered into a million little pieces. She had felt so safe and secure after Noah and Carl came to their rescue. Then it turned into a nightmare. They would have been safer to have just stayed in the dumpster. Her love and admiration had been wasted on a monster, and she wondered if she could ever love or trust anyone again. Could she ever allow herself to put someone on a pedestal again? The man driving the car was another person she had developed affection for, and was deceived by him too. She was glad she hadn't known him for too long.

And her faith in humanity had also taken a real licking today. A man she had loved and respected told her that innocent lives didn't really matter in the grand scheme of things; at least not as much as world supremacy, standards of living, and of course, oil.

How do people come to think that way—how had they been influenced to twist their brains and their humanity into pretzels?

And now here they were with Sam, or Bob, or whoever the fuck he was, driving to Connecticut, handcuffed and helpless.

Kerrie was shaken out of her daydreaming by the feel of the car slowing down and turning off the highway. She looked ahead of them and saw that they were turning down a dark country road, following a "rest stop" directional sign. She hoped that Sam just had to take a leak, but her instincts told her to be scared.

Sam pulled into the rest stop, which at this time of night was abandoned. It was slightly illuminated by one single light over the usual tourist map attached to a billboard, and one other light that would guide the way to the washroom doors.

Sam got out of the front seat and opened the door on Jack's side. He barked, "Get out, both of you—on this side."

Kerrie could see that in his right hand was a large pistol with a silencer screwed to the barrel.

Chapter 40

It was already quite dark outside, and Jack knew that it would be highly unlikely for anyone to drive into this rest stop now. And if some Good Samaritan happened upon them, what chance would he really have against a gun-wielding professional assassin like Sam. They hauled themselves out of the back seat and followed the direction of Sam's gesturing gun to a rustic narrow pathway along the side of the rest stop. Jack could see that the pathway led to the back of the building near the men's washroom entrance, surrounded by thick forest on three sides. As they left the car, Sam had opened the trunk and pulled out a fluorescent "Closed for Maintenance" sign, and placed it on the ground at the front of the building. This didn't make Jack feel any easier, except knowing that at least some poor bugger who had to take a leak wouldn't get a bullet in the head instead.

Jack started thinking of his list of regrets, not the least of which was his insatiably curious mind compounded by his boring retirement. If those two factors had not been present in his life, he and Kerrie wouldn't be in this predicament. Why couldn't he have just left well enough alone? Why hadn't he listened to Meagan's warning about being in way over his head? Did he have a death wish? And if he did, was he that selfish that he had to expose other people to it?

Jack shook his head in disgust. If he had to do it all over again, knowing what he knew now, he would have just ignored Mule's stupid microchip and continued on with his boring life. Boring would be nice right now.

He thought about Heather and Josh, and how nice it would be to just hang out with them again. Soak up their simple happy lives. He wondered if everyone who was about to die had these thoughts—the grass was so very green when you knew you wouldn't see it anymore.

He looked from side to side to see if there was some remote opportunity. He figured they could try to run off into the woods, but knew that Sam would react quickly to that and they would just get it in the back. The fact that both him and Kerrie had their hands cuffed behind their backs also limited their options. He glanced behind him ever so slightly to gauge how far away Sam was positioned from his deadly feet. Sam was smart. He was keeping himself at least eight feet behind them, so lashing out with a kick was not going to work. The only thing Jack would hit would be thin air.

Kerrie was walking along beside him like a zombie, seemingly resigned to her fate. She looked defeated and demoralized. He leaned his head toward her and down in front a bit, trying to catch her eye. She stared straight ahead as if Jack wasn't even there. He wondered if his own face was conveying the same look of resignation. More than likely, his face was starting to show signs of panic—panic that intensified as his heart rate quickened. Jack knew that by now he should have taken some aspirin and an anxiety pill. Silly for him to even think of such a thing now. A stress attack was the least of his worries.

Physically though, he felt like he was almost back to normal now. Whatever they had slipped in his drink had been pretty potent stuff, and must have had a lifespan of about two hours. His legs were still a bit stiff and his mouth was dry, but at least his tongue had reduced down to normal size. He recalled biting it by mistake several times while it was swollen, and he was paying the price now.

He tried telling himself this wasn't over yet. He was confident that even with his hands cuffed, he would be able to give Sam a run for his money if he got half a chance. He knew that his legs, while not back in top form yet, were still deadlier than the average bear. Jack was determined to take the chance, whether or not he got the perfect opportunity. He knew that at best he would only get one shot at it, and if it was going to be his last shot anyway, what did he have to lose?

They marched on. The only thing Sam said to them during their hike was, "Keep going, to the rear of the building." That alone was an ominous statement.

When they arrived, he ordered them to stop. He motioned Jack to move several feet away from Kerrie, then removed a key from his pocket and reached behind to her handcuffs. All Jack could think of at that moment was that Sam was either going to let them die with some dignity, or more likely he wanted it to look like they had been executed by some crazed maniac. Handcuffs on the bodies would draw too many questions.

He willed Kerrie with his mind to do something, anything, just to give him an opportunity. She could yank her leg up behind her and kick Sam in the balls. That would be enough to give Jack a fraction of a second. He could see that Sam was being careless as he was un-cuffing her. He had the gun pointed toward the ground and not at either one of them.

Once the cuffs were off, Sam threw them into the woods. He passed the key to Kerrie and ordered her to remove Jack's. He backed away from both of them. Kerrie leaned down behind Jack and slipped the key into the handcuffs. She twisted the key and the cuffs came off. Sam pointed to the woods and she threw them back there to join the other pair. Then she stood beside Jack and they both faced Sam, waiting for the inevitable. Jack felt her hand grab onto his, squeezing it hard. Her palms were sweating.

It was so silent, and dark—some slight illumination was coming from the outside washroom light, but that was about it. No full moon to offer assistance. Jack felt like he had stopped breathing. All three of them were standing still, not a word spoken. What was taking him so long? Why didn't he just get it over with? Jack tensed his body, waiting for the bullet.

Instead of a bullet, a set of car keys came shooting towards him, which Jack reached out and caught in one deft movement. Then Sam raised his gun to shoulder height and Jack braced himself again. But to his surprise Sam flicked his wrist, sending the gun flying behind him up against the building.

In a monotone voice, sad and expressionless, Sam said, "I want you two to get out of here, fast. Your knapsack and purse are safely in the trunk. I told them we were going to Connecticut, almost a three-hour drive from New York City. We've been on the road here for about forty-five minutes, so by the time you get to the airport you'll have at least an hour's head start before they get concerned that I haven't contacted them. Even a little more time than that probably, because they'll allow me a bit of grace for highway slowdowns."

They just stood there, stunned. Jack glanced over at Kerrie and saw that there was once again life in her eyes. Neither of them knew what to say; they had both conditioned themselves for a pitiful ending.

Sam then took out his wallet and tossed that to Jack also. "Put that in the glove compartment. In case someone finds me soon after you leave in my car, it will guarantee your head start if I can't be traced too quickly. Also, make certain to put that 'closed' sign back in the trunk."

Jack asked in a low voice, "What about you?"

"I want you to put me out, Jack. You're perfectly capable of doing that. I don't want you to kill me, even though it may be hard for you to resist. I have a wife and kids, and I want out of all this. It has gone way too far for me to stomach. I can't be a part of it any longer.

"For the record, I need for both of you to know that I had no knowledge of Operation Avalanche until I heard you and Noah talking tonight, Kerrie. I heard rumors over the years of course, within the Agency, and a little voice inside told me that it could have been us but I chose not to believe that it was possible. It was too horrible to believe.

"Not that I want you to think better of me. I don't. In fact, I don't care what either of you think of me. What's important right now is what I think of myself, and what my family thinks of me."

Jack could see that Sam had a frown on his face now, as compared to the deadpan expression he had shown over the past few hours. He was experiencing some kind of redemption, and must have been thinking long and hard during the drive here as to what he was going to do. Jack thanked God that Sam had listened to the right voices in his head.

Sam continued, speaking quicker now. "You guys have stumbled onto something huge here, and you need to either go as far away as possible as fast as you can, or protect yourselves with the documents. If you're not going to run, get all of the documents to a safe place. And then let these turkeys know that you have them and that they will be released if anything happens to you."

Kerrie asked, "What would you do if you were us, Sam?"

"That's a hard one. With my training and skills, I would probably hunt for the documents and get them to a safe haven. However, neither of you are trained for these risks. If I were you, I'd run. Leave the country and never come back. Go to a country that doesn't have an extradition treaty with the U.S. and change your names—and then never, ever, contact anyone in this country under your old names again. That's my best advice to you."

Kerrie persisted. "What about just giving everything to the media?"

Sam laughed, in a mocking way. "That would be a joke, Kerrie. None of the media would touch this. For all intents and purposes, we own the U.S. media. Sure, they would probably play along with you, invite you in for an interview, act shocked, ask for copies of your documents, then promptly call someone like me just like Noah did. You would then disappear just as you were supposed to tonight. You were lucky that I was in charge of your file, and Noah had already been instructed by my superiors to contact me if he heard from you. If it had been someone else, you would already be dead."

Sam took a deep breath and continued. "So many shocking stories over the years have been brought to the attention of the media by good, naïve witnesses, only to have those stories squashed and the witnesses perish in 'accidents.' Those good citizens were just footnotes on page three, and write-ups in the obituaries. That's the only coverage they were able to get for their trouble and their lives. And normal people like you who read the news, were never the wiser."

Jack piped up, "All the media?"

"Well, at least all the major ones here in the United States, and I would expect your country too, Jack. Canada in a lot of ways is a puppet of the U.S., sad to say. Oh, and there are of course those 'conspiracy theory' media outlets who would probably be more than thrilled to publish your documents. However, no one ever listens to them even though a lot of what they say contains some truth. We at the CIA have done a marvelous job of smearing them all as freaks and nut-bars. The public has an image in their minds now of that media, and nothing is going to change that. So, as far as we're concerned they can publish anything they want—the government is safe. Just goes to show the power of counter-branding, doesn't it?" Sam chuckled in a cynical tone.

"So even if we get the documents and get them safe, what would our threat to release them do? How would that protect us, if as you say, most of the media are in the pockets of the CIA?" Kerrie asked.

"Think beyond our borders, Kerrie. Think of those who hate us and would just love to get their hands on that stuff. Think hard. It will come to you. It's a fairly long list. For now, though, we're running out of time," Sam said.

"Okay, Sam, how do you want to do this?" Jack asked, with clear dread in his voice.

"The first thing you need to do is break my gun-hand wrist with a kick. I've thrown the gun behind me, so you need to make it look like you kicked it from my hand. My wrist has to survive scrutiny; it must look like it was broken from a kick and not a twist. I'm going to hold it out like this and I want you to just do it—now!"

Jack didn't hesitate. He went into position, fixed the target of Sam's hand in his mind, and spun in a 360. He heard a snap and Sam's arm dropped limply to his side. The wrist and hand were now at an odd angle to his forearm. Sam showed a flash of a grimace, but that was all. He was clearly accustomed to handling pain.

Jack heard a gasp escape from Kerrie's mouth. He turned around and saw that she was looking in the opposite direction now, with her hands covering her ears.

"Now, I want you to leave marks. Batter me in the face, and launch a couple of kicks to my side and chest as well. You'll need to break a rib or two."

"Sam, I can put you out just by pressing the back of your neck, you know that. Why put yourself through this?" Jack asked, with genuine concern in his voice. The stress of this bizarre situation was taking its toll on him. This was not why he had learned karate, to beat the shit out of a willingly defenseless man. And he had three emotions going on at once—anger, sympathy, and gratitude—all directed at Sam. He only needed the anger one to deliver this beating, but the other two were fighting back.

"Because, while this is probably not important to you, you'll be saving my life if you do it the way I tell you. We have CIA doctors who examine every injury suffered in the field, to make sure there was no collusion. My injuries have to look genuine; otherwise, they'll make sure I'm dead within days. If you do this right, they'll be convinced that I suffered the injuries legitimately, because by now a lot of people are well aware of what you, Jack, are capable of. I can use that to my advantage."

Jack nodded soberly. He understood why, for Sam's sake, it had to be done. He looked back at Kerrie. She'd moved further into the trees and still had her hands over her ears. Jack moved in close to Sam, and threw a lightning punch to his mouth. Several teeth went flying as Sam's head flung backwards. Then Jack sent three more quick punches his way, around the eyes. Sam held up his palm for a second to catch his breath. He was bent over, panting, blood gushing from his mouth. Jack could see that the man was already bleeding hard around the eyes as well. His wrist looked painful but Sam didn't seem to care. He stood erect once again, with his hands at his side, and nodded for more.

Jack bent over and removed his shoes and socks, then he spun, delivering a vicious kick to the chest. He heard a snap as at least one rib broke. Then he kicked again with the upper part of his foot, curling it around Sam's side and back at impact, to leave a mark around the kidney area. He knew that one would be very painful for him. Sam went down, but struggled back to his feet again. Jack could hear Kerrie's heavy breathing in the background, and her voice, begging Jack to stop. Sam was struggling for breath and he held up his hand for Jack to pause again.

"Now...you need...to break my...jaw...and put me out. Before...that... remember, take...my advice. Just...get out...of this godforsaken country... and...don't come back! Be...smart!"

Jack looked at Sam hard. He hoped this last kick wouldn't kill him. While he didn't have any particular affection for Sam—or Bob as Jack and Kerrie had known him, in these last few minutes he had come to admire him. Sam was a true patriot; he was nothing like that power-hungry madman, Noah Hendridge. Sam had a conscience just like Mitch had. Noah was a sociopath, if not a psychopath.

But Jack hesitated. He looked at this defenseless man in front of him and it sickened him knowing that he had done this damage to someone who was not prepared to fight back.

"Do it! You're running...out of time!" Sam pleaded.

Jack still hesitated. He knew Sam was right, but something was holding him back. His conscience or humanity, he guessed, which he had always hoped everyone had at least a bit of somewhere deep down inside.

Sam gestured to him to approach. When Jack got close, Sam rasped into his ear. "Connie... and her brother...are dead. Chopped up...into little pieces." Jack felt a sudden pain in his chest and his hands balled up into fists. His fingernails cut into his palms, he was squeezing so tightly. An image of sweet, harmless Connie flashed into his brain. Her demure smile, her innocent sense of humor, her dedication to her brother. And the horrors she had endured—too many for any one person in a lifetime.

Her parents' deaths in the south tower, her ordeal with Mitch and watching him die. Now finally the ultimate insult of dying herself at the hands and tools of these cruel spooks. He felt like he was going to throw up, but he had something to do first.

Sam braced himself. Jack could tell. He now had his bloodied eyes closed and was doing his best to stand still, but he was swaying on his feet. Blood had now covered most of his face. Jack took a few steps back and went into his stance, focusing on Sam's chin and jaw. Then he spun. The heel of his bare foot connected right to the exact spot he wanted, but he had lost the discipline to pull his kick like he'd planned to do. Sam went down in a crumpled heap on the ground, and stopped moving.

Jack dropped to the ground beside him and felt for a pulse. Then he vomited.

He donned his shoes and socks, pulled himself up, and wiped a sleeve across his face as he walked back to Kerrie. He put his arms around her and whispered in her ear. "He's alive, Kerrie. He'll be fine. It's time for us to go."

He felt her muscles relax a bit in his arms, and he knew she was relieved. She started to turn back from the woods, but Jack said, "Shield your eyes with your hands as we walk by. It's not a pretty sight. You don't want to remember Sam this way." She nodded and covered her eyes. Jack clutched her tightly as they made their way back up the path, past the bloody scene.

Jack stole one last glance at Sam and his once handsome face, and saluted him as he passed. That's one brave man, he thought to himself. And deep in his gut, now that his anger had been released, he knew that Sam had had nothing to do with Connie's death.

Jack grabbed the sandwich sign off the ground and threw it into the trunk. He saw that the knapsack and purse were in there as Sam had promised they would be. Once in the car, Jack stuffed Sam's wallet into the glove compartment.

He asked Kerrie if she wanted to drive, but she said she would prefer to just give directions to him. She knew her way around these highways very well, so Jack would be counting on her to find the fastest way to the Long Island airport.

He maneuvered Sam's powerful BMW back onto the highway, in the direction of where they had come from. Jack handed Kerrie a small piece of paper that he had taken from his pocket. "Kerrie, can you call the pilot for me? I called them at 3:00 and it's now 10:00. They must be wondering what the hell happened to us."

Kerrie told the pilot they would be there in about ninety minutes. The captain assured her the jet would be ready for immediate take-off when they arrived, fully catered this time. They discussed the flight plan as well—back to Helena.

Jack looked over at Kerrie after she hung up. "I heard you tell him Helena was the destination. Are you sure? Should we just fly south instead? Do we want to run?"

Kerrie took a moment to think, and then glared at him, fire in her eyes. "No fucking way, Jack! Let's finish this! I'm not looking over my shoulder the rest of my life! Helena it is."

"Glad to hear you say that. Let's give this our best shot. I don't want to hide either, and why the hell should we?"

*****

It was 11:30 p.m. when they boarded the aircraft. The pilots greeted them, and this time there was a flight attendant on board to serve them since there would indeed be food on this flight. The pilots had waited for them so long, they just went ahead and took the initiative to have the plane catered. Jack and

Kerrie were glad they did.

They stretched out in the comfortable chairs and strapped in. The jet took off a few minutes later, and no two people were ever so glad to be in the air.

"Do you think Bob will be okay?" Kerrie asked.

"Remember, his real name's Sam, at least we think it is, and he'll be okay. I have no doubt about that. He'll be out of action for a while, but it sounds like he wants out permanently anyway. He's a tough guy, Kerrie. He can take a lot."

"I was blown away by what he did for us. I thought for sure we were goners," Kerrie mused.

"Me too. Not to take anything away from Sam, but what he did, he did more for himself than for us. That was his moment more than ours. He finally did the right thing for his own soul." Jack decided not to tell Kerrie about Connie. Sam had clearly used that to provoke him, and the tactic had worked. But Kerrie didn't need to hear that right now.

He did some quick calculations of the time factors. The flight would take about four hours tonight according to the captain, so that would get them into Helena around 3:30 a.m. New York time, and 1:30 a.m. Montana time, Saturday. Then the three-hour drive to Bigfork meant they would arrive at Kerrie's house at about 4:30 a.m. It would still be dark—a good thing.

He and Kerrie discussed the risks of going back. The discussion didn't last long. They had no choice but to check out the house and try to gain access to the attic. They were convinced that Mitch's final clue was designed to lead them to those guns, sitting in that trunk in plain sight.

They knew they first had to see if the house was being watched. The head start Sam had given them, and the fact that it might be quite a while before he was discovered at that rest stop, might just give them the edge they needed. Also, since they knew that Jack and Kerrie had a plane at their disposal, the CIA might immediately assume that they would just take the opportunity to fly out of the country, scared out of their minds. Jack had to admit, he had thought of doing that.

The attendant came out of the galley with the meal service one hour into the flight. Kerrie had already moved back to the couch, so she enjoyed hers there. Jack folded out his table and dug into the crab salad and Kobe beef tenderloin. There were vegetables on the plate too, but Jack didn't notice. He asked for seconds of the Kobe, and the attendant was more than pleased to bring him another sumptuous serving.

Then a three-stage dessert of cherries jubilee, coffee, and a well-needed nap.

*****

The Audi pulled into the last turn from the town of Bigfork, heading toward Kerrie's house. It was 4:15 a.m., Saturday morning, still pitch black outside. They were about a mile from the house when Kerrie motioned to Jack to pull off the road into an empty lot. She directed him to park the car in the middle of a stand of trees.

"I don't feel good about driving any farther, Jack. I think we'd be taking a chance. If someone's there, they know your car by now."

"You're right. Good thing you're on the ball here."

Before they started their hike, Jack went back to the trunk, pulled the mini cassette out of his pocket, and stuffed it into a zippered pocket of the knapsack. He left the knapsack there, and Kerrie threw her purse into the trunk as well. But first she took out her cell phone and clipped it to her belt. She checked to make sure it was turned off.

Then one last item. Jack reached into a rear compartment and pulled out a flashlight that was plugged into a charger. They were ready.

They made their way down the dark road toward Kerrie's house. The moon shimmering on the lake gave them a good directional. Jack kept the flashlight off. They stayed near the trees on one side of the road to minimize their chances of being seen. It was very still—no sounds, no lights. The great state of Montana was still asleep. Jack could feel his heart pounding so hard he was afraid it was going to pop through his chest.

After about fifteen minutes, they could see the huge, majestic bed and breakfast looming in front of them, and Kerrie whispered that despite how she now felt about the place, it was good to be home.

They stayed low to the ground as they walked, and came closer to the side of the house. One portion of the front porch was now in view and the house seemed deserted. They both knew that what they were doing was incredibly dangerous, but after what they had been through the last couple of days, and the second chance Sam had given them, they didn't want to waste the opportunity to do what needed to be done. And what would life be like living in fear, hiding, wondering when the bullet would come? That wouldn't be life. They had no choice but to finish this, and protect themselves with the complete story and the evidence that they felt they were so close now to getting their hands on.

Suddenly Kerrie grabbed Jack by the arm and quietly pulled him down to the ground. She put her finger to her mouth, and pointed down to the lake. At first he couldn't see anything out of the ordinary and wondered if Kerrie was imagining things. Then he saw it.

The dark silhouette of a man standing on the dock. They would have missed him completely if he hadn't been smoking a cigarette, flicking the orange embers into Flathead Lake.

Chapter 41

They could hear his shoes clicking against the dock boards as he paced back and forth, smoking his cigarette. Sound traveled very well around bodies of water. They had to be careful themselves, as the night was still and any unnatural noise would resonate. Kerrie knew they were far enough back from the lake not to be noticed right now, but they were a bit exposed lying there in the grass. She motioned to Jack to move backwards so they could hide themselves in a nearby cluster of trees. Together they slithered on their tummies, slowly and quietly, back to the trees, making sure that the two thickest trees would be between them and the lake.

Kerrie breathed easier now. They stayed flat on the ground as they peered around the trunks toward the house and the lake. They were about 100 ft. to the north side of the house, and at least 200 ft. from the dock. She looked longingly at her dock, where she had spent so many peaceful afternoons. Now an intruder was flicking his ashes into her lake. She felt anger building up inside of her. She couldn't even enter her own house because of these bastards.

She looked over at Jack in the dark and could tell that the wheels were turning in his head. What were they going to do next? They both watched the man on the dock as he paced, hearing the faint click of his footsteps meshing with the sloshing of water up against the rocking structure.

Suddenly their eyes were drawn to the left of the lone figure. A stocky silhouette appeared, walking along the shoreline to the edge of the water. Another one! He hailed the man on the dock, who turned and started walking down to the ramp leading to the beach. They could hear their faint voices, but only caught a couple of words: "moon" and "exposed".

Both of the men walked away from the dock back toward the porch. Then one of the men raised his hand and motioned to someone else out of their view. Jack looked over at Kerrie and held up three fingers. She nodded.

She whispered to Jack, "We could try for the back door, but I keep the key for that one hidden in the shed. I don't think we could slide those metal doors open without being heard."

Jack nodded. "We'll need to do something within the next ninety minutes or we'll lose the cover of darkness. I suggest we give ourselves half an hour to figure this out, or we head back to the car."

Suddenly they heard another footfall, this time over to their left and to the rear of the house. Someone was walking from the main road, down along the side of the house toward the front porch area where the others were. They could see his dark image as he passed within fifty feet of where they were laying. He rounded the lake side of the house and was soon out of sight as he joined the others on or near the porch.

"So, there are at least four of them. They're hoping we're going to pull up in our car from the road, which is why they're staying out of sight on the lake side," Jack whispered.

Kerrie could feel her heart pulsing in her neck as she lay helpless in the grass. Trapped on her own property.

They both reacted to the noise at the same time. From a few dozen feet behind them came a sound of nature that made their blood run cold. They knew instantly what it was. Snorting, throaty growl, thrashing of heavy paws through the brush. They didn't have to turn around to look. Jack demonstrated frantically to Kerrie to get into the fetal position, and then folded his arms down on each side of his face with his hands clasped behind his neck. She followed suit.

The sound was very close now, and they could hear the bear's heavy breathing, signaling that it had discovered their presence. From its terrific sense of smell, it had probably known they were in the area several hundred feet ago, but now was getting excited. Its pace had quickened as it closed in on their hiding place. They were easy prey, lying there on the ground. And they had nowhere to go—killers in front of them and a killer behind them.

The bear took Kerrie first, pouncing on her, clawing at her back and the hands that were protecting her neck. Kerrie could feel her flesh tearing away along with her clothes. Its claws were like knives; searing pain engulfed her as it scratched along the entire length of her back. It was trying to get her hands unclasped from her neck, but she held them together for dear life. She wanted to scream, but she knew she couldn't. She also knew she had to play dead for as long as she could, or at least until she really was dead.

****

Jack turned his head sideways with his hands still clasped, and saw the bear trying desperately to turn Kerrie over onto her back. She was doing the right thing, stubbornly resisting in the fetal position, but he knew that it wouldn't be long before the bear stopped playing with her.

He could see that it was a black bear, and a big one, at least 400 lbs. Its throaty growls were getting louder. Suddenly the bear stopped tearing at Kerrie's back, reared its head and roared. Jack knew this was a sign that it was now going to get serious.

Jack quickly unclasped his hands, brought his fist back and rammed it directly into the bear's nose. He could see the look of surprise on the beast's face, and saw it open its huge jaws and shake its head. Jack's punch had hurt for sure, but only enough to make it more curious, and more enraged. The animal turned its attention to Jack, and swung a paw directly at his head. Jack could feel the claws as they sheared across his scalp, tearing out a patch of hair along his forehead and leaving blood dripping down into his eyes. It took a second for the pain to register, but now it was burning him. He felt like his head was on fire.

Jack was no longer facing away after his shot to the creature's nose and he realized he had broken a cardinal rule. The thing dropped its front paws onto Jack's chest and started tearing at his jacket and up towards his throat. Jack then did the only thing he could; he brought two fingers up into the "V" position and jammed them right in the direction of the beast's eyes. He could feel the huge mushy eyeballs give way to his thrust, and could smell the bear's rank breath as it opened its jaws in shock. Then it reared up and roared once again.

Jack quickly rolled over on his side into the fetal position as before, bringing his knees up as close to his chin as he could, his hands protecting the back of his neck.

The sounds of muffled shouts came from the lake side of the house. Jack could see two dark figures advancing toward their position, in a crouch, about 100 ft. away. "It sounds like a fucking bear!" could be heard amid the roar of the animal, disturbing the early morning stillness.

The bear now ignored the two figures on the ground, and turned its massive head in the direction of the lake. It let out another roar, clearly angry at this intrusion. It pulled itself off Jack's exposed side and started towards the men. It had to negotiate its way between the two trees in order to advance but bumped hard into one of the trunks, snarling in disgust. Jack figured the beast was blind but just didn't know it yet.

"I can see him now, he's coming our way!" one of the men shouted.

"No guns! Use the crossbows!"

Now there were three men silhouetted against the lake staring the bear down. Two of the dark figures raised their menacing crossbows—weapons that had not been meant for a bear today, but instead to silently take the lives of a man and a woman.

The bear charged, blind but fully guided by its keen sense of smell and hearing. Jack heard the sound of two soft twangs, and the thud of one of the arrows into a tree right in front of them. The other one zipped over their heads, the whoosh sound so clear, so close. Jack could see the men reload and fire again.

Jack wondered if they'd hit the bear. He figured the agents didn't know either. They stood still for a second perhaps expecting the beast to fall, but it didn't. Then, each of them frantically loaded another arrow, drawing them out of carriers on their backs. The bear was getting close to them now. Its sense of smell was drawing it to them like a magnet. The third man yelled, "Run!"

One of the men took that advice without argument, but the other one held his ground. He quickly fired another arrow as the creature came within about 30 ft. There was an anguished cry from the bear as the arrow sliced right through its neck. But it kept charging, close enough now to swat the man off his feet. Then the beast was on him, tearing, slashing, lunging for the man's throat. The man screamed in agony with each swipe of the massive paws.

One of the dark figures mercifully reappeared from the porch side of the house, raised his crossbow, and fired. Another soft twang sound. The huge beast went down, shuddered, and then expired with a heavy sigh, flopping its bulk across the prone shape of his prey.

*****

Jack glanced at Kerrie as they both lay in the grass behind the clump of trees. Under the dim light of the moon, he could see that the back of her jacket and the blouse underneath had been shorn off, her bare back displaying the souvenirs of the bear's attack. Horrible scratches that looked as if she'd been whipped with a rope of nails. He removed his jacket, tore a sleeve off his shirt, and started gently dabbing at the wounds. She was lucky—they weren't too deep. The backs of her hands were bleeding badly, and Jack tore off his other sleeve into two pieces and tied on makeshift bandages. Kerrie was a cooperative patient, and lay still while he quietly attended to her. She seemed okay otherwise but was still shaky from the ordeal.

He looked down at the scene towards the porch, and there was noisy activity now. Three men were attempting to roll the bear off their buddy, grunting and swearing as they did. There was no sound coming from the man on the ground. Jack laid flat on his stomach and looked down toward the lake. Two of the men were now carrying the body of the fallen agent back to the porch side of the house. The third man was talking to them in hushed tones. Jack couldn't make out any of the words.

Kerrie leaned up on her elbows and grimaced in pain. "What are we going to do? It'll start getting light in an hour. We have to decide now." Her whisper sounded strained, hoarse.

"I have an idea, and I think it's the only option we have other than going back to the car and giving up."

"Tell me."

"We can use that tunnel from the outhouse. It's only about 200 ft. away and the agents are hiding on the lake side. We can crawl around the back of the house and won't be seen, as long as no other agents show up from the road."

Kerrie looked at him, long and hard. Then, with new determination she rasped, "You're right. I don't think anything can ever scare me again."

Jack leaned across to her and kissed her cheek. "Okay, let's go. We're in this together and we'll finish it together. And we have a golden opportunity now while they're distracted with their friend, who may be dead or close to it. They'll be in shock and busy for the next few minutes, at least."

They turned in the direction of the back of the house and started their long slither. They had 100 ft. to cover before reaching the back of the house and they were safer to do it flat on the ground. They went single file, slowly and quietly. Once they got to the protection of the house, they rose to a crouch position and started their cautious approach to the far side of the structure where the outhouse waited for them—perhaps just as Mitch had intended.

Jack noticed Kerrie slow down and peer through several windows as they eased across the back of the house. She nodded and made the "OK" sign with her thumb and forefinger. So, it appeared as if the agents were staying outside, a stroke of luck. They clearly intended to pull off an ambush in the driveway. The arrogant bastards had severely underestimated them.

After several minutes they finally reached the faux ramshackle outhouse, Mitch's deceptively genius construction. Jack led the way, carefully opening the door which if it were truly an old outhouse would have made an eerie creaking noise. In this case, it was wonderfully silent. "Thank you, Mitch," Jack whispered under his breath.

They entered the outhouse, and Jack quietly flipped up the four clamps holding the seat and its base down. He now had the flashlight on. They had no choice and had to take the chance. He shielded it with his jacket and motioned to Kerrie to go down the shaft first. She didn't hesitate. He lit the way down the shaft until she reached the bottom, then he followed down the rope ladder as quickly as he could. It swung sideways due to his speed and he smashed his shoulder against the shaft walls several times, but he didn't feel the pain. In fact, after the bear attack, he didn't think he would react to pain again for quite some time.

As soon as he reached the bottom, he guided Kerrie over to the tunnel. She looked at him curiously under the reflection of the flashlight, and then took it out of his hand. She flashed it at his face and gasped. "Your scalp! Part of it's missing!"

"Don't worry about it, I'm fine."

"You're not fine. It's bleeding, and your chest is bleeding too!"

"I'll be okay. The bear took a good swipe at me, but the blood's starting to dry up. At least I won't have to worry about my hair falling down over my eyes," he quipped.

"Always the jokester, huh?" Kerrie ripped off a sleeve of her blouse and tied a bandana around Jack's forehead with her wrapped hands. Then she pulled apart his torn shirt under his open jacket and examined his chest wounds.

"You're lucky. The chest looks like it'll be okay—but that forehead, my God. You're probably going to need plastic surgery on that."

"Something to deal with later. Let's get going."

They headed down the tunnel with Jack leading the way with the torch. When they arrived at the spot where the gun case was hanging from the wood supports, Jack took it down and slung the strap over his shoulder.

"What's that?" Kerrie asked.

"Guns your dad left us. We may need them." Kerrie nodded grimly. Jack figured nothing would surprise this girl anymore.

They crawled their way to the end of the tunnel and then stopped short of the rope ladder. Both of their chests were heaving. The air was very thin and musty, and they had already been short of breath from the bear scare. And they had crawled through the tunnel too fast. Now it was hitting them.

"Kerrie, before we…climb…let's take…a moment to try and…breathe more evenly." The two of them leaned over with their heads close to the ground, and took short shallow breaths.

Kerrie waved her hands frantically. "I'm suffocating…" she gasped. "Have to get…to…fresher air…"

Jack nodded, knowing she was right. If they didn't climb up there now, they were likely to pass out. He led the way as quickly as he could muster, up the rope ladder to the top of the shaft. Then carefully, and quietly, he put his shoulder to the trap door and eased it upwards a crack. He listened carefully for any voices or sounds. Feeling safe, he put his hands to the contraption and hefted it the rest of the way, holding it upright. They eased out of the shaft, and collapsed on the floor. Jack drank in the fresh clean air and saw that Kerrie was doing the same. Jack felt the desperate need to cough but held back. After a few minutes Kerrie nodded, indicating that she was okay to carry on.

They were now in the passageway that connected the main house with the tower section. Jack slipped the leather case off his shoulder and opened it up. He pulled out the two Uzi guns.

"Which one are you most comfortable with?" Jack whispered.

Kerrie reached for the pistol, checked to make sure the safety was on, and slid it into her waistband. "Now I thank God that my dad taught me how to use a pistol."

Jack raised the Uzi sub-machine gun and checked to make sure the selector lever was on safety. Then he shouldered the leather case that contained the extra magazines. He nodded and they began to move, slowly, cautiously.

Kerrie led the way now, taking the flashlight from Jack and turning it off. "I know every nook and cranny, even in the dark," she whispered confidently. "Follow me."

She opened the door into the main house, and luckily it was another silent one. They crept along the hallway until they reached the kitchen. This room was slightly illuminated by the moon, and Kerrie motioned for Jack to crawl. They both got down on their hands and knees and moved their way slowly from the kitchen to the main foyer. Jack glanced toward the door window overlooking the front porch and could see the outline of one of the thugs standing just outside the door. Kerrie held her finger to her mouth and pointed with the other hand toward the darkened stairway to the second floor. She led the way on her hands and knees.

They made their way up the stairs and reached the second floor hallway. Still no sign of anyone in the house. Kerrie reached up and grabbed the handle on the trap door to the attic, and gently pulled. The attic stairway came down quietly but made a slight 'thunk' as it came to rest on the floor. Kerrie cursed under her breath. They listened. Nothing. Jack crept back to the top of the landing and looked down. No activity on the porch. They had caught another break.

Kerrie climbed the stairs to the attic with Jack following close behind. Once up there they wasted no time—going straight to the trunk with the guns and carefully, slowly, lifting the lid. It made its usual squeaking noise but that couldn't be helped. Jack crawled over to the attic opening and listened again. All was quiet.

He went back to the trunk and turned on the flashlight, once again shielding it with his jacket, and started rummaging through the guns. There were about twenty deadly weapons, all packaged in bubble wrap. One by one, they unwrapped each of the guns, examined them, and put them aside. Jack remembered the last clue Mitch had left them in his letter, the quote from Mao Tse Tung: *"Political power comes from the barrel of a gun."* He knew in his gut that they had to look for a Chinese weapon—it was the only thing that made sense. Mitch had quoted that for a reason. From all that Jack had learned about Mitch, he always had a reason and didn't waste words.

After unwrapping the tenth weapon, he found what he was looking for. One of the weirdest looking weapons the military world had ever seen. He recognized it as a Mauser C96, originated in Germany, but unauthorized versions had also been manufactured in large numbers by the Chinese. He remembered from his Asian history studies that this gun was widely used in the Chinese Civil war, as well as the Sino-Japanese war. The Chinese had been simply enamored by this weapon and loved it so much they had also adopted it for use by their domestic police service. Jack remembered seeing photos of Chinese soldiers proudly holding this weird pistol. It was nicknamed the "Broom-handle Mauser," because the grip of the pistol was shaped like a broom-handle. But the strangest part of this pistol was a wooden shoulder stock mounted to the grip, which also had a lid that allowed the stock to be used as a carrying case. The Chinese just adored it.

The "Broom-handle Mauser" had become a popular collector's item. Jack guessed that this gun would be worth in the low five figures right now.

He was excited. He knew this had to be it, and his hand shook as he held the gun under the flashlight and carefully examined every inch of it. It looked unblemished, until he slid his hands over the wooden shoulder stock. He could feel slight indentations on one side. He looked closer and held the light down to an inch from its surface. He could barely see notations carved into the wood: *"GCI BK 189762."*

"Kerrie, that's where the money is!"

"Where, what are you talking about?"

He pulled her closer and showed her the carvings. "I'm betting those notations stand for 'Grand Cayman International Bank,' and the numbers that follow must be the numbered bank account. That's all you're going to need to access the funds. I was fairly certain after reading your dad's letter that he would have hidden his money in a tax shelter country. Grand Cayman is one of the most commonly used off-shore centers for that purpose."

"Jesus Christ!" Kerrie gasped.

"Kerrie, memorize those numbers. Focus. Lock them into your mind." Jack urged.

Kerrie stared at the wooden stock for a few seconds, and closed her eyes. She took a second look then closed her eyes again. "Okay, got them."

Jack whipped out his tiny Swiss army knife and carved distortions into the wood. Within minutes he had the carvings so ruined that no one would ever be able to make out the original notations.

He then turned the gun around again, and held the flashlight close to the side of the barrel. He carefully examined the shiny long cylinder, and lifted the lid on the wooden stock. There was nothing inside the stock, which would have been the most logical place to hide something. Undeterred, he flashed the light into the interior of the gun barrel itself. Then he turned to Kerrie and whispered excitedly, "I see something!" He fiddled with his army knife and swung out a thin screwdriver, which he slid down inside the barrel of the gun. He pulled upwards and out slid a rolled-up plastic baggie with what looked like sheets of microfilm inside. He held the package close to his flashlight, nodding his head in recognition. It was indeed microfilm.

"This has to be it, Kerrie. *'Political power comes from the barrel of a gun.'*" This microfilm has to be the evidence that your dad wanted you to find—all hiding in plain sight."

Kerrie stared at it and gulped. Then Jack saw a sudden look of panic on her face.

"The sun will be up soon!"

Jack nodded in agreement and stuffed the microfilm into the side pocket of his jeans. "C'mon. Let's get the fuck out!"

He swung his flashlight around and they started moving to the top of the attic stairway. Suddenly, in unison, they stopped dead in their tracks. They heard voices and footsteps down in the front hall of the grand old mansion.

Chapter 42

"I've found some bandages down here," a man's gravely voice traveled up from the front foyer. "Check upstairs to see if there's any ointment or something. But don't turn on the lights."

Jack and Kerrie stood frozen, afraid to make a move that might be heard. Jack flicked off the flashlight, and placed it on the floor. Luckily there was a thin gleam of light from the moon that was finding its way through the attic dormer window, giving them a small amount of visibility. But the attic stairway was still in the down position; they had no time now to raise it back up. Kerrie strained to hear the man make his way up the stairs to the second floor. She could see the dim glow from his flashlight.

She hoped he would use his torch to light the way to the washroom at the other end of the hall, and not flash it toward the attic stairs.

Jack motioned to Kerrie to get down on her knees, and directed her to slide over directly in front of the stairway opening. She looked at him, puzzled. He made the sign of a gun with his fingers. She nodded, and withdrew the pistol from her waistband and flicked off the safety. Then Jack made a pointing motion with his hands, indicating to her to hold the gun in front of her directly at where the man's head would make an appearance if he came up through the attic opening. Then he held out his open palm signifying a stop sign. Jack then slid quietly around to the other side of the opening, facing Kerrie. They were now covering both the back and front of the stairway trap.

They waited. Kerrie could feel her heart pumping harder and harder. The pulse in her neck felt like it was going to burst through her skin. Her hands were sweaty and her grip on the Uzi pistol felt unstable, like if she put any pressure at all on the trigger the handle would slip sideways. She was terrified that if she had to shoot, Jack would be the one to get it. He was right in the path if she made a bad shot, or if the guy ducked just as she was pulling the trigger. Or the bullet could go through the man right into her friend. Kerrie shuddered at the images in her head.

She thought way back to her father's lessons. After formal instruction at a firearms academy, he took her out to practice. The first day they went out to an open field to shoot beer cans off stumps. Mitch tried to get her to learn how to use a rifle, but she'd resisted. She felt better about a pistol if she was going to learn how to use any weapon at all. Somehow, she was able to kid herself into thinking that a pistol was less deadly.

She remembered asking her dad to demonstrate a rifle's performance. He had brought a compact case with him in addition to the Glock pistol that he was teaching her to use. He obliged her request and opened the case. It was felt-lined, and several different pieces were comfortably organized into compartments. It looked complicated. Her dad calmly sat down on the grass, and in less than a minute he had assembled an impressive instrument of firepower. His hands had worked fast, grabbing all of the pieces one by one—and there were about eight of them—and snapping them into place. His hands twisted and turned, his fingers made adjustments, and a scope got attached to the top of the rifle in the blink of an eye. When he was finished, a long sleek rifle was the product, and he swung it up to his shoulder like the expert he was.

Remembering that image, she thought back to the mini cassette—the recorded conversations between her dad and whoever. Her dad had been addressed as "Sniper." That code name resonated with her now as she thought back to that first day in the field, when he raised the rifle and asked her to pick a target. She pointed to a "No Hunting" sign about two hundred yards away, laughing, being a smart-ass, thinking her dad didn't stand a chance.

Mitch had shrugged, raised the rifle, sighted the target—and the next thing she saw was the sign being split in half. Kerrie was astounded, and remembered feeling a weird combination of horror and pride at the same time.

Thinking back now, she knew that she was naïve, or in denial, or something. How could somebody be that expert at a skill like that, if he hadn't been trained by serious people to use that skill? It had a purpose, a purpose she really hadn't wanted to know in all honesty. Of course she was fully aware that something was odd about her dad's occupation, and the general description of what he did. But in being totally honest with herself today, she had to admit she never really probed him for more information. From what she knew now, he probably wouldn't have been able to tell her anyway. That day in the field a little voice in her head had told her that her dad was a killer, but she hadn't wanted to believe it. She had preferred the alternative—staying innocent.

Mitch had put the Glock in her hand, and showed her the workings of the pistol. The most important lesson he gave her was to control her breathing as she prepared herself to shoot, the inhale/exhale stuff at just the right moment of squeezing the trigger. And to not pay any attention to cop movies or cowboy movies that showed one hand holding the gun. Two hands were needed, he had stressed—one hand holding the gun, the other hand holding the hand holding the gun. The rest was accuracy, he had told her. You either had it or you didn't. Hand/eye coordination made the difference between hitting your target or not. Kerrie was lucky. She had discovered through several destroyed beer cans over many weeks of training with her dad, that her accuracy was first-rate. But a beer can was a lot different than a human head.

Now, years later, she was kneeling on a floor facing an attic opening, one bandaged hand holding the gun, the other bandaged hand holding the bandaged hand holding the gun, and she silently thanked her father for having had the foresight to train her.

Her eyes had now adjusted to the dim moonlight lacing through the attic. Kerrie looked across the opening at Jack and could just barely see a look of fear on his face—the same expression he probably saw looking at her. They looked into each other's eyes for what seemed like the longest time—speaking without speaking. But the longer she looked at him, the more confident she felt. He was afraid just like her, but he had the most reassuring look of determination at the same time. He winked at her, and gave her a grim smile as if saying, "We'll get out of this, together." Just like he said to her as they lay behind the trees after the bear attack. She remembered the tender kiss he had planted on her cheek, and she remembered feeling at that moment that they would be okay. She felt that again now with his wink. They would be okay.

She looked affectionately at his face, still handsome even with the bandana wrapped around his ravaged forehead and the dried blood staining his cheeks.

They waited, and listened. The beam from the man's flashlight had found its way down the hall to the bathroom. They could hear him rummaging around in the cupboards, doors quietly opening and closing. Then footsteps again. The beam of light was heading back down the hall to the top of the stairway. Then the footsteps stopped. And Kerrie felt like her heart stopped.

The beam of light now flashed right at the attic stairs. Footsteps started again, this time in their direction. He wasn't going down the stairs to the first floor after all, but instead down the hall for a little detour. He must have noticed the attic stairs in the down position.

Kerrie looked up at Jack and he held his finger in front of his mouth. She noticed that his Uzi was laying on the floor beside him. The man below was flashing the beam of his torch up the stairs into their open space. Kerrie was far enough back from the opening that the beam didn't catch her, and Jack leaned back on his knees to make sure he was also hidden in case the guy flashed it around the opening.

Now he was starting up the stairs, obviously curious about the attic. Kerrie knew that he probably didn't suspect anyone was up here, as he and his buddies had been watching the house carefully for a few hours at least. There had been no noises to tip him off and no light. He probably wanted to snoop around a bit before going back down. At least this was what Kerrie preferred to think. Their only hope was the element of surprise.

Kerrie's hands, and the gun, started to tremble. Jack shook his head slowly at her, and her hand suddenly became steady. The man was near the top, the dark image of the top of a head reached a level position with the opening. One more rung and his head would be in their sights.

The figure broke the opening, flashlight in one hand, the other holding onto the landing. Kerrie leveled the gun straight at the forehead, knowing that the agent would not be able to see her until he raised the flashlight. Jack did not want her to shoot—he had signaled the stop sign to her with his palm when they were getting prepared. They couldn't afford the noise. She reasoned Jack only wanted the shock value of her gun, and he would do the rest from behind.

Kerrie couldn't contain her gasp as the head burst through the opening. It was a woman who stared up at her and the menacing image of Kerrie's Uzi pointed at her forehead.

The agent was clearly stunned. She opened her mouth for a fraction of a second, but her killer reflexes hesitated a moment too long. Kerrie was still trying to process the fact that a female killer was standing there on the ladder looking straight into her eyes, when she saw both of Jack's hands move in a blur. There was no gentlemanly hesitation on his part in seeing a woman instead of a man. He just moved like a precision instrument. The agent's flashlight allowed her to see Jack's left hand swing from behind and around her mouth, and squeeze so tightly that her cheeks puffed out. Surprise and fear swept over the woman's face and from the coldest eyes Kerrie had ever seen in her life. She moved quickly to snatch the flashlight out of the agent's hand before it went crashing down the staircase.

Jack made his next move. He reared his right hand back and formed his fingers out straight like a dagger, his third and fourth fingers slightly elevated from the others. His hand rammed forward like a javelin into the soft fleshy area at the base of the woman's skull. Her cold eyeballs rolled upwards and her body fell instantly limp. Kerrie watched Jack let go with both hands, and in another blur, shift them down under her arms as she began to fall. He yanked her silently up through the opening, gently laying her on the floor. Kerrie swung the dead agent's flashlight in Jack's direction. He was wiping the blood and brain matter that was clinging to his fingers onto the woman's jacket. "My God," Kerrie whispered at the sight.

Jack placed his other hand on Kerrie's shoulder, squeezing it gently. He whispered, "There were at least five of them, not four as we had thought. We didn't see the woman out there. So, counting the guy mauled by the bear, two of them are now out of the picture."

"We…should hustle ourselves out…fast. They're going to…come looking for her. We'll be sitting ducks…up here," Kerrie stated in a shaky voice. She was still stunned by what she had just witnessed.

"Keep her flashlight—it's better than ours—and keep your gun out as well, safety on, until we get down these attic stairs. The others must be waiting for her outside. If we're lucky, we can get down and crawl along the hallway to the tunnel before one of them comes back into the house. Are we good to go?"

Kerrie nodded and lit the way down the stairs with the flashlight. Jack went first, slowly and carefully. He was going down with his back to the staircase. Kerrie worried that he could easily slip going down that way, but she assumed that he didn't want to risk taking a bullet in the back.

Kerrie came down next and she handed Jack the flashlight, which he shielded once again under his jacket. They moved tentatively down the hall and reached the top of the stairs. So far, so good. Jack went first, slowly, quietly, one step at a time, staring at the front door as he moved down the staircase. Kerrie was right behind him. The flashlight was now off, and Jack held it in his left hand while his right hand held the submachine gun, the case slung over his shoulder. Kerrie had her pistol extended straight out in front of her and aimed at the front door, as she moved down two steps behind him. Both hands supported the gun and it was as steady as Gibraltar.

They were now close to the bottom of the stairs—just two to go. The moon, now quite low on the horizon, was lighting up the first floor landing and hallway. Kerrie began to breathe a bit easier. She resisted the overwhelming urge to leap over the last two steps and dash to the relative safety of the tunnel.

Suddenly the front door burst open to the sound of a man cursing. "What the fuck is taking you so..." Then he saw them, and dove to the floor yelling, "Gun!"

Jack flicked on the flashlight and beamed it right at the agent's eyes, momentarily blinding him. The agent reached into his shoulder holster and pulled out a pistol. Jack aimed the Uzi at the man's chest, pulled back the bolt on top of the weapon, and squeezed the trigger. Nothing! In that split second Kerrie saw him fumbling with the safety selector switch and she realized what was wrong. She imagined a beer can, and pulled the trigger. The loud blast from the Uzi pistol seemed to echo around the room, and the agent's head was flung back slamming against the wall. As she lowered the barrel, she could see a hole above the bridge of his nose, with blood pooling quickly on the floor.

No need for silence now. They jumped off the stairs and ran down the hall. They could hear shouts out on the porch in reaction to the gunshot. They kept going and didn't look back, slamming through the fire door leading to the passageway to the tower section. Jack grabbed the trap door and hefted it with all his strength. He motioned for Kerrie to go first, and he swung around and faced the direction they had come, with his Uzi pointing at chest level. He had the safety off now.

Kerrie was down the rope ladder faster than she had ever thought possible, then she yelled up at Jack to hurry. He jumped onto the ladder several rungs down and yanked the door down with a loud 'thunk.' Kerrie knew the agents would find this tunnel now, no question about it, but at least Jack was making sure they'd have to lift the heavy trap door themselves.

Kerrie was already halfway down the tunnel on her hands and knees by the time Jack had reached the bottom of the shaft. And she was doing that in the dark, as Jack still had the flashlight. He shone it ahead, illuminating Kerrie and the path in front of her. He moved after her in a crawl that would have broken Olympic records if crawling were an event. Kerrie was now at the end of the tunnel with Jack quite a few paces behind. The moonlight lit up the shaft to the outhouse quite handily, and she looked upward with her hand on the first rung. "Jack, hurry up!" she screamed.

"Get going, Kerrie. I'll see you at the top."

And with that, she was gone.

*****

Jack heard the worst possible sound—the sound he knew would come, but prayed that it would come *after* he had left the tunnel. A loud 'thunk' echoed down the tunnel, then the soft sound of feet landing on earth. He knew he was in trouble now.

Suddenly Jack was bathed in light from a powerful torch. A man was on his stomach about twenty yards behind him.

He whirled around to face back down the tunnel, and quickly checked to make sure the Uzi was on automatic. A shot rang out, and slammed into the wood timbers just to the left of his head. Jack cursed in anger as he squeezed the trigger of the sub-machine gun. It started rattling in his hand and seemed to have a mind of its own. The power was immense, and the gun seemed to want to just jump into the air. He let up on the trigger and positioned himself on his stomach, squinting towards the light. Jack pointed his flashlight down the tunnel to give some kind of blinding counteract. He then propped his left elbow onto the ground and grabbed the front grip of the Uzi with that hand. Then he pulled the trigger with his right hand for dear life, aiming it directly down the middle of the tunnel. Dust was building in the thin air, and with the two torches shining directly at each other, that dust became a thick cloud almost completely obstructing any view. Jack's cartridge was empty in seconds. He reached into his case and grabbed another one. He slammed it into the handle, pulled back the bolt, and squeezed the trigger again. Bullets rained down the tunnel and Jack had no idea if he had even hit the guy yet. Only that one bullet had come his way so far. His opponent obviously didn't have a machine gun, which gave Jack an edge.

Then suddenly out of the dust, he saw a figure burst along the side of the tunnel wall, in a crawling sprint. The guy had been avoiding the middle where Jack had been aiming. He was only ten yards away now, trying desperately to shield his eyes with one hand while struggling to move forward on his knees. The pistol hand aimed blindly in Jack's direction.

Jack pulled the trigger again, and a hail of bullets slammed the agent back against the flimsy support columns. The columns gave way to the weight, combined with the force of several bullets that had torn through the wood's integrity. The wall sagged, then the ceiling supports in that spot started to rupture, and Jack could hear a sickening creaking sound. The ceiling supports fell along with the sheet metal and dirt above them. The entire tunnel was turning into a house of cards.

Jack scrambled to his knees and turned around to face the opening to the shaft landing, several feet in front of him. He crawled, then was knocked to his stomach by a heavy beam directly above him. Mounds of dirt began to fill in the gaps, and he knew he was going to be buried alive in only a few moments. Jack threw the flashlight and the Uzi ahead of him into the shaft landing, and began digging his hands into the dirt, dragging himself out from under the beam. It was slow going, the dirt was becoming thicker as more ceiling supports gave way. He lurched forward and scratched with his fingers to drag himself along the tunnel floor. Just a few more feet.

He got his head into the shaft just as a major section of the ceiling fell onto his lower legs. But he had the leverage now to completely drag himself out. He pulled his body through the heavy dirt just as the rest of the ceiling in the tunnel collapsed behind him.

Jack rolled onto the shaft floor and glanced back at where the tunnel used to be. It was now completely plugged, with dirt and dust pushing into the shaft where he was now standing. He made a quick sign of the cross.

Jack picked up the flashlight and the Uzi, putting the gun back on safety for the trek up the rope ladder. He climbed two rungs at a time, swinging into the walls, not caring in the least at the pain. This time the breathing was a bit easier, as he had made it down the tunnel at a record pace. The tunnel collapsing behind him had also pushed whatever air there was, up into the shaft.

He came up into the outhouse, hoisting himself up and onto the floor, gasping and drinking in the beautiful fresh air. The door was open, but he didn't see Kerrie outside. Jack slammed a fresh magazine into the handle of the Uzi, yanked back the bolt, and put the shifter on automatic again. He left the flashlight off as he exited the outhouse. The moon was very low now and the sun would be up to take its place within about thirty minutes, Jack guessed.

He crouched and started moving slowly and cautiously away from the outhouse toward the main road behind the house, Uzi thrust out in front. Jack knew there should be only one agent left standing, assuming the mauling victim was out of commission. He did a head count just to make sure: a dead guy in the tunnel, a dead one in the front foyer, and a dead lady in the attic. He looked from side to side swinging the machine gun, and called out in a loud whisper, "Kerrie!"

His heart lifted as he heard her call out, "Over here!"

He turned to his right and walked toward an opening in the trees in the direction of where her voice had come from. There, thirty feet away, stood the stocky man they both knew as Stan Trundle—the agent who had pretended to be the brother of the man who had begged Jack to beat him senseless only a few hours before. Stan had one arm firmly wrapped around Kerrie's neck, squeezing so tightly that her face seemed to be swelling. Jack could see that she was struggling to breathe. Her gun was nowhere in sight.

The free hand of the agent held a large pistol extended outwards, aimed directly at Jack's head.

Seeing this left Jack numb. He yelled out "Kerrie!"

Then, yelling even louder, with panic in his voice, "Just let her go! I'll give you what you want!"

The cold voice from the last agent standing stated matter-of-factly, "Yes, you will indeed sir, but I won't be letting her go."

Chapter 43

Two blocks away from the shores of Flathead Lake, a doghouse in a large backyard began to shake.

It was early morning and the sun was just starting to rise. But it was already too late in the morning for a Border collie. Generations of these dogs had always been up and working well before dawn. Work was what kept their blood flowing; having something useful to do was their reason for existence. Without that, there wasn't much purpose.

A handsome specimen of the Border collie breed crawled out of the doghouse, stretched, and looked around the yard hoping for something to do. His coat was thick and as smooth as silk. He was the classic combo, with a back that was jet black up to his shoulders. At the shoulders, his coat changed to an arctic white, forming a large ring right to his underside. His belly was entirely white as were his two front legs. His back legs were black just to make things interesting, and so was his tail—except for the white tip. Ears were black and pointy and his face was almost entirely white. God had painted a little masterpiece when he had painted Mule.

He sniffed the fresh mountain air and yawned. That nice lady would be bringing out his breakfast soon, but he was hoping to get in some exercise first. He did have a buddy out here with him for the first couple of days, but the lady finally gave up and took the other one inside at nights. They each had had their own little dens, but the other one just didn't want to play. When it got dark, it only wanted to sleep, and no matter how many times Mule had nipped at its feet, it wouldn't cooperate. It was good that the other one was now inside at night. If he didn't know how to behave with company, then he deserved to be on his own.

Mule didn't know if he liked sleeping outside or not. He hadn't decided that yet in his analytical brain. He was accustomed to sleeping on a bed with his partner, but he hadn't seen him in several days now and wondered if he ever would again. However, like all Border collies, Mule was adaptable. Wherever his partners wanted him to be, he would be. He suspected this lady was his new partner, so he would just have to get used to it. He missed his old partner though, so much so that sometimes at night Mule would cry. He knew no one would hear him, but it made him feel better. This lady was his fourth partner now, but the last one had been his favorite. They had done everything together and the man always seemed to anticipate Mule's thoughts. Mule was also able to anticipate his. He was gentle, fun, loved to wrestle and run. They had developed some good routines together, particularly when they went to the park. He would throw a ball or disc, and Mule would catch it—usually in mid-air. Mule loved to jump. At those parks there were always lots of creatures that he could go to work on too, and his partner usually let him. Mule could round up any number of moving beings into a tight circle with very little effort. He didn't know what possessed him to do that, but he absolutely had to every time he saw something move.

Movement always created an instant reaction in Mule. He couldn't control it. His head would drop low to the ground, his ass would be high, and he would tuck his tail between his legs with just the nice white tip sticking upwards. But Mule knew that the main power he had in rounding up things was in his eyes; another thing he couldn't seem to control when it looked like creatures in a park needed to be organized. He could feel his eyes lock on to the creatures, and it almost felt as if he could will them in the direction he wanted them to go. His gaze was intense and didn't waver until his job was done. His legs always followed his eyes.

But when it was done, he always felt like he hadn't quite finished. He needed more. His old partner always let him have more. Until he got impatient with him, and his voice always let Mule know. Mule loved that partner so much he would do anything for him, and if a command were given he would obey it, despite always secretly wanting to disobey. That was just his independent streak. He didn't really need his partner for survival, but he wanted him. He felt lost without him.

Why had he left? What had Mule done to cause him to leave? He guessed he would never know, and he would just have to adapt. But it made him sad, and he was bored.

It was not a good thing for a Border collie to be bored. A dog like Mule needed stimulation because his brain was so quick and calculating, always searching for something to do. Mule needed to feel that he was contributing. Fun things that he used to do with his partner helped satisfy most of Mule's needs, because at least those things involved activity. Energy just surged through Mule's muscular physique and at times without warning. When that happened, he desperately needed to wear it off.

He had learned a lot of things from his three previous partners, and all of those lessons had stuck with him. Virtually none of them needed practicing because everything a Border collie learned, it retained as if it was fresh. Mule could retrieve a trick or technique in an instant, either through a command or the right stimulation.

But no one had ever taught him how to herd, and he did that as if in a trance. He loved it when he went into that trance. Only his partner's commands could shake him out of it. Sometimes Mule felt the herding instinct come over him even when there was nothing to herd. Mule enjoyed it every time. Something rushed through his body whenever that happened.

He trotted around the backyard looking for anything at all that needed doing today. He stopped at the little swimming pool that he had burst with his teeth the other day. He decided that the thing had to be pulled over to the corner of the yard next to the fence. So he did that, which took him no time at all. He stood erect and looked once more at the pool. He decided to pull it back to the middle of the yard again. Mule sat down and admired his work. Two robins landed in the far corner of the yard and Mule couldn't help himself. His head dropped and in his trademark hunch, he silently moved over to the birds, intending to convince them to stay together in one spot. They saw him at the last minute and flew away. Mule whirled around and saw a squirrel near his den. The trance came again, and something deep inside of him pulled him low to the ground and moved him in graceful fashion towards the pesky little creature. The thing ran up a tree. Mule never wanted to hurt these creatures; he just wanted to organize them, and he didn't understand why they didn't seem to like that.

He lay down on the grass and sighed. He thought about the partner who had left him a few days ago. He liked to remember his voice and the way he looked. He could picture his face in his mind, a face that had always made Mule feel comfortable and happy when he saw it. He missed seeing that face. His new partner didn't seem to want to do things with him. She didn't like to throw, or go for long hikes. Mule missed the excitement of herding something, anything. She didn't seem to need him; didn't need anything done. He felt frustrated by that. He desperately needed to feel useful again.

He ran over to a garbage can in the corner of the yard and knocked it over. Then he put his front paws on it and started pushing it in circles, round and round. There, that was better. He sped out to the middle of the yard and promptly dug three holes, just because he could.

Then he saw some bees hovering around near a bush. He ran over, leaped into the air, and swatted with his paws. They moved on to the next bush. He followed them and did it again. That felt good.

Mule sat down again and gazed thoughtfully at his den. He then ran over and used his substantial strength to knock it onto its side. He had done this several times already and his new partner always came out and put it back up again. He laid down beside his den and sighed once more. Then up for a drink of water from his bowl, then back down again.

Suddenly his ears perked up. What was that? He knew that voice—the partner he had before the last one, the soft one. He listened carefully. Nothing more. Then he heard something that caused his heart to ache. His last partner's voice clear as day, and he sounded scared, frantic. He needed him. Mule cocked his head to one side, ears still perked, and listened harder. Nothing. Mule barked—then again, louder this time. His partner didn't answer.

He could feel the energy surging through his body, and he whined. His partner was in pain and he needed him. He had to get to him. He had come back for him. Mule had to prove to him that he was useful enough to take back.

His keen sense of hearing told him the exact direction where his partner was. He looked at the high wooden fence around the yard. Mule had already tried to jump it once and had gotten stuck at the top hanging on with his front paws, falling to the ground. He had to try again. Mule set off around the yard at a trot, then went down into his classic hunch and picked up speed. Very few creatures alive were a match for the speed of a Border collie, and Mule was confident about what he was capable of. Mule didn't like the direction he was heading for the angle he wanted, so he made an abrupt turn and started running in the other direction. He loved to turn at full speed; it was fun and he knew there were very few creatures who could match that turning skill. He fixed his intense eyes on a spot at the top of the fence and headed straight for it, leaping at full speed as he approached the structure. He sailed upwards but slammed into the top of the fence, a little bit higher though than the first time he had tried this. At least his mid-section was resting on the top. But he couldn't hold it and couldn't get a grip with his hind claws on the wood. He fell backwards onto the grass.

Mule growled to himself and scrambled to all fours. He set off once again, first at a gentle trot as he surveyed the landscape, then put on a burst of speed as he circled the yard. As he moved in his wide circles around the perimeter of the large yard, he put his intense gaze to work analyzing the height of the fence, looking for an anomaly. He saw it and fixed the position in his mind. One section of the fence seemed slightly lower than the others, and he was confident he could clear it. Mule picked up speed as he circled the yard, faster and faster. He had to do this. He was needed. He forced himself to go even faster, and he knew that this was probably the fastest he'd ever run in his life. He started crying softly as he raced, worrying that he may not be able to get to his partner. He was depending on him—that's why he had called out. He had to get to him.

Mule finished his last circle and headed straight for the section of fence that he wanted. His speed was blinding at this point and he lifted himself into the air at just the right moment. His speed was right and his height was right. He sailed over the fence and landed nimbly in the grass on the other side.

Without missing a beat, Mule raced toward the lake. His nose was guiding the way. He knew where the water was, and he knew where the house was that he had been staying at before. He was in his zone now. Even though he wasn't herding anything, the intensity and the adrenaline had triggered his trance. He was in his hunch, eyes focused ahead, racing with the wind. Nothing could stop him. Out of the corner of his eye he noticed three deer. Under normal circumstances Mule would have turned abruptly toward these creatures and herded them into their proper place. But today he gave them only a fleeting glance. They would have to wait until later. It was hard for him to resist though, and for a second he felt conflicted. He cried to himself in frustration. However, his disciplined brain shoved that feeling into a corner to deal with at another time.

He flew over two ditches, and headed for the road. He leaped over a metal fence and had to maneuver to avoid two huge potholes. Easy tactic for a Border collie. He picked up speed again and practically flew towards where the sound had come from. His instinct told him exactly where that was.

As Mule advanced closer and closer to where he knew his partner was, he raised his nose into the air for a danger check. He could smell both of his friends clearly, but there was another smell that he didn't like. It was someone who he had smelled before. He didn't like him then and he liked him even less now. His instinct told him that this man was the cause of his partner's cry for help. Mule had to fix that. He was needed to fix that. He had real work to do and it was exhilarating to have that feeling again.

He was approaching the last corner close to where he needed to be, and he forced himself even lower to the ground as he took the corner at breakneck speed. He almost lost his edge, but compensated instantly to prevent a wipeout. He leaped over another ditch and broke into a clearing. His tail was still tucked neatly between his rear legs, giving him leverage with each twist and turn.

Mule saw them now, still a fair distance away, but his intense eyes flicked from one figure to the next, sizing up the situation. He recognized his favorite partner, the one he was making this mad dash for, and could suddenly feel his heart beat faster. He wanted to yelp with joy, to let him know that he was coming, but a deep primal instinct told him that would be a mistake.

He then saw the man whose smell he despised, holding onto his other partner, the soft one, in a way that seemed unnatural and threatening. His eyes picked up the despised one's arm, extended outward in the direction of his partner. He recognized an object in the man's hand. He recognized this from work that he had done long ago with his first partner. He knew from his training that the object was being pointed at someone that it shouldn't be pointed at, and Mule's quick brain instantly retrieved the process that he had been trained to follow. He had been trained to correct that.

He continued at incredible speed, close to the ground, his intense eyes fixed only on that object. It gleamed in the early morning light, and that gleam was all that Mule could see now. He allowed himself to go into his trance, because his instincts told him there was real work to be done here.

Chapter 44

A weariness enveloped Jack, as he began to face the inevitable once again. Their luck had finally run out, and a cold-blooded killer now had a vice grip on Kerrie's neck with an arm as thick as a small tree trunk. She was clearly struggling to breathe and the sight of her that way pained him to his core.

This was no agent with a conscience, like Sam Summerfield. There would be no last minute reprieve from this man, Jack knew in his gut.

The Uzi was in Jack's hand but down at his side. He knew he could try to swing it up to take a shot, but Stan already had a pistol pointed at his head. Jack would be no match in an open field gunfight against a trained assassin. Uzi machine guns were not known for their accuracy—they were merely for slaughtering. He was just as likely to hit Kerrie as he was to hit Stan.

If his gun had been set to semi-automatic instead of automatic, then it would shoot one bullet at a time as opposed to blasting a dozen bullets in Kerrie's direction. He knew it would take only a slight movement of his finger to slide the shifter to semi, but he would probably be dead before he managed to get his finger to the right spot.

As he raced through his options, he heard the sound of a dog barking some distance away. It sure sounded like Mule's bark, and that thought made his heart ache. His little buddy was only a couple of blocks away, and here he was in this deadly predicament. He hoped Sarah would appreciate Mule and take good care of him.

"Jack, drop the Uzi. Don't do anything stupid." Stan spoke in a calm monotone.

"Please let her go. She can't breathe," Jack pleaded.

"Drop the gun and I'll consider it."

Reluctantly, and with a feeling of finality, Jack let the machine gun slide from his fingers onto the grass.

"Now, move a bit closer to me, away from the gun."

Jack took a couple of steps and stopped. But Stan didn't release his grip on Kerrie. She had her mouth open with her tongue drooping out of one side.

Her eyeballs were starting to bulge as Stan's grip tightened on her. She started kicking with her feet, and Stan effortlessly lifted her off the ground by her neck. Her blouse and jacket were hanging in shards off her shoulders from the bear mauling, and as Stan twisted her sideways, Jack could see the blood streaking her back.

Jack felt like he was going to be sick. His own heart started pounding in his chest, and his throat went dry. He found it hard to swallow, and impossible to produce any saliva.

"Hand over what you found in the house. Do it and I'll lighten my grip."

Jack believed deep down in his gut that their only chance of survival was to give this prick the hope of getting something, instead of actually giving him something. Once Stan had what he wanted, the two of them would be of no use to him. Jack had to buy some time. He figured the more time they had, the better chance Stan might make a mistake. Where there was life, there was hope.

"We found nothing in the house. But we have information that we found in New York. You can have that."

"I was told that you found a letter from Agent Joplin, and a cassette tape that you both listened to. Is that correct?"

"Yes."

"And you found no supporting documentation in the house here?"

"No."

"I'll have to search both of you, and your gun case as well."

"Sure, go ahead." Jack tried to sound confident. He was at least confident of one thing. Even with Stan holding a gun, if somehow he could lure him to within reasonable distance of his feet, he could kill him with one targeted kick. If Stan managed to search his pocket without Jack getting a shot at him, the man would find the microfilm and their chances of living after that were slim to none.

"Where's the letter and tape?"

"Hidden a short distance from here. We can show you."

Suddenly, out of the corner of Jack's eye he caught a blur of movement in the tall grass, about a quarter of a mile away. The grass was bending towards them as a creature was hurtling through it at incredible speed. He tried not to look directly at it, because he knew in his heart what it was: black and white, low to the ground, and running as if his life depended on it. What Mule probably didn't completely understand was that Jack and Kerrie's lives depended on it.

He continued the conversation, to keep Stan's eyes directed at him. He was terrified that Stan would turn slightly to his rear left and spot the heroic canine streaking silently through the grass toward him. "It's only a short walk, but you can't drag Kerrie like that. Let her go. You have the gun and you can keep it on both of us."

Stan grinned in a menacing way. "Maybe I'll just leave her here. I really don't need both of you, do I?"

Jack shuddered at the implication.

He thought quickly. "Actually, you do. I hid the tape, and Kerrie hid the letter. Neither of us knows where the other item is." Jack allowed his eyes to wander slightly off to the side. He could see Mule now leaving the tall grass and rocketing through the open field directly towards Stan. The determined dog didn't even look in Jack's direction. His eyes were locked on only one man.

"Well, wasn't that sly of you? I guess I will need both of you after all. Take off your jacket and shirt and lay down on the grass, Jack. I'm going to get Kerrie to pull out your pockets and pull down your pants so I can have a look. Then you can do the same to her."

The man was smart. He had heard what Jack could do, and he wasn't going to take any chances by getting too close to him. As Jack knelt down in the grass, he could see his little black and white beast barreling toward the killer. He was only about thirty yards away and he knew Mule would be airborne at any moment now. Jack wanted to yell, "Go Mule, Go!"

"Take off your jacket and shirt and lie down now! Quit wasting my..."

Stan turned as a blur of movement launched toward him. Instinctively, his gun hand reacted, but he wasn't nearly fast enough to get the jump on Mule.

Mule was a thing of beauty as he flew through the air with sheer grace and force. His front paws extended forward, tail locked between hind legs that were stretched straight behind him for aerodynamics. Jack's heart cried. Mule was five feet off the ground when he latched onto Stan's wrist, chomping on it with his powerful jaws and then, even before he hit the ground, shaking it viciously to make the gun come loose. He knew exactly what he was doing.

Stan screamed out, probably in equal amounts surprise and pain. The gun flew out of his hand and he went down, taking Kerrie with him. Mule held on to the killer's now mangled wrist and wouldn't let go. Kerrie was free. She put her hand up to her throat and began gasping for breath.

Jack started running toward the commotion on the ground, but he knew he wouldn't get there in time. He saw Stan reaching behind with his good hand, pulling Kerrie's Uzi pistol out of his back waistband hiding place.

Everything from that point on seemed in slow motion. Stan brought the pistol around in Mule's direction and started to take aim. Jack heard Kerrie scream "No!" and somehow she found the strength to lash out with her foot at Stan's hand. Jack heard the roar of the gun and a loud, piercing yelp. Mule rolled off Stan's wrist onto the grass beside him, and for a moment lay in stunned silence. Kerrie's kick had knocked the gun loose, but not before the bullet had found Mule. Jack felt for a second that his world had just collapsed.

To his astonishment, Mule dragged himself to his feet, and in a snarling rage, lunged for Stan's throat as the thug was struggling to get up. Mule's jaws were wide open, teeth bared, and Stan didn't stand a chance. Within seconds, Mule's protective instinct and intense drive for survival caused the centuries-old wild beast in him to emerge—for at least that moment in time. Mule pounced on Stan's neck, oblivious to the man's pounding on his back.

Mule's forty pounds of fury were an overpowering force against Stan's two hundred pounds of panic. He tore Stan's throat wide open, deep, and Jack could see the horrified look of inevitability on Stan's face. He could almost see the question "What just happened?" in those dying eyes.

The cold, evil man was gone within seconds, but the blood continued to spurt. Mule rolled off him once he sensed the danger was over, and started dragging himself toward a tree several yards away as if ashamed. Jack could hear him crying as he crawled. He called out, but Mule ignored him. Jack ran over to Kerrie and helped her up. He called out again to Mule, but the dog kept crawling. He was in a different zone now, one that didn't include loved ones. They could see blood coming out of Mule's rear side area, staining the silky fur right at the spot where it transitioned from black to white. They could also see that his mouth and chin were blood red, but they knew for sure where that had come from. Jack spoke softly. "He's crawling away to die. In his mind, he's protecting us again. He doesn't want his carcass to attract predators to us."

Tears were streaming down Kerrie's cheeks. "We can't just let him die," she pleaded.

"You bet your life we can't," Jack said.

They followed the little fellow's blood trail to the large tree he had now laid behind. Jack held out his hand to slow Kerrie down. "We have to be slow and gentle. Very primitive instincts are driving him now. He won't be the same dog when he's in this state. He might try to bite us, to chase us away to make us protect ourselves. Prepare yourself," Jack said.

They got onto their knees and slowly slid up to where Mule was laying. He was on his side and panting hard. Jack took off his coat and laid it on the ground. "We'll use this as kind of a stretcher," he whispered.

He then ripped off what was left of his shirt, and handed it to Kerrie. "You'll need to bind this around the wound to slow down the bleeding. I'll talk to him while you're doing that."

Jack went down close to Mule's face, and he heard him growl. He started talking to him in a soft voice but the growling continued. Kerrie eased Jack's shirt underneath Mule, and he whimpered. She started gently tying the makeshift bandage around where the wound seemed to be.

Suddenly Mule snarled and snapped up at Jack's face. Jack pulled back just in time. Mule started to cry, almost as if apologizing. Jack then used the command that always worked with Mule: "Calm". He repeated it several times. Mule closed his mouth and started licking his lips. He turned his eyes and looked directly into Jack's. He whimpered as Jack gently stroked his head.

They were done. Jack didn't know whether Mule would live or die, but they were going to give him the best chance they could.

They eased Mule over onto Jack's coat, and he cried out in pain. It broke Jack's heart. They lifted carefully, one at each end of the jacket, and started making the trek back to Jack's car parked about a mile away. It would be the longest mile they had ever walked. Jack watched Mule's eyes off and on the whole way to make sure he was still with them. But he didn't have to do that. He could tell by his high-pitched wail that he was feeling every step.

When they reached the car tucked away in the trees, they laid Mule down in the back seat, still on the jacket, and Jack retrieved the knapsack and purse from the trunk. They would need their documents as they crossed the border. If they were lucky enough to cross the border. But they had somewhere else to go first.

As they sped away from Flathead Lake and the Lighthouse Inn, Jack wondered if Kerrie would ever return to this bloody place, a place that had apparently served her father as a waiting room for the revelation of the most gut-wrenching secret imaginable.

*****

An hour later they pulled into the town of Whitefish and Jack headed straight for the house that he had stayed at just a few weeks before. To the house where the cute veterinarian had told him that he might be crazy, and that he had better do his utmost to ensure that no one he loved got hurt in his quest for answers. He should have listened to her.

He needed her now and prayed that she was home. It was just after 9:00 Saturday morning, so he knew she wouldn't be at her office.

He parked in the driveway and they both lifted Mule gently out of the back seat, still on Jack's coat. They carried him up to the front door, noticing that he was a lot calmer now, which could be a good sign or a bad sign. He was still breathing steadily though and his eyes were half open, watching the proceedings carefully. They knew he would have preferred that they had left him to die behind that tree. They were going against his primal instincts and they knew that must be very unsettling for a creature that was driven so powerfully by instinct. But, so be it. He had to live. Hopefully Mule would eventually forgive Jack for his interference. He knocked on the door and within seconds Meagan was standing there, still dressed in pyjamas, a stunned look on her face.

"Jack, my God, what happened? Get inside, quickly!"

She led the way into her treatment room without any questions, and directed them to lay Mule down on the surgical table. She attached straps gently across his mid-section. "Look at the two of you. You need to get to a hospital!"

"No time, Meagan. We have to get across the border. As you can guess, we're in danger. Mule has been shot in his lower side and we need you to pull off a miracle here. Please."

"Go, both of you. I have extra clothes in the basement. You'll never get across the border looking like that. See if you can find some things that are comfortable. They're all second-hand, but clean. My house is a drop-off for donations to the poor, so I'm well stocked."

They ran to the basement and picked out some pullovers and jackets that would work. Not great, but they'd do. Jack also grabbed a baseball cap to help hide the bloody bandana across his sheared scalp. Kerrie pocketed a pair of light gloves to hide her hands.

When they came back upstairs, Meagan was already anaesthetizing Mule through an IV tower, still in pyjamas. Jack came up behind her and gave her a grateful hug.

"Thanks, Meagan. Please, please, do what you can, everything you can. I can't lose him. He saved our lives today. I don't care what it costs, just don't let him die."

"I won't, Jack." She held out her hand to Kerrie. "I'm Meagan, by the way."

Kerrie smiled and shook her hand. "I'm Kerrie. Sorry, I'm so distraught that I forgot we hadn't met before. Jack has talked so glowingly of you, it's as if I already know you."

Meagan smiled back at her. "Do you want some food for the road?"

"No, no time to eat," Jack piped up. "We need to go, but I'll be in touch with you as soon as I can. But if you don't hear from me, or Kerrie, could you keep Mule and give him a home?"

"I promise you this darling dog will be okay. I'll get that bullet out in a few minutes. You guys bandaged him up pretty good; the blood loss wasn't that great. I'm keeping my fingers crossed that no internal organs were damaged. Okay?"

Jack smiled at her and wiped away some tears, having heard the words that he so desperately wanted to hear. He bent over and kissed Mule on the forehead. Kerrie did the same. Then they were out the door and gone, towards the Canadian border as fast as the throaty roar of the Audi's turbo engine would take them.

Chapter 45

"Hi, Heather, it's Jack."

"Oh my God, Jack—I've been so worried about you! Where are you? Are you coming home?"

"I'm on my way right now. I have Kerrie with me, my friend from Montana. We need your help."

"I haven't heard from you in days. What's wrong? Are you okay? How far away are you?"

"We just passed through the Canadian Border gate south of Waterton, so I'm guessing three hours tops. We're in desperate trouble. I need you to get in touch with the senior partner at your law firm, and meet us at your office downtown."

"Christ, it's Saturday, Jack. I hope I can reach him."

"Please try, try hard. We need to engage him today for an important legal service, and we also need access to a microfiche reader. Do you have one in the office?"

"Yes, we do. Listen, let me off the phone so I can set this up. I'll call you back."

"Thanks, Heather. I can't tell you how urgent this is. And before I go, how are Josh and Buster?"

"They're both fine. Josh will be so excited to see you again and so will I! We've missed you!"

"I've missed you guys too. Glad to hear you're all okay."

They hung up and Jack left his cell phone on for her callback. For a couple of days now, since their time in the dumpster in New York, they had thrown caution to the wind and used their cell phones. The alternative would have been hunting perilously for phone booths that were almost extinct now. They would have wasted precious time, and been overexposed far too often. So while they were nervous about using them, their cell phones posed the safer of the two alternatives.

Within minutes Heather called back. "Hi, Jack. Scott will be at the office waiting for you. I'll be there too—I'll meet you in the lower lobby to let you in. Scott is more than anxious to help you with whatever the problem is. You'll like him, he's very nice."

"What's his last name, Heather?"

"Dennison, Scott Dennison."

"Okay, tell him thanks. God willing, we'll be there in about three hours' time. And, Heather, prepare yourself and Scott. We look in pretty bad shape, but it looks worse than it really is."

"Oh, God. Did you consider maybe going to Emergency first?"

"Can't, and can't go home either. We need legal help first before we can do anything else. Trust me."

Heather was silent for a few seconds. Then she asked softly, "Jack, what have you done?"

"A lot, but we're the good guys, Heather, so don't worry. You won't be harboring fugitives. We know some things and we need to get that knowledge protected so that we'll be protected."

He heard her sigh. "Bye, Jack. See you soon. Please be careful."

He could tell she was puzzled and worried, but definitely glad to hear from him. He was looking forward to seeing her too. It seemed like forever since they had made love together, and he missed her warmth. He also missed Josh. Jack had started becoming more than just a Big Buddy to him. He had been imagining lately what it must feel like to be a father, so it was obvious the loving little guy had made a serious impact on him.

His thoughts were interrupted by Kerrie shaking his right shoulder. He turned to face her.

"Jack, are you okay? I don't think you heard one word I said."

"Sorry. I must have been daydreaming."

"You miss her, don't you?"

"Yes, I do, and her little boy."

"That's nice, very nice, to have people to miss." Kerrie looked through the windshield, deep in thought, far away.

"So what was it you were asking me?"

"Oh, just, are you sure we're doing the right thing?"

"Yeah, I'm sure. In fact, it's the only thing we can do."

Kerrie nodded.

They had had a lengthy discussion before, as they made their way north to the Canadian border. Kerrie was angry and wanted to just release what they knew to the world. But Jack had reminded her of what Sam had said to them before he knocked him unconscious at the rest stop. The U.S. media were influenced—they would fall into a trap if they contacted them, and probably wouldn't be alive very long afterwards to even realize it. And he also reminded her of what that monster Noah had said. He actually had spoken the truth. If they were successful in making these facts public—and having them believed—there would be unfathomable chaos in the country and in the country's interests around the world. Jack was sure that the U.S. would degrade into anarchy, and trade relations with civilized countries would end. Allies would abandon America en masse. So, in reality they would be doing more harm to the American people by making this public than just remaining silent.

"We can't save the world. What's done is done. Horrible as it is, no one gains if we make this public. We need to be more concerned with trying to make sure it never happens again—that some wings get clipped and power is better controlled in the future."

Jack sipped his water, and briefly took his eyes off the road to look over at Kerrie. "Our first priority is making sure that you and I survive. We want to live. This could end our lives if we kid ourselves into thinking we're saviors. We're not. We're just normal people who stumbled onto something we shouldn't have, thanks to a dog named Mule, and an inquisitive prick named Jack Howser. Now we just have to get on with our lives. The world will unfold as it should, with or without us, and with or without this information becoming known.

"If I were a betting man, I would bet that neither of the last two administrations—the people at the top—knew about Operation Avalanche beforehand. I'm betting they only knew about it after the fact, but they realized just like us, that releasing it would be too dangerous. Actually, your dad alluded to this in his letter. He was convinced it was a rogue operation, and had been told as such. So it became a locked-up secret probably like so many other things. The CIA most likely acts on the premise, *'Begging forgiveness is preferable to asking permission.'*"

Kerrie looked through the windshield at the road ahead. Jack knew that deep down inside she agreed with him, but she was fighting the need for immediate vengeance, retaliation against those who had killed her father and thousands of Americans. She was the type of person who needed instant gratification. It was more than just mere impatience, it was a drive she possessed. He had noticed that about her during their time together—a quality that also helped make her the appealing and charismatic person she was. Kerrie was not boring or predictable, he knew that for a fact.

He continued. "There is so much power that is within the hands of the CIA and all of their black ops divisions, that there's probably nothing they can't pull off, or haven't already pulled off. It's a government within a government, and each new U.S. administration over the last few decades has probably been absolutely terrified with what they became privy to when they came into power; but ironically were powerless to do anything about it. The President is probably just a mouthpiece, a puppet. He probably doesn't have any real power in the grand scheme of things, sad to say. Maybe that will change now."

"It's ominous to think of it that way, Jack. I just have such a tough time grappling with it."

"I know, me too. Your dad's quote from Mao Tse Tung: *"Political power comes from the barrel of a gun"* is probably more factual than most people realize. When you think hard about it, what really keeps a government in power? What keeps the people on the streets from rioting and rushing in to destroy all the trappings of office, and those who hold that office?"

Kerrie nodded. "The military."

"Absolutely. Without the threat of lethal force, no government would survive. And when you think back over almost every coup d'etat that has ever happened around the world, it was the military that either turned their backs to let it happen, or just executed the overthrow themselves. Just think of the not-so-subtle blackmail that might exist over the President of the United States and the leaders of most militarized countries, with respect to every important decision they make, or don't make. I shudder when I think of it, and before this past week I never really thought of it in those terms. I sure do now."

Jack turned on the radio, hoping to hear some nice music. He realized that he hadn't listened to a radio or watched television in over two weeks. He settled on one of his favorite stations, and they heard chatter about Michael Jackson's death. He and Kerrie exchanged surprised glances. With all that had been going on, they hadn't even heard this news. They listened to mindless debating from talking heads about whether or not Jackson had molested children, then discussions about the various secret rooms in the Neverland Ranch. Then the announcement about how several thousand tickets would be available on a lottery basis for the Jackson memorial service. Jack shook his head in disgust, and switched stations. It didn't make a difference. Every station was reporting the same news, and engaging in the same brainless speculations.

He turned it off. "That's the real news Kerrie. That's the type of crap the media is confident that Americans really want to hear," Jack said cynically.

Suddenly Kerrie's cell phone rang. She picked up and said a series of "uh-huh," "uh-huh," and finally "Okay, thank you for checking."

Her face was white as a sheet. "The police went out to my place and found nothing, inside or out—absolutely nothing. No bodies, no blood, no guns. Oh, they did find a dead bear, but no arrows in the bear. They suggested that was probably the disturbance I had heard about, some illegal hunting."

Jack punched the steering wheel. "The injured guy, the one who was mauled, must have made an urgent call to get picked up and have the scene sanitized. Amazing, incredible. There's a good reason why these people are called 'spooks.'"

A couple of hours ago, Kerrie had insisted, against Jack's better judgment, on phoning the Bigfork Police, to have her place checked. She told them she was away in New York and heard from a neighbor that there was some disturbance at her property, some gunshots. The police agreed they would go out and check around. Jack had tried to convince her not to phone them, but she was concerned because it was her property and there were guns lying around. She said there were lots of children at the lake from time to time, and she also didn't want her nice neighbors stumbling across dead bodies. Or the police tracking her down later treating her like a suspect. Jack had found it hard to argue against her points. But in the end, it didn't matter—the spooks beat her to it. And the more he thought about it, it was better that way.

They were both silent for a few minutes, absorbing this new information. Jack checked his rearview mirror as he'd been doing every minute for the last several hours. So far, their trip had been uneventful, which was a nice change. Even the border crossing had been painless. Of course, he was dealing with Canadians this time around, compared to the clowns he had had to deal with a few weeks ago when he crossed to the American side. The Canadian border folks actually said, "Welcome back." They had no idea how glad he was to be back on his own soil.

They were making good time. Jack figured they should be in downtown Calgary by mid-afternoon, barring any surprises along the way. With that thought his foot got heavier on the accelerator and he pushed the speedometer up to 140 km. an hour. Kerrie pulled out her cell phone again, and began dialing.

"Who are you phoning now?" Jack asked.

"Belinda. I want to find out if she's been able to locate Connie yet. I'm worried about her."

Jack felt a lump in his throat. He had to tell her now. This was the time.

"Kerrie, hang up."

"What?"

"Hang up." He reached over and took the phone from her hand. "Connie's dead. And so is her brother. Sam told me."

*****

They were cruising north on Calgary's Deerfoot Trail at 2:30 in the afternoon, and it was a bright sunny July day. The Calgary Stampede, the world famous rodeo and fair, had just started the day before and would continue for the next nine days. So traffic was busier than usual, and they could see that occupants of almost every vehicle were decked out in wide-brimmed cowboy hats. The city would party for the next week and a bit, and Jack knew that it was one of the best parties on earth. He wouldn't be participating this year, but wouldn't really miss it either. Partying was not at the top of his list right now.

Kerrie had been silent for the last couple of hours, ever since he had given her the news about Connie.

She finally came out of her cocoon, turned her head and glared at him, fire in her eyes.

"So when exactly were you planning on telling me about Connie?"

"I would have told you eventually. I just didn't want to hit you with any more shocks. You'd been through enough."

"You had no right to make a decision like that. I deserved to know the truth. What am I, some delicate little flower that you have to protect? You should know by now that while I may shed a tear once in a while, my tolerance for hurt and stress is pretty high."

"You're right. I'm sorry."

"We're partners in this, Jack. You better remember that. Is there anything else I should know?"

"No…well, yes. I guess you should know that old redneck sweatshirt you're wearing has some words stitched across the back: *'Let me light your fire. I'm a hot piece of ash.'*"

Kerrie lost her angry face. First she broke out into a giggle, then lowered her head in a prolonged laugh. Jack started laughing too. They had needed a silly moment to release the stress. They were near the end of an incredible ordeal, and both of them were surprised that they were still alive. It was almost over, and they really needed something to laugh about. Kerrie's tacky second-hand sweatshirt, borrowed from the needy, was it.

"I'm going to miss your sense of humor, Jack."

He followed Deerfoot Trail to the Memorial Drive exit, and followed the

4th Avenue fly-over to downtown Calgary, a gleaming metropolis of glass and steel. He loved this city, and was damn glad to be back. He felt much safer being on his own turf again.

He left the Audi in a pay-parking lot off 4th Avenue. They grabbed the knapsack and Kerrie's purse and started walking the one block distance to Heather's office tower.

They passed several wannabe cowboys along the way, and no one seemed to notice their beat-up appearance all that much. There was so much dressing-up during Stampede week, almost anyone blended in. With their bruised and bleeding appearance, some people probably even thought they were rodeo stars.

As promised, Heather was waiting for them just inside the lobby doors. She let them in and Jack introduced her to Kerrie. She then stood back and studied him. She gently removed his baseball cap and examined his blood-stained bandana.

Then she gave Jack a hug and kissed his cheek. She looked into his eyes and said, "I don't know what you've been doing, but I am so relieved that you're back. After this meeting, I'm taking both of you to the hospital. I've been so worried since your call."

Heather led the way to the elevator bank, and inserted her card. They rode up quietly to the 20th floor. She ushered them into a conference room just down from the front hallway. When they entered the room, Jack could see that the microfiche reader was already set up for them, as was a laptop computer. A pot of coffee with mugs and a jug of water and glasses were waiting for them on a side credenza. Jack asked Heather to leave them alone for about an hour, and then bring Scott in to meet with them.

He zipped open the outside pocket of the knapsack, removing the cassette and the tiny microchip that had been removed from Mule's shoulder. Kerrie opened her purse and brought out Mitch's letter. Finally, Jack reached down into his side pocket and took out the plastic baggie containing the several sheets of microfilm.

He turned on the microfiche reader, and flattened out one sheet of microfilm. The little sheets were a little out of shape from being rolled up in the barrel of the Mauser, but luckily didn't appear damaged at all. Jack and Kerrie huddled over the reader and Jack turned the handle slowly to scroll down to the first exhibit, then the second, then the third...

They looked at twenty-five exhibits, which consisted of detailed engineering diagrams and Thermate demolition specifications for the three WTC towers.

They were all date-stamped and approved with the CIA seal. They were signed, with names of the signees typed underneath the signatures. Then there were the memos—from individuals with fancy titles within the CIA, NCS, SAD—and then one from an official in the Pentagon itself. All labeled "Top Secret," and all referring to the project code name 'Operation Avalanche.' Some were addressed to Mitch, some to other CIA officials, all giving assurances as to the purpose of the project being as benign as Mitch had been led to believe. Then another microfilm sheet showing timelines on official letterhead specifying when each stage of the project had to be completed.

None of the documents mentioned any planned coordination of demolition with attacks by airliners, and none of them mentioned Bin Laden. According to Mitch and Noah, it was all a coordinated plan, but there was nothing in writing about that. However, anyone viewing this documentation could easily put two and two together. The American public had been led to believe that the collapse of the towers was due to the impact by airplanes. There had been no admission of programmed demolitions. In fact, that had been vehemently denied whenever conspiracy theorists raised the point. Thousands of people had died when the towers collapsed, when there might have been time to save them if the buildings had been left standing. So the lie about that deadly part of the story made the entire story a lie.

Jack and Kerrie could barely breathe. It was a damning mountain of evidence and the implications were immense. It was more blatant than even they had speculated about after reading Mitch's letter. They knew he had something, but they didn't think it was anything as detailed as this. It was eerie, and incredibly horrifying.

Scott Dennison came into the room and introduced himself. A nice guy, about Jack's age, mid-fifties, dressed in golf clothes. This was, after all, a Saturday. Jack was sure there was somewhere else he would rather be. He did a double-take when he saw the condition of the two of them, but composed himself quickly. Heather must have prepared him nicely.

Jack explained what they wanted to do, and Scott listened intently. He did not tell Scott what was in the various documents they had, but stressed to him that it was serious enough to have threatened their lives. He was honest with Scott. He told him that the information they had was probably the most incendiary political information anyone could ever imagine. He explained to Scott the services that he wanted his firm and others to provide.

Scott nodded as Jack explained, and merely replied with, "Incendiary is what we do. Protecting our clients is what we do, no matter what it is as long as it's nothing illegal. You can consider that what you want done, will be done."

Jack exchanged relieved glances with Kerrie. "How soon can this information be protected, Scott?"

"Is today soon enough? We can do everything you want and we can do it today. Just remember not to tell me or anyone else in this firm or the other firms we use, what it is that will be protected. But it will be useless protecting it if you don't tell your pursuers today that you have it protected. That has to be communicated before you can safely leave this building. Only then will you be immune from whatever it is that's been haunting you."

Jack nodded and held Kerrie's hand. She squeezed it and smiled, a smile that looked to Jack as one of absolute relief.

Scott continued. "And one more thing. It won't be cheap. It will cost half a million dollars for your two lifetimes. One flat rate. Are you prepared for that? There's a danger factor here for our firms that has to be addressed in the cost."

Jack whistled. "That's a hefty price, but I guess we have no choice. Our lives are worth far more than that, at least to us!"

"Okay, make your phone call, and then you can draft your letter. We'll take care of the rest." Scott stood up, and came around the table to shake their hands. "Good luck to you both."

Scott left the room, and the two accidental fugitives stared at each other. Then they smiled. They knew they were going to be okay. Their nightmares might remind them occasionally about how close they had come to becoming statistics, or as Sam had put it, "obituaries," but they could at least enjoy their waking hours now and breathe sighs of relief. They were finally safe, and they would continue to be safe. They were sure of that. Jack pulled out his cell phone.

"Who are you calling?"

"Noah Hendridge. We should use him as our conduit. He's obviously still well connected and had a prominent role in the 9/11 horror. He also assassinated your dad. He's the perfect first contact for us with what we're going to do. He'll inform whoever needs to know, I'm confident of that. The man thinks of himself as a patriot."

"To hell with you, Mr. Howser!" She snatched the phone out of his hand. "You're not phoning Noah. I'm doing that. It's the least I can do for my father." Jack knew she was right. He had done it again—trying to control something that was not within his right to try to control.

He nodded to Kerrie. "Go ahead. You're the one who should do it. I agree. I'll be right here beside you for moral support." He passed over to her a sheet of paper with a list of countries and news media outlets that he had compiled on the plane trip back from New York. The on-board computers were great for surfing the net, and Jack had made good use of his time.

Kerrie smiled at him, and whispered, "Thanks."

Jack noticed how tired her eyes looked, but she still seemed alert. It had been a long time since either of them had slept. He knew his eyes probably looked the same as hers. It was amazing how long one could go without sleep, he thought, when adrenaline was dominating the body. Well, lots of time to sleep after this last part of the ordeal was over. He was looking forward to getting to his house, and crawling into bed—maybe a nice scotch first, though. Heather's intention to take them to the hospital may have to wait.

*****

Kerrie punched in the number. She could sense that her smile had been replaced by a face of sheer rage. She couldn't see what she looked like, but she could sure feel what she looked like. And she knew it wasn't pretty.

"Hello?"

"Carl, get your boss on the phone."

A few seconds later, "Hello? Is that you, Kerrie?"

"Fuck off, Noah. Listen carefully."

"Kerrie, let me phone you back on my secure line."

"Fuck your secure line. It doesn't matter anymore. You stay on this *insecure* line and just listen. And if you haven't started recording this conversation yet, I suggest you begin now."

Noah went silent. Kerrie began what she needed to say:

"We have the documentation detailing Operation Avalanche. It is clear and concise. It names names. It shows approvals. It shows specifications. There are also some bonus documents that my dad must have gotten his hands on giving even more detail. It's all shocking, disgusting, and murderous, and the American people deserve to hear it." Kerrie paused to let that sink in. "But they won't, unless either Jack Howser or myself are dead. We see no advantage in the greater interests of the American people, or the world for that matter, in broadcasting what monsters you people are. The calamity that would result would be huge and irreversible. Two wrongs don't make a right.

"So we are prepared to remain silent, and we have protected ourselves by securing all of the information we have with one legal firm as lead solicitors, and two additional firms as subordinates. All of the information will be replicated and placed in secure vaults with each law firm. If either Jack Howser, or I, Kerrie Joplin, happen to perish from whatever cause imaginable, the information will be released to the media. So it will be in the best interests of the government of the United States of America, to keep both of us alive for as long as possible.

"Because even if we die from natural causes, or one of your so-called accidents, the first one who dies will trigger the release of these documents. So you had better hope for a long and happy life for both of us. What should be obvious here, is that eventually the American people will know what really happened on 9/11, because inevitably both of us will die of hopefully just old age. The documents will be released after the first death.

"The lead law firm will expect to hear from both of us each year, using pre-set code words on a set date, to confirm that we are alive. If they don't hear from us, death records world-wide will be scanned automatically to ascertain if one of us has died."

Noah interrupted. "You don't know what you're doing, Kerrie. If you think the threat of media release is going to protect you, think again. Your best play is to just hand over everything you have, and we'll leave you alone."

"As I said before, fuck off and listen old man. Learn to pay attention." Kerrie took a sip of her coffee, and continued.

"We're not stupid enough to threaten to release documents to some of the weak-kneed American media who are basically beholden to you maniacs. I'm going to read you a list of countries and news media that would just love to see what we have. These are the outlets that will receive the documents, dad's letter, and the cassette tape if one of us dies. These are countries who are not particularly fond of the 'Land of the Proud and the Free.'" Kerrie paused, then snarled, "I won't be repeating myself:

"Germany – *Der Spiegel*

"France – *Herald de Paris*

"Russia – *Pravda*

"Spain – *Barcelona Reporter*

"Italy – *Il Manifesto*

"Venezuela – *El Globo*

"Honduras –*El Libertador*

"China – *People's Daily*

"North Korea – *Pyongyang Times*

"Iran – *Tehran Times*

"Syria – *Al Baath*

"Lebanon –*Al Markazia*

"Cuba – *Ahora.*

"Oh, and last but not least, how could I forget Qatar and the infamous *Al Jazeera.* In fact, our lawyers will be instructed to make sure they receive everything first. I'm sure Al Jazeera would prefer to have all this, instead of a Bin Laden video any day. They deserve that at the very least, being the most watched and trusted news media in the Middle East, an area of the world you murderers seem to be particularly obsessed with.

"In addition to this phone call to you, of which I fully expect you will inform all who need to know the minute you hang up, we will be sending letters giving details and names to high-ranking officials of the U.S. government, including the White House, Department of Defense, CIA, FBI, National Clandestine Service, SAD, and anyone else we might think of. We will share enough detail that will convince each of the recipients that we do indeed have authentic documents pertaining to a project called Operation Avalanche. After they receive these letters, it is a certainty that they will want to investigate further and uncover what you madmen have hidden.

"We will include in those letters the demands I have just cited to you as to our safety. The letters will go out by special courier today. I would expect that you, your collaborators, and superiors will be on Washington's radar for a long, long time.

"And the minute I hang up the phone with you, I want Jack and I removed from that No Fly list. If we are not removed by Monday morning as an act of good faith, all bets are off and our lawyers will release the documents that afternoon. So, get busy!

"Finally, Noah, you might want to pay your boy Carl a little bit extra to watch your cowardly back a little bit closer for the rest of your miserable life. Rot in hell, you bastard!"

Epilogue
June 2010

Jack leaned in close to the mirror and began peeling the bandage from his forehead—slowly, carefully. God, it hurt. It was looking better but still a long way from normal. He had just undergone his third skin graft procedure, and this one seemed to have taken hold pretty good. It would be a while before hair would grow back in again on that part of his scalp. He rubbed on the ointment that he was required to do twice a day, and applied a fresh bandage.

Jack sat down in his living room and turned on the television. Same old news. He switched it off and stretched out for a nap. He had been exhausted since this last operation, and seemed to need several naps a day to compensate. Within seconds he was assaulted by a flying ball of fur. Mule would never let him nap alone—he had to be there. And he had his favorite spot too, right down near his feet, and Jack would have to open his legs wide to make room. Then the dog's butt insisted on snuggling up close to Jack's crotch and inevitably his legs would stretch out and kick Jack in the balls. Same routine every time, and Jack enjoyed every single minute of it.

He was so glad to have Mule back in perfect form. He reached forward and pulled the dog's head back towards him and gave him a big hug. Mule groaned appreciatively.

Meagan had done a wonderful job of bringing Mule back to life. Jack was so afraid he was going to lose him, but he was a tough little guy. He thought back many times to that vision of Mule flying through the air to their rescue. It had been a sight to behold, particularly considering how desperate their situation had been at that very moment when Mule made his fearless appearance.

It had been almost a year now since Jack and Kerrie had parted at Calgary International Airport. She had boarded a flight to Grand Cayman via Miami and it was a heartbreaking goodbye to say the least. Jack was not one to cry that easily but he sure did that day. They both did.

They had been through such an intense experience together, parting almost felt like an amputation. Kerrie had kissed him lightly on the lips as they said their goodbyes. Both of them had tears running down their cheeks. She turned on her heel and headed for the security gate.

He watched her go. Then suddenly she turned around and came running back to him. Their lips locked and it seemed so natural, so fulfilling. He held her tightly and she whispered in his ear that she had fallen in love with him. Then she ran before he could say anything. He watched the blonde goddess, with her father's cleft chin, maneuver through security and disappear. She didn't turn around again.

He had watched through the observation deck as her plane lifted off. He wondered if he would ever see her again. Then he thought about Heather and started to feel guilty. Should he be feeling this way about parting with Kerrie? What did that say about his feelings for Heather?

Jack walked away from the terminal back to his car, rationalizing in his mind that it was only natural to feel this way with the ordeal that the two of them had gone through. He and Kerrie were confusing love with survival intensity. Both involved powerful emotions, and both evoked feelings of longing. They had been to hell and back together.

Of course they would feel close to each other. That was only being human, he guessed.

Now almost a year later, in the rainy month of June, he was still a bit confused but becoming less and less so each day. He lay there on the couch thinking about both women, when Mule suddenly turned around and crawled up on his chest. He laid his chin beside Jack's face and whimpered. Jack hugged him again and thought that the only true love he was sure about right now was what he felt for this brave little dog.

He had seen Heather and Josh many times over the past year, and their relationship had been developing nicely. They were a wonderful little family and Jack felt honored to be a part-time member. He knew he cared for both of them deeply, but something was missing. This bothered him, and for quite a while he hadn't been able to put his finger on it. The last few weeks, however, he had been coming to the realization with the help of his therapist, that the excitement and spontaneity was missing. And he had to decide how important that was in a relationship, and was it realistic under normal everyday life to even expect that. His time with Kerrie had not been normal, to say the least.

His brain was comparing Heather unfairly with the adventure he had had with Kerrie, adventure that had occupied the entire time he had known her. This made sense to him. He and Kerrie had never really spent any time together when they weren't either figuring out clues or running for their lives. It certainly hadn't been a normal relationship, and he might not feel the same sense of anticipation with Kerrie if they spent some normal calm time together. Did he owe it to himself to find out?

He hadn't confided in his psychologist completely as to what they had endured or discovered. He said just enough for the man to understand where his mind was at now, and where it had been. He had been seeing this shrink at the suggestion of his plastic surgeon. The surgeon felt that Jack needed help, mentally, to get through the surgical procedures and to deal with the memories of his frightening ordeal.

Not just the ordeal with the mystery itself, but most importantly the ordeal of losing his wife. His shrink told him that he had never really come to grips with that, and his search for excitement and the insatiable need to satisfy his natural curiosity were his methods of coping—which could be dangerous methods of coping. Boy, was he right on!

Jack's mind brought it all down to adjectives: Heather was domestic, safe, happy, close, predictable, loving, and attentive. Kerrie, on the other hand, was adventurous, exciting, unpredictable, distant, stubborn, temperamental, and had a hint of danger about her.

And most importantly, each relationship had developed under different environments and circumstances: one exciting and intense, the other relaxed and comfortable. It was impossible to compare them, as they weren't on a level playing field.

Who did he feel the most tenderness towards? Heather, no doubt. Tenderness, however, was far different than excitement. One was wonderful, the other was intoxicating.

But despite the intoxication, lately there was just something about Kerrie…

*****

Kerrie had called him for the first time from the Cayman Islands about a week after she arrived. She told him about how she had accessed the numbered bank account with Grand Cayman International Bank—what Mitch had carved into the wooden stock of the Mauser. Luckily she had written down the account number a few days after she had memorized it up in the attic. The bank accessed the records and told her that her father had actually opened the account in both of their names. The rest of the paperwork was easy since Kerrie had possession of the account number, which was all she really needed in that famous tax haven.

Mitch had left his daughter $20 million American in that account. Kerrie was astounded. Jack was even more astounded. She joked that she now had enough money to start her own small army. Jack was pretty sure she was joking.

He heard from Kerrie again about a month later. She told him that she had decided she would never return to the United States. She said she was ashamed to be an American citizen and was putting the wheels in motion to become a permanent resident of the Cayman Islands. It was beautiful there, she told him, and she urged him to come for a visit.

Jack wanted to, but his head injury from the mauling was so severe that he had to stick around for regular treatments, and the three surgeries. His life was on hold.

The next month she called him again, this time announcing that her resident status had been fast-tracked due to the large amounts she had invested in the islands. She had gone ahead and purchased a large villa on the separate and more remote island of Cayman Brac. She said it was beautiful, sitting high up on one of the bluffs the island was famous for, overlooking the Caribbean. She emailed Jack some photos and he had to admit, she had found her place in paradise and her own beauty blended in perfectly with the surroundings.

As Jack thought of tropical paradises, he couldn't help but remember his long-gone wife, Susan, and how much she had always loved those kinds of vacations. Part of the fun of going away with Susan had been the preparations ahead of time. She would buy travel books for whatever destination they were headed to, insisting on becoming an expert on the place by the time they got there. She was always so excited, even months before they left, and this always got Jack excited too. She was like a little kid, which was such a contrast to her high-powered business life. Then the packing. She started days in advance. Jack always made fun of her, and once he even snuck in and unpacked all of her things and replaced them with items she had never planned to take. He could still remember laughing to himself, watching her standing in their bedroom looking into her suitcase, wondering to herself what on earth had possessed her to pack winter clothes for a tropical holiday.

Jack shook his head and wiped away a tear. It had been almost nine years since his wife died, and he still wasn't over it. It was tough, knowing now how deceptively she had died, that her wonderful life had been wasted due to a scheme hatched by power-drunk madmen. Perhaps that was why his love life was still confused. He was still unable to get Susan out of his mind, and perhaps somewhere deep inside his subconscious he was still comparing both ladies to her.

He thought back to the house on Flathead Lake. It was sad that Kerrie felt she could no longer return to her own country. Jack had tried to convince her otherwise. A handful of cowardly killers did not make a country. And she had put such heart and soul into that house. It must have been a wish of her dad's that she would live there. But he had left terrible secrets and surprises in that house. It was naïve of Mitch to think that she could have lived there comfortably. The attic that housed its military shrine, guns, and 9/11 documentation, and the tunnel that now contained a body buried in its earthen tomb. Kerrie felt there was no way she could go back to that. Jack understood, but still he thought it was a travesty that she was harboring such resentment to an entire country for the acts of just a few.

In hindsight, Jack thought it was kind of ironic he had started thinking this way. For years he had harbored the same feelings of resentment for his wife's death. And one would have thought that after what Jack had discovered in that storage warehouse, that his resentment would now have grown to rage. But it wasn't that way at all. Perhaps finding out that Operation Avalanche was a scheme hatched by a coven of crazies ironically helped him put a lot of the resentment towards America behind him. He had some answers now and some closure. It was still horrifying, but now his resentment was focused in the right direction and no longer irrational.

He and Kerrie had heard nothing from anyone since their letters had gone out last July. He was a bit surprised by this, considering the enormity of their extortion. He felt safe, kind of, but also unnerved from the deafening silence. But, he was just glad he was alive. They'd pushed the envelope and were lucky beyond belief. The world was a weird place right now and if the words in Mitch's letter, about the manipulation of power by keeping America in a state of perpetual war, were true, the implications were scary. There was nothing a simple man like Jack could do about it, except hope that sanity would return one day.

He had naively hoped that their letters to U.S. officials would have made a difference, but lately he'd had serious doubts. There had been a string of terror warnings over the last few months, including one about a dud bomb in some clown's underwear, of all things. He wondered if these threats were real or fake. Mitch's words from the letter came to mind: *'When we allowed war to be declared on terrorism, it basically meant that we are in a war that will never end.*

And if things settle down and people think the war is over, all that has to be done is fake another terrorist attack to keep Congress and the American people in a state of fear."

Kerrie told Jack that her realtor had been successful in selling her house for $2.5 million to a retired man and his family from the Glendale area, just outside Los Angeles. He had recently become disabled, now on a government pension, and had always longed to live on a lake. It was just what he had been looking for apparently. Kerrie had given power of attorney to the realtor so it could be sold without her involvement. She didn't care who bought it and didn't need the money anymore either. It was better off going to a good cause, and a cause that her father would have approved of. So, Kerrie donated the proceeds from the sale of the house to a New York charity that provided college funds for children of 9/11 victims.

He and Kerrie had chatted on the phone at least once a month. He enjoyed the conversations but something had changed. Either he was past the intense experience with her, and things were just more, well, normal, or he was wrapped up more in serious thoughts about Heather. Or maybe it was something else. He couldn't pin it down, but something was nagging in his mind that Kerrie was a different person than the one he had come to know, or at least thought he knew. Or maybe he was different?

And she hadn't yet offered to pay her share of the big legal bill, or for the chartered aircraft in Montana. He had never made that a condition, but in light of her new good fortune, he had expected at least an offer. One part of his mind told him he was being petty, but the other part said her half of $650,000 was not petty.

As for Jack, boredom luckily had not yet set in again. He figured he had had enough excitement to last him a lifetime. His shrink told him that for the good of his recovery from everything, he should fight back against his curious mind. That mind had been a tonic for him, but now he had to grow up and let it go—or at least let it function through safer outlets. Jack couldn't disagree with the good doctor's advice, but then again the good doctor didn't know what Jack knew. What advice would he give, he wondered, if he knew what mind-numbing secrets he was harboring?

A big part of Jack's recovery and treatment was a project that he figured would keep him occupied and out of trouble for quite some time. He had spent the last year jotting down notes, plot outlines, and character descriptions. In fact, this project was unfortunately becoming another one of his obsessions and he felt he had no choice but to just go with it. He knew what he could be like.

Jack rolled off the couch, taking Mule along for the ride. "Okay, boy, are you coming? I need to get started, and you have one of the starring roles."

Mule gave Jack an impatient snort, tail wagging, no doubt wondering what on earth his partner seemed so excited about now.

Jack headed straight for his office and sat down at his desk. While he and Kerrie had promised in the letters they had sent to various government officials that they would not release the documentation they had on Operation Avalanche, Jack did not promise that he wouldn't write a fiction novel. And that's exactly what he intended to do, but under a different name of course.

He sat down at the keyboard and got ready to write. The visions clear in his mind that he wanted to portray. The characters clear in his mind that he wanted to bring to life. He began the Prologue without further adieu:

Mitch Joplin looked in the mirror as he went about his morning routine. Not bad looking after all these years, he thought. Tall, well-built, still lots of hair. And his most striking feature of all—his eyes—still penetrated, right back at him from the mirror.

*****

Jack awoke with a start as the sound of the phone jarred him from one of his rare pleasant dreams. "Hello?"

"Hi, handsome. How's your half-bald head doing?"

"Hi, Kerrie. Great to hear from you. As for the head, I think every day it's looking a bit better, but that may be just my male vanity speaking."

"Email me a photo and I'll give you my honest opinion."

"I don't think I want to do that. You'll never want me to visit if you see what I look like!"

"I doubt that very much. So, when are you coming? I miss you more than I can say. It's been almost a year now!"

"I know, time flies when you're under a scalpel. I do want to come Kerrie, but not yet. I need to sort some things out first, not the least of which is a scalp that probably couldn't stand the tropical heat for more than a minute or two!"

"I have several lanais, so that's not a good excuse."

"I know, but I'll be down there soon. I promise you. We have a lot of catching up to do."

"Jack, I wanted to tell you that it was my dad's birthday a couple of weeks ago, June 10. He would have been seventy-three years old if he'd lived."

"I hope you managed to enjoy some nice memories of him that day. You owe yourself that."

"Yes, I did force myself to recall some nice ones. And I actually placed an 'In Memoriam' column about him in the Obituary section of the *New York Times* a few days later. I think it appeared on June 13. Search it online if you're interested in reading it."

"I will. But right now, I've gotta run. Let's talk again real soon, okay?"

"We definitely will. Oh, and Jack, while you're searching out my dad's memoriam, scroll down a little bit further in that same issue. You'll see an interesting obituary."

Jack easily located Kerrie's memoriam on her dad, Mitchell Bernard Joplin, in the June 13 online issue archive of the *New York Times.* It started off with his birth date of June 10, 1937, and then the date of his death, February 13, 2003.

It was a brief column, written clearly from Kerrie's heart. She wrote about how proud she was, and how she admired the strength that he had shown throughout his life, right until the day of his death. She closed the column with a dramatic heartfelt statement:

You tried real hard, Dad, but you failed to make things right. But that's okay. Your strength and goodness came through in the trying. I learned from that, admire you for that, and hope that during my lifetime I can emulate that.

Jack scrolled down further as Kerrie had suggested. The obituary caught his eye right away:

Noah Robert Hendridge; Born April 6, 1935; Died June 10, 2010. Passed away suddenly.

Cause of death undetermined.

Noah was a loyal and dedicated father and grandfather, whose commitment to family always came first. He will be remembered as one who made time for his family despite the demands that came with serving his country for most of his life. Noah served first in the military and then dedicated his life to pursuing peace, in the foreign service as a career diplomat. He will be missed by his colleagues as someone who valued human rights and freedoms above all else, and fought to preserve those rights around the world.

Survived by his loving daughter, Sheila Winston, and grandson, Jason Winston. Service will be private. No donations or flowers please.

Jack's eyes rode up to the top of the obituary again. He had read both notices quickly, but there was something eating at him. Then he saw it—the date of Noah's death. It was June 10. Mitch's birthday.

*****

Mule always got anxious at the sound of the computer keyboard. Jack figured that Mule knew fun times were on hold as long as Jack was sitting at the desk, pounding away.

Connie couldn't help herself—she screamed and buckled to the floor as her knees finally gave out. Mitch leaped over the counter as if he were bouncing off a trampoline. He wrapped one strong arm underneath her and gently helped her up—as he did, she could see him reach under the counter and press the button himself. He seemed to know the exact spot—no fumbling around.

The phone did the job for Mule, pulling Jack away from his computer.

"Hello?"

"Hi, Jack. Tell me what you're doing today."

"Hi, Kerrie. Nothing special, just drafting some notes for a speech I have to make in a few weeks," Jack lied. "However, I may try to get in eighteen holes later on. How's it down there in Margaritaville?"

"Beautiful. I'm sitting out on one of my lanais right now, the one I've reserved for you as a matter of fact. It has the most shade for that sensitive head of yours."

"That's nice of you. Continue to reserve it for me. No youngsters under seventy-five years of age allowed, okay? I can't handle the competition." She laughed. Jack was a flirt and he knew it.

"Jack, did you have a chance yet to search the New York Times?"

"I did."

"You're a bright guy. You must have noticed the strange coincidence."

"Yes, that was strange indeed." Something stopped Jack from commenting any further. And there were actually two coincidences, not just one. First, the memoriam on her dad appearing in the same issue as the obituary for Noah, and second, Noah dying on Mitch's birthday. Was it possible what he was thinking? Was she baiting him? Jack shook his head, as if to clear his mind. His head hurt. Kerrie must have sensed that he was holding back, because she quickly changed gears.

"Do you remember that I kept a copy of my dad's letter before we handed all the stuff over to our lawyer?"

"Have you lost it?"

"Oh no, actually I just got the courage today to read it again. I haven't looked at it since that day in the warehouse."

"Okay." Jack didn't know where this was going.

"Let me read a part of it to you. It caught me by surprise, and I had completely forgotten about it." She read: *"As well, there is an old video located in the box. It has nothing to do with the subject of this letter, so it will not help you find the documentation. I have included it only as a throw-in. You can view it one day after you have recovered from this shock, if you want to. You might as well know completely who I really am. Needless to say, it won't matter to me anymore."*

Jack felt like there was an explosion in his brain! He had forgotten all about the video! He remembered asking Kerrie if she wanted to view it back at that motel in New Jersey, and she had declined. He had then stuck it safely away in an inside pocket of his knapsack.

"Hold on, Kerrie!" Jack dropped the phone and ran to his bedroom closet. He yanked out the knapsack stashed in the back, and threw it onto the bed. He zipped it open and reached inside, then unzipped the inside pocket. There it was! He pulled it out—the old videotape with the CIA seal on the cover. Jack ran back to the phone, and struggled to catch his breath.

"Kerrie, I've still got it!"

"Oh, thank God. I was worried that I might never find out what was on it. Dad said in his letter that it was old and had nothing to do with the documentation, but I'm hoping, praying, that there might be something on that tape that will help me know my father just a little bit better. Maybe it's a personal message to me."

"Do you want me to courier it to you?"

"No, not yet. I'd like your assessment as to whether or not I can handle it first. Would you mind terribly viewing it for me?"

Jack hesitated.

"Jack?"

"I'm still here. Yeah, I can look at it for you. Are you sure you want me to see it first? It might be something very private, meant for your eyes only."

"I trust you. Do this for me, please?"

"Okay, I'll do it. I'll call you after I've seen it."

"Thanks so much, Jack. Talk to you soon, and take care of yourself, okay?"

"I will, I promise."

*****

Jack was pacing the living room floor. Mule was watching him curiously—back and forth, back and forth.

Why was this bothering him so much? It was just a video, for Christ's sake.

It had been a full day since he had talked to Kerrie, and he still hadn't watched the damn thing. She was probably getting real impatient by now. She sure did seem empowered lately, he thought. He detected new strength in her voice, a demanding confidence that had been missing before. Of course, now she was relaxed and not running for her life anymore. That alone would make a huge difference.

But there was something off. Something in her tone maybe? She had clearly bounced back quite nicely, whereas he was still having nightmares. She was also living in a tropical climate, wealthier now than she could have ever imagined. Kerrie didn't have a care in the world anymore. Of course, Jack was wealthy too, not to the extent she was now, but he didn't have many cares either. He thought that maybe the new feelings he was having had more to do with jealousy as to how well Kerrie seemed to have rebounded. That must be it. He wanted to put it all behind him as handily as she seemed to have done.

But the two coincidences from the *New York Times* were also bothering him. And he knew for a fact that he could not spend the rest of his days relaxing on a lanai. He found it hard to believe that she could either.

Jack sat down at his computer and decided to finish off the final paragraph for the Prologue of his novel—a good excuse for procrastinating on the video a little bit longer.

...She dove to grab the detonator, but knew it was too late. The button popped up with a resounding "click" that she decided, in that one horrifying moment, was the loudest noise she had ever heard in her life.

He reviewed the entire Prologue and was satisfied. Chapter One was next. Perhaps he'd start it later in the evening over a scotch.

Jack knew that he was putting off the inevitable. Why was he afraid? It felt a bit like if he viewed that video, he would be no better than a Peeping Tom. That video was not meant for him. Also, part of his brain was listening to his shrink and trying to fight off his natural curiosity. He was in a conflict, almost like fighting to resist an addiction.

He picked up the phone and dialed her number.

"Jack, did you look at it?"

No niceties, no "How are you doing?" Just in his face, and right down to business. For a fleeting moment Jack thought of that famous saying, "The apple doesn't fall too far from the tree." A little voice was telling him that something had changed, and whatever that change was, it was not sitting well in his heart.

"Not yet."

"Why not?"

"I wanted to ask you something first. What if there's nothing nice on that video? Do you want me to tell you about it, or just burn it? You've started a new life down there, and that life sounds like a pretty good one. Do you really need this?"

"I'll leave that to you to decide, Jack. I can handle whatever your judgment dictates."

"Okay. I'll call you tomorrow."

"Don't keep putting this off. Please. I'm getting anxious, and I must say I'm disappointed in you. Procrastination is not one of your lovable traits, Jack."

Jack hung up the phone, knowing in his gut that he himself was already well beyond anxious. He went to the bathroom, poured a long cold glass of water, and popped an anxiety pill. He couldn't ignore it any longer.

Jack was actually proud of himself. His trademark curiosity was not driving him to slide the video into the machine. A few months ago, he couldn't have restrained himself. He would have watched it in a flash if Kerrie had let him back in that motel room. Now she was begging him to and he was balking. He guessed that his therapy sessions were working. He was trying to leave well enough alone, just as he was counseled to do.

Enough. He went to the bar, poured himself a tall scotch, and pulled the video out of its official government case. Turning on the television, he slid the video into the machine. He went over to the couch with his scotch and Mule jumped up beside him. The pill, scotch and Mule were making him feel better already, but there was a nagging little voice that was telling him to just burn the damn tape. He was half-hoping when he had suggested that to Kerrie, that she would have taken him up on it and decided that neither of them should see it. But she didn't.

So here he sat—Kerrie's surrogate. He took a big gulp of his scotch and scratched Mule's ears. He braced himself for whatever he might see.

The tape began to play. It was black and white, no sound. He could tell from the images and grainy quality that this was an old movie, shot with probably an Eight millimeter or Super Eight movie camera. It must have then been converted to video later on. The hand of the person holding the camera was not very steady. The shaky images challenged Jack's eyes. It looked to be a bright and sunny day. There were reflections of light off an old railroad boxcar.

Suddenly the door to the boxcar slid open, and in single file, four men jumped down onto the grass. They were dressed in old clothes, but their physical conditions and their confident swaggers belied how they dressed. They were bums who didn't look much like bums. Each of them wore old long coats, and their exaggerated movements proved that the film was old. Their pace was unnaturally fast, jerky.

As they crossed the field closer to the camera, their features became more distinguishable. The first two were older—fortyish, with lined weathered faces, wearing hats. They looked sullen, and seemed to be deliberately holding their heads down so the camera couldn't completely catch them.

Jack gasped as the third man came into view. He first saw the cameraman's free hand partially in front of the lens, motioning for this third guy to come directly to the camera. He did as he was told. This man was younger—twenties, broad-shouldered, over 6 feet tall—and bore a striking resemblance to the actor David Soul.

Then the fourth man came within close range, and again the cameraman's hand motioned for him to come directly toward the lens. At the sight of him, Jack choked on a chip of ice and started coughing. He had seen Kerrie's photo of her dad when he was younger, and this was without a doubt, Mitch Joplin, otherwise known as the CIA killer, Sniper. He towered over the other three, and walked with a stride that was as menacing as it was captivating. He glared into the camera with the most intense eyes Jack had ever seen, then abruptly spun away and walked in the direction of the other three men.

Jack couldn't turn away. His old curiosity was back at full throttle. He took another gulp of scotch. The adrenaline was pumping and his eyes were riveted to the screen.

The cameraman now followed behind the four men. They approached a fence with a growth of trees on the other side. Mitch went ahead to the fence line, and the other three lined up behind him, as if deliberately blocking him from view. The camera angle caught sight of a roadway off in the distance beyond the fence, lined with people. Then the filming stopped.

When it started up again, all it caught at first were three large black umbrellas tilted back and touching each other, completely blocking the heads of the three men holding them, as well as the fourth man in front. The three umbrella men seemed to be acting as an impromptu kind of screen. The fourth man was Mitch. There wasn't a rain cloud in sight.

Then the cameraman started walking, the images in the lens jerking as he did. The lens went around the men with the umbrellas and focused on Mitch standing at the fence. As if on cue, Mitch withdrew a rifle from a sling pocket on the inside of his long knee-length jacket. His fingers expertly attached a scope that had been concealed in another inside pocket. The cameraman motioned again with his hand and Mitch turned for a second to face the camera, holding the rifle up as if posing. The umbrella men stayed in their spots.

The camera clearly caught the moving images of a motorcade, weaving its way along the road in the distance. Mitch raised his rifle and lined his right eye up with the scope.

Jack knew exactly what he was watching. He didn't have to be a student of history to recognize it. He could feel goose bumps running up his back as he sat with his eyes riveted to the screen, could hear the ice clinking in his glass as his hand began to shake. Some of Mitch's last written words once again haunted him: *"Foreign policy in reality is dictated by intelligence services and the military—the President really has no say. If he disagrees with a course of action, he can be easily coerced or threatened. If he still won't tow the line...well, trust me on this, things can happen."*

He saw a convertible coming into view now, with four passengers waving to the crowd. He could see Mitch focusing his rifle across the top of the fence. A confident index finger pulled back smoothly on the trigger, and almost instantly in the distance Jack could see the head of the iconic figure in the rear seat of the convertible snap violently backwards.

Jack clearly remembered where he was on that day in history so many decades ago. A horrifying moment that had been almost too surreal to believe, especially as a young, naïve child.

The moment that gave new meaning to the anthem *Hail to the Chief.* That moment when Camelot was destroyed in the blink of an eye.

About The Authors

Peter Parkin was born in Toronto, Canada and after studying Business Administration at Ryerson University, he embarked on a thirty-four year career in the business world. He retired in 2007 and has written seven novels with co-author Alison Darby.

Alison Darby is a life-long resident of the West Midlands region of England. She studied psychology in college and when she's not juggling a busy work life and writing novels, she enjoys researching astronomy. Alison has two daughters who live and work in the vibrant cities of London and Birmingham.